AMBROGAE

THE PROPHECY OF SEIKE

ZACHARY DUNFORD

Ambrogae

Tellwell Talent
www.tellwell.ca

ISBN
978-1-77941-078-8 (Hardcover)
978-1-77941-077-1 (Paperback)
978-1-77941-079-5 (eBook)

ACKNOWLEDGMENTS

This book wouldn't have been possible without the support of my family and friends. I would especially like to thank my parents, Joanne and Gary Dunford, for reading each chapter of this novel as I was in the process of writing it and encouraging me along the way. A special shout out goes to my friend Paul Mackay, who had an integral role in the creation of this book. He read the prologue and more or less insisted, strongly, that I had to make a complete book out of it. He also read the book in its entirety once it was finished. Without his enthusiasm, I may never have gone further than the prologue. Thanks Paul.

The editing process was undertaken as a collaborative effort by all who read the novel. It was mainly undertaken by my father, who is a huge reading aficionado and a perfectionist by nature. He has always had a keen eye for how well-written a book or novel was, with an ability to find mistakes in finished works that I feel certain most people wouldn't notice. He was able to find the typos and small errors that had escaped being found by anyone else, including myself.

Lastly, I would like to thank my grandmother, who has always thought that I could do anything that I put my mind to, including writing. She's always supported me, through both the good times and bad. Thanks, Nanny.

PROLOGUE

Several times he tried, heaving with most of his strength while maintaining control of it. The hinge at last gave its first creaking sigh, letting Seike know that his efforts hadn't been for naught. He was calm, before, considering the situation. At present, he decided to let a bit of confidence creep into his mood.

Time for a break.

He stepped back from the gargantuan door that held him within his confines. Many years ago, he would have never dared let himself believe that it was possible for a single man to throw a car, starting at the chest, and have it land a dozen or so meters from the point at which it was thrown.

At first, when he was put in this room, he experienced the same disbelief, accompanied by an unwelcome sense of powerlessness, when the door seemed to be as unmovable as it would have been when he was still just an ordinary fellow.

Now he surveyed the room, taking special time to stare deep into the lens of the camera at the front left corner, a blank expression on his snowy face. Dressed in all black as he was probably only lent to his sinister appearance. A part of his mind, which he had come to think of as the Serpent, had invaded quickly and soothed his initial rage at the thought of truly being confined. It did so with the cool caress of some cold, unknowable void. Seike knew then that not destroying the camera was to be the first of many progressive changes in his approach to his present situation.

Two guards were posted outside his door. He knew them intimately within very little time of being put here.

He knew what Karl Schultz, thirty-nine, of Minnesota was planning to have for his dinner that evening. Steak and potatoes, very cliche. He knew that his partner Barry Clarks, thirty-three, also of Minnesota, was a compulsive masturbator. He was thinking of it when he arrived on duty and hadn't stopped for more than a few moments at a time since. It was getting close to his usual time for a bathroom break, and he was looking forward to not having to think about it for a half hour or so, afterward. Pathetic.

Everything they said, he heard. Most things they thought, he knew. There were other things he knew, as well. Many things. The sound and rate at which each of the two guards' hearts beat. The music of it. The smell that wafted from the two of them. So wonderful it hurt.

Adding to the sweetness of that scent, he now knew that this door wasn't going to hold him.

"But what exactly is he, sir?"

From within S-47 Command and Communications, General Tristram Kelloway stared at the screens before him. Especially at the big one in the center. He registered the question that the young sergeant posed, but ignored it for the time being, instead holding up his hand to forestall further speech. The young man quickly retreated one step back, and one step away, snapping to attention.

Though the soldier couldn't see it from his vantage point, the General allowed himself just a bit of a smile. He was respected and a little feared by his subordinates. He believed that being the hardest of the hard asses made his men and women the hardest and sharpest company of soldiers, of any kind, in North America.

Kelloway was seven-star. He made that up himself. It was one of the perks of being the general of an army that the world didn't know existed, but that fought and held against threats every bit as dangerous as terrorists, possibly more. Definitely a hell of a lot scarier.

The eyes of the man inside the newly constructed cell seemed to stare directly into his own. Moreover, they seemed to stare directly into him, into his soul.

This one was new and had easily smashed his way out of a cell that had never posed a problem when holding others of his kind. He fed on the guards, though not fatally. Then, he had just stood there, allowing himself to be recaptured. The liquid-crystal high-definition display on the monitor highlighted a certain detail that deeply disturbed him. Those violet eyes of his. They were the brightest and most beautiful eyes he had ever seen. Looking into them made his own eyes water.

Also, they scared the ever-loving shit out of him.

"He's a vampire. He drank some of our troops' blood, remember? Nearly killed them."

"Permission to speak freely for a moment, sir?" The young sergeant, Willams, allowed his voice to crack slightly at the end of the question. Tsk Tsk.

Kelloway turned and regarded the soldier with his blue eyes, which, for a human, were very cold and piercing. "Yes," was all he said.

"He nearly killed Larch and Weaver, sir, but he didn't. He could have but chose to withdraw. I am sure of this, sir." Willams' voice was clear and confident, again. He met the General's eyes evenly, determined to enforce his certainty. There was no need to inform the sergeant that he had already considered this. This sort of thing occurred somewhat often in his interaction with subordinates. He felt that there was nothing wrong with the fact that Willams had voiced his own thoughts. It wasn't the first time the young man had done that. He liked him more because of it. There was a future colonel somewhere in that boy.

This new cage had been built over the course of the last week, the strongest yet. It was built just for this man, while he awaited with triple the guards on duty in a second Ambrogae containment unit. The General had contained a very large number of very strong and strange classified individuals in his time working here. And he had been here since the facility was built, thirty-five years ago, roughly. The Ambrogae were the reason for this whole damned mess. Vampires, whatever fancy-ass name they liked to call themselves.

It started back in the mid-eighties. Really, it had started a much longer time ago. It was just noticed by a lot of prominent members of government, including the United States Army behind them, in the eighties.

The late twentieth century was the perfect time for these assholes to show up more often in human circles. The army was getting ready to go off to fight another little war and the people were many. Lots of goths in the eighties, vampire culture was hot then and has been hot ever since. It was the perfect environment for these demonic bastards to start getting ballsy. Easy to be just another face in the crowd.

In January of 1984, a certain former US senator was found dead in a five-star hotel room. Top floor, corner suite. The local police station's forensic report was messy. Four people were found dead in the room. They were identified as two males and two females initially, as the bodies were in such a state that they were only identifiable by the clothing strewn across the blood-spattered carpets of the hotel room. The dead appeared milky-white and grey in complexion, bluish veins and arteries starkly apparent on what seemed to be just skin and some meat hanging over their skeletons. No blood inside. The senator and his bodyguard were identified by the IDs in their wallets, which were found in their suits. The women appeared to be escorts, but no IDs were found.

The next morning, a man showed up at the police station claiming to be the deceased senator's bodyguard. He had a very wild story to tell, and it garnered attention from some higher-ups. He claimed that a third prostitute had done it all. He said that she turned into a monster with red eyes and slew everyone at the height of an orgy that she had coerced the senator to arrange to celebrate a business deal. The bodyguard had pissed himself, and the stink and stain were still on him. He had acted angry and demanding, but he was scared shitless. He hadn't wanted to participate in the orgy, but the senator and the red-haired prostitute made him record it all with a video camera. He had the tape, as well as proof of identification. After the positive ID, he wouldn't give the tape to anyone, but instead wanted to be confined in the most secure cell they had with it. After making his phone call, he stayed in the cell corner, clutching the tape, until some people came and took him away.

Those people were Kelloway's people, now. Back then, he was just a colonel. He was very good at it, and apparently his psychological profile fit the bill for a job like this.

At first, he was very happy with those people for thinking so highly of his mental stability, as well as very happy with his ability to cope with the realization that humans were not the only intelligent animals out there. Now, he thought those same people were just a bunch of old fuckers, and the pride at his reactions to this crazy new world had long since washed mostly away, though he still had his moments.

The General recalled those tapes in his mind. Nasty. Very nasty stuff. This fiery-haired bitch was showing them all the time of their lives when it came to a very violent halt. They were all climaxing simultaneously while she laughed and worked her magic. The details were something he tried to forget. Their screams didn't last long, anyway, though the damage done in so short a time was obviously more than any human could have done. She drank them all very quickly after killing them, first looking at the bodyguard holding the camera and commanding him to shut his mewling mouth, then telling him to keep filming. When she finished, she looked at the camera, laughing like a panther, and said "We're here to stay. You're all on your way out."

She had then leapt out of the window, not bothering to open it first, glass shattering.

When Kelloway was shown the video for the first time, he didn't question its authenticity. No one involved questioned it, and it wasn't long before more reports started coming in from various sources with the corpses looking the same. Field Base A-92 was eventually established in the central location of Minnesota, and the rest was history.

Turned out that the Ambrogae had been here all along. They lived underground. Go figure. Odd as it was, sunlight didn't do much to them. Made them weaker, but still quite able to massacre a squadron of soldiers in the right circumstances.

Some of them were actually working alongside the military, though under the most cautious of circumstances. It was impossible for the 'good' Ambrogae to disguise their nature. These good ones, fewer in number, were mostly former humans. They had blue eyes unlike anything you would ever see without the use of colored contact lenses. The bad ones had ruby red eyes with cold black pupils when they turned their faces on. The features of their faces changed, too, though not always. The oldest ones underwent pretty hideous transformations.

This guy had purple eyes. Did a red one and a blue one fuck and spatter purple all into the canvas of reality? Who knew? The blues never told the humans a thing that they didn't have to know, and the red ones just ate the humans.

General Kelloway had only ever spoken face to face with one of the blues. She never gave her name, but she was the only one who had personally set foot into the base. She was a bit cold, but she seemed to have a very human personality. He never knew what to think of that, because the blues still needed human blood to live. Animals were not an option, for whatever reason.

The blues got most of their human blood without the human ever knowing, and without any harm done, but it still creeped Tristram out, being in the same room with one. Her pretty ivory face and perfect shining black hair didn't change that.

Bringing himself back to the moment at hand, he acknowledged Willams' opinion.

"I think you're right, Sergeant. After seeing this vampire in action, I'm beginning to wonder whether he doesn't actually want to be in here."

A red light began flashing on the ceiling overhead, accompanied seconds after by the blaring of the alarm. Somewhere along the line, that sound had become the source of all the General's fears. Images started switching rapidly on monitors as the security AI focused images of areas surrounding the hazard site. The central monitor stayed the same. The new cage was now empty. And broken. Shit.

Activity swirled chaotically in the command center as several response teams were dispatched to their assigned locations. Fear permeated every action, as it always did. And it made everyone very efficient, as it usually did. These people all worked here for the same reason he did. Stability.

"Sir?" Willams waited for an order from him, as he was the only person in the room who outranked the sergeant, currently.

"You go with Alpha, Willams, and report directly to me on the comms."

"Yes, sir!"

The first seventy-two hours of an Ambrogis' or Ambrogess' existence are crucial.

This is what Seike and every other human were told, in some form or another, when they were made into a vampire. During these three days, their ultimate nature would take form. Most succumbed to the darkness, taking on the being of the Leviathan. Legion, as some holy folk would later refer to it as. Others, fewer in number, had taken on the being of the Serpent, Seline.

Most Ambrogae believed these tales, of the vampire God and Goddess. Most priests believed in God, too.

When he was told these tales by his sire, he regarded them with doubt, despite the obvious evidence to the contrary. Even though he had not been an atheist in his human life, he believed in human potential more than anything else. Becoming something other than human had unnerved him, but he had first noted that he was still himself. And with that sort of mind, he still regarded most things theological with doubt. Ambrogaeic myths, human myths. Tomato, tomahto.

-Please, you must side with the Serpent, Seike-

A haunting voice arose in his memory. His sire. Selinda.

The name meant 'moon lover' in the ancient tongue and she had indeed loved the moon. She had been a blue and had given him a second chance at life. He had loved her in a way that hurt him now even more than he thought the pain of the final thirst would. She was the reason that he was here, in this cell. She should have never doubted that he would serve any cause that was hers.

He smoothed over his thick black hair, standing and staring at the next door. The alarm didn't sound in this room, but Seike was aware of the smart security system that an installation like this would have. Besides, he could hear it in many of the other rooms that it was going off in.

Shultz and Clarks were napping soundlessly at their card table. He had not fed off them, because Larch and Weaver had provided him enough sustenance for nearly two weeks, barring bodily injury. Once he had at last obtained the information that he needed from a stray thought somewhere, the door had proven to be an easier task than he thought. Three blows instead of one. He sensed four frightened minds in the second guardroom on the other side of the wall. The lights were probably going off in there, no doubt those men were the first informed of this little mishap. For him, it wasn't really a big deal. Those men were about to begin experiencing a great deal more fear, though.

As he was taught, he let the void of the Goddess flow into his mind, inky and frigid. Charging his body with the resulting psionic energy, he smashed the thick, gleaming steel door. It crumpled like foil and flew several feet, landing heavily on the floor on the other side. Four sets of completely stunned faces had absolutely no time for reaction as Seike blurred from one to the other, hitting each lightly on the neck. The strikes themselves were hardly more than caresses, but the psionic jolt he sent into their brains flattened them. They, like the other two, were merely asleep. Their heads would hurt a great deal upon waking, a thought which made him smile. He imagined some of the communications officers spilling their coffees at that smile, as they watched this all go down on a screen somewhere above.

Conveniently, the cell he was looking for was very close. He easily smashed his way through the next two groups of soldiers that he encountered. They were armed with the same high voltage rifles that he had feigned electrocution from twice already. They made him feel all tingly when they shot him. Regardless of their ineffectiveness, though, Seike thought again about how futuristic this place was.

He arrived in the correct corridor and knew that the cell was around the right corner of the T-section straight ahead.

At that moment, four more soldiers came around both corners at the end of the hall. Seike recognized one. He was the same sergeant that had responded to his first breakout. The young man's name was Jake Willams.

Sensing amiability underneath the fear, he decided to try talking first this time.

"Boy, stand down. I have business here, and then I will be gone. I mean no one here any harm. On the contrary, I find what you do here very respectable in comparison to most branches of government."

The young man raised his hand, smartly signaling his men to stand down for the moment.

"I have orders to detain you by any means necessary. Communication would be my preferred method. I'm not an idiot. I've seen what you can do."

"I am not going to let you detain me this time. The first time was no accident. The second time wasn't either, but you already know that." He refrained from using the soldier's name. Telepathy was one of the features of the Serpent that humans didn't need to know about.

Willams hesitated, then hit a button on the communications device on his outer shoulder. A response came through. "Report, Willams."

"Sir, the… the Ambrogis says he has business here. He wants us to stand down." Seike noted the hesitation with a half-smile. Many Ambrogae despised the name vampire because to them it symbolized the humans' ignorance of their world. The only thing popular fiction ever got right was the drinking of human blood. And to a lesser extent, the transformation aspect. Seike never really cared what anyone called him.

The other soldiers waited as Willams listened to an earphone response. Seike wasn't supposed to hear the response, but he heard it anyway.

"Like hell! He comes in here causing all this shit like he's a red, and now he's asking politely? Fuck him. Ask him what he wants."

Obviously nervous, Willams relayed the reply, omitting everything except the question.

"I need to see an old friend one last time. You would know him by name, I think. Emilio."

Not a single soldier held his composure at his mention of the name. Yes, they had most certainly all heard of the famous Emilio. "Heart-ripper" is what these particular men thought of him as. A very good idea, actually. He was caught almost two decades ago for crimes against humanity and the Ambrogae of Seline. After his capture, the roots of interaction and cooperation between the Ambrogae of Seline and the soldiers of Field Base A-92 were set. For the first time in history, a joint trial was undergone between both human and vampire. Who would get to exact punishment?

It ended up that the Ambrogae won the right, and their folly was in their arrogance and sureness in dealing with the situation. He would be put to the final death by ancient rites and ritual.

Ancient rites and ritual made it easy for the old vampire to escape. He took the lives of four blues in the process. He took Seike's will to live that night, something that was very hard to get back. Even still, he would never be the same. He wasn't there for her when he could have been.

It took eleven years to recapture him, and this time the humans did it. They had kept him, a right that the Ambrogae acknowledged. Even when he was human, Seike found it difficult to understand why governments always let their most dangerous criminals live for so long after capture. In this case, it was likely for experimentation, but still.

He couldn't let the humans have Emilio, though. He wanted him all to himself.

The General responded openly. "I would love to, but you've killed, too. We can't just let you go like that. Wouldn't be good for morale." Through a hastily made decision, the violet-eyed vampire had been forced to kill one of the soldiers when he was 'captured' originally.

"Then I will make you a deal, sir. You let me have visiting hours with Emilio, I let you lock me back up." He didn't intend to keep that promise, of course.

There was silence for a while as the soldiers fidgeted nervously, guns pointing mostly steadily in his direction. Finally, the General responded. "Alright, you know what? If it means none of my men have to die tonight, then you have a deal. Order your men to let him pass, Willams."

At that moment Seike felt a strange and strangled mental tension from one of the soldiers, and he knew the man was about to disobey that order. A hate that had managed to hide during the confrontation resurfaced at the General's acquiescence and seized control of the man's thoughts. The furious current of it was so strong, Seike was impressed that the man had been able to hide it from him. This person had lost someone dear to a red Ambrogis. Feeling this kind of rage from a human caused his mind to pool and form a curious question. He wondered if Legion and Seline were restricted to influencing only the minds of vampire kind. This man's hate felt like something dark and corrupting.

The trooper had a gun holstered at his side, but he quickly snatched the weapon out of it and raised it to fire. Seike sensed a thought from him. Silver. Really? Once most people knew vampires were real, they were ready to believe just about anything. The soldier started firing, but Seike already had a layer of psionic energy forming a kinetic shield between himself and the bullets. They ricocheted off of what appeared to be air only inches in front of him.

Seike first saw the red spot appear on Willams' head. An instant later, he felt the four soldiers become three as gravity took over the lifeless body of the sergeant, dropping it heavily in place.

That the unfortunate young soldier had lost his life in such an unlikely way was something he couldn't bring himself to feel even a moment's sympathy for. The cold part of his mind instantly knew this would dampen his relationship with the men and women of S-47 just that much more, but there was no time to consider the consequences of the last five seconds. Seike rushed into the three remaining soldiers, felling all three before they could respond. He rounded the corner, and his vision sharpened as his heart sped up. He saw the door he was looking for.

He hastily smashed the steel door down and saw exactly who he was hoping to see. An emaciated Emilio, red eyes glaring into his violet ones. The Ambrogis was old and came from below. All of their kind began existence with pitch black hair, which became progressively lighter as they aged. Emilio's hair was a silvery-white in color. He smiled, baring his many small razor teeth.

"So, you've come to kill me, yourself? I thought you were better than that."

The ancient one looked like he was about to say more as Seike drove his fist into the bastard's chest, pulling out his heart and crushing it completely before its owner's very eyes. Red blood so dark it was nearly black spattered in every direction as the organ exploded.

For the first time, he saw fear in those arrogant eyes, and he felt a strange elation. Placing his bloodied hand onto the face of Emilio, he sent a vicious blast of energy into the red's brain, cooking it in seconds. An agonizing death that left Seike feeling momentarily satisfied.

She was avenged, now.

"I did it, baby." he whispered to the air. His voice, though quiet, choked slightly. He knew his bright purple eyes shone with emotion.

For nineteen years, his thoughts had been consumed too often by vengeance and pain. Now there was only the pain, and a yearning emptiness. As he made his way out of the base, his thoughts drifted back to her. His Selinda. She was still gone, but now her murderer was gone as well. Hopefully to some sort of eternal hell.

Selinda had become a memory of pain greater than he imagined the final thirst would be. But now, even as he shed a few salty tears for his loss, the memory of her face brought him peace for the first time since she had died. He felt as if her ghost were there, comforting him and at the same time telling him to let go of his pain.

Seike wanted to listen, but he couldn't let her memory go. He would never again see her. Never smell her or hear her. His body quivered in response to his misery, even as he rushed out of the base and into the night forest.

Be it dull or sharp, pain was his new world.

CHAPTER ONE

Haley Stafford had a lot of determination, and what she felt was a good dose of self-confidence. She stared into the mirror in her new suit, turning left and right, testing out her smile and her handshake. Opportunities like this didn't come around for everyone, and she wasn't going to let this one go to waste.

Triaclon Industries was a corporate giant, with products all over the market. One of their specialties was pharmaceuticals, and it was with this branch that Haley had scored an interview.

She was a chemist, and formulating pills to be popped had been a dream of hers since her college years, when she herself was popping just about anything that came across her way. Turned out she had been smart regardless of her adventurous spirit, and her Bachelor of Science and specialization in chemistry had not proven too much for her to handle. Her marks were mostly Bs with the occasional A or C+.

All in all, a very good student who turned out to be a competent chemist, and though her work record wasn't long as she was still young, she didn't feel too overwhelmed going in. Or she would, once she got out of her apartment and down to the branch's headquarters on 5th and main.

Calling a cab did no good in a city as big as L.A. After a little hailing though, she found her ride. She was early, anyway. She'd rather take no chances. The ride was a little slow going, but that was no sweat off her back.

Twenty minutes before her appointed interview time at four forty-five PM, she was standing before the doors to what she hoped would be her new place of employment. She took a deep breath and went inside.

There was a female receptionist who took her name and asked her to take the elevator to the eleventh floor where she would be directed further. As she expected, there was a mild looking man with puddle brown hair and eyes waiting for her as the door opened after the elevator had taken her up.

"Miss Stafford?"

"Yes, that's me."

"Very good. My name is Gregory. Your interview is with Mr. Crawley, if you'll follow me."

He turned and she followed. They went through a small maze of hallways before arriving at a small sitting area. At the end of the room was an old-style wooden door of some kind, Haley didn't know her wood so she couldn't say what it was made of, but it was dark and reddish.

Gregory turned back to her and for a moment it was as if his eyes were different somehow. She looked again, but no, they were brown. She must have been seeing things.

He smiled. "If you'll please sit here, Mr. Crawley will see you at five PM."

Five? What happened to four forty-five? Haley guessed that they must have just wanted her to show up on time. She thought this guy was a little weird. "Oh, okay. Thank you."

"Of course."

He silently walked away down the hall, turning the corner left at the end of it.

She sat and checked her phone. Four thirty-five. The ideal time for a cell phone game, but she had never been into video games of any kind. She didn't have a book to read either, so she just settled in to wait.

Checking her watch a few times over the ensuing minutes, she was now looking at it as it said four fifty-nine. It turned over to five, and seconds later a man emerged from behind the wooden door. He was tall, at least a little over six feet, and he looked older, but it was hard to say how much older. Fifties maybe? Late forties? He had no gray in his black hair.

She stood up to meet him, extending her hand. "Haley Stafford."

He took her hand in his and then oddly put his other hand over top of hers in a small caress. "Robert Crawley," he said with a smile, his bright brown eyes striking. "Please, come into my office, Miss Stafford."

He leaned back and then waved his arm toward the wooden door he had just emerged from.

Haley felt uncomfortable for some reason, but she figured it was just that gross handshake. He might be a perv, so what? She didn't think she was about the be raped or anything, as this was an official situation. She went into the office, he came in behind her and walked past her, moving to the chair behind his desk. He sat down. There was a turned-out chair on the other side of the desk, of inferior quality to the cushy one he himself sat in. He motioned to it. "Sit, if you will, Miss Stafford."

She took a seat, smiling. Already feeling better about her momentary case of the heebie jeebies, she now felt she had to comment on the office. It had a very cool, very gothic look.

"This is a very nice office you have here, Mr. Crawley. Is this desk made of the same wood as the door?"

"Why yes, it is, Miss Stafford. But we're not here to discuss interior decoration. We're here to discuss you."

A smile spread across his lips. "You smell simply amazing, Haley."

The discomfort was back, times ten. There was something up with this guy. Her internal alarms were sounding.

"I thought this was an interview? I don't see what me smelling like has to do with anything."

"I conduct all of my interviews at three PM. Every day that I have them. Five PM is dinner time."

Suddenly there was a transformation in his face. His brown eyes shifted somehow and became red, and his smile turned into a grin full of wickedly pointed teeth. Haley sat there with her mouth open in shock. She had seen vampires in the news and on television, but they were rare, and most people never had to meet one.

"You're a vampire." She was in shock; she couldn't believe this was happening. She knew the proper name to use was Ambrogis, but she couldn't think.

He laughed. "And you're dinner."

She screamed, then. It did her no good.

"Damn it, Seike! Damn it! Do you know the repercussions that will occur now that you have done this?"

Elder Kesel paced the room, stepping over books scattered around. This old library was the place the Elder called home. He was muttering in the ancient tongue now, which Seike hadn't bothered learning much of in nearly a century of being an Ambrogis, or vampire. He didn't care for either name, really.

The Elder abruptly turned from his mutterings, locking eyes with him.

"We of Seline already have a tenuous enough relationship with the human world. What you did won't become public knowledge. Instead, only the human elite will be informed, which is far worse."

Up until now, Seike had just let the Elder tirade over him while remaining silent. He was honor bound to report to Kesel whenever he had dealings with the human world beyond passing through it. The Elder was the father of his late sire. Those of the blue eyes could sometimes procreate naturally. Though it was a small chance of happening in general, it was still very hard when trying to conceive.

He always tried to speak with care towards the Elder and did so now.

"I admit it didn't go nearly as smoothly as I planned. I was aiming for zero casualties-"

"You shouldn't have been there! S-47 is no joke, and they only tolerate those of the blue eyes because of our connections throughout the rest of the human world. We wouldn't need to give them much reason to change their minds about that tolerance."

"Not to sound brazen, Elder, but I believe the color of my eyes curbs blame being lain at the feet of the people of Seline."

The Elder scoffed at him. "Though you're not really known in the human world, there are those who do know of you, and they have come to associate you with my kind. They know you follow our rules, at any rate. Or at least, did."

"I still do."

Kesel hesitated. Seike was sincere in his words, the Elder read it in his eyes. Plenty of Seline's brood were hot headed while still young, and it would seem he of the violet eyes followed that same trend. Not for the first time, though, the Elder wondered about Seike's proclivity toward the whisperings of the Leviathan. It was an old worry, from an old worrywart.

"She wouldn't have wanted this, young man. You must know this is not what she would have wanted," Elder Kesel stated after the brief hesitation.

Seike visibly flinched at those words, and Kesel could see he had wounded him in saying them. It made them no less the truth, however. The look of pain in those strange eyes at first made the Elder regret that he hadn't chosen his words more carefully. It didn't take long for Seike to ball his hands into fists, though, anger radiating from eyes that were now glaring at the Elder.

"That's not fair. I couldn't stand living anymore knowing that that sadistic son of a bitch was still alive out there. It was only by chance that I found his location at all, and once I determined where he was being held, I tried going the diplomatic route first. I really did, Elder. They didn't want to talk. They were too afraid for talk."

Seike's hands kept clenching and unclenching, his anger wavering between rage and sadness. The boy was right, Kesel concluded. It wasn't a fair thing he had said.

The elder let out a long and sad sigh and propped his bottom down on a stack of books. He investigated Seike's eyes. They weren't so angry, now. The sadness he knew the young Ambrogis was experiencing had proven to be a balancing point, of sorts. Perhaps there was no need to regret the stinging words he had just used, but there was a need for an apology.

"I am sorry, Seike. I spoke out of my heart, without using my head. Truly, I am glad that Emilio is dead. I loved her too, you know." The last words came out as a hoarse whisper.

For long moments, the two men just stood there, looking at each other, remembering Selinda. They both felt one another's sadness as something real and tangible, not in a simply empathetic way but in a truly empathic fashion. There would be no more arguing over what was already done, the Elder knew. It was time to move on in the discussion. Time to decide what would be done in the future as a result of past actions.

"The council is going to want to mete out some form of punishment for me." Seike stated. It was not a question in his mind.

The Elder sighed again, this time exasperated. He shifted his position on the books to rest his chin on the palm of one hand. His blue eyes were thoughtful, and Seike wondered again just how old the Elder truly was. His hair was almost completely white, and that was saying a lot for any of the Ambrogae.

When an older human was turned, despite whether they ended up being of the Leviathan or of the Serpent, they regained a good portion of their youthful appearance. A man in his seventies was once turned into a vampire, and he looked like he was thirty again after the transformation had completed. He ended up being a red, though. Seike had dispatched him personally during his feeding frenzy.

The feeding frenzy was a pseudo-ritual that every newly made Ambrogae who ended up siding with the Leviathan went through. Legion would tighten its grip on their mind by getting them to kill and feed from as many humans as possible once their eyes went red, for a period of one full day. There was some kind of ranking system involved, Seike knew. It was more than just bragging rights. The more humans that were killed, the greater the measure of respect that was offered to the new vampire among his brethren.

Those of Legion had their own form of telepathy amongst themselves, and though they could not readily read the minds of humans, they had various forms of mental coercion and mind control that they could utilize on their victims.

Just when Seike was about to say more, Kesel spoke up.

"I can handle the council. I stand at their head, after all." A sly smile crept onto the old man's face. Seike wanted to grin just from seeing that expression, but he was still worried.

Too often, the council had been made to overlook certain transgressions of his, because he stood apart from the two known factions of the Ambrogae, and yet he fully sided with the blues. Despite the uniqueness of his eyes, he had proven to them over time that he had indeed kept his humanity, which to them meant that he was a blue, for all intents and purposes. And, like many young Ambrogae of Seline, he was prone to making mistakes that required intercession.

Up until this point, though, he had never killed any humans. This was a much more serious offense compared to any of his earlier insubordinations, even if the deaths were accidental. Despite what Elder Kesel perhaps believed, there would be consequences for Seike. He might even be banished from the harbors of the safe havens.

"I will accept whatever punishment is bestowed upon me, Elder." Seike said calmly. All that remained now was to face whatever was to come with all the dignity and poise that he could muster. In the weeks following Selinda's death, he had been suicidal. He had deprived himself of blood and was likely near fatal starvation when Kesel had had some choice words with him that changed the course of his life and gave him the courage to keep on living. Those words were similar in content to what he had just said about what she wouldn't have wanted. But instead, they were what she would have wanted.

She would have wanted him to keep on living. And so, he did.

It didn't take very long, however, for his thoughts back then to turn toward the cold hate that he had borne until the moment that he had ripped that bastard's heart out. He had been consumed with the idea of revenge for the better part of the last two decades. It had driven him. Now he felt hollowed out, again. Not suicidal, but lost.

The Ambrogae of Seline were not telepathic with one another in the sense that they could read each other's minds like they could read human minds. However, they had deep empathic connections that could give each other very good ideas about whatever they might be thinking about. The connection between the blues was so strong that they could feel the presence of their own kind a mile or more away. They could sense those of Legion in a similar manner, though not at quite that distance. Perhaps close to a mile, but not beyond. That was how he had stumbled upon Emilio's location. He had felt the old creature nearly a mile below his feet while on a sojourn through the Minnesotan forest. Unlike a typical blue, Seike was able to discern identities through the telltale psychic signature of another Ambrogis or Ambrogess, as long as he had met the individual at some point, face to face.

He would accept whatever the punishment would be, and he would continue on with the kind of life that was considered normal for a good-natured vampire. Stopping reds, feeding from blood bags and the occasional sleeping human. At least, that was assuming he wasn't to be banished from the few places of safety for blues around the country. If that were to happen, his life would most definitely change course in comparison to what it had been like for nearly a century, now.

Elder Kesel may as well have been reading his mind at that moment.

"I know you believe you are going to be banished, my friend," the old one intoned. "Do not think for a moment that I am going to allow that to happen. Other blues have on occasion killed humans either in self defense or through some accidental means, and they are rarely banished for it."

"I just have this feeling," Seike responded. "You know Jurai doesn't like me. He has never fully trusted in my humanity. Ferana has always seemed to disdain me as well." That last part came out sarcastically. Heaving out his own sigh, the young Ambrogis found a spot on the floor devoid of the clutter of books and plopped himself down, resting his hands on his knees.

"It is my opinion that this entire endeavor of yours has only proven you to be more human. For what could be more human than to be driven by the pain of losing someone dear to you? Driven by it to the point where you do something reckless and regretful." The Elder stood up, then, placing his hands behind his back. It was a pose familiar to he of the violet eyes. Kesel was about to give a little lecture.

"Long ago, I was young and foolish, too, you know. And I never told you this, but I lost someone dear to me as well. This was before I met Selinda's mother." Pain flashed in the Elder's eyes, causing them to shimmer momentarily. Seike knew it could be regarding his daughter, or his wife. Ludia was still alive, in another haven on the other side of

America. West coast. She left Kesel after their daughter was killed. Or, Seike thought, it could be that he was remembering this other individual who was dear to him.

For a moment it seemed the Elder might not continue. He just stood there, clearly remembering something that hurt, brows furrowing together. Then he cleared his throat and began a slow pacing as he spoke.

"He was my brother. He was not an Ambrogis, no... He was human. I myself had only been turned for a mere handful of years when it happened. I was still trying to keep my human life, you see. My parents had passed away many years before I became an Ambrogis, as had their siblings, all of whom had not had any children. Only my brother and I remained in our entire family as far as I knew. In my human life I had rather piercing blue eyes.

"At the time I thought it was good fortune that I did, for I was able to maintain a relationship with my brother, who only noted at times that my eyes seemed somewhat bluer than usual, but otherwise was none the wiser, nor suspicious at all. Now, thinking back on it, I believe it would have been better had I not been able to disguise my nature, and simply stayed away from him."

The Elder was clearly struggling to keep his composure, now. How much pain this old man must have gone through throughout who knew how many centuries of existence. Seike had never really given it much thought before, but he did now. Kesel continued.

"This is something I try not to think about, much less talk of with anyone. My sire was a red. Actually," Kesel's eyes met Seike's, his gaze sharpening. "My sire was... Emilio."

Seike knew it was coming before the name had been stated. Even so, his heart sped up to the point where his vision slightly blurred for a moment before going into a crystal-clear focus. He had never guessed, and no one had told him in nearly a hundred years of being what he now was. Emilio was a figure that all those of Seline were educated on early into their new lives. Had Selinda known he was the sire of her father? More questions bubbled to the surface of his mind, but he forced himself to empty his head and slow down his heart.

Kesel had noticed Seike's reaction to this information and was regarding him with a strange expression, head tilted slightly. Once Seike could meet the Elder's eyes again, the old one gave a small, almost apologetic shrug.

Then it dawned on him. There was no way he was going to be banished for putting Emilio to the final death, even if two human lives were lost in the process. As if Kesel had been reading his mind yet again, the Elder chose that moment to allow himself a small smile.

"Seike, you and I and many, many others did not want that horrible old monster to continue living. That includes most of the council. He killed my brother, though I blame myself that it happened. But that's a story for some other time. Emilio was responsible for a great deal of pain caused among those of Seline throughout most of North America and Europe, over the centuries."

Suddenly Seike felt another presence enter the library. A voice he had come to dislike spoke from the archway separating the library's two main chambers. "That being said, you will still have to serve some sort of penance, and we will soon be discussing just what that will be."

Through the archway strode Jurai. He wore a frown, as he always did whenever he was in proximity to Seike. His black hair was generously streaked with silver, indicating numerous centuries of life as an Ambrogis. And where there was Jurai…

"There you are, Kesel," Ferana walked silently through the arch to stand beside her husband. She pursed her full lips in disapproval as she looked at Seike. "Preparing this one for his inevitable punishment, I hope? Perhaps some lashings and a few years in service to the nobility will cool his head." A few years in service to her is what she meant. Like the dog she saw him to be.

Elder Kesel gave a quiet chuckle, meeting Seike's eyes briefly before striding up to the two newcomers. That look said for him to keep his tongue from spitting venom, as he had been known to do from time to time with Ferana. He could hold his peace around Jurai, as the councilman was honest as a person, as far as Seike could tell, and despite not liking the violet-eyed one, he spared him from unnecessary insult.

Ferana, on the other hand, liked to verbally abuse Seike. She wasn't on the council, so sometimes he would insult her in retaliation. To do so on this day would be unwise, however. He knew that. He picked himself up off the floor, though. He'd be damned if he was going to just sit there and let that bitch look down on him literally as well.

"I assume the council will be convening soon," Kesel said, bringing both of the other two Ambrogae's stares toward him.

"Yes. In one hour," Jurai stated. His tone was rather detached, as it usually was. He seemed cold at times, but mostly it was simply that he didn't allow his emotions to get the better of him no matter the situation. "Come, my dear, let us go and inform the others."

Ferana gave one last callous look toward Seike before turning on her heel and following her husband out of the library.

Jurai was second only to Elder Kesel on the Central Council, which operated out of this haven that they all called home. The haven was called the Central Haven and was located in Iowa. His rank called for the gathering of council members for meetings whenever the Elder was otherwise occupied. Kesel must have informed him of his intentions to meet and speak with Seike before the young Ambrogis had arrived back at the haven. They would have all sensed him coming. According to Kesel, Seike's presence felt a little different from other blues but was otherwise still quite pleasant when compared to someone of Legion. Seike did not doubt that the difference in feeling had been a cause for many to distrust him, as much as his eyes were.

The Elder watched them go, waiting a few moments after they silently closed the library doors behind them, before turning back to Seike.

"She's afraid of you, you know. She masks the fear well, but she's always been afraid of you. That's why she treats you as she does." Kesel's eyes held sympathy for him, but Seike didn't want sympathy. He didn't really mind being mostly a loner, with few friends among the Ambrogae of Seline, and nothing but enemies among the reds. Unlike the blues, he had the ability to turn his eyes, for a time, back to their original color. In his case that was brown. That was a trait of those of the Leviathan. They could also change their eyes back to whatever color they had been as an ordinary human, or in the case of a pure blood Ambrogae, who were all of Legion and born as offspring, they could disguise their eyes whatever normal human color they saw fit to.

Many blues didn't like that trait of his, but it suited him just fine. It made it easy for him to move about the human world without attracting notice, and if he ever got lonely, he found walking among humans to be pretty therapeutic.

He had even managed to befriend a couple of humans in the last decade, though it wouldn't be much longer now before they noticed he wasn't ageing.

Jackson Houston and Fergus Harrelson were drinking buddies he had met in Iowa City about seven years ago. They had gone to college together and didn't take life too seriously. Both of them had work near the city, but nothing that had anything to do with their Bachelor of Arts. They were both in construction. Different outfits. They loved to joke about how they were each other's competition in both work and social life. They even made sport out of competing for the same women at times. They were a couple of ordinary fellows that helped Seike feel both ordinary and not so lonely. The former feeling was of course an illusion, but the dissipation of loneliness was genuine.

It was easy to have a good time with those boys. They were both nearly into their thirties now, and both still retained the youthful appearance of their college days. Ferg attributed that to 'the dope' as he called it. Marijuana. They both liked their joints, and Seike didn't mind smoking and drinking with them, even though alcohol and weed had no effect whatsoever on him.

That was actually how he got to know them. He drank them both under the table the night that he met them, to their high praise later on.

"Ferana has no reason to be afraid of me after all this time."

The Elder drew his bushy brows together as he frowned. "Whether you mind it or not, you're an anomaly, Seike. There isn't any lore on you or on any kind of purple eyed Ambrogis or Ambrogess. No one has anything to go on. Add that to the fact that you're as powerful as a thousand-year-old when you are in fact barely a century old, and you have a recipe for fear and distrust."

The frown took on a worried look as he continued speaking. "You won't try to go anywhere, I hope, while the council convenes? Protocol dictates that you remain here in the haven until we decide what we are going to mete out as your punishment."

"Don't worry, I'll stay put. Right here in this library of yours." Seike managed a smile.

"Good," was all the Elder said. He seemed as if he wanted to say more, but after a moment's hesitation, he merely murmured that he must leave to inform certain members of the nobility of the council meeting. Only the nobles were allowed to attend council without being on the council, and only then upon invitation by someone from the council.

Elder Kesel departed, leaving Seike alone with his thoughts. He looked at the grandfather clock located at the end of the chamber. Nine o five. They would be convening at ten PM.

He wondered what Jack and Ferg were up to. It was a Friday night, so they were probably at The Old Doll, their favorite pub in downtown Iowa City. Probably just getting started for the night. He couldn't call them, because cell phones and other technology were not permitted within the haven. Technology could be tracked. Seike kept a small bachelor pad in Iowa City that was sparsely adorned with furniture and things such as a cell phone and laptop. He even kept some food there, and not just blood bags. Although he didn't get any real sustenance from human food, he could still eat the stuff. It didn't hurt him. And so, he sometimes would eat something just for the flavor. He was far from the only vampire that did that.

What the Elder had said just before they were intruded upon by Jurai and Ferana stuck in his head.

He was ready for anything, but now he had a hope for a lighter punishment. Something that wouldn't take up too much of his time. Perhaps he would even be able to drop by the pub later.

He sat down at one of the four desks that this chamber of the library had arranged about it. He picked up a book that was lying within arm's reach on the desk and read the cover. 'Legends of the Olde Gods' was written on it, in English. He thumbed through the book a bit. Old English. There was no year or author stated anywhere that he could see, but it looked like a very old book. Well preserved, but very old. Probably at least a few centuries.

He noticed a piece of folded paper between two of the pages. Then he noticed the heading at the top of the left page. 'The Purpul God' was written in an Old English flowing script, larger than the script of the page's actual content. Seike was perplexed. He read the first few paragraphs. A God that was robed in purple and smelled of lavender, but nothing about purple eyes. He, or it, was called the Purpul God because apparently, he had declined to ever give a name, so the ones who identified him simply named him after the color of his clothing.

Bullshit, just like all the stuff on the old gods as far as Seike was concerned. But why the page marker? It could have been Kesel, but it could have just as easily been anyone else in the haven. Seike thought of the library as Kesel's home only because the old man spent so much time here, but in reality, he had his own quarters within the haven just like everyone else. The library was for all who lived in this place. Seike had his own quarters too, but he spent around half of his time at his apartment anyway, as he rather liked technology. And people that didn't look at him sideways.

The other Ambrogae were curious about him, it seemed. Someone was anyway, as the page marker was a bit of paper that didn't feel like Kesel, though Seike couldn't say who it was. His psychometry wasn't the best. He particularly excelled in psionics. It was like he was made for combat.

At that thought, he went to the shelves in pursuit of a book on psionics. He found one he hadn't yet read after only a short time in the 'P' section. There weren't many left he hadn't read already. This one was titled 'The

Philosophy of Psionic Energy'. He remembered seeing it over the years, but it never really sounded all that interesting to him, as he had never considered himself much of a philosopher.

Apparently, a lot of people felt the same way, as he could tell by the book's condition that not very many people had perused it over the years.

He began at the start of the book, reading the introduction first. It was by an Author called Vladimir Blak.

He found himself re-reading the first two pages, unable to keep his attention on the book as he kept looking up at the clock. Before finishing the second page, he rested his head between his forearms and just lay like that, facedown on the desk, listening to the ticking of the clock.

He kept his head down even after the clock struck ten. This particular grandfather clock was silent other than the usual tick tock of the pendulum. It didn't chime as was common for clocks of its kind. Someone had disabled the mechanism for that long ago.

Before much longer, he felt someone enter the library. Moments after, he heard a throat clear. He didn't sense any fear, though. That was good. Of course, he didn't sense it from Ferana either. Ambrogae learned to disguise their emotions well with time.

He lifted his head to regard the clock first. Ten fifteen. They convened for only fifteen minutes to decide whatever fate they had in store for him. Probably a minute or two less than that. He then turned his head to see a youngish noble that he recognized but couldn't remember the name of. There were over three thousand Ambrogae in this place, and he had never bothered to get to know most of them, though he knew the face of each and every one after spending the better part of forty years here.

"They're ready to receive you," the young noble said. "They asked me to tell you not to delay." And with that, the man left as quietly as he had come.

Seike got up from the desk and did a quick cat stretch before heading for the archway into the other chamber with the exit. Time to get this shit over with, he thought to himself.

CHAPTER TWO

It wouldn't be long, now.

Coranthis waited with patience on his throne atop the dais. He and probably some of the other ancients located around the central United States areas had felt Emilio die. The death scream, as his kind called it. Any who had known him personally could tell it was him. What was unclear was *how* he had died, but within the next few minutes Coranthis would know more.

For years those of the true God, Leviathan, had wondered where one of their most prominent of brethren had gone. That he had been captured a second time within a decade was not in doubt, they had heard of that incident. But they did not know at all where he was being held. With his death, there was information to be gleaned. The foolish followers of that false Goddess Seline did not know the extent to which the devout were connected to one another.

When a being of the Leviathan perished, his or her death could be felt for at least a hundred miles all around, by any other Ambrogae who followed the true path. Not only could it be felt tangibly as a feeling of the expiration of that individual, but the direction of the dying one could be ascertained by anyone with sufficient experience. Someone like Coranthis, who was in truth the monarch of this country that the humans called the United States of America.

A dead Ambrogis or Ambrogess who was of the true God released a special pheromone that could only be detected by others of their kind. This scent could be smelled for many miles even weeks after their death, allowing others to home in, with accuracy, on the location of the body. The initial release of the pheromone was psionically amplified and in the case of an ancient like Emilio, could be felt for over a thousand miles. The older the Ambrogae, the further the amplification reached. Another thing those blue-eyed idiots had never learned about. The true Ambrogae were very careful not to reveal as much of their nature to their enemies as they could keep hidden.

The damned human enemy knew about the pheromones, though. They did not know just how effective their release was, however. The psionic aspect to their becoming airborne was something that the humans had never figured out. Even their best scientists were terribly ignorant of the esoteric nature of the world, and their distrust of all Ambrogae, regardless of the color of their eyes, had prevented the humans from sharing their little secrets with the followers of Seline.

Coranthis knew that the humans were the ones who had been holding Emilio for the last several years, but he had never been able to find out which little compound that the exalted one was imprisoned within. A fact which had irritated Coranthis to no end.

Emilio's death was a blow to all true Ambrogae, to be sure. Even Coranthis felt the sting of it. That someone had been able to kill him was bad enough, but that it may have been humans that committed the act was completely infuriating. The monarch was patient and in control of his emotions, though. He was even smiling now, a small smile. The scouts had returned, he could feel them in the palace, making their way toward the throne room in haste. Haste was good, that meant that the news was likely going to be informative.

The large ornately gothic doors to the throne room began to open. Coranthis did not realize he had been leaning forward in anticipation, and he settled back into his throne. Appearances were important, after all. He kept smiling that small smile.

The four scouts who had been dispatched to locate Emilio strode in confidently, and in unison they all went down on one knee before the dais, heads bowed.

Their leader, a reliable man called Olinar, spoke after a moment.

"My liege," he intoned. "We have located the place where Emilio had been held before his untimely death. It is a human compound that they call Field Base A-92. We were fortunate to run into a surface patrol and were able to extract many details from them before killing all but one, who we took prisoner."

Coranthis smiled more deeply now. The news was better than he had hoped. Not only did they find the exact location, but they brought home a meal for their monarch. A meal that may be informative before becoming delicious. They had plenty of prisoners already, of course, but most of them had been bled for weeks if not months, and the blood lost its flavor after so much of this. A healthy human soldier sounded like a welcome reprieve from the recent supply.

"So, am I to take it that you did not enter this compound, then?" Coranthis had hoped they did not. Not yet.

"That is correct, my liege. Though I am sure they are on high alert after a patrol of theirs failed to return, they do not know any details of us. Almeidra was able to use her abilities to shut down all nearby cameras temporarily, so we were not seen by anyone besides those we took down, and our prisoner."

"And I assume you four had a good feeding off the patrol that you dispatched?"

"Yes, and we burned all evidence of the bodies, as is protocol. Do you have any further orders, my liege?" Olinar raised his head as he said these words, gazing at the face of his monarch but keeping his eyes from meeting those of his king. Respectful. Coranthis had always liked Olinar. He was just courageous enough to be frank with his superiors without being disrespectful.

"And I also assume," Coranthis began, ignoring the man's question, "that this particular compound is important to those damned human fleas. And as such, will be well-guarded should we return."

Olinar only nodded before again lowering his head.

The monarch of America considered the situation. He had learned over his long life that rushing was usually not the option to take. Subterfuge was almost always the best road taken, and the long road taken. Given enough time, the humans would let down their guard. Better to try to do this with no loss at all among the Ambrogae. Better still if he could learn even more about this Field Base A-92. No doubt it was run by that damnable S-47, that collection of humans that had taken it upon themselves to capture and kill those of the Leviathan. Even experimenting, sources had informed Coranthis, on the prisoners.

They were indeed infuriating little fleas.

Since before the surface-dwelling human population began recording the years of history with any accuracy, the true masters of this world lived under the earth, coming up to the surface at their leisure to walk completely unbeknownst among mankind. The Ambrogae, for the longest time, only reproduced among themselves. Humans were food, nothing more. This had always been the way, but at some point, some humans had been left alive after being bitten. They became what the pure-blooded Ambrogae would later call half bloods.

Some true Ambrogae must have thought this a good thing, for there had been many humans and few Ambrogae, and with the advent of the half bloods, there could be many more Ambrogae made from the cattle. Their kind had always found it difficult to reproduce, and their numbers increased very slowly. Half bloods could not reproduce at all. This must have been regarded as a solution to the Ambrogae of the time. Damnable ancestors, Coranthis thought.

An Ambrogis or Ambrogess could live for a very long time, but they were not truly immortal. As far as

Coranthis knew, none had ever lived naturally beyond ten thousand years, and most succumbed to the final thirst long before then.

After one of the Ambrogae became too old, they would be unable to ingest and keep down any blood. Inevitably, they would begin vomiting up any that they drank, no matter how fresh or pure the blood was. They would live their final days in great pain unless they were otherwise killed. Since time immemorial, this is why the rites of the final death were devised. Any who became old enough for their bodies to begin rejecting that which sustained them were able to choose of their own volition to be ceremoniously put to death by others of their kind. It was a choice almost always made, for the pains of the final thirst were an agony that could scarcely be imagined.

Coranthis himself was a true Ambrogis. He was nearly two thousand years old and had a long time ahead of him, yet. His father and mother ruled most of Europe and were each well over four thousand years old. They were also both pure-blooded. Monarchs could never be half bloods. It had always been that this world was ruled by the true Ambrogae, and it would always be so. They told him stories of how the first Ambrogae of Seline arose among the half bloods not long after they were born.

Even his parents were unable to say where the source of the scourge began, however. They seemed to begin popping up in many places all over the world at once. Blue-eyed cockroaches. Something other than the Ambrogae, as far as many pure bloods were concerned. Like them, but not the same thing. After some time, it was found that these creatures worshipped some sort of Goddess that they called Seline, and they claimed that this being whispered to them that they should live in harmony with humanity, to spare those they fed from.

Whatever this so-called Goddess was, it was clear to Coranthis that this had been a ploy. And still was. Humans that were spared death had a chance to turn, and humans that were turned had a chance to become more of those blue-eyed vermin. This being Seline, whatever it was, clearly wanted to propagate itself.

Even more maddening to Coranthis was the tendency of the followers of Seline to choose new Ambrogaeic names for themselves after they became what they were. Instead of keeping whatever name they had called themselves in their human life, they in their perversion of the Ambrogae thought of themselves as really like the true Ambrogae. To the point where they had adopted a similar system of nobility and monarchy, even. It was despicable. And the worst part of all was that they could reproduce amongst themselves as well, like a pure blood, though apparently it was just as rare for them to conceive. When they did though, it guaranteed another blue-eyed imposter Ambrogis or Ambrogess.

Coranthis was brought out of his musings when he noticed that the four scouts, especially Olinar, were fidgeting slightly. They were nervous.

"You have not told me everything, then?" Coranthis posed the question, but it was more of a statement.

It was again Olinar that spoke.

"We were able to find out who exactly was the individual responsible for killing Emilio, my king. It...

was Seike." The scout leader cleared his throat and swallowed audibly.

Damn. Damn that freak of nature. Emilio would make the second of the exalted ones that this Seike, this absolute perversion of what the Ambrogae were, had killed. During humanity's second world war, that bastard had managed to kill a cousin of Coranthis', an Ambrogess called Tiahmra. She was exalted for many centuries before meeting an early end at that monster's hands. And now he had done it again. Coranthis had had a deep respect for Emilio. That man had brought in more livestock for the true Ambrogae than any other of their kind in all of North America. He had been committed to the cause. A true saint.

Naturally, though the scouts were a bit nervous, they had no reason to be afraid. Their king was not known for fits of rage, nor unjust punishments. They could not be faulted simply for bringing him information that he found disagreeable.

"Rise, and depart. I will call on you again when needed. Tell the steward to have the prisoner brought up from the dungeon on your way out."

Clearly relieved, the scouts rose from their knees and quickly left the foot of the dais, departing the throne room through its large doors.

Coranthis could hear Olinar relay to the steward in the antechamber the order he had been given. He heard the steward leaving to carry it out. A good man, that Olinar. Strong and smart. And most importantly, respectful. The king sat on his throne and settled into deep thought.

Perhaps there was a silver-lining to be found here. In recent decades, this purple eyed abomination had been encountered numerous times by those of the Leviathan. Most of those times had been somewhere in the central United States. Wyoming, Illinois, Kansas. Not much in Minnesota, but a number of times in Iowa. Now where could he be hiding? That he associated with the blues was no big secret, but what was less well known, though Coranthis knew, was that this Seike was able to change his eyes back to what they looked like when he was human. So, he probably spent a lot of his time among the humans. That much was easy to deduce.

The thing about this Seike that Coranthis hated most was that he was very hard to detect in proximity. Like a blue. They were not easy presences to feel, nothing like the true Ambrogae. Sometimes they had to be closer than a mile to one of them before their presence could be faintly felt, and even then, it was hard to discern direction. This was by far the most annoying trait of those who followed this Seline. Otherwise, they would have been hunted down and exterminated long ago. Coranthis himself could feel the presence of a true Ambrogae, or even a half blood, for two dozen miles or more in any direction. Most of the pure bloods could come close to matching that feat, and even many half bloods could still feel any others of the Leviathan for several miles in any direction.

It was high time to start a more active mission to scout for the one called Seike. To make it a priority within Coranthis' conclave. For years now many had tried to find and capture or kill him, without success. But a large-scale operation to do so had never been undertaken. That's what was called for, now.

He would order the mission to begin in Minnesota and extend to the surrounding states. The order would be for the detainment of Seike. Coranthis wanted to kill him personally.

The smile had crept back onto the ancient king's face.

Field Base A-92 was on high alert now, and General Kelloway had no intention of slacking, or allowing his soldiers to relax. A five-man patrol had gone missing topside yesterday evening, only a day after that purple-eyed prick had escaped once he took out their prize prisoner. This had been one hell of a week, so far.

They hadn't found any bodies of their missing troops, but that still meant they were likely dead. The cameras around the area of forest that the patrol was in had gone screwy, the image freezing even though the timer was still counting. Sure, that could be due to the intervention of some terrorist humans, theoretically. However, the systems in place in the Command and Communication center of S-47 were not only top notch, but most of the tech wasn't even public knowledge. The likelihood of human hackers was zero, as far as the General was concerned.

To make matters worse, Tristram Kelloway wasn't too keen on his new chief sergeant. The boy's name was Justin O'neil, and he reeked of inexperience. He seemed a little too nervous at his new posting for Kelloway's liking.

He missed Willams already. The soldier that had gone and disobeyed the order to stand down was still in the brig, awaiting further repercussions. The General saw the whole thing on camera and knew the vampire had just put up one of those psychic shields some of their kind could put up. In all honesty, Kelloway knew the blame for Willams' death was on the head of the soldier in the brig. That little fucker's career was over.

Double duty had been assigned to watch the topside cameras three times as closely. God knew it had taken far too long for the boys and gals in security to notice that frozen image discrepancy. It's a good thing it was daily procedure to go over footage that had already been recorded, or they might not have noticed anything at all until the crew topside had failed the report in.

As things were, one girl in the security room had found the frozen images just shortly before it was time for the patrol to report in. Kelloway had a gut feeling at the time that those boys on the surface were not going to give their hourly report, and had tried contacting them immediately, but there was no response.

And now he had a really bad feeling in his gut. He knew they had been compromised. Maybe they should have told the blues about the pheromones that dead reds gave off. Kelloway was reasonably sure that the oddity that they had had in the newly reinforced cell a couple of days ago was ignorant of that fact. He wanted to believe that. He was pretty sure the blues didn't know about the death scent that reds gave off, based on past intel. He was also positive that even though that one had purple eyes, he was aligned with the blue-eyed vamps. Also based on intelligence reports.

"O'neil, have the crates of ammo all been delivered and secured to the storerooms near the topside doors?"

"Yes, sir. All ammunition has been counted and delivered, sir." The boy sounded a little too enthusiastic about such a simple feat being carried out successfully.

"Good. Make sure the soldiers charged with manning the turrets are getting their practice in the simulators."

The new young sergeant snapped to attention and turned on his heel, boots squeaking as he did so, to leave and go check on the turret cadets, as Kelloway called them. Good, the General wanted the boy out of his hair for a few minutes at least. His nervous energy was becoming contagious. Or maybe, the General had to admit to himself, he was nervous too.

This was an event of unprecedented proportions for Field Base A-92. They had never been compromised before. They had never lost patrols on local soil.

"Sir," one of the communications officers, a corporal named Sarah Lisgard, spoke up suddenly. "There's a call for you on the red line. It's not The White House, sir." She sounded taken aback at whoever it was. Which could only mean one thing. Kesel.

"Put him through, corporal."

"Yes, sir."

"What do you want, Kesel?"

The voice on the line was not Kesel, however. It was a voice that Kelloway nonetheless recognized.

"I've called to apologize, General. And to inform you that I am going to be reprimanded for my actions the other day. Elder Kesel wanted me to let you know that he is also sorry for what I have done. The council would like to express their grief over the loss of two of your men. And I would, as well. I would like to begin by sharing my name with you. I am called Seike."

So, he was with the blues for certain. This was information that could prove useful down the road. Up until the other day, Kelloway and most of S-47 had only heard rumors of the violet-eyed vampire that ran around killing reds with recklessness. He was an unknown quantity. It seemed that might be about to change.

"You little prick!" The General was fuming at the sound of that voice, trying to sound sorry for the situation he had brought about. "You have no idea what you've done. We're compromised." May as well let them know about the pheromones, now. No reason to keep it a secret any longer, the General thought.

At first there was no response. Kelloway heard a slight intake of breath, then a moment of silence, then, "How?"

"I'm only sharing this with you because I've come to believe it is information your kind should know about, but I want help from you in return. And I don't just mean more information. Dead reds release a pheromone that others of their kind can smell for miles. We don't know how they can smell it from so far off, but they can. Yesterday we lost five more men, and we're sure it's because you killed Emilio."

Again, another silence, then Kesel's voice rang out of the intercom. "Why didn't you tell us this information?"

"We figured it was need-to-know. And you didn't need to know. Listen, we can tell you more, but you need to send us a team of your blues, and after seeing what Seike can do, we'd like him to be on that team."

"Seike is being punished, presently-"

"This can be that fucker's punishment! And yours too, if you want. We don't know when the reds are going to show up again, but we know that if one of our patrols has gone missing, then you can bet your ass they know exactly where our doors are. It's only a matter of time before they show up again, and in force."

Another silence, longer this time. Kelloway could hear indistinct conversation and the sound of some breezy wind on the other side of the line. Were they on a cell phone? Jesus Christ.

"You'll get your team, General Kelloway." Kesel, again.

"And Seike?"

"He'll be on it."

"When can I expect this team? My troops are nervous as it is, and though you guys give us the willies, I think we'd all be breathing a little easier with your powers to match with our firepower."

"First, you have to promise us more information on the pheromones you mentioned."

"I can promise you we'll share everything we know about it, which isn't much more than I've already said. You can have the scientific details when you get here."

"We'll send one of our scientists, as well, then. Perhaps we can learn more on the topic, together. Expect us before the next twenty-four hours is up. And please, don't point your guns our way."

"I promise we won't shoot. We had a loose cannon, I'm sure your Seike has already told you about it. We went over his profile and discovered why. We don't have anyone else on staff who hates vampires so much that they would shoot at the good ones." Kelloway could scarcely believe his own words, but they were true enough. The blues *were* the good ones, and no one else seemed likely to go A.W.O.L.

"That will do. You'll see us on your cameras sometime tomorrow. We'll be wearing blue shirts and jeans, so don't mistake us for some of those of the Leviathan."

"Perfect. General Kelloway out." He nodded to his communications officer, who promptly cut the line.

"Make sure that cell phone wasn't tracked and find out where the call was made from."

"Yes, sir."

Kelloway waited the few minutes it took for his communications officer to work her magic. She might only be a corporal, but everyone in this room was chosen because they were exceptional. Even that O'neil, Kelloway had to grudgingly admit.

"No trackers," the corporal stated after several minutes. "The call was made from Iowa City, sir."

Iowa City, huh? Unlikely in the General's opinion that that was their base of operations. Maybe since they would be sharing some research, the blues could be coerced to reveal their base of operations in this part of the country.

Yeah, when pigs fly, thought Kelloway.

Still though, he couldn't discount it as a possibility. After all, the relationship between their factions had always had a level of caution on both sides, but until this little fuck up, it had never really been considered strained. Maybe this would turn out well. Maybe both of their factions could bring the fight against those Legion cocksuckers to a conclusion in this part of the country.

Probably not, but a man could dream, couldn't he?

CHAPTER THREE

The fire was spreading and there was nothing he could do to stop it. The house was burning.

Jeremiah Williams had always hated fire. He wasn't afraid of it exactly, but he never liked its capacity to destroy everything in its path. There was nothing he could do as he stood helplessly outside the large house, besides watch it burn. All the memories of his family were in there.

Tears began to streak down his face. He wished he could use those tears to douse the flames. His parents and his sister had all died three years ago, in 1918. That damn Spanish flu. There were photographs of them in that burning house. And his sister's diary, which he was shamed to admit he had read front to back since she had died. It was all he had left of them; besides the objects they had owned, which were also in that house.

And now those memories were all being erased. No, not the memories, he told himself. Just mementos of the memories. He was the one that held the actual memories themselves. He wouldn't let them be forgotten so easily, house or no house.

"What happened here?" A woman's voice.

He turned his soot and tear-streaked face toward the most beautiful woman he had ever laid eyes on. She had the most lustrous and shining black hair, and oh God, those blue eyes of hers. How could they be so damn blue? They were beautiful.

He didn't have any control over what he did next. He just rushed into her arms, sobbing like a little damn baby.

"All the memories of my family are in there," He was crying uncontrollably in her arms, and a small part of his mind expected her to push him away, but instead she hugged him back. She made little shushing noises and smoothed his hair, then rubbed the tears off his dirty face as she looked into his eyes.

"It's alright, Seike," she whispered softly. "Everything is going to be alright."

Who was Seike, he wondered as he stared back at her. Did she mistake him for someone else?

He stared back at the burning house. Something wasn't right. It couldn't have burned that much in just these last few moments. He turned back to the woman. She was looking at him in the most sympathetic way. Something was familiar about her.

"Wait… Selinda?"

Seike jerked awake.

That dream, yet again. Always when he slept it was the same dream with only slight differences. She didn't usually call him by his Ambrogaeic name. In fact, he was fairly certain that whenever she called him by any name in the dream, it was Jeremiah. His name when he had been human. Strange, but not overly odd. The dream always had these little differences. It was the only dream he had had since the day of her death.

It was mostly just a memory though, for that's how the two of them had met. He was standing outside his burning house, and she came to ask him if he was alright. That's how it had all begun. Thinking back on it now, he experienced a moment of clarity in which he realized that being what he now was could be regarded, in a way, as a gift. A gift, because the memory of his family was still alive in him, even after all this time. He was partly glad that it was the only dream he had, because it helped him remember his human life more clearly when awake. He was also partly glad that the need for sleep was very seldom as an Ambrogis. Perhaps a few hours every week was all. If he had to sleep every single day and dream that same dream, he might have ended up going mad with grief years ago.

He was in his private chamber in the haven. Elder Kesel had ordered him to get a few hours of sleep in, to help his mind stay focused on the task ahead.

The council, most notably Jurai, was displeased that Seike had been personally requested by the General. Well, demanded, really. He had received thirty lashings upon the final statement of his punishment, the first of a three-phase penalty. They had healed already. His back was as smooth as it had always been. The second part was to contact Field Base A-92 and personally apologize for the commotion he had caused, as well as to relay the council's own apologies. The third part was something Seike truly hadn't seen coming, and something he very much despised.

He was ordered to stay in the haven until he became 'fairly adept' at the ancient tongue, a language known only to the Ambrogae and known usually by that moniker. Officially it was called Ambrogaeic. He would not be allowed to leave until, through tutelage and personal study of the library's collection, he had acquired a comprehensive knowledge of both speaking and understanding the language, as well as writing it.

Elder Kesel knew that their stay at the base could extend to quite a while, so he had convinced the council that while there, the young scientist, whose name was Marikya, would tutor him in the language. She was extremely adept and spoke it as fluently as many of the oldest Ambrogae of Seline. She also took her duties very seriously and Kesel had no doubt that she would not let Seike get away without his lessons. From Seike's point of view, her one saving grace was that she was far too curious about him to be afraid or disdainful. She asked him too many questions, though, whenever he was around at the same time as she was. Sometimes the questions were a little too personal for Seike's liking, so he had come to find Marikya rather annoying over time.

Still, he didn't mind her despite that. Maybe it was even because of that. Most of the other blues ignored him or only spoke to him when necessary. She was one of the few who actually sought him out, of her own volition, at times. As for the other two who were assigned to the team, one was the young noble who had come to gather him for the deliverance of his punishment. He had since learned the man's name was Tannik. The other was an individual who didn't like Seike, nor trust him. None other than the spawn of Jurai and Ferana themselves. Their one and only son, Kaisimir. Another noble. And one who was far too stuck up his own ass for Seike to ever like him either.

Kaisimir was noble by birth, whereas most of the nobility gained their status through age and experience. Even the 'young' Tannik was over four hundred years old, though his hair was still completely dark, with not a single white or gray hair on his head. Kaisimir was barely older than Seike, if you included Seike's life as a human. Not even a hundred and fifty years old. He was considered something of a prodigy in the area of psychometry, Seike's worst area of the esoteric studies. And that was the reason he was chosen for the mission. Supposedly.

Seike knew it was probably because Jurai and Ferana wanted a close eye kept on him for the duration of their stay at the base. After this mission was done, Seike was to return to the Central Haven and stay put for however long it took him to learn how to speak the ancient tongue. He was a bit pissed about the punishment, still. He would do it, of course, but it pissed him off. He was certain that the punishment was Jurai's idea. He knew that Seike had almost no interest in the ancient tongue and even less interest in most literary works of any kind, even those in English.

Moreover, the part that really irked Seike was that he had to stay within the haven indefinitely until he displayed a sufficient understanding of the language. Jurai knew he liked to walk among the humans as stress relief.

Elder Kesel maintained that it was really a rather light punishment, in his opinion. Seike knew that Kesel was actually looking forward to the young Ambrogis learning the ancient tongue, however he tried to hide that fact. Seike thought, though not seriously, that he might have preferred to be banished from the havens.

Yes, it was just punishment, even he had to admit that to himself. He took two lives, however indirectly. And here he was moping about having to learn a language that he really should have learned long ago. He shook his head, berating himself. He could see things from the old ones' perspectives. He was acting like a young and spoiled brat, which is exactly what he was to them. Young, spoiled, and inexperienced in the ways of the Ambrogae. He had to change that. He wouldn't shirk his duty to the haven, nor his penance.

On the plus side, he had managed to convince the Elder to allow him to make a call while they were in Iowa City. He had dialed Jackson. He convinced Elder Kesel that it would be in the haven's best interest if he had a reason for disappearing from Jack and Ferg's radar for a while, in case they wondered too actively what was going on, maybe enough to ask around town. Kesel had thought it wasn't a bad precaution to take, so Seike told Jack that he was going out of town for a while, though he wasn't sure how long. He told him that it was work-related. As far as Jack knew, he was Jeremiah the IT guy, computer whiz extraordinaire. It was easy to convince him that he got a temporary position outside of Iowa, and that he'd be back eventually. Jack would relay that information to Fergus, and all would be well on that front.

He let a few more minutes pass before sitting up on the bed. A small yawn escaped him. He looked at his watch, which was analogue rather than digital. That was as technological as this place got. Clocks and watches. He had slept for nearly four hours. Plenty of sleep, he would be good for a while now.

A light knock came at his door.

"Come in," he said.

The head that popped in was not an entirely unwelcome sight. It was Marikya. A petite woman of youthful appearance. Young looking especially considering that she was almost four hundred years old herself. She probably only had another few decades before being raised to the status of noble.

"Sorry to intrude, Seike. I know you just woke up."

There was no need to ask her how she knew that. Marikya was especially empathic. She could detect Ambrogae with more distance and clarity than most of Seline's brood. That was the second main reason that she had been chosen for the assignment, aside from the fact that she was an extremely adept physicist and biologist, with a good education in various other sciences as well. Apparently, she had known Galileo personally.

"That's okay, Marikya. Don't worry about it."

"The Elder asked me to give you a small lesson before we set out, which will be only two or so hours from now."

"Okay, no problem."

She raised her eyebrow at him, a little smirk forming on her face. "Well, it *is* a problem that you've been an Ambrogis for very nearly a century now and you probably don't even know what my name means, or the Elder's name means, in Ambrogaeic."

"The Elder's name means 'He who flies'."

"*One* who flies," Marikya corrected. Seike could tell this was going to be an arduous time, indeed.

"Right. Sorry."

"And your name?"

Seike had come to be proud of the meaning of his name. "The light of the fire," he said automatically. Selinda had named him so, when he was ready to leave behind his human name. It was a rite of passage for a sire to name any brood they might have.

"You can also just think of it as 'fire's light', but you are correct. And my name? Do you know what Marikya means in the ancient tongue? We'll be starting with names, in case you haven't guessed."

Seike just shrugged. He honestly had no idea. Marikya smirked a little, again.

"It means 'lover of flowers'."

Seike must have had a strange look on his face, because Marikya gave a quiet chuckle after seeing his expression. "I thought you were a biologist," he said, maybe a little sarcastically.

She shrugged. "I make a fairly good botanist, as well, when the need arises. And I do love flowers."

Seike couldn't help but allow himself a bit of a smile at that statement. He couldn't really picture this woman spending time with plants. She had always been more interested in formulas and books, or so he thought. He didn't really know her well, of course.

"What does the name Jurai mean?"

"Hole of the ass."

She actually laughed at that. "Oh, this is going to take some time, but I imagine it will be fun." Seike didn't think it was going to be fun, but at least he didn't mind his tutor. She then informed him that the name Jurai actually meant 'oath keeper'. Seike couldn't really argue with that, as Jurai had always been a man of his word, even if the two of them didn't get along well. Elder Kesel had respect for him, at any rate.

As she began to list off the names of people within the haven and what their meaning was in the ancient tongue, Seike thought that there could have been worse punishments doled out to him. He couldn't really think of any, but he felt sure that things could have been worse.

Olinar didn't like the situation, as it stood. Nor did Almeidra. The other two scouts, Ignusai and Woitan, seemed content with their lot.

King Coranthis had appointed the four of them to be leaders in a larger force that was to explore and inquire throughout the human realms in the central United States. At present, they were still in Minnesota. Ignusai was to take his force to North Dakota and make his way down throughout South Dakota, with Woitan going from Minnesota to Wisconsin and then Michigan. He and Almeidra would go to Iowa and check that state out together, then split apart to check out the surrounding states. He would go to Nebraska and Kansas, and she would go to Missouri and Illinois.

It had just been the four of them as a team for years, and now they would be going their separate ways before long. Ignusai and Woitan had little experience in leadership, and Almeidra wasn't much better off: She was smart enough to know that her inexperience could mean trouble, but the other two were all too happy to get to barking orders.

Of course, Olinar didn't question the wisdom of his liege. He was merely of the opinion that perhaps either Ignusai or Woitan wouldn't be up to task. Or both of them. In any case, like it or not, orders were orders. The forces they had been assigned were all devout men and women, and all were pure bloods. That mattered most. Olinar didn't want any half bloods mucking up the situation any more than Coranthis himself wanted it.

The city of Saint Paul had been a bust, they had found nothing there. A few times they thought they could feel some of those blue vermin, but the rats had scuttled away from them. No human that any of them had spoken with could recall seeing any individuals with unnaturally bright blue eyes, either. They had searched most of the surrounding small towns as well as combed through the forests, keeping away from the spot where those S-47 scum were, as ordered. Again, nothing.

Olinar's phone rang, and he swiped right to answer the call. It was Almeidra.

"Nothing here either, sir," she sounded disgusted, whether with the situation or her own inability to find anything concrete, he wasn't sure. "There's no trail to follow, we haven't even found any of the Seline worshippers. How are we supposed to find this prick?"

"I feel you, Almeidra. It's only going to get more difficult and take longer once we leave Minnesota. We're almost done here, but we can't rush things. It would be better, obviously, if we could find even an inkling before leaving the state."

"I understand that. I'll move on from Grand Rapids and head towards Bagley then, sir."

"Sounds good. Happy hunting," it came out in a sarcastic tone, but Olinar couldn't help himself. He could almost feel Almeidra smile on the other end. He hung up.

He was presently in Redwood Falls, a quaint little den of humanity. Small town, basically a village in today's world. Very rural. Easy hunting grounds. Most of Minnesota was easy hunting, really. Lots of rural areas, lots of people that tried their best to pretend they were living in a world without the Ambrogae. He was still perfectly sated from their previous meal of S-47 soldiers, but he could eat. Maybe he could find a hot little number at a local restaurant before he left town. Poke around for info before settling in for a snack.

He was still musing over the possibility of getting in a kill and some fresh blood when he felt it. That barely tangible, but indisputable presence. He couldn't tell which direction it was coming from, but there was most definitely a blue nearby. And they were getting closer. Slowly. Slow enough to be on foot rather than in some kind of car or truck. Okay, so that was something to go on.

Olinar himself was seated in his Ford Mustang. He actually didn't much like Ford, but he did like his Mustang. Emerald green, 1977. He decided to stay put and see if the blue kept coming closer. After a few more moments, he did indeed feel that whoever was out there was getting progressively closer. A thought then occurred to him.

Whoever they were had probably felt his own presence by now, and they were still closing in.

Olinar wasn't scared, because they were close enough now that he could sense with certainty that it was only one person. He felt very confident that he could take on one blue, no matter who they might be. The oldest of the blues tended to stay in their little places of safety, wherever those might be. It was almost a sure thing that this one was young.

It was almost midnight, and no one was on the streets that he could see. Another minute passed, and he saw someone slowly walking up the road, after turning from a corner street. It was a man, and he was looking around like a hunter. Looking in windows of both cars and the buildings near him as he passed. The man was heading Olinar's way. And he was definitely the blue, Olinar could feel him distinctly at this distance. What genuine luck, he thought. The man was hunting, but little did he know that he was the prey.

Closer the man crept, until he was only a few cars away from Olinar's. If he had been seen, the man gave no indication of it, as he still seemed to be searching. Olinar contemplated firing his silenced pistol directly into the man's heart. That would put him down easily, then the scout leader could capture him and question him. Pride got the better of him, though, and he opened his car door and stepped out onto the sidewalk. The rest of his forces were lurking nearby. Doubtless some of them, the closer ones anyway, had felt this blue's presence as well. All Olinar had to do was press a particular button on his phone, and they would come.

If it was even necessary.

"Yo, looking for someone?" Olinar was larger than most men, his skin was snowy white like all pure bloods, and his hair was black and shaggy. He looked a little like Jim Morrison on human growth hormone. He towered over the startled Ambrogis in front of him.

"Yeah. You." The man had quickly regained his composure and seemed totally unafraid. He even had a smile on his face. "Well, not you in particular. You or any of the others of your kind I can feel around here. Pass this message along to your buddies. Leave town, now."

Olinar couldn't help but have a chuckle at the man's audacity. He could see the man clearly at this distance, and he could feel from the presence that this was a fight that Olinar would win. So why was this guy being so cocky when he knew that he was facing off against not only one superior opponent, but was in fact surrounded by multiple foes?

He asked as much. "Do you understand the gravity of the situation you're in, my man?"

The man only smiled. Then he did something unexpected. He clapped his hands together once, loudly. Suddenly, Olinar could feel another blue close by, then another...

Within the next ten seconds, he couldn't accurately count the number of blues he could feel nearby. Shit. Shit, shit, shit. He didn't know they could hide themselves like that. Did anyone of the Leviathan know? What he did know was that the tables had suddenly turned. He had six more men in this town, not including himself. There were definitely more blues here than that. He contemplated pressing the button on his phone but decided against it.

"Alright. You want us to leave? Have it your way, we're done in this place anyway. Just let me phone one of my buddies to pass along the message, yeah?"

"Sure man, knock yourself out." Cocky motherfucker. Seemed like he had a reason to be cocky, after all. Olinar would be too in a situation like that. Hell, a minute ago, he had been feeling pretty cocky himself.

He dialed one of his boys here in Redwood Falls. "Yeah, we're leaving." After those words, he hung up the phone, and got back in his Mustang. He didn't need to say any more than that, because the rest of his crew could feel them out there too. He who runs away, lives another day. Close enough, anyway.

He started up the engine and looked just once more at the man outside his car. The man gave him a little wave, and Olinar wanted to give him the finger. He didn't, but he wanted to.

He could already feel his boys getting the hell out of dodge. Time to join them.

The man, whose name was Samaiel, watched the green Mustang drive out of downtown Redwood Falls rather hastily. He whistled appreciatively at the sound the engine made as the vehicle accelerated. Beautiful car, really. Too bad it was owned by such a piece of shit. He would have liked to have taken the guy out just for the car, but it was a risk he couldn't take. Already he was feeling the strain of what he was doing. He wouldn't be able to hold the net much longer.

He gave it another couple of minutes, until he couldn't even faintly feel the presence of any of those murderous Legion dicks. Then, he clapped once loudly. The net dropped, and the feeling of others of his kind around him vanished slowly. There was no finer empath than Samaiel among those of Seline. At least, that's what he liked to think. Certainly, that was one trick none of the other empaths had ever been able to replicate. He had never gotten to use it around a group that large before, though. Usually no more than one or two wandered through this town at a time, and this was the first time in years that he had encountered a pure blood.

He was hoping they would go around telling others of their kind that the blues had more power than they realized, and to stay the heck out of Redwood Falls. He hoped, but he didn't count on it. Those creeps were looking for something, or someone. And he was almost positive that the one they were looking for was Seike. Not completely certain, but reasonably.

Man, what to do? Samaiel was a known wanderer, and he spent less time in the Central Haven than even the violet-eyed one himself. His solution was simple. Sunglasses, even at night. He had never had any issues with humans just because he had sunglasses on even in the middle of the night. Plenty of weirdos who were just normal humans wore sunglasses at night. Thank you, Corey Hart. He had taken them off for the encounter with this pure blood, of course. He had wanted the prick to see his blue eyes clearly.

It seemed like he was going to have to pay the haven a little visit. He only hoped he could avoid that old windbag Kesel while he was in. He really didn't feel like another lecture about the dangers of travelling alone as an Ambrogis of Seline.

Ah well, he might as well suck it up and go grace the place with his presence yet again. And he felt like this was something that should be done sooner rather than later. No walking, as much as he loved to walk.

He had better take his Chevy.

CHAPTER FOUR

Robert Crawley was staring out of the large window, which was the entire wall, of his boardroom. The meeting had concluded a few minutes ago and he was now alone again. Alone to mull over the situation here in California.

That whore Ludia and her merry band of do-gooders had been a serious pain in his neck lately.

He gazed out at the cityscape of Los Angeles. His city. As much as that wench and her kind would like to believe otherwise, the entire west coast was his. Not theirs, not the humans. His. He had been around since the thirteenth century, becoming that which he had grown to love being before the turn of the fourteenth century.

His sire had never known the likes of him. And the old fool had not seen his own death coming. That had happened before the turning of the sixteenth century, and Robert had taken that arrogant man for all he had been worth. Which had been a pretty penny. He had killed his sire himself, not long after refusing to take on an Ambrogaeic name. He had been born Robert Crawley and that is who he would always be. He had grand plans and ambitions for his own future and the future of the world. He would be the crows that infested the clearing, as was his namesake.

One day, he would be a king. Not of the Ambrogae, and not of the humans. But of the world.

Triaclon Industries was his creation. He had built it from the ground up. He had stocks in many other businesses, because more money was always good, but his own company was where the real magic happened. His kind was known to the original Ambrogae as half bloods, those who had been human before being turned. They looked down on what he was, but they were fools.

At Triaclon Industries, everyone that held a position of leadership was an Ambrogae. To be more specific, a half blood. And all of them proudly used their human names, even those who had been offered to be named by a sire. Robert detested the so-called pure bloods. Most of his employees shared that resentment. He didn't openly reveal that to them, of course. Instead, he pretended to be one of their pawns in surface world affairs, while secretly playing them for the fools he knew them to be. He made moves against the followers of Seline mostly according to the whims of those who considered themselves his masters, but really it was always in his best interest to make those moves. And whenever he took out a player, he took them for everything they were worth. Whether they had blue eyes, or red ones.

Every day his ambitions were getting closer to becoming realized. Half bloods usually only lived for a few thousand years as most, as opposed to a more than double that lifespan among the pure bloods. No one knew for certain how long the followers of Seline could live, only that it was longer than a half blood. They had not even been around for five thousand years, but several of the original ones were still alive. A fact that played into Robert's plans.

Robert Crawley planned to live forever.

Not only that, but despite not even being a thousand years old, he had already managed to become more powerful than that putz Coranthis. And that wasn't by measure of his own ego, either. He had conducted all the necessary tests and went through simulated scenarios to determine the authenticity of such a claim as scientific fact. Leviathan had bestowed him with certain rare gifts. Gifts that allowed him to grow rapidly in knowledge and power over the course of the centuries, when coupled with his own personality and ambition.

His specialty was twofold. He was telekinetic, which was rare among those of the Leviathan, and rarer still among those of the Serpent. But what had truly allowed him to grow in power over the years was his very particular skill in psychometry.

When he drank blood, he gained the knowledge of the victim, so long as he took their life in the process.

This was something that he alone could do, and he knew of no one other than himself that could. Centuries ago, there was one other he had known that possessed this singular and potentially unique gift. His sire. Had his sire been alive today, Robert was sure that the old creature would have done away with him before this point in time. Once they had found out each other's secret, it was only natural that one of them had to die.

The Leviathan had chosen Robert, though, in the end. Not his pure-blooded sire. The circumstances that had brought about the opportunity he had been presented to end his sire's life could only have been arranged by a God. Coincidence was simply impossible. And so, Robert was a believer. A true believer. He was the chosen one, after all. How could he not believe?

That delectable Haley Stafford had been yet another successful piece to the puzzle that he was in the process of completing. It was her imagination, more so than her actual intellect. She had had a way of looking at the molecular make-up of the building blocks of reality. She had seen things from unique angles. Probably as a result of all the drugs she had done in her teenage and college years.

And besides that, her blood had an absolutely exquisite flavor. He had even saved some of it for later. Not for the knowledge it brought, he had already acquired all of that. Simply for the taste.

It was mostly thanks to his unique psychometric trait that he was probably one of the most powerful of the Ambrogae on or inside the planet, but it was also due to his willingness to use himself as a guinea pig for the research he and his collaborators conducted. In the last decade, he had injected himself with numerous solutions, and most had proven extremely beneficial to him.

He allowed his collaborators to inject themselves as well. They were all in this together after all. A new world, for the true future masters of it. Besides, he was older and far more powerful than any of them. Not to mention a thousand times more intelligent.

He gazed out of the floor to ceiling window, settling his eyes on a building about two miles off in the distance. One of Tesla's office buildings. Tesla had been irritating him lately on the stock market, influencing some of his interests toward a downward trend.

Charging his telekinetic energy, he made a slight waving motion with his left hand, and watched as the building began to slowly collapse. He didn't laugh, or smile. He was detached from what he had just done. He only did it to increase his funds for future research.

Again, Samaiel cursed under his breath. Just his luck.

His baby, his Bertha, was dead.

The old brown '85 Chevy C10 was toast. The Silverado had ridden its last rodeo. Sad times.

He was still a good twenty miles from the entrance to the haven, and he wasn't going to risk hitchhiking any of the rest of the way. Looks like he would be walking, after all. He considered running, but he felt there was no need to rush that much. He was sure Seike was alright. The man could take care of himself.

He considered he of the violet eyes to be a friend. He didn't have a lot of friends, but not because his personality wasn't stellar. He could talk the talk just as well as he could walk the walk. He just considered friendship to be a bond forged in fire. And he went through most flames himself. He was a loner by nature, but he and Seike had been through some tough times together. That, and their personalities just meshed. They both saw the world through very similar colored lenses.

Shades of grey, man. Not black and white.

He left the truck by the side of the highway, taking a few minutes to put the important stuff in it into his backpack. If anyone saw him walking on the side of the road, they would probably imagine that he was going to stick out his thumb, because he looked the part of a hitchhiker in his plaid shirt and jeans, baseball cap and sunglasses, and backpack.

It was a sunny day in Iowa, ladies and gentlemen. And Bertha wasn't here anymore to bask in it. That truck had lasted him since he had bought it in the early nineties from a used car lot. He had mostly lived in the thing during that time, unless he was in one haven or another. For the last two decades, though, Iowa and Minnesota had been his go to states. And for the last four years, he had spent most of his time in or around Redwood Falls.

He did his best thinking while walking, anyway. It was on one of his longer sojourns that he had first devised and implemented what he had come to think of as his echo location net. That handy trick had gotten him out of plenty of tight squeezes, not that he couldn't handle himself. At nearly three hundred years old, he had gained a lot of combat experience over time, and his psionic abilities were nothing to shake a stick at.

But telepathy and empathy were his main gig. He was exceptional as a psychic, and he had gained an incredible understanding of human psychology as a result. He could put Jordan Peterson to shame. He also loved casinos. They were how he made his cash. Yeah, he sometimes cheated, but mostly he just used his own not inconsiderable skills with knowing odds, observation, and keeping a great poker face.

He would actually be passing by one of his favorite casinos on the way to the haven, but he wouldn't be stopping there. He had enough money right now, anyway. Plus, he could sense that he needed to go to the haven with as much haste as he could muster without running all the way. He had learned to trust his gut over the years, and it was telling him now that he needed to be there. Something was going down. Something big. A real game changer.

Besides, he was hungry. Some goth chick that was into vampires let him drink about a pint of her blood last week, but he hadn't had any since. They always had plenty at the haven.

He whistled as he walked the highway. In about another ten miles it would be time to leave it and follow a certain road that would lead to a bar where those going to the haven from this direction had to park their vehicles. He would see what kind of info he could pick up while he was there. The last several miles to get to the haven had to be traversed on foot, even if he still had his Chevy.

He missed her already. The sound of a solid truck had always been alluring to him. She hadn't sounded very healthy for the last few miles of her life, though. Not healthy at all. Something inside the engine block had finally blown at the end of it. No coming back from that one.

An unpleasant memory flashed into his mind as he walked. Seike, standing over Selinda's lifeless body.

It had gone down at the Central Haven. Very unpleasant business. He had taken Seike's side in that he believed they should just fry that prick Emilio and be done with it. None of that rites and ritual bullshit. If the council had listened to them, Seike's one and only would probably still be kicking. He hated to think about that fact. Almost as much as he hated more than half of the council for voting against him and Seike and Selinda, as well as the others of Seline who had taken their side in the debate. Jurai, odd as it was for him, had voted in their favor. He usually went against anything that Seike was invested in, but in that case he had seen the right of it. So had Kesel.

The other old coots for the most part were too set in their ways, which were old and archaic, just like them. Outdated.

Not for the first time, Samaiel thought there should be some newer blood on the council, instead of it being solely determined by the age of those on it. The thirteen oldest in the haven were the council members. They had been the same people for all of Samaiel's life. And he had grown to resent them, more than a little.

In fact, the council itself was one of the key reasons that Samaiel didn't spend a whole lot of time within the haven. The only reason he did go back there was to check in on some folks he actually gave a shit about, like Marikya. He just adored Marikya. He'd date her if she'd have him, but she had never seemed interested in him in that way. Or anyone else, for that matter. She just liked her books and her boards and her research. She had a lab in Iowa City that she worked at sometimes. One could find her there pretty much any time that she wasn't in the haven itself.

He looked up at the sun. For the millionth time he wished he could tan, but at the same time he was glad that he couldn't get a sunburn. He remembered sunburns from when he was still a human. They sucked.

It was taking a while, but he was steadily closing the distance to the bar. Now that he thought of it, someone there might have a blood bag with his name on it. Lots of blues frequented the place, and the owner was a sympathizer to the cause. He was a human by the name of Brad Hennick. A good guy, for sure, who had no problem with the children of Seline. In fact, he probably saw them as the only chance the world had to get back to normal. Which was most likely true. Well, as normal as it had ever been, anyway, whatever normal was supposed to be.

He did have to wonder, though, if humanity would accept a world that had just blue-eyed vampires that were all friendly towards ordinary folk.

He always thought that the government and military would turn on them if they ever got to a point where there were no more Legion vamps on the surface, at least. It was an opinion, and not a fact. But it was a reasonable assumption. Those sorts of folks probably wouldn't be content with just wiping out those who were of the Leviathan. They weren't likely to stop there, if the world ever got to that point.

Who was he kidding, though? There were maybe a million followers of Seline in the whole world, and probably more than three times that number of those Legion fucks. They were fighting a losing battle, really, as much as he hated to admit it. The best bet was to just do their best to survive and take out as many reds as they could at any given opportunity while maintaining their own numbers.

Yeah, survival was the best any of them could hope for. He wished that a blue who turned a human could guarantee another blue, that would even things out. But sadly, the majority went red. That was just the way things were, as depressing as it was.

Some of those of Seline had taken it upon themselves to turn humans who wanted to become vampires. They made it their mission. They would watch each and every person that they turned very carefully for the first three days, and if they went red, they would do them in. Simple as that. Samaiel wasn't part of that crew, and he wasn't sure what to think of them. He knew their intentions were good, in essence, but he wasn't certain of their morals in the matter.

Shades of grey, man.

He had been walking the road off the highway for a while now, and finally he could see the bar in the distance. The bar's road sign was clearly visible to him. Just for Kicks. Samaiel liked that name for a bar. He found the name rather suited the place too, and more so it suited Brad Hennick. The guy didn't take life too seriously, and he knew it was short. Even still, while he was around, he was determined to fight the good fight.

The parking lot was mostly empty. Not a big surprise for a bar in the middle of nowhere. There were more trucks than cars, as was the case every time that Samaiel had come to the place. Brad himself owned a Chevy. Post millennium, though. Yuck.

Already, he could feel the presence of a few blues. Good stuff. If there were some of his kind there right now, chances were good that Brad had gotten a shipment of primo blood bags recently. Samaiel was elated at the thought of them. He was far from starving, but oh man was he hungry. Maybe he'd get a burger and a beer too. Why not?

As he approached the door to the bar, he was more than a little surprised at who walked out before he could walk in. It was Jurai. He recovered from the surprise quickly though and shot him the customary greeting.

"It's been a while, old dude."

Not a laugh, not a smile in response. As usual, Jurai seemed cold and distant. Samaiel wondered what he was doing here. Council members rarely left the haven.

"Hello, Samaiel. Heading to the haven, are we?"

"Yeah. Got some news to share."

"You can share it with me, right now. Then go and feed, you look famished."

"I am hungry, councilman. Not why I came though. There's something going down in Minnesota."

The councilman regarded Samaiel for a moment, head tilted to one side slightly. Then he responded. "I'm afraid that you've been gone too long yet again, my young friend. I take it you've come here about an incursion of reds in that state? We're already aware of that. A man of your unusual talent might be needed for a certain task that I have in mind, however. A good thing I encountered you here."

A good thing indeed. What *was* the councilman doing here, anyway? Samaiel decided to ask as much. "You don't usually leave the haven, Jurai. What brings you here?"

The councilman smiled a small smile then. "I wanted to be a part of the patrols that we recently sent to scout out the perimeter of the haven. We're checking all the hot spots, and even a bit beyond them."

Samaiel whistled a bit as he realized that the situation might be even more dire than he had thought. He asked the obvious question next.

"Where's Seike? Has he been here?"

"It's funny that you ask that, as I would like you to join him at his present location. He's at Field Base A-92."

"Are you fucking kidding me? What the fuck is he doing there?"

"Language, please."

"Sorry, Jurai. Seriously though, what is going on? I felt that I needed to return and that something big was going on, cause I had a crazy encounter myself, in Redwood Falls. But I didn't expect… wait, is it just Seike there? Or did you send others?"

The councilman leveled his gaze at Samaiel. "A team of four, including Seike. And my own son. And Marikya." That gaze sharpened at the mention of Marikya's name. Jurai knew how he felt about her, and he knew that he had him now, hook, line and sinker. Samaiel let out a breath that he didn't know he was holding in.

"Your skills would be an asset for the assignment, Samaiel, but I can't force you." He just did though, that clever old fart.

"I'm gonna need a drink, first," Samaiel said in resignation.

Jurai smiled again.

CHAPTER FIVE

The rain pattered softly on the leaves of the trees overhead. Kaisimir was rather fond of rain, he had been since he was a child. Tristram had the four of them spread out around the forest, trying to feel for the presence of any of the children of the Leviathan. So far, they had found no sign other than an area with some ashes, which Marikya had informed them had likely been the remains of the patrol that went missing. Kaisimir had run his hands through the ash, feeling that they had indeed once been human. They had reported as much to the General, who cursed and swore about it before ordering them to continue sweeping the area.

At the moment, the four of them were separated, and so Kaisimir was alone to think on their present circumstances. Naturally, he blamed Seike for this mess. He of the violet eyes was the reason that the four of them were in this precarious situation. Never mind the fact that it was the first time that those of Seline were cooperating with S-47 directly, rubbing shoulders with the distrustful humans. Seike killing Emilio was the real problem.

Granted, a part of him was glad that Emilio was dead. He felt sure that every child of Seline that had heard about the death felt some kind of relief from the information. The problem, however, was what had been revealed to them about those of the Leviathan releasing pheromones upon dying. In Emilio's particular case, those pheromones had led the reds to discover the location of Field Base A-92. Once they returned to the base from this sweep, Marikya was to be brought up to date on everything that S-47 knew about their chemical make-up.

Kaisimir was no fool, despite his youth. The reds had been here and since left, which meant that by now the location of this base was no longer a secret to a great deal of their kind in the area, if not the entire central United States.

He looked up at one of the cameras that were positioned throughout these woods. A thought then occurred to him.

In the report that his team had been given, a sergeant by the name of O'neil had told them that the cameras had their images frozen for the duration of the incursion. Presently, Kaisimir approached the tree to which this camera was attached. It was fairly high up, far too high to reach from the ground, but that posed no issue. The camera had followed his movement and was now pointing directly down at him. He began to quickly climb the tree towards it.

He gently laid his hand on the device once he reached it and allowed his focus to heighten. At first, he couldn't sense anything. After a few moments, however, he felt what he had suspected. A tangible residue of psionic energy. He used his psychometry to try to delve further into the residue. There. A female. Full of malice at the time she had disabled this camera. He tried to probe even further… Damn. He had reached the limit; it had been too long since the camera was tampered with. He was unable to ascertain a name or anything else. With a sigh, he let himself drop lightly to the ground below.

Static buzzed momentarily on the intercom badge he and the others had been given before departing the base for this sweep of the area. Kelloway's voice came through.

"What the hell was that all about? You got some kind of fetish or something?"

Kaisimir chuckled lightly. He couldn't help but like the General, he admitted to himself. The man was full of nervous humor that he used to mask the seriousness of the situation.

I was seeking out information on the intruders, General," Kaisimir and the others had been told before they left the haven that this was to be an unprecedented level of cooperation between their haven and the people of S-47. As such, the humans were going to inevitably learn more about the Ambrogae, and in turn the people of Seline were going to learn more about what the humans had themselves learned so far. "I was able to discern that it was certainly a red that disabled your cameras. A woman. Unfortunately, I couldn't get a name or any other information, aside from the fact that she felt very predatory at the time of the incident."

He heard Kelloway whistle appreciatively over the intercom. "You figured that out just by feeling up my camera? That's psychometry, right? I thought that was something only rarely done by us humans. Are you tellin' me that it's something that all of your kind can do?"

The young noble was aware that the General was phishing for any information he could use in the future, but again he reminded himself that this was to be an unprecedented level of cooperation. "Yes, General. Though, most of us have very limited levels of skill with the ability. I was put on the team because it's something I excel at."

"What about the reds, can they do it too?"

"Unfortunately, they can, General Kelloway. We're all Ambrogae, and we share most of the same kinds of powers and abilities."

Kaisimir listened as the General swore over the intercom before replying. "Well, that's just perfect." Sarcasm was another of the General's emotional defense mechanisms. Sarcasm and humor. Kaisimir really did like the man's personality.

"General, we have been out here for over two hours, now." Closer to three. "There are no reds out here, and I don't think we're going to find anything else."

Another sound of static as Kelloway switched off the channel briefly. Moments later, the intercom activated again. "Alright you four, come back to the base. We've got some things to discuss, anyway." There was a pause, and then, "You managed to gather some solid intel, good job out there." He actually sounded like he meant it. The man had obviously earned his rank, as far as Kaisimir was concerned, and didn't seem to bear any particular grudge against his kind, despite that they were Ambrogae.

The rain chose that moment to increase in downpour. It was coming through the canopy more heavily now, and Kaisimir's blue shirt and jeans began to get even more saturated than they already were. Good timing. He didn't mind, though. Rain was beautiful, to him.

Tristram Kelloway watched as the four black-haired, ivory-skinned people before him toweled themselves off in the debriefing room. They really seemed to act just like any other human. He leaned back in his leather chair at the head of the table as they finished drying themselves. A soldier stood ready to take the towels. After they were dry, the General merely motioned for them to take seats on either side of the table.

Once they were seated, Kelloway spoke up.

"Okay. So before you four went out there, we were still completely in the dark about the details of events the other day. Now we know for certain that my men are dead, and we know the reds are responsible. We also know that at least one of them was a woman, and that she used some kind of ability to screw with our security system. That's a hell of a lot better than having nothing to report."

The team Kelloway had immediately sent out to scour the perimeter upon failure of the patrol reporting in had uncovered sweet fuck all. Already, the General was feeling he made the right call in demanding that Kesel send a team over to his neck of the woods. He had done so in a sort of panic, he knew, but his gut had told him it was the right call at the time and that was the only reason he went through with the demand. He was also glad that his men didn't seem *too* perturbed at having a group of vampires in the facility. It was something they weren't completely unaccustomed to, anyway, as they held several reds there at any given time.

The soldiers weren't used to the blue eyes being here, however. Other than the woman that Kesel used to send over occasionally, many years ago, there had never been any of the blue-eyed ones allowed into the base. All communication was accomplished electronically. He was proud of his men and women at their ability to cope well with having vampires walking around the base outside of a cage. Even if some of them seemed a little more nervous around this Seike. Hell, that one even made the General himself a bit anxious. Considering their last encounter, that was no surprise. Give it some time, the General thought.

It was the woman who spoke first in response. "I would like to examine these pheromones as soon as possible, if that's alright with you, sir." She was the only one that called him 'sir'. The other three had thus far referred to him by his rank or name. Kelloway didn't care, though. These weren't his soldiers. They were allies, but not technically under his command.

"Of course, Marikya, was it? I get your name right?" He waited for her nod before continuing. "Yes, I'll have my lead biologist begin his collaboration with you posthaste, Marikya. In fact, I'll let him know you're coming right now. Corporal, would you escort our guest down to lab nineteen?" The General had turned his steely blue eyes toward one of the soldiers standing on either side of the door to the debriefing room, silently daring the man to so much as stammer.

The man snapped a crisp salute. "Yes, sir! If you'll come with me, miss, I will show you the way."

As Marikya got up from the table, the general said to the corporal, "Introduce her to Doctor Peterson, once you get there. I'll radio him right now and let him know you're on the way." Kelloway did just that, pressing the intercom on his suit, and letting his leading biologist know about the visitor he was about to receive. He hoped the little bastard wasn't going to ask her to submit to some experiment or another, he didn't want to dampen his relationship with these vampires, now. They were too close to fostering a stronger partnership with one another's factions. Something that Kelloway felt there was a need for, now that Field Base A-92 had finally been compromised.

Once Marikya left the room with the corporal, Tristram again regarded the three blues still sitting at the table. Each of them were regarding him, as well. "So, in the dossiers that Kesel had you four bring me, it states that your specialty, Tannik, is combat. You as strong as Seike here?" The General doubted he was, and Tannik admitted as much.

"No, General Kelloway, I am not. I would wager that I am vastly superior with any kind of firearm, and perhaps better at martial arts, but as far as I know, there are not any people of Seline that are as skilled as Seike in the psionic arts. I must admit, I would probably only last a few minutes against him in hand-to-hand combat. At most."

The general chuckled. "A few minutes against him, eh? Sounds like you're pretty damn tough, to me, just based on that alone. Over a dozen of my men didn't even last a few seconds against him. Good. So, we have two combat specialists, a scientist, and someone who can glean information from any kind of object."

"And people," Kaisimir put in. "If I touch a person, I can get information about any physical actions they performed within the last day or two. It's not reading their mind. It's reading their body." The General didn't say anything right away, but instead considered the implications of an ability such as the one this Kaisimir possessed. He would make an incredibly useful spy. A damn super spy. He noticed the reproachful look that Tannik shot toward Kaisimir as the young man spoke. So, the older Tannik was indeed the wiser, and figured maybe young Kaisimir was being a little too forthcoming. That's alright. They were all going to have to learn to be a little more trusting over time, that was all there was to it. That included himself.

Time to reveal to them what Kesel had reported while they were out. "Your faction is sending over another team member. Someone named Samaiel. What are you grinning at, purple eyes?" The general saw that Seike's face lit up and a sort of stupid grin had spread across his face at mention of the new one's name. A friend of his, maybe? Or something more? Was the man interested in other men, perhaps?

"Samaiel is a friend of mine. We've been through a lot of fights, together. He's going to round out this team nicely." The purple eyed freak was still grinning. So, not a lover, then. A brother-in-arms. Another soldier. That was good. Kelloway had a feeling, another gut feeling, that they were going to need as many blue eyes as Kesel was willing to send his way, and the more that specialized in being soldiers, the better.

"He going to bring a dossier on himself too?" The General asked. The other three exchanged glances, and Seike just shrugged. They kept glancing at each other, and now even Tannik was smiling. Just who the hell was this Samaiel, anyway? He noticed that Kaisimir now wore a small frown.

"Am I missing something, here, fellas? Please enlighten me." Kelloway didn't like being kept in the dark. "What's got you all so worked up over this guy?"

"He's a bit of a loose cannon." This from Kaisimir. Great, so that's what had Seike smiling like a fool. They weren't sending another professional his way, they were sending a damned renegade. Someone who vibed with this reckless purple eyed vampire. Not that it bothered Kelloway too much. If the man could fight, and was going to fight on the General's side, then he was a welcome addition. He just hoped that this Samaiel had more respect for authority than Seike did.

"Take what Kaisimir says with a grain of salt, General," Tannik said. "Samaiel is going to be a welcome addition to the team. He has some unique abilities, and I would put his combat prowess on par with my own. He's a warrior."

Unique abilities, huh? Well, that sounded interesting. At any rate, if he could go toe to toe with Seike for a few minutes as well, then Kelloway would welcome him with open arms. More manpower was always a good thing, and these vampires seemed to think pretty highly of this Samaiel, even if he was, as Kaisimir put it, a loose cannon.

Tristram had been something of a loose cannon himself in his younger days, and it had proven to be an asset more so than a detriment. Helped him think outside the box.

"Can you tell me more about these unique abilities of his?" Kelloway couldn't help but ask. It was Seike who responded.

"He can sense the presence of reds further off than any of us here, for one thing. As well as being more precise with the direction they're in." Well, that did sound pretty damn useful. Seike continued, "He's a bit of a joker, General, but I think you'll find him to be pleasant company. And he's careful. Even if he knows exactly where a red is, he never gives it away with his body language. On the contrary, he usually plays stupid with them. To his advantage."

So, whoever this Samaiel was, he was some sort of strategist. That was good, too. Renegade or not, if he had a military mind, he would definitely be welcome in Kelloway's company. He already liked the rest of the team that Kesel had sent, aside from Seike. He still couldn't bring himself to like that one. Maybe in the future his opinion would change, but for the present, he couldn't let go of the fact that one of his soldiers had died by that purple eyed bastard's hands. Even if it had been accidental. He recalled the incident.

When Seike had first shown up at the base he had tried talking, to his credit. When the troops opened fire before being given the order, Tristram had known things were about to get messy. In the ensuing skirmish, one of the soldiers had managed to sneak close enough to the violet-eyed vampire to put a gun right up against his temple and was about to pull the trigger when the soldier was elbowed by Seike. The General knew now that it hadn't been intended to be a lethal blow, but at the time, accident or not, it was. Seike's elbow had connected a little too close to the soldier's heart and had sent the man flying. A broken rib had managed to pierce the man's heart, either from the blow itself or connecting to the wall, and he was instantly dead. Since coming back to Field Base A-92, Seike had again apologized to the General, and he did seem sincere in it. God knew accidents happened, but Tristram was still wrestling with the notion of forgiving the vampire for killing one of his men. Even if it hadn't been on purpose and was sincerely in self-defense.

After all, Kelloway had had to tell the man's family that their boy had been killed in action. The official story was a terrorist attack, of course. It stung him to have to lie to any family members of any of his men, but he had grown used to that over the years. It was a necessary evil.

Then of course there was Willams, but the General didn't find fault in Seike for that incident. In fact, he blamed himself for overlooking that aspect of the insub's files. It was right there in the paperwork. The man's girlfriend had been raped and murdered by a red. When he had initially gone over the soldier's dossier, Kelloway thought it would probably give the man grit. He was wrong about that, he knew now. It had made the man bitter and resentful, and he couldn't have that kind of instability happening within S-47. It had only been days since Seike had initially come to this base, but already Kelloway had ordered an update on everyone's psychological profiles. He didn't want any kind of repeat of that nature.

He looked now at the violet-eyed vampire, making himself meet those eyes. "So, you say you and this Samaiel have been through thick and thin together, huh? He older than you?" Tristram was aware that they were aware that he was consistently phishing for information from them, but he wasn't about to stop that little game. Anything that they could give him could be used in the fight against the reds, and age was something that these immortal beings never seemed to discuss much, whether they were allies or prisoners.

"Yes," Seike replied. "Quite a lot older, actually. Not as old as Mirakya or Tannik, but older than Kaisimir and I." Fuck it, thought Tristram. He was just going to ask straight out.

"If you don't mind telling me, how old are you?"

Again, the three remaining vampires glanced at one another. Kaisimir looked a little uncomfortable. Tannik just raised an eyebrow at Seike. For a moment, the General thought he was going to decline to answer. But answer he did.

"I'm well past my first century of life. I'm the youngest of us here."

The general had involuntarily been leaning a little forward in his chair, and now he sat back into it. He had honestly figured that the violet-eyed vampire was a lot older. Something gave him that impression. But he was new to their kind. Truly young, in Kelloway's estimation.

"Why are your eyes purple?" He just blurted it out, it was the question he and every man and woman on the base had been wondering about since the day this vampire had first arrived on location. Why purple eyes? It scared him, and it scared all his men. He needed some kind of answer. They all did.

Seike let out a slow sigh. His eyes weren't looking at the General now, or at anyone in particular. They just stared, unfocused, at the room. "That's a difficult question to answer, seeing as how I'm not sure myself. What I can tell you is that I possess all of my humanity and have no desire to kill the humans that I must feed from. I follow the ways of Seline, not Legion. I seem to possess a lot of power and strength for my young age, as well. I was born a human, and it was a blue that was my sire. The people of Seline have been trying to figure me out for a hundred years, but I content myself with the fact that I know for certain that I am good. I am not evil."

Seike met the General's eyes then. They really were stunning to look at, if unnerving. So, this Seike didn't even know why his eyes were like they were. He claimed to follow Seline, but he was a mystery to himself despite that. Kelloway almost felt sorry for him, imagining him being questioned and scrutinized by the other vampires for the last century. The ones who were supposed to be on his side. No wonder he was a bit of a rebel. Shit, Tristram probably would be too, were he in the man's shoes.

Just then the intercom on Kelloway's jacket buzzed. It was Doctor Peterson.

"General, sir. Could you perhaps send the one named Kaisimir to the lab? This Marikya has already found something astounding, even though she just got here. Apparently, it's something you need to be a va- er, an Ambrogae to be able to detect, but she's currently modifying one of my instruments to show me how it can be physically detectable as well. Very exciting, sir. However, we need the particular… talent. Yes, the talent that Kaisimir possesses. Psychometry. Marikya maintains that he will be able to give further information on the pheromones by coming into physical contact with Emilio's body. Fascinating notion. I've already sent for it. The body, that is. Is Kaisimir still with you?"

The General met the young vampire's eyes, who nodded and said, "I'll go right away, but I'll need an escort as well. I've no idea where the lab is." Just then the corporal that had escorted Marikya returned and offered yet another crisp salute before returning to attention at his side of the door.

"There's your escort." The General smiled at the timing. "Corporal, I'm gonna need you to escort Kaisimir here to lab nineteen, as well."

The young solider snapped another solid salute, with a "Yes, sir!" in a voice that didn't waver at all. Briefly, Kelloway considered promoting the young man just for being so professional with the present company of guests. Of course, more was needed than a good salute and an unwavering response to an order. Still though, he acknowledged to himself that this corporal did S-47 proud.

Kaisimir rose and followed the corporal out of the room. Kelloway gave another look toward Tannik and Seike. Time to offer a little hospitality, though it made him a little queasy to say what he was going to say. "We keep blood bags on hand for the prisoners. You two are welcome to some of them if you find yourselves in need. I'll contact Sergeant O'neil to show you to your quarters.

There're some blood bags in the mini fridges in those rooms. Again, good work on sweeping the perimeter. Dismissed."

Remarkable, Marikya thought as she examined the pheromones under the microscope. How had no one among the children of Seline, including herself, ever thought to look for these before?

Perhaps because those who were of the Serpent had none of these kinds of pheromones themselves. If one of them died, the only way that anyone else close enough would be able to tell would be by the dissipation of their telltale psychic signature.

These pheromones were emitting a psionic waveform, however. Barely detectable to her own senses. The implications disturbed her greatly. Just how far off could others of Legion detect them? Probably many miles, at least. But if that were so, then what were the odds that a group of reds, or even one red, had been in the forest to 'smell' them when Emilio had been killed? According to what they had been told, it wasn't until the next day that the patrol had gone missing.

These factors had caused Marikya to have a disturbing notion. What if when Emilio had died, the psionic waveform was initially magnified? Many miles could have become many more miles, even if just for a short time.

Doctor Peterson had been hovering over her since she had arrived, but she understood that he was just intensely curious and interested. He had some strange thoughts, but his mind was very much a scientific one. Thus far, he hadn't imagined dissecting her, at least. But he had thought several times to ask her if she would be willing to participate in some harmless experiment or another, though he hadn't voiced those thoughts out of politeness. He was worried about offending her, which she actually found rather endearing.

At the moment, she was periodically making adjustments to the electron microscope's ability to determine electrical signals, occasionally looking through it to see if her tinkering was having any effect. She made one more adjustment, then looked again. Eureka.

"Have a look, Doctor Peterson." She moved aside to allow the excited scientist to peer into the outer lens of the device.

"Oh my. They are emitting electricity. How is that even possible?" He looked at her briefly, then looked again into the microscope. "This microscope was already equipped to detect all known electrical frequencies. Is this even really electricity that I'm seeing?"

"What you're seeing is psionic energy. But yes, it is a form of electricity, more or less. It's simply of a much higher oscillation than what you've always known as electricity. Also, it produces waves that your microscope can't detect, not just the particles that it can."

Marikya smiled as Doctor Peterson exclaimed, "Wowee!" He was feeling like a kid in a candy store full of candy that he had never tried before, she could tell. It was time to sober him up a little, however.

"This is grave news, Doctor. I'm afraid that it may be that Emilio's death was able to be felt by others of his kind in a very large radius, and they may have been able to even determine the direction of it." Immediately after these words, she felt the Doctor become afraid. He was brave, though. He fought the fear. And what she had said did indeed have a sobering effect.

"That's not good," was all he said. He wasn't smiling anymore, and Marikya felt bad for having to reveal the gravity of the situation to him. It had to be done, though. After a moment, his head jerked slightly, and his eyes widened noticeably. "I must tell the General. This is something he needs to know right now."

"Of course. Let's just wait and see what my associate might be able to reveal, though." The Doctor just nodded, though he was fidgeting.

Hurry up, Kaisimir, Marikya thought. The body was just being delivered to the lab, and now she needed the young noble to see if he could verify what she already suspected.

A minute passed after they had left the body on a lab table, which really was just like an embalming table from a mortuary. Then Kaisimir arrived. Marikya didn't have to say a thing to him. She and Doctor Peterson only looked as he strode over to Emilio's body, though he didn't touch it right away.

"I won't be able to tell what he was doing before he died. It's been too long since he was killed."

"That's not what we're interested in finding out. Don't aim for the body. Aim for the pheromones." Marikya noticed that Kaisimir seemed to have a eureka moment of his own at her words. He placed his hand over Emilio's bare chest. At first, nothing happened as far as Marikya could tell. Nearly a minute passed before Kaisimir, whose eyes had been closed, suddenly jerked his hand away as if it burned.

"Oh Goddess." He said dramatically. "By Seline, I had no idea they... I didn't..." He turned toward Marikya and the Doctor, seemingly at a loss for words.

"What? What is it?" Doctor Peterson could hardly contain himself in the suspense of the moment. "Spit it out!"

"They emit waves. When he died, they emitted waves."

"We know," Marikya began, but Kaisimir spoke over her.

"No, when he died, the waves were a hundred times stronger. I'm not sure for how long. But if they were that strong..." He didn't need to finish the sentence. Marikya had been thinking dozens of miles, but if Kaisimir was right...

"Hurry up and contact the General, I've got to contact Kesel. The haven doesn't have any phones, though. How do I contact Elder Kesel?" Marikya was panicking, she knew. She couldn't help it though. Dozens of miles? More like a thousand miles. And that would mean the death wasn't felt solely in Minnesota, but in surrounding states as well. This was really bad.

"The Elder is scheduled to call in less than an hour from now," Kaisimir stated. Good, that took care of that part of her worries. Kaisimir looked at the Doctor. "What are you waiting for? Get Kelloway on the line. Now!"

CHAPTER SIX

The neon sign on the front of the nightclub read 'Black Mamba'. Olinar had the place surrounded. His squadron of Ambrogae had placed themselves to watch from various points every way in and out of the building.

He and Almeidra as well as four others had stationed themselves across the street and were scanning the faces of everyone who came and went from the club. So far, they had all been human. He could feel the blues inside, though. At least a dozen by his count. He knew that they were undoubtably aware of the fact that they had been surrounded by the followers of the Leviathan.

King Coranthis had not seemed at all put off by his report of the encounter in Redwood Falls. On the contrary, amusement had tinged his voice as he stated that the orders remained the same. Find Seike of the violet eyes.

Not long after that incident, they had finished combing through the state of Minnesota, and were presently in Iowa City. Half of each of his and Almeidra's forces had come with them to the capital of the state, Des Moines, and their search there had provided clues that Iowa City was a den of those Seline miscreants. The other half of each of their forces was spread throughout the state, searching for any information they could find pertaining to the whereabouts of this Seike. Now, he and Almeidra had the entirety of the Ambrogae that had been with them in Des Moines surrounding this club. Forty men and women, not including them.

Olinar had never met he of the violet eyes in person. He'd only heard the stories. Apparently, the son of a bitch was a legendary warrior, despite his youth. He'd killed a shitload of Olinar's brothers and sisters in arms. And even more half bloods. As loyal as Olinar was to his liege, part of him wanted to kill mister purple eyes, himself. Orders were orders, of course, but perhaps when he found Seike, there would be an unfortunate accident or occurrence of some kind. Olinar felt sure that he would be forgiven if he had no choice in the matter, if the situation evolved into a life-or-death kind of outcome. He knew Almeidra felt the same way.

Right now, he was concerned that there might be more than the dozen or so blues in there that he was sure of. He wasn't the only one. The other men that had been with him in Redwood Falls were part of the force that now had these blues locked down. Each group of them had a team leader that possessed a small but expensive walkie talkie. Olinar had the one for his group, and he pressed the push-to-talk button now.

"Anyone see any targets leaving from the other exits?"

He knew he was just making chit chat; his troops would have radioed him the second they had seen anyone. He was letting nerves get to him. That encounter in

Redwood Falls had him thinking all kinds of crazy shit. Like what if there were more blues than there were those of the Leviathan? What if they had just been cleverly hiding their numbers this entire time? Thoughts like that had him on edge. He'd been feeling this way nonstop since his encounter with that cocky little prick. His king didn't seem worried for some reason, but he hadn't said anything to Olinar to alleviate his worries.

Each of the other three larger groups finished radioing him back with a negative. Suddenly a piece of information just clicked in Olinar's head as yet another small gathering of humans left the club. For the last twenty minutes or so, people had just been leaving. No one had been going in. He radioed his people again to ask if they had been seeing people leaving from the rear and alley exits. They all radioed back an affirmative. He pressed the push-to-talk button again.

"Well, everyone, seems to me that they've been slowly clearing the place out. I want five of you over on alpha team to head toward the front doors. We'll meet you there." Alpha was comprised of the strongest of his combat veterans, other than the three Ambrogises and one other Ambrogess that were with him and his second now. He looked Almeidra's way. She nodded. They crossed the street, meeting up with the five Ambrogae who rounded the corner from the left side alleyway. His heart was beating a little louder and faster now, but it wasn't from fear. This was the kind of shit he lived for. He'd always been an adrenaline junkie.

The eleven of them stood there together, meeting one another's eyes. Every eye was red and eager. No need to go in disguised, they all knew this was going to end in bloodshed. He radioed the other three teams again.

"Okay. Alpha, Bravo, Delta, hang close to those entrances and be ready to pour in on my signal." He always put himself on team Charlie whenever the groups were divided into three or more squads. It was because he used to have a dog named Charlie, a while before he started serving Coranthis. Charlie had been a good dog, a German Shepard. He had lived a healthy fifteen years. That's a very long time for a Shepard to live.

It was time to make an entrance.

"Alright, boys and gals, let's go," Olinar said. He patted his pistol out of habit just before opening the doors and checked his watch. Twelve fifteen AM. He and Almeidra took the lead as they filed in three abreast into the fairly large double-doored entrance of the nightclub. Of course, they had been expected.

As Olinar scanned the place, he noted that there were still a few humans there. Techno music was still playing, too, though the volume had been turned down a few notches. The humans all seemed to be employees, such as the bouncers. Usually, a bouncer would be at the door to see someone's ID, but these guys were off to the left and right sides of the club, and they were packing heat, it seemed. They were close to the side doors and had been watching them before turning to see Olinar and his gang enter through the front. He noted the holstered pistols strapped to their hips. There was a large dance floor in the center of the building's interior. Empty now, of course. Some tables off to the sides still had people sitting at them. There were people at the bar in the back of the place, too.

All of them were Ambrogae. Blues. They all turned their heads from quiet conversation to regard Olinar's group with piercing blue eyes.

"I count fourteen," whispered Almeidra. It seemed her count was accurate. Then there were the bouncers, who numbered six. There were two bartenders. One was human, a middle-aged blonde woman. The other was an Asian follower of Seline. He was rubbing a glass clean with a cloth as they had walked in, and it was he who broke the silence.

"Care for a drink?" He had a slight accent. On closer inspection, Olinar could tell he was Chinese. The accent, despite being thin, sounded like Mandarin to Olinar's ears.

They must know there were others still waiting outside, but Olinar couldn't feel any fear radiating off them. Just like in Redwood Falls. He hadn't sensed fear from that smarmy little man, either. And Olinar had a nose for the scent of fear. He decided to play along with the Chinese man's invitation and motioned for his crew to take seats at a table in the corner of the dance floor, where they could watch the tables that held the other blues, as well as having a perfect view of the bouncers on either side of the large room. He and Almeidra walked casually up to the bar, seating themselves at two of the three empty stools in the center of it. On either side of them were two more blues. Five at the bar, including the bartender. Nine at the tables on either side of the dance floor. The stage is set, Olinar thought to himself.

"Always was partial to whiskey," he said a moment after taking his seat, looking directly at the Chinese man.

"Top shelf?"

Olinar chuckled. "Sure, top shelf."

"On the rocks?"

"Naw, I like mine neat. The more it burns, the better." Olinar watched as the man poured from a bottle of a brand that he actually did like to drink sometimes. He turned to Almeidra. "Thirsty?"

She looked directly at the female bartender. "Yeah, I could use a drink."

The woman didn't smell afraid either, Olinar noted. She met Almeidra's red eyes levelly, then took an unlabeled bottle out from under the counter. She poured its contents into a wine glass that she got from the rack behind her. It was blood. Smelled pretty good too. *Almeidra will know if there's anything funny in it*, Olinar thought as he watched his second stir the liquid with her pinky finger.

After stirring for a few moments, she withdrew her pinky, sniffing it as she made a small moan of pleasure, and then used her tongue to lick her finger clean. She then took a generous swallow of the blood. "Good, actually," she said, still looking at the woman bartender like a cat eyeing a mouse. "This stuff have a name?"

The woman just stared at Almeidra for a moment before saying, "Cherry."

"And what's your name? Is it Cherry?" Almeidra asked, sounding as innocent as she could manage, red eyes glinting in the club's neon interior.

"Yeah," the woman said. Then she put her hand on her hips and swished her hair, her own light brown eyes widening slightly. "How'd you guess?" Her tone was sarcastic. *Oh, bad move, babe.* Olinar knew how

Almeidra felt about humans. The same way he felt. They were for consumption. He wondered how Almeidra was going to react to her potential meal taking on a sarcastic tone with her. He watched with interest as he downed his whiskey in one gulp.

The Asian man moved closer to the human bartender. Almeidra shifted her gaze to meet his eyes. "We're looking for someone. Maybe you can help us find him."

The Chinese man leaned on the bar, looking rather relaxed. "Let me guess. The man with purple eyes? Word travels, you know. We heard about many pure bloods asking those very same questions all around the state. We even heard that there were some of those same questions being asked in Minnesota, only days ago. And," suddenly Almeidra was sailing quickly through the air, crashing into their crew's table in the corner of the dance floor, sending chairs and bodies sprawling. "We heard about you killing people in both states when you didn't get the answers you were looking for."

The Chinese man looked Olinar's way, and he found himself also flying through the air, landing directly on top of Almeidra's prone form. His team had scattered out of the way in time for him, but some of them were still picking themselves up from Almeidra's impact when he landed.

"Get the fuck off of me, Olinar," she said from beneath him. "You weigh a ton." She was fine, and he was starting to feel pretty fired up himself. So, a telekinetic? He hadn't encountered a telekinetic blue in over a century. Not personally. He knew they were around, but they were few and far between.

And he was their antithesis.

He could already feel his body being charged by the telekinetic energy that had just been used and was still within the room residually. He sucked it all up. He waited, though, to see if the Chinese man was going to try doing it again. He'd be ready this time.

Judging by the sudden look of fear on the Chinese man's face, he guessed he wasn't about to get more charge. That was fine, he had plenty to work with. The guy was a strong telekinetic. And apparently a man of experience, as the fear that was now radiating from him told Olinar that the Chinese man realized exactly what he was.

Olinar smiled. "You guessed it, buddy. I'm your worst fucking nightmare."

Olinar raised his hand, drawing from the energy that was now in his body. The Chinese man exploded into rapidly spreading flames. He screamed for about a second before dropping lifelessly to the ground. The fire had lit areas of the bar on fire, and the female bartender's shirt had caught as well. She wailed in a high pitch as she slapped the fire on her body in an effort to put it out. Olinar saw a blur speed past him and within a moment Almeidra was on the woman, ripping out her throat as she said, "Shut up, bitch." The woman forgot about her shirt as her hands went up to the gaping hole where her windpipe used to be. Only for a few seconds, though, as she dropped to the floor beside the Chinese man's flaming body.

Olinar still had about half of the charge he had gotten from the telekinetic. He didn't use it right away, though. His crew had recovered themselves from the surprise of being pummeled by Almeidra's flying body. They looked at him calmly, awaiting an order. Most of them weren't aware that Olinar could do what he had just done, but these were hard people, used to surprises. And this one was to their benefit.

"Take the bouncers. I got the table of five. I want prisoners from the table of four." Olinar didn't wait to see that they obeyed his order, and he saw Almeidra already taking out the four Ambrogae who were still at the bar. He turned toward the table of five surprised blue-eyed faces. They had clearly not seen this shit coming.

Olinar pointed at them with his finger, thumb raised. "Poof, motherfuckers," he said as he brought his thumb down. They tried to move, but too late, as the table exploded outward in a violent fiery blast. Five flaming human shapes started running around the dance floor, screaming. Ambrogae were just as susceptible to fire as any ordinary human would be, so long as they were engulfed by it. They couldn't regenerate from burns nearly as quickly as from other types of wounds. Olinar took out his pistol and put a bullet through four of their hearts, the easiest way to kill one of their kind. Quick and accurate shots. He missed the last one's heart, a woman, who dropped to the ground dead just as he fired. That bullet went into her head, instead.

Olinar surveyed the scene before him. It was pure chaos at the Black Mamba, now. The smell of charred bodies brought back pleasant memories.

The bouncers didn't stand a chance. A few of them managed to graze some of his squad in the ensuing fight, but his people were too fast and got out of the way of most of the bullets fired. It was a brief encounter, overall. He watched as all six of the burly men were quickly dispatched by his band of trained killers.

One of the blues at the table of four, a man in a nice dress shirt and jeans, got up and charged with rage at Olinar. He was fast, reaching the twenty or so feet to his target before the big man could react, and throwing a flurry of potent psionic punches. Olinar didn't have any telekinetic juice left to use, so he just took the hits. They didn't hurt him very much, anyway. At six foot five and close to three hundred pounds, Olinar was a brute of a man. He specialized in psionics to enhance his own physical strength and toughness, sacrificing speed for muscle.

In this case, it was working out in his favor. After the first nine or ten inhumanly fast punches, the man stopped with his eyebrows raised, momentarily stunned by their lack of effect on Olinar. The man then turned his head slightly and hollered to the others still at the table. "I'll hold him here, you guys get the hell out!"

Mister hero man, Olinar thought. This one probably wasn't going to answer any questions, but just in case, he would be taken alive. All four of them would be. Olinar threw one of his moderately hard punches as the man finished saying his heroic words to his friends. Right into the guy's breadbasket. The man flew back into the table where his friends were, knocking it over, and started gasping for breath. The other three men went to their friend, making sure he was okay.

At this point, the bouncers were dead, as were most of the people that were in the nightclub when Olinar's crew had walked in. And all eleven men and women of the Leviathan inside were still alive. This had turned out to be pretty easy. How fortunate that the Chinese man had been telekinetic. They were so very rare, these days, as was Olinar's kind. Pyrokinetics needed the energy from telekinetics to use their abilities. It was like the Gods had made him just to kill those uppity object-moving bastards. If Olinar hadn't been what he was, they would certainly all be dead right now. They wouldn't have stood a chance against a telekinetic, which explained why the blues had all been unafraid in the first place. Hell, that one man likely would have killed them all, including his people outside.

He almost forgot about the rest of his and Almeidra's forces outside. He picked up his walkie and pressed the push-to-talk button. "Yeah… So, party's over guys. We're taking some prisoners, but come on in. There's blood behind the bar. In bottles and in bodies."

Almeidra chuckled as she and the rest of the gang inside surrounded the four blue-eyed Ambrogises at the overturned table. They were clearly terrified. He began to whistle a tune, which brought their swiveling heads snapping back toward him, eyes looking at him in fear. Fear that he could smell. Much better.

He sauntered up to the bar as he whistled. The bottle of whiskey was still there, completely unscathed. Damn, what a lucky night.

He grabbed the bottle and began to down its contents while keeping his eyes fixed on the four petrified blues before him. He finished it, then tossed it behind the bar roughly, where it smashed. He cleared his throat and sat on a stool, still looking their way.

"So, like the lady was saying... We're looking for someone."

It didn't take very long to get the cowards to talk.

CHAPTER SEVEN

A few days had passed since Seike and the rest of his team had arrived at Field Base A-92. The compound had been full of constant activity since they had made the terrifying discovery that had led them all to believe that they may be in imminent danger. Activity not only inside the base, but all around the perimeter of it as well.

Portable turrets had been deployed throughout the forest at key strategic locations. Patrols were constant, and just yesterday an additional two hundred of America's finest soldiers had arrived to bolster their numbers. Field Base A-92 wasn't S-47's only base of operations, though it was central. The new troops had arrived from a number of other established facilities from around the country. An air of readiness permeated the place.

Presently, the five of Seline's brood were standing around in Command and Communications, the main operations room of the base. Samaiel had arrived early yesterday as well, shortly before the first of the additional S-47 members began to show up. They were all watching the action from the many screens that were located on the room's walls. All of the human men and women around them hardly batted an eye at having them around, at this point. Their nervous energy was directed into the organization of their defense against the real threat. Seike found this redirection of energy to be most welcoming. He hadn't liked the level of anxiety that many of these men and women had directed his way when he and his team had first arrived on site. The soldiers had been a bit standoffish with the other blues with him as well, but he had sensed that they had been truly afraid of him, personally.

Now it seemed that when they looked his way, it was almost as if they were regarding him with a sort of hope. He could feel their thoughts, and how many of them, especially Kelloway, saw him as some kind of secret weapon that they had in their arsenal. Seike really didn't mind being seen that way. If he could help these people survive what was to come, maybe he would be able to stop feeling guilty about the deaths he had inadvertently caused to happen to a couple of their own. He wanted redemption for his hastily made past decisions.

Kelloway himself was standing amongst their team, all six of them in an upraised section of floor that was in the middle of the room and had several more important technological workspaces and staff manning them. He was currently observing the tactical action that was being carried out by his men and women outside the base. General Kelloway had focused most of his attention on the outdoor cameras in the last twenty-four hours, as within the facility most preparations had already been completed. Seike could sense that he was worried that they would be attacked at any moment. The General hadn't stopped being ready for a shitshow for a single minute since Doctor Peterson had reported back from the lab with Kaisimir's and Marikya's startling discovery, almost three full days ago.

"I've noticed that you haven't slept since the lab report came in, General Kelloway," Seike said. He decided to risk finally stating this fact. The General's thoughts were becoming slightly erratic after days of absolutely no shut eye.

"Neither have you. Neither have any of you," Kelloway snapped back. "I'll have myself a good nap when this nightmare is all over."

"We don't need very much sleep compared to an ordinary human," Samaiel put in, glancing at Seike before returning his eyes to the monitors. "We can go a couple of weeks without it before we start to go a little crazy from the lack of it. Mostly it's just a few hours a week, for our kind." Seike was truly glad to have an actual friend in his present company. That didn't happen very often, for him.

The General gave a small, mirthless laugh. "I'm aware of that. But it hasn't even been close to a week since I've slept. My mind is still sharp. Sharp enough, anyway." He held up a mug in his right hand. "Besides, I got my cup of joe."

Seike couldn't argue with that. It was true that the General's mind was a little more chaotic than usual, but the man was far from unstable in his present condition. He could likely go a few more days before his mental health would be at risk. Samaiel looked Seike's way again, smirking with a little roll of his eyes. Seike smiled as well. Marikya was frowning, but her attention was fixed on a tablet that she held in her hand. She was still going over the genetic make-up of the pheromones from Emilio's body. Kaisimir and Tannik were standing with their arms folded, both looking serious as they watched the screens.

"You already know how to kill our kind," Tannik suddenly said. The General paused with the cup halfway to his mouth, raising an eyebrow in Tannik's direction. His face had more than a five o'clock shadow, grey whiskers were bristling on his cheeks. Tannik turned to regard him. "A bullet in the heart usually does it, though depending on the gun used, it can take more than one bullet. These turrets you have should be able to blow heads clean off, which would also do the job, but just to be certain, and to make aiming a little easier, I would have your troops aim for the chests of the enemy. Judging by the size of the ammunition those things are equipped with, the resulting hole should take out the heart even if the right side of the chest is hit."

The General made eye contact with one of his communications officers, a woman Seike had learned was named Sarah Lisgard. She made an inquisitive gesture, to which he responded, "Relay the order, Corporal Lisgard."

"Right away, sir." She said, then turned back to her station and began opening the necessary channels. She then relayed the statement that all personnel manning the turrets should aim for the chest of their targets when the invasion began. After another moment, she sent a reminder to the men and women of S-47 that shots to the heart would work best against the enemy. It was a good call as far as Seike was concerned, because he knew from the General's mind that there were more than a few green soldiers on location. The General was satisfied as well, Seike could tell, though he said nothing further.

"Thanks, Tannik," Kelloway said a few moments later. Reluctantly, he added, "I should have thought of that. Maybe I do need an hour or two of sleep. Damnit. Samaiel, do you feel anything out there?"

"No, sir. Nothing yet." Samaiel had immediately taken to calling the General 'sir', as he was a soldier once, himself. It wasn't just because Marikya referred to the General in the same way. Seike knew that Samaiel still considered himself a soldier in the grand scheme of things, more than any other sort of vocation.

"O'neil, you have the room," Kelloway stated. "I'll be back in ninety minutes, unless we're attacked in the meantime. You five, be ready to get outside on a moment's notice." Seike nodded, while Samaiel and Marikya both said, "yes, sir," in unison with Sergeant O'neil. Tannik and Kaisimir exchanged glances, then went back to carefully watching the flurry of activity on the outside monitors as the General left the room. The five of them had fully agreed to take the fight to the enemy if and when they were attacked. The soldiers of S-47 knew that the vampires dressed in blue shirts and jeans were allies and were not to be fired upon.

Justin O'neil was someone Seike rather liked. He was nothing but grateful that the Ambrogae of Seline had sent a team to assist S-47. He had admitted to being a bundle of wracked nerves until they had shown up. Even General Kelloway had commented that the sergeant seemed to be doing a lot better since the arrival of the 'boys and gal in blue' as he had put it. He told some of his other men that they should follow O'neil's example, which had made the sergeant beam proudly.

A sergeant was the highest-ranking enlisted soldier in the S-47 command structure, Seike had learned. Every other base throughout the country had a colonel that was in charge, and colonels were the highest-ranking officers in the S-47 command structure, aside from Kelloway, who was the leader of the entire force of S-47. According to the General, the 'S' stood for 'secret', which Samaiel had found rather amusing. Seike thought it wasn't very creative.

The General had given some solid reasoning behind the seemingly low-rank command structure of the organization, however. Each man or woman who served in S-47 was hand-picked by the General and the colonels themselves. They were chosen right after they had completed their basic training and were all specifically recruited based on a very rigid set of requirements, which included extremely solid psychological profiles, as well as a preference for men and women without children, especially preferring those without any familial attachments whatsoever. These people were all but leaving their civilian lives behind, after all. They were not allowed nearly as much leave as an ordinary military recruit.

In order not to arouse suspicion in the outside world, their ranks were all kept low, aside from Tristram, who was officially only a lieutenant general, three star. He had made a joke about being the only seven star general in the world, but that rank wasn't officially documented in any way. Still, Seike had to give the man merit. He felt that the General deserved to call himself seven star. The man was rock solid. Here he was, constantly under threat, secretly hunting those of Legion for decades, and he could still make light of life, with a sense of humor that was largely intact. Seike had come to actually admire the man.

Sergeant O'neil approached Seike, looking uncertain. He clearly had something to say.

"Seike, I was wondering something," O'neil said hesitantly. He was fidgeting with the insignia on his shoulder that denoted his rank. His eyes were downcast, but Seike could tell he was gathering the nerve to say whatever was on his mind. He raised his eyes to meet Seike's own, his gaze level. "How many Legion Ambrogae have you ever had to tango with at once? I only ask because I have a bad feeling about the situation. It's been days and there's been nothing, but I have discussed my feelings with the General, and he feels the same. We have this unsettling feeling in our gut."

Seike understood completely, because he felt the same sense of danger. So did the others. "I once fought and killed over twenty half bloods. That's my personal record." Seike hoped his honesty would be able to put the man at ease. "And before you ask, there's really no difference between half bloods and pure bloods in terms of threat level. It's more about how old the Ambrogis or Ambrogess is. And also, what kinds of unique powers or abilities they might wield. The ones I just mentioned were mostly older than me. They didn't have much going for them as far as special abilities, though."

The sergeant nodded at this and did seem to be placated by Seike's remarks. Then he asked, "Do you have any special powers? Something we might be able to use?"

Seike smiled sympathetically at the man. "As Elder Kesel has told me more than once, I'm still young." The sergeant sighed, so Seike added, "He also tells me that my psionic power is that of an experienced thousand-year-old. Every one of the Ambrogae can use psionics, though. Elder Kesel assures me that I am still learning and getting stronger all the time. He also says that it's likely that I will end up developing a unique power or ability, if not more than one, based on how strong I am for my age."

"Kesel doesn't know what you are any more than the rest of us," Kaisimir interjected, with some venom in his voice. "For all we know, you could lose your humanity at any moment."

"Shut up, Kaisimir," Samaiel said. "Before I smash your stupid noble face."

"This isn't the time for this," Marikya said sternly, alternating her gaze between Samaiel and Kaisimir. She then leveled it in Kaisimir's direction. "Samaiel is right though, Kaisimir. You should know better than to speak of that which you know nothing about. Seike is one of us, and he always has been. That's not going to change." She smiled at Seike, and he could tell she was being sincere.

Kaisimir scoffed and said, "I'm going to my quarters." He left the room looking like a teenager in angst, which, they all knew, he basically was. He was born an Ambrogis, and was still very young for one. Tannik gave Seike an apologetic look. He then shrugged and turned to follow Kaisimir.

"Let me talk to him," was all he said as he left Command and Communications. Tannik didn't seem to hate nor be afraid of Seike, so the violet-eyed Ambrogis hoped that the man could calm Kaisimir down, noble to noble.

Seike again met O'neil's eyes. The sergeant didn't seem put off by Kaisimir's remarks. Instead, Seike detected a note of sympathy in the man's mind, though he kept it out of his facial expression.

"I'm not going to lose my humanity," Seike said. He didn't know what else to say besides that. He knew himself, and he had never stopped being himself since he had become the vampire with the violet eyes. The transformation into what he was had been painful in ways, and strange in others, and for a short while during it, it was like his mind had struggled with the Leviathan itself. But he came out of it the same man he had been going into it. The only thing he was truly certain about was who he was on the inside. He was good, and he knew it.

Marikya came up to him then, patting him on the arm. "We know that Seike. I don't think Tannik thinks like Kaisimir. Hopefully he can talk some sense into that boy." Seike smiled at her, appreciating the gesture. He knew how Samaiel felt, but it was nice to see that Marikya was in his corner, as well.

"I think you're on our side, and you're going to stay on our side," O'neil said after a moment. He made a brief hesitation before adding, "Forget what that asshole just said to you."

Samaiel laughed and said, "O'neil, mah man! That's right Seike, forget about that asshole!" He clapped Seike on the shoulder, then turned toward the sergeant and raised his hand for a high five. At first, O'neil looked bewildered. But then the man smiled and gave Samaiel the high five he was looking for.

They all shared a laugh. Laughter had been a rare commodity these last few days.

The map was spread out onto the ground. Olinar looked upon it as Almeidra traced a circle in red marker along the center of a rather forested region of the state of Minnesota.

"My guess is that's about the area of their perimeter," she said, sounding certain of herself. "Maybe not exactly, but roughly for sure, based upon the camera setup they had on our first visit there."

Olinar stroked his bare chin as he stared at the map. Back in Iowa City, it hadn't taken long to get the blues they had captured to talk. It had turned out that the heroic one had a weak spot. The lives of his friends. In exchange for their lives, he had talked. He had heard that the violet-eyed one was sent to Minnesota for some sort of mission, but he hadn't known many details. That information was all that Olinar had needed to know. He had disposed of the hero's three friends before the blue's eyes, taking special time with each one. The hero had begged and pleaded for Olinar to spare them. Olinar had promised to spare them, he had mewled. After the three friends were dead, Olinar ripped the hero's head off. It had taken a few good twists, but it had come right off, in the end. He had laughed at how the hero's head blinked several times at him as he held the disembodied head in his hands.

"We go in at three AM. We'll be able to see better than a human with night goggles." Olinar was rubbing his hands together. He couldn't wait for this bloodbath. "Is everyone all set?" He directed the question at his second, and she nodded.

"Yes, sir. We're all well outside the perimeter, but completely surrounding it at roughly the same distance from the center of their little base. Ready to go on your mark." Almeidra sounded pretty eager, herself. Olinar had grown rather fond of her in the years that they had served king Coranthis together. She had a few rather interesting talents. She could psionically infiltrate technology with a precision that he had never seen before. She was also good at using technology in general.

They were still numerous miles away from the enemy. Nearly a hundred pure blooded and eager Ambrogae in total. They had decided to do this themselves, he and Almeidra. They had taken all of each of their forces on this mission but hadn't bothered notifying Woitan and Ignusai of their intention, instead seeking the glory themselves. Olinar couldn't be sure if this Seike was there or not, but he had a very strong suspicion that that was the case. And according to the blues they had interrogated, Seike hadn't travelled alone to Minnesota. One could never be too careful. They had to stay far enough away within the forest, just in case Seike or anyone he was with could sense them before they could sense him. But when the time came to move, they were going to move fast.

They felt certain that a hundred pure bloods could wipe out this base. It shouldn't be an issue. Besides, everyone on his force was heavily armed with gunnery. And Ambrogae were far better shots than human soliders.

Olinar didn't share his age with very many other Ambrogae. Not even Almeidra knew how old he really was. Coranthis and the royal family knew, of course. It was a large part of the reason that he was immediately given a position of command upon coming into his king's service.

He was over twelve hundred years old. Vikings used to worship him as a God, at one point in time. But times were changing. People didn't worship Gods anymore. They worshipped money and technology. That was fine by Olinar, as he was never really into being worshipped, or known at all for that matter. He found his current circumstances to be quite pleasing. Mostly he just spied and killed for his king. No one really knew who he was, or what his history was, and that was the way he liked it. Whenever he wasn't on an errand of some kind for his liege, he could just blend into the background of society.

He kept periodically rubbing his hands together, anticipating the moment that he would come face to face with Seike. He wanted to pluck those violet eyes out of the man's head, take them to his king and present them as a trophy. He knew that Coranthis wanted Seike alive, but now that it had come down to the moment, Olinar had decided that a story about how his hand had been forced would be the better option. Realistically speaking, the violet-eyed Ambrogis wasn't likely to go peacefully, anyway. And if the tales he had heard about were even half true, then Seike would be very difficult to keep as a prisoner.

He checked his watch. Almost midnight. He hated waiting, but that was all there was left to do, now. All the preparations had been made.

"You still have any of that Cherry left?" He posed the question to Almeidra, who sniggered and dug into a bag that was close by. She pulled out a wine bottle and tossed it to him. He caught it effortlessly, smiling as he pooped the cork and took a generous swig.

He really did like Almeidra. She was a woman after his own heart.

CHAPTER EIGHT

Elder Kesel had considered Xiang Lau to be a dear friend. He had been one of those few of the followers of Seline that had desired to keep the name he had in his life as a human being. Such a decision was respected among Kesel's kind, though most blues had a tendency to take on a new Ambrogaeic name not long after they had been turned. Of course, every person who was born as an Ambrogis or Ambrogess was named in the ancient tongue. Some Ambrogaeic names sounded much like a typical human name, though most didn't. Selinda, his daughter, had been named a name that sounded very human, but the meaning of it had its roots much further back in history.

The report had come to him last night, along with over a dozen bodies. All of the dead Ambrogae had been members of the Central Haven, including Xiang Lau. Part of Kesel's mind still couldn't believe that the man had been killed. He had been around for over a thousand years and had been through so much hardship, only to end in this way. Kesel had actually met Xiang Lau in his home country of China over two hundred years ago, not long after the man's own Ambrogaeic clan had been slaughtered by an army of the followers of the Leviathan. During that incident, Xiang Lau had been away from the place his clan called home. When he had returned, he found only the dead waiting for him. It had been tragic, and when Kesel had first encountered him, the man had nearly been at his wit's end. After they had travelled together in China for nearly a month, Kesel had extended an invitation to Xiang Lau to return to the then young United States with him, which the man had graciously accepted.

That was during an era of exploration for the Elder, when he had travelled the world seeking more of his blue-eyed brethren. Kesel could speak over a dozen languages, including Mandarin. He had learned much over his nearly fifteen hundred years of being in this existence. For the last hundred years, however, the Elder had spent most of his time in the haven that he had been appointed to oversee.

Kesel was very worried, now. He hadn't known there were any pyrokinetics in his region of the United States. He knew that there were none among the blues of the Central Haven, and it had been so long since he had heard of the defeat of a telekinetic, he had assumed that there were no Leviathan pyrokinetics around, either. Both were exceedingly rare breeds, but the Elder suspected that pyrokinetics were perhaps the rarest of all types of Ambrogae. To have one in the area, one who was of the Leviathan, no less, was a cause for great concern among the members of the council. They had been avidly discussing matters regarding the incident at the Black Mamba since the previous night and had still not arrived at a decision of what to do. Presently, they were all yet again sitting around the long table that they held council meetings at. This was the third time in less than a day that they had convened.

"Either we send more people to Field Base A-92, or I'll lash you myself, Kaolirus!" Jurai was almost yelling, which was rare for the normally levelheaded man. Elder Kesel understood his frustration. The old fools on the council were far too reluctant to send reinforcements to the General's base of operations. Not too long ago, they hadn't wanted to quickly do away with Emilio, either. They had wanted the creature to have a ceremonious death, as if it would please the Goddess to have it that way. This situation reminded Kesel of that time, with him and Jurai against the rest of the council. Only this time, it seemed it was Jurai's child who was in danger, as well as the others that had been sent to Kelloway's compound.

The Ambrogis that Jurai had just addressed sneered and leaned forward in his chair. "We've already lost fourteen members of the haven, and now you want to risk more lives! I do not disagree that there may be a danger, but we do not know where that danger lies, or what its intentions are. For all you know, they could be looking for the haven." Murmurs of assent came from the others on the council, and Kaolirus sat back in his seat, looking far too satisfied for Kesel's liking.

For the last several minutes, Kesel had been letting Jurai handle the wordplay with these stubborn fools who were so set in their ways, but now he spoke up. "Perhaps we should let the people of the haven decide for themselves what to do. If any of them want to volunteer to go and help Jurai's son and the others, then so be it. If they want to stay, then that should be their decision too. After all, they are our wards, not our prisoners." At this, there was muttering and mumbling from everyone at once, aside from Jurai. These idiots couldn't even respond to a suggestion in an orderly fashion, let alone make life or death decisions at anything resembling a reasonable pace. They had coddled themselves for far too long, staying holed up underground in safety, afraid to go into the outside world. It had addled their minds, as far as Kesel was concerned. He was the oldest of them, but except for Jurai, these men and women seemed almost senile to him, at times.

An Ambrogess by the name of Gerlanyeil spoke in response to what Kesel had just said. "If we allow our warriors to go and aid the humans, we'll be weakening our own defenses. As Kaolirus said, we can't be certain of the enemy's motivations or movements. We do not know what their intentions are. For all we know, they could be targeting us, not the humans." More murmurs of agreement followed her words.

"I've had enough of this!" Jurai *was* yelling, now. "I'm going to take Elder Kesel's suggestion and put it into action. I'm leaving this damned room, and I am going to see who wants to go and who doesn't among those who are our fighters. Curses upon you decrepit morons and your protocols and procedures! My son is in danger, I just know it!" Jurai almost knocked over his chair as he got up from it. Eleven shocked faces just watched him storm out of the room.

Elder Kesel glanced at the grandfather clock at the center of the back wall of the council's meeting room. It was shortly after midnight. He had a feeling that Jurai was correct. Kaisimir, Seike and the others were in danger, not to mention Kelloway and his force. The question was, were they too late already?

"This meeting of the council of the Central Haven is now concluded." Kesel got up from his own chair, watching out of the corner of his eye as the others on the council merely watched him leave the room. He allowed himself a small smile, as he fully planned on helping Jurai in his efforts. It would only take a matter of hours for a force of their own to join Kelloway and the team that their haven had sent. He hoped again that they were not too late.

"As I've said, I think Seike can be relied upon. You have too much of your mother's opinion of him in you." Tannik was sitting in a chair against the wall of Kaisimir's room. The boy himself was lying on the bed, moping like the child he still was. He had been trying to mollify the young noble for nearly an hour now. "I understand that Seike is a phenomenon that we know next to nothing of, but you can't be too judgmental of him. He has always proven himself to be a valuable member of our haven. You can't deny that fact."

Kaisimir was just staring at the ceiling with his arms crossed upon his chest. He offered no response. Tannik sighed for about the tenth time. Ferana's fear and distrust of Seike had been too ingrained in the young man. Tannik wasn't afraid of Seike and saw him as an ally of note. He couldn't understand why so many of those of Seline were disdainful toward he of the violet eyes when Seike had proven himself time and time again to be not only on their side, but a great warrior for their cause. A true defender, and a potent hunter.

Fear was the main cause, Tannik supposed. He himself had never been afraid of anyone or anything. It just wasn't in his nature. He had been turned into an Ambrogis of his own volition by a sire who was no longer in America, nearly four hundred years ago. He was a young human living in England, only twenty-two years old, when he had been offered the choice. He didn't accept out of fear of death. He had accepted out of loneliness.

Tannik had been an orphan on the streets for the entire memory of his life as a human being. He had never made any friends and had been treated poorly throughout his early days in England. Originally, he had had an English accent, but he'd been in America for so long now that the lilt had all but been replaced by the typical way of speech for this country. His sire was from England as well and had returned there after visiting America for a decade over a century ago to make sure that Tannik had solid foundations in his new haven. After those years, his sire left to return to the isle of Great Britain. Tannik had occasional contact with him to this day. He was doing well, the last the noble had heard.

He wished that Kaisimir and Seike could just get along. Whenever the violet-eyed one wasn't around, Tannik found Kaisimir to be rather pleasant company. The boy was smart, and wise for his age, typically. He wasn't usually prone to fits like this.

After several more minutes of silence, with Tannik just sitting there staring at Kaisimir while Kaisimir ignored him and stared at the ceiling, the intercom badge on both of their shirts buzzed onto an open channel. Sergeant O'neil's voice rang through.

"We have a problem, gentlemen. Samaiel just radioed after a quick run around topside. He says he can feel the enemy in every direction when approaching the outer areas of the perimeter. They're miles away from our forces, but he can feel them. They're surrounding us. He says they weren't closing in at the time he felt them, and he was sure they were too far away for them to have felt his own presence." O'neil stopped talking for a moment, and Tannik heard him clear his throat over the comms. "We're sending you all up topside, right now. Samaiel is already there. Orders have been sent to all the troops above to tighten ranks, including the portable turrets. We were spread out because we didn't know what direction they might be coming from. Now that we know they're going to be coming from every direction, it only makes sense to gather our own forces a little more tightly together. The moment has arrived, so if you would please join your friends at the main doors, that would be lovely."

Tannik and Kaisimir exchanged wide-eyed glances only briefly after O'neil had finished talking. "Let's go," Tannik said, and they both hurried out of the room.

Kaisimir reached the door first, and as Tannik followed him out, he saw that there were soldiers running in the direction of the main doors to the facility. There were orange rotating alarm lights shining in both directions of the hallway. No sound of an alarm, just the lights. That was more than enough for the men and women of S-47. All commands had been relayed over secure channels to every soldier in the base, and everyone knew what their task was.

Tannik looked at Kaisimir one more time, and the young Ambrogis just nodded, his face serious. That look said it all. The boy would put aside his fretting, at least for now. Seike was an ally and would be with them for this fight. Good enough.

Together, they ran through the hallways and up several ramps that would lead to the main entryway. Tannik still didn't know the layout of the base very well, but he knew enough to go upward when trying to leave the place. Kaisimir seemed to know where he was going, but Tannik suspected that he was just following the consistent stream of running soldiers. After a few minutes of running through halls and up ramps, they arrived at the familiar site of the elevator that led to the surface and would take them to the bunker that served as the main doors of Field Base A-92. In truth, it wasn't just the main door, it was the *only* door. There was no other way in or out of the compound. A passcode was needed to operate the elevator, and the five of them had been given the code by Kelloway in a moment of trust.

Tannik reached out and grabbed Kaisimir by the shoulder just as they approached the elevator doors. The young Ambrogis looked at him questioningly. "Hang on a moment," Tannik said, as he pressed the button on the intercom badge. Something had just occurred to him. He waited for the sound that indicated a channel had been opened in response.

"This is Kelloway. Go ahead, Tannik."

"General, are you aware that fire is particularly harmful to our kind?"

For a moment there was no response, then, "We've lit Legion prisoners on fire to see what it would do to them. They seemed to be able to take a lot more heat than a human would have been able to in those circumstances. Lived for a while after being lit up, too. Still died though. We also noticed that those that survived took a long time to heal. What are you getting at? We've got incendiary grenades, napalm, things like that. All a part of what we use on the regular."

"Were you aware that our kind, mostly, is particularly afraid of fire? I mean really afraid of it."

There was silence for a few moments before Kelloway responded. "No, son, I was not aware of a particular fear of it shared by all vampires. You're thinking of some psychological warfare, then?"

"Not just psychological, General. If you could light the whole perimeter on fire, like a ring of fire that would surround us and all your men, it would not only deter the enemy, but it would obscure their vision. Plus, we're a little more flammable than a typical human, so if any of the enemy did want to risk going through a wall of fire, there's a good chance they would light up in the process."

"Might end up lighting the whole forest on fire, if we do that. But fuck it, let's do it. We could use a man like you in S-47, Tannik. You have a military mind. I see you and Kaisimir are by the elevator," A camera was pointing right at them, Tannik noticed. "Seike and Marikya are going to be joining you in a minute. I want you four to hang by the main doors until I give further orders. For now, I'm gonna light a camp fire and roast some marshmallows."

The intercom went silent, and Tannik settled in to wait for their two companions. Kaisimir was looking at him a little strangely, but he said nothing. Tannik knew that the fire could spread and be a danger to them, but he had weighed the risks in his head, and apparently the General agreed with him on it. Besides, trained soldiers could probably somewhat control what they lit on fire, and it had rained just the other day. Tannik felt that the risk of an out-of-control blaze was minimal given the circumstances.

Seike and Marikya ran up the last ramp to join them. The four of them entered the elevator together. Kaisimir glanced more than once at Seike but didn't seem to want to say anything. Tannik had hoped that the boy might offer a quick apology before they went into battle, but apparently not.

When the elevator had arrived at the surface, Samaiel was waiting for them in the bunker. He was grinning, despite the situation. "Took you guys long enough," he said. "They're enclosing us in a ring of fire right now. I heard General Kelloway on a sergeant's comms a minute ago and apparently, they're going to make a controlled blaze that lasts as long as it takes for the enemy to arrive. Hopefully we're not the ones who end up getting burned." Samaiel shot a quick glance at Marikya. Tannik smiled. The man would never give up trying to court her, it seemed.

Over the next few minutes, Tannik heard from the soldiers that the blaze would be inside the perimeter and would be a wall of flame that was thin enough to control, but thick enough to keep the enemy on the other side. The troops had high-tech goggles that apparently included a mode that allowed them to see through the flames. Tannik and the others were each offered a pair of these, but the five of them refused. The General wanted them to stay back, anyway, to meet any of the Legion forces that managed to penetrate the wall.

After another several minutes of waiting, Tannik saw Samaiel cock his head to the side. They all knew what that meant. Samaiel then pressed his intercom badge, and within moments the General's voice came through the little speakers.

"I suppose that our guests have arrived." It didn't come out as a question.

"Yes, sir," Samaiel replied. "They're moving in fast. I'm guessing they saw the smoke and decided it was now or never." The General cursed on his end. They heard him bark orders over all comms that the enemy was closing in, and to prepare for battle. He then returned to the channel dedicated to just the five of them.

"If any of those bastards get through the fire, give 'em hell. Kelloway out." And with that the intercoms went silent.

Tannik and the others all just looked at one another. The time had come, and they all knew this was a life-or-death scenario. They hadn't heard from Kesel since the night before, which worried Tannik. Certainly, it worried all of them. Something must have happened back in Iowa, and Tannik just hoped that Kesel and the rest of the haven were all right. No time to really think about it now, though.

Suddenly the sound of gunfire and shouts began to permeate the air. At first it was just a few shots and several voices yelling, but within seconds it became a cacophony. The place sounded like a warzone. The five of them rushed outside together, to scope out the situation outside the bunker. They knew that they were to stay close to the main doors, but the General hadn't specified for them to stay inside the bunker, so they didn't. What they saw as soon as they reached the other side of the doors shook Tannik.

The wall of fire was almost completely out.

Apparently, the enemy had foreseen this possibility, somehow, and had brought flame retardant sprays with them. Tannik could see some of the Legion troops in the distance still spraying the flames as even more of them came through the perimeter. They were all armed as well. Tannik had grabbed a rifle just before leaving the bunker, and so had Samaiel, but he noticed that Kaisimir, Marikya, and Seike appeared to be unarmed.

"Why don't you three have guns?" Tannik asked. There was no time for him to wait for an answer though, as a firefight was just breaking out only a few dozen meters from their position. About ten Legion Ambrogae had engaged with a company of soldiers who outnumbered them, but Tannik watched in horror as the Ambrogae fired their rifles with deadly accuracy. Over twenty S-47 soldiers became only a handful in several seconds, and then Tannik began to open fire on the Ambrogae, himself.

He managed to kill three of them with shots to the heart before they noticed him. Just as the remaining seven enemy troops were turning their guns toward him, he saw Seike running past him directly into their line of fire. Had the man gone mad?

The enemy Ambrogae all turned their attention to Seike, firing at him simultaneously. The bullets bounced off of air in front of the violet-eyed one as he rapidly closed the distance between himself and the seven Ambrogae. Once he reached them, Tannik watched in awe as the violet-eyed warrior danced from one enemy to the next, punching each one so hard in the chest that his fist fully penetrated their bodies, destroying each of their hearts with power and precision. Tannik had never seen Seike in action before, he'd only heard the various stories from people who had. To watch the man kill seven trained Ambrogae within seconds had almost left him breathless.

Tannik turned back to where the others had been and saw Marikya standing behind Samaiel, using her psionics to shield him from incoming fire. She had created a shield that allowed Samaiel's bullets to pass through from their side, while incoming bullets ricocheted perhaps three feet away from where Samaiel was standing. Samaiel was raining hell on a group of enemy Ambrogae that were about twenty meters from his position. One of the enemy was able to create his own kinetic shields, but only large enough to defend himself. He watched as his comrades dropped one by one from Samaiel's gunfire.

Tannik couldn't see Kaisimir. Where had the young noble gone to? He scanned around, walking carefully as he looked. Two Ambrogae fell to his rifle while he searched for Jurai's son. He killed them almost casually without stopping his stride as he hunted for any clue as to the whereabouts of the boy. Jurai had asked him to keep an eye on Kaisimir, and he didn't want to let the councilman down.

While he searched, he saw that things were not going too well for his side in this battle. Most of the bodies he saw were S-47 soldiers. The mobile turrets that he passed were either destroyed by some kind of explosion, which he had begun to hear plenty of in the last little while, or they were simply unmanned. How many soldiers did Kelloway have out here? A little more than two hundred, wasn't it? He wondered how many enemy troops there were. Samaiel had said they were surrounded, but Tannik knew that didn't mean that the enemy had more troops than S-47. It didn't seem to matter if the Legion forces had less, though, as it was pretty clear that these were some seriously trained Ambrogae that they were dealing with.

While he searched, he was lucky enough to see enemy Ambrogae before they saw him. He managed to kill three more that were also prowling about solo, as he was. He had seen them first, and so they died.

Finally, he saw what he had been dreading. Just beyond some trees, he saw a woman holding Kaisimir by the neck, apparently saying something to him. He didn't wait, he just fired. The bullets bounced off of the air around her. So, this one had some skill in psionics. Damn.

She turned her head toward Tannik, smiling. She was holding Kaisimir with her left hand, and her right hand was out of view. She turned her body fully toward Tannik, dropping Kaisimir as she did so. He seemed to be unconscious. At least, Tannik hoped he was just unconscious. Almost too late, he saw the pistol in her right hand come up and begin firing. He managed to get his own kinetic shield up just in time for the first of the bullets. They ricocheted only inches in front of his face. The woman laughed and said, "Alright, let's settle this the good old-fashioned way." Then she ran faster than a cheetah directly at him, dropping her gun as she did so. Tannik dropped his own gun as she approached.

She leaped at him once there were only several feet between them, but Tannik was ready. Her kick landed on his chest, but he had formed a barrier over his skin to toughen himself up for the fight. The kick hurt considerably, and he gritted his teeth, but he didn't go down. He threw a right cross directly at her face, but she blocked it with one of her arms. This woman means business, Tannik thought as he launched a series of jabs and crosses at her, each one being deflected by her speedy hands and arms.

Back and forth they danced, for how long Tannik couldn't say. Minutes seemed like hours in a fight like this one. Every time he managed to land a blow, she would counter with a successful hit of her own, and her strikes were painful. What infuriated him the most was the wicked grin on her face the entire time. He wanted to see if Kaisimir was ok, but he couldn't even spare a single moment to glance in the young Ambrogae's direction.

Suddenly, she threw a high kick right at Tannik's neck, and landed it. His vision blurred, and the psionic barrier he had spread over his skin was undoubtedly the only thing that kept him from losing consciousness from the blow. Realizing she had gained the upper hand, she redoubled her efforts with kicking, throwing kick after kick into Tannik's body, some of which he managed to block. She then attempted to kick him in the neck again, but this time he was ready.

He used his opposite hand to block the kick, simultaneously grabbing her ankle and then getting a grip on her calf with his other hand. He managed to use her momentum in this instant to lift her by the leg she had used for the kick, spinning her and slamming her body into the ground. He then tightened his grip on her ankle with both hands and began to swing and smash her body onto the ground over and over again on either side of himself. He did this five times, until he saw that she was unconscious, if not dead.

He took a moment to examine her, making sure she wasn't moving, before going to check on Kaisimir.

The young noble was breathing, thank Seline. He was indeed unconscious, but Tannik managed to rouse him with a few shakes. He smiled up at the older noble from his muddied position on the forest floor. "I just ran," Kaisimir muttered. He laughed bitterly, choking slightly as he did so. "It was like I lost all control of myself, and I just started running. Then she came out of nowhere."

Kaisimir looked over to the unmoving form of the woman. "Is she dead?" He began to pick himself up off the ground. Slowly, he regained his footing. "She was demanding to know where Seike was."

Seike? Tannik and the rest of them had all figured this was about taking out an S-47 facility. What did she want from Seike? He decided to check to see if she was still alive, and maybe ask her some questions. He began to walk toward her, noting that she was still unconscious.

Suddenly, he felt an impact in his chest. He looked down to see a large red spot had formed on his blue shirt. The next thing he noticed was that his legs would barely hold him up.

"You really did a number on Almeidra." A voice came from some trees in front of him. Out from behind one of them stepped a very tall and burly man with shaggy black hair. "I don't take kindly to having my people fucked up like this."

What was he talking about? His people being fucked up? Tannik couldn't really think straight anymore. His vision began to darken.

"I really only need one of you to lead me to that purple eyed fucker." The man raised a gun toward Tannik. Where had that gun come from?

"Run, Kaisimir," Tannik said, though it came out as a weak croak. He wished he could see Seike fight like that one more time. It had been such an amazing display of combat prowess. Suddenly, things were clear to him. This was the end of his story. Over four hundred years of life had come down to this final moment.

The man smiled as if he had read Tannik's thoughts. That smile was the last thing that he ever saw.

CHAPTER NINE

Seike didn't know how long he had been fighting. The battle seemed to go on for hours, though that much time couldn't have passed. He had killed dozens of the enemy. They had kept pouring out of the forest at him and had taken to trying to best him in hand-to-hand combat once the bulk of their forces realized that guns were useless against his kinetic shields. A few times they had thrown grenades at him, but he had gotten out of the way of the resulting explosions. He was sweating with exhaustion.

He'd seen Tannik run off somewhere but hadn't seen Kaisimir since the initial skirmish. He hoped they were both alright.

He looked around the area right after pulverizing the heart of yet another Legion trooper. The man had been good enough to strike Seike more than once, though the barrier that the violet-eyed vampire had over his body had shielded him from any real damage.

Samaiel and Marikya were still near the bunker doors. Seike observed as Samaiel unloaded a magazine from his rifle and replaced it faster than most seasoned soldiers would have been able to manage. His friend immediately took to scanning the trees once he had reloaded, but there were no more Legion Ambrogae to be seen, for the moment.

Seemingly satisfied that they had reached a momentary lull in their part of the battle, Samaiel turned his head toward Seike, taking the time to look over the pile of Ambrogae bodies that were strewn about the ground around them. His face took on a note of sadness as he saw that there were just as many dead S-47 soldiers in the area as well.

"There couldn't have been as many as I thought there might be," Samaiel said. "Are you alright, Seike?" There was a great deal of blood covering Seike's arms and clothing, but none of it was his. Still, he looked down at himself and imagined what he must look like from their perspective. Marikya was looking at him with concern, as well. He just shrugged, a half-smile on his face.

"Fighting's messy business," He replied. "Did either of you manage to see where Kaisimir and Tannik went off to?"

"I saw Kaisimir bolt into the woods as the first Legion troops began to come through the trees at us," Marikya commented. "Tannik must have gone after him shortly after." Samaiel's expression grew grim, and he shook his head despondingly.

"That little son of a bitch," Samaiel muttered. "He chickened out."

"He's never been in a real fight, before, Samaiel, so be easy with the poor boy once we locate him," Marikya admonished. She turned her attention to Seike. "I've never seen anyone fight the way you do, Seike. I'm glad you're on our side. Kelloway wanted us to stay here and wait for the enemy to come our way, but I don't see any more of them at the moment. What should we do, now?" Both she and Samaiel were looking at Seike askance. He wasn't supposed to be their leader, their team had none of them officially in charge, but Seike had learned that in situations like this one, people tended to turn toward him in that regard. He had grown used to it, after this much time.

He looked around now, noticing that there were still a few S-47 troops standing. All eyes were on him, awaiting some kind of suggestion or order. He could sense that there were still more people behind the closed bunker doors. He was able to hear their hearts beating rapidly in between the occasional reports of gunfire in the near distance. During the time they had been fighting, Seike had seen several Ambrogae fall to the soldiers of S-47, but he'd seen many more of those brave men and women fall to the bullets and hands of the Legion forces. He noticed one of the men still standing was the sergeant that had offered them the special goggles, and he addressed that man now.

"Take your remaining men and get inside the bunker," Seike said to the sergeant. "You all did well, but protecting that elevator should be prioritized, now. I don't feel a lot of enemy Ambrogae left out there. We'll take it from here. Tell General Kelloway that we're taking the fight to them."

Samaiel nodded at this, then said, "There isn't more than a dozen of them left out there. There are also some more members of S-47 judging by the gunfire we're hearing, and we should get out there and try to save as many of them as possible." He was addressing the sergeant, but at the end of his statement he spared a glance toward both Marikya and Seike. Seike couldn't agree more. He was already feeling distraught at seeing so many dead bodies that had been their allies in this fight. He wanted to get out there and save as many as he could.

"Yes, sirs!" The sergeant snapped a salute. "Let's go people. Into the bunker." The rest of them didn't hesitate, following the sergeant's lead. Seike and the others stayed until they were all inside and the doors were shut behind them. Then he turned toward his two companions.

"You want to take point, Samaiel?" He asked his friend. He knew the man was able to sense those of the Leviathan with pinpoint accuracy at this distance. Not just them, but others of Seline as well. "Do you feel the other two out there?"

"A lot of those I feel are a little far off, but I can feel at least one of our own due north. And closing in on our location." Only one? Seike knew that Samaiel had thrown in 'at least' in the spirit of hope, but if his friend could only feel one blue out there, then that meant either Tannik or Kaisimir was likely dead. He could tell by his two companions' expressions that they were thinking the same thing. No time to mourn right now, however.

"Okay, due north it is." Seike stated solemnly. "On second thought, though, I'll take point." The violet-eyed vampire walked past Marikya and Samaiel, motioning for them to follow his lead. Together, and feeling grim, they headed north through the darkened trees and brush.

There were still spots of fire here and there in the distance, and the fight had gone over to the outside of the perimeter around the bunker, as well, by this point in the battle. Cries and sounds of guns going off could be heard, sometimes close, sometimes further off in the distance. As they travelled, they felt the presence of an enemy Ambrogae that was coming toward them along with the presence of one of their own. This made Seike uneasy, as he imagined why that might be. It was likely that one of the others had been taken prisoner, by his estimate.

He suggested as much to Samaiel. Turning sharp blue eyes toward him, his friend said, "Yeah, they feel like they're rubbing shoulders. And I can't see either of them choosing to betray us, not even Kaisimir. And especially not Tannik."

Seike agreed with Samaiel's assessment. The distance between them and the incoming individuals had closed enough that Seike could sense that whoever was coming toward them was walking at about the same pace that they were. They were very close now, but there were enough trees in the way that they couldn't see very far ahead. After another minute of walking, Seike felt that the other presences had stopped their advance.

"They've stopped moving," he said to the other two. "They should be just up ahead." As he said this, the trees gave way to a grassy clearing. In the light of the moon, it was easy to make out two figures on the other side of the open glade. One was a tall and muscular man with shaggy hair. He had his hands on the shoulder of a more diminutive form, and Seike could see from this distance that it was Kaisimir. The three of them stopped and stared at the big man and their companion.

"Well, well, we meet at last," the large man yelled out. "Your little friend here doesn't seem to like you very much, Seike. He blames you for this whole mess, you know." The clearing was perhaps thirty meters in diameter, and from the other side of it, Seike could see that Kaisimir was glaring at him.

"Where's Tannik?" Marikya yelled back, her voice tinged with fear. They all knew the answer before the large man gave his response.

"Your other friend won't be joining us. He beat my second in command senseless, and I just couldn't let that stand." The man shoved Kaisimir to the ground roughly and produced a large pistol, pointing it at Kaisimir's head. The boy didn't seem to notice as he continued staring a hole through Seike.

"It's you they're after, Seike. Everyone that died here today, died because of you. Tannik is dead, because of you." The young noble's lower lip was trembling as he finished spitting his words. The tall man laughed.

"Let him go, and I'll come along with you, if that's what you want." Seike met the man's red eyed gaze. The burly fellow began to rub his bare chin with his free hand, making a show of considering Seike's words.

"My orders *are* to take you prisoner, Seike. But after all this," he waved his hand around the clearing, indicating the events of the night. "I have a better idea. I'll let the boy go, if you fight me. I really want to pull those eyeballs out of your skull, myself. I lost a lot of reliable people tonight, and that's on your head, as far as I'm concerned."

Seike was willing to indulge in this man's ambition to kill him. If it meant that Kaisimir didn't have to die, he would gladly fight whoever this guy was. From this distance he could sense the power behind the man's presence. He had never felt such strength from any follower of the Leviathan before, but he wasn't going to let that fact dissuade him.

"Deal," was all he said.

Samaiel and Marikya didn't protest, but instead Samaiel lowered his gun and threw it off to the side. The big man laughed and did the same with his own weapon.

"Run along home to mommy, you little shit," the man said, booting Kaisimir in his rump hard enough that the boy's face planted into the grass before him. "I've got to deal with the grown-ups, now."

Kaisimir raised his head from the ground, glaring again at Seike before picking himself up and walking across the clearing. Seike began to walk forward himself. Samaiel and Marikya stayed where they were. As the violet-eyed one passed Kaisimir, the boy whispered viciously at him, "I hope he fucking kills you."

Seike just kept walking, taking only a moment to turn his head enough to see that Kaisimir reached the other end of the glade and was safely next to Marikya and Samaiel. He stopped several feet away from the hulking man, who looked him up and down while grinning maliciously.

"You don't look so tough. My name is Olinar. I want you to know the name of the one who is finally going to end your little spree of killing my brothers and sisters." The man adopted a stance like that of a boxer. Now that Seike was this close, he could feel the man's presence and strength even more clearly. It didn't surprise him that Olinar was the leader of the invading force. For the first time the violet-eyed vampire wondered whether he was going to come out of the situation on top. He truly had never felt a presence like this one from any of those he had fought in the past.

"Someone else is coming," Samaiel called from across the clearing. "Just warning you. Just one, but they're coming fast."

"That would be my second, Almeidra. She's gonna sit this one out once she gets here, though." Suddenly a spark of recognition dawned in the man's eyes as he looked at Samaiel. "Hey, I remember you. Where are all your friends now, smart ass?" Seike heard Samaiel chuckle behind him.

"Still in Redwood Falls," Samaiel retorted. "Waiting for the next group of shitheads to wander into town."

Olinar laughed. "Yeah? Maybe I'll pay the place another visit, with a much larger group of shitheads, once I finish up here."

Suddenly a woman ran through the trees behind Olinar. She was bloodied and looked furious. "Where's that cocksucker at?" She directed her question at Olinar, but then her gaze fell upon Seike and his companions, and she smiled. "Oh, you found him."

"You didn't notice the corpse of the man who pounded the snot out of you? Tsk tsk, Almeidra. Where's your situational awareness?" Olinar didn't take his eyes off Seike as he said this, still wearing his evil grin.

"Whatever, Olinar," Almeidra sniffed. She wiped her nose, and her hand came away bloody. "Let's do this." She assumed a fighting stance as well, looking right at Seike.

"Naw, I made a deal. You're on the sidelines for this one, my dear. Me and mister purple eyes are going mano a mano." At first, Almeidra frowned at Olinar's back and looked as if she was about to argue, but then she smiled and plopped herself onto the grass.

"Wish I had some popcorn," was all she said, leaning sideways and propping her head up with one arm. She reminded Seike of a cat, somehow. She definitely looked the part of a predatory animal and didn't appear very worried about Olinar's safety. On the contrary, she exuded an air of confidence.

Olinar advanced toward Seike, and Seike backed off for a few meters. He exercised caution, wanting to put some distance between them and this woman, just in case. Suddenly, the large man charged at him with a ferocity and speed that Seike hadn't expected from a man of his size. The violet-eyed one parried the haymaker that Olinar threw at his head, but the force of the attack sent him staggering sideways. Even through the barrier over his body, Seike felt the pain of the blow. This Olinar was truly cut from a different sort of cloth compared with opponents that Seike had faced in the past.

He wasn't about to be deterred by the bigger man's assault, however, and quickly recovered, landing a blow of his own right under Olinar's chin. Seike expected to send him flying with the punch, but instead the huge man barely seemed to register it. Clearly this man had a very strong psionic barrier strewn over his own body. This wasn't going to be easy.

"I actually felt that," Olinar said. "Let's see if you feel this." He threw an underhand directly at Seike's stomach, but Seike managed to block that, as well. It also hurt his arm, even though it hadn't connected as intended.

Olinar grimaced at being parried a second time and began to step it up. He threw punch after punch at various points on Seike's body, but the violet-eyed vampire managed to duck and block every one of them. The big man was fast for his size, but Seike was faster. They began to circle one another and were now roughly in the center of the clearing. Seike decided it was time to go on the offensive.

He punched Olinar repeatedly in the face and body, connecting with almost every shot. The first few hits barely fazed the large man, but at the end of his barrage, he managed to land a particularly hard punch right into Olinar's solar plexus. The big man grunted and stumbled back a few steps, bringing his hand up reflexively to grope about his stomach where he had been struck.

Olinar looked like he was about to say something, but Seike didn't give him time. The violet-eyed vampire launched a roundhouse directly at Olinar's head and felt the satisfying crunch of the man's nose as he fell backward onto the grass. The huge man grabbed at his face and screamed wordlessly. He was back on his feet almost instantly however, blood dripping from his shattered nose.

"I can see why so many of the Leviathan are afraid of you, Seike." Olinar sneered at him. "You broke my fucking nose. No one's ever broken anything of mine." He put his hand up to his face and over his nose and made a twisting motion. Seike heard it crack back into place. The large man then spat some blood and ran again at the violet-eyed vampire.

He started jabbing this time, quick forward punches that Seike was having difficulty escaping the impacts of. Every time one of the hits connected, Seike briefly saw stars. Olinar's punches were harder than any Seike had ever taken before. After one of those stunning jabs, Olinar brought his knee up into Seike's stomach, fully connecting.

Seike couldn't believe it, but he was flying through the air. He landed on the grass only meters away from the woman called Almeidra. His body automatically curled up with the pain that his lower torso was experiencing. He heard Almeidra laugh behind him. He looked up to see Olinar steadily advancing in his direction, walking confidently now.

Once Olinar was close enough, he leaned forward and whispered, "After I kill you, I'm going to kill your three friends over there. How do you like them apples?" Again, Almeidra chuckled behind Seike.

In that moment, Seike was filled with a rage that he hadn't felt before in his entire life. It wasn't like the anger that had taken his heart and mind after Selinda had been killed. That anger had made him feel powerless and helpless. This rage inside of him now had him feeling like he could do anything. Like he could conquer the world. His body was positively humming with it. Without really knowing what he was doing, he raised his hand toward Olinar.

Out of his palm came a bolt of electricity as thick as his arm. It looked like he had plucked a lightning bolt from the sky and was now launching it at this man who had just threatened to kill his friends. The bolt struck Olinar square in the chest, and the man went flying back with much more force than Seike had flown from Olinar's knee to the stomach.

As the big man's body flew in the direction of his three companions, they all cleared out of the way. Olinar struck a tree behind them with a resounding thud, then fell to the ground.

Seike then turned to look at Almeidra and saw in her face that she was now terrified. She got up and ran into the woods that she had previously run into the clearing from. He turned back and saw that his three companions were approaching him. They were looking at him with a sort of stunned awe, as if they could hardly believe what had just happened. Even Kaisimir was looking at him in this way. He didn't know how to feel about those looks.

Samaiel was the first one to speak after a few moments of silence between them. "I feel a large group of our people coming in from the southeast."

Seconds after Samaiel had said this, Seike could faintly feel the same thing. He couldn't tell how many there were, but a large group of those of Seline were definitely coming from that direction. He felt relieved and scared at that moment. Relieved that the battle seemed to finally be over and scared of himself. At whatever he had just done. He had never heard about an Ambrogis or Ambrogess that could launch bolts of electricity. He'd always had a very high degree of psionic skill, to the point where he could electrically fry either flesh or circuitry by physically touching them. This was a first, for him, though. Judging by the faces of his companions, it was a first for them as well.

"I can hardly believe what I just saw," Marikya said after a minute. "I don't think I've ever heard or read about any Ambrogae that could do what you have just done."

"You sh-shot lightning," Kaisimir stammered out. "How..?"

"I don't know how I did it. Let's not talk about it right now." Seike realized he was still on the ground and picked himself up from it. "Let's get back to the bunker."

The others didn't seem to mind the change in subject that Seike sought from them, and Samaiel gave his shoulder a comforting pat before the four of them began to head back. On their way, they noticed that Olinar's body was nowhere to be seen. Apparently, the bolt of energy hadn't been enough to kill him, and he'd also fled. Seike didn't care, he was just glad the four of them had made it through this night.

"Tannik. He's dead..." Seike said, shortly after they had left the open glade, and were heading back toward the bunker. "We need to get his body. He deserves a proper burial."

"Yes, he does." Marikya looked at Seike with sympathy. "This isn't all your fault, Seike."

He didn't know what to say. If they had been looking for him, how could it not be his fault? Those of Legion had only come here because they were seeking him out. They only found the base in the first place because he had killed Emilio. The chain of events leading up to this night seemed to Seike to indeed be mostly his own fault. He didn't say as much, but he certainly thought it.

They decided to turn back and look for Tannik's body. After a short search, and thanks to Kaisimir's direction, they found the noble laying on his back, his eyes closed. He looks at peace, Seike thought as he gazed down at Tannik's face. They all stood there with him, taking a moment of silence for their fallen comrade. Tannik had lived and died a warrior's life and death.

Was that how Seike would someday go out? Not from being a thirsty old vampire, but in battle, while he still had plenty of natural years left ahead of him. He wondered if he might prefer things that way. Certainly, the prospect of the final thirst did not hold any appeal for him.

He looked around at the bowed heads of his brethren. Marikya was shedding tears silently as she looked upon Tannik's lifeless form, and Samaiel and Kaisimir looked incredibly sad as well, despite their lack of tears. He knew he must look the same way.

"He spent part of his last hours saying everything he could think of to convince me that you are good, Seike," Kaisimir said into the silence. "And then he saved my life... But tonight, you saved the rest of our lives. That Olinar wouldn't have let us go. I just know he wouldn't have. I'm sorry about what I said to you before you started fighting him." Kaisimir met Seike's eyes evenly. His words sounded sincere, but his eyes assured Seike of his sincerity.

"It's okay, Kaisimir." Seike replied. He didn't have it in him to say much else, for the moment, but he meant his acceptance of Kaisimir's apology. He didn't fully feel like he deserved the apology in the first place, but he was glad of it.

Kaisimir bent over Tannik's body, lifting him up and cradling him in his arms. They said nothing more as they made their way back to the bunker.

CHAPTER TEN

It's a damn shame, Kelloway thought, not for the first time since Seike's team had returned to the facility. It had been two days since the invasion, and they were all still recovering from it.

Not only had he lost over one hundred and fifty men and women to this first ever assault on Field Base A-92, but the blues had lost Tannik, as well. In the short time that he had spent in the company of the blue noble, Kelloway had grown to like the man. He had had sharp instincts, and a soldier's intuition. The wall of flame they had spread around the perimeter hadn't kept the enemy out, but it had bought them all some time. It might have even been the deciding factor in their hard-won victory, as the Legion vampires had to take the time to put the fires out.

His people and the team of blues had managed to kill nearly one hundred of those bastards. The enemy had come in force, well-armed and fully prepared to take the base out. Shortly after the conclusion of the battle, thirty-eight more blues had shown up, in the now-customary blue jeans and shirts. They were too late to aid in the fight, but their leader, a noble named Isaius, had offered for him and his platoon to stay on site and lend whatever aid they could in the restoration process, as well as to be on hand for any potential future assault. Kelloway wasn't reluctant in accepting.

The General had learned from Seike that the enemy had apparently been targeting him. Their leader, an individual named Olinar, had escaped after a brutal confrontation with the violet-eyed vampire himself. The General knew that Seike had triggered the situation that had led to the present circumstances, but he didn't blame him for it. Cause and effect was a tricky thing, and the General knew that sooner or later, his compound would have been compromised in some other way. Besides, with things as they were now, it seemed that a new era of cooperation was dawning between the blues and his own people.

Shortly after Seike and his band had returned, Marikya and Doctor Peterson discovered that if the bodies of the dead Ambrogae were burned, it terminated the release of the pheromones. Furthermore, if one of those Legion pricks were put to death by fire in the first place, the pheromones would be stopped in their tracks. There wouldn't even be a release of the dying super-wave, as they had come to call the initial release of pheromones that could give away the location of a dying red for hundreds of miles.

Up until the present, Kelloway had been lucky. In previous years, every vampire prisoner that his people ended the life of had been young for one of their kind. Marikya maintained that the radius of the dying

Ambrogae's super-wave was largely dependent on the age of the individual. The older they were, the further away their death could be felt. She had ascertained that most of those that Kelloway had killed on site in the past, that weren't burned alive, had only put out the signal of their dying for roughly a hundred miles, give or take, in every direction. There wasn't much more than forest and a few small dens of humanity for a hundred miles in every direction. It had all come down to the luck of the draw.

No one knew how old Emilio had been, but it was known that he was by far the oldest and most powerful prisoner they had ever kept. Kelloway had had his body burned along with the rest of the dead Ambrogae topside. No need to take any risks. The bodies of his own troops of S-47 had been collected, and Kelloway was still in the process of informing family members of their dead kin. He took it upon himself to make most of the calls, but a few of his subordinates had been helping with the notifying of the deceased.

Kelloway had about two hundred and fifty men and women left. Some of those had been the reinforcements that had been called from other sectors, but they were all now commissioned to stay at Field Base A-92. More people would arrive periodically over the next week. This facility was the first S-47 base that had ever been compromised. The other colonels were more than amiable in sending more people Kelloway's way.

It had been a busy couple of days since the incursion. Kelloway had caught a few hours of sleep here and there, but he was tired. Right now, he was in his office, looking over the dossiers of the new S-47 members that would be arriving at his location over the course of the next several days. The only reason he had slept at all was from a feeling of some degree of safety due to having the new platoon of blues around. They were all warriors, like Tannik had been. He was going to miss that man. A damn shame.

A knock sounded at his closed office door. It was the middle of the afternoon, so it could have been anyone.

"Come in," he said. Even his voice sounded tired.

The door opened to admit the noble named Isaius. The man was built well and wore his hair in a crew cut. Apparently, he'd served America in both World Wars, passing himself off as human despite his piercing eyes. He'd managed to hide his true nature as an Ambrogae even from the American government, back then. Kelloway could imagine it, as the man had enough color to his skin tone, not being as ghost white as so many of their kind. He looked almost human, even to Kelloway's trained appraisal.

Isaius saluted as if he was one of the General's own men. "I just got off the line with Elder Kesel and councilman Jurai, sir. Our haven is going to send another platoon of men and women our way. Elder Kesel says they're all willing to stay on a semi-permanent basis as well, if you'll have them. They're going to bring an ample supply of blood, either way, to offset diminishing your own supply, sir."

Isaius stood perfectly at attention as he informed the General of this most welcome news. "That in any way your doing, sergeant?" Kelloway had taken to calling the man sergeant almost right after he'd arrived. He'd learned that Isaius had attained the rank in World War One and

Two, climbing from private to sergeant in both of those wars, separately. The man had expertly forged documents just so that he could serve. The General found that quite admirable.

"Yes, sir. I put in the request early yesterday morning during Elder Kesel's check in."

Kelloway was beginning to like Isaius more than he already did. He'd take all the help he could get, at this stage of the game. His own people had already grown rather accustomed to having these blues around, and Kelloway was sure that they would all welcome the reinforcements as well. "Good work, sergeant. The more, the merrier. Any idea how many extra people? It would help to know the number, so I can arrange quarters for them all in the meantime."

"Thirty more, sir. All seasoned warriors like those of us who've already come."

Very pleasing news, Kelloway thought. That would bring the number of blues on site to over seventy, plus Seike. The General had heard stories from his men about the violet-eyed vampire's role in the recent battle. They said he had been a killing machine, taking out nearly two score of the enemy himself. The Legion fucks had known right where the bunker entrance was and had homed in on its location as soon as they had breached the perimeter. A good thing that Seike and the others were there at the time.

"That's welcome news, sergeant. I'll have O'neil begin preparing quarters for them in the next hour. Thank you for vouching for us. Dismissed." Kelloway watched as the man gave another perfect salute, with a perfect about turn before he left the office. If the General was a betting man, he'd bet that Isaius was feeling right at home here at the base. The man had been comfortable from the moment he had arrived, fitting in well with Kelloway's own S-47 soldiers. All of the platoon of blues had been getting along well with the General's people.

He was going over the new dossiers for the next several minutes, then the phone on his desk rang. He picked it up and heard Corporal Lisgard's voice on the other end.

"Call for you on the red line, sir. It's Elder Kesel."

Good timing. He wanted to thank the Elder for becoming so cooperative in these tough times. "Put him through, corporal."

"Yes, sir." He heard the click of the changing of lines.

"Good afternoon, General Kelloway."

"I just received the report from Sergeant Isaius, Elder. I'm glad you called. I wanted to thank you for your support in the matters at hand." The General reflected for a moment on the level of amiability he now felt towards Kesel. Just last week he would have never thought of addressing him by his proper title.

"Sergeant? Ah, yes. I do seem to recall that Isaius had been a soldier for the American army in the past. That explains why he was so eager to volunteer to go to your aid. You're most welcome of course, but I am calling to discuss another matter." A serious tone had entered the Elder's voice, and Kelloway braced himself for whatever the old Ambrogae was about to say.

The Elder continued. "The name of the one that led the assault was Olinar, correct?"

"That's according to Seike and the others. I doubt they would get the name wrong. What of it?"

"Well, I happen to have found records at the Central Haven regarding the man. I knew that the name sounded familiar, and so I looked into it. Apparently, he's been in active service to King Coranthis for the last century or so, though I don't have anything to state in what capacity. He's a bit of a mystery, it seems. There's not much on him, but I have a report here from a reliable source that some of us that have previously survived an encounter with him heard him mention the name Coranthis. That's not much to go on, I know, but if he mentioned the king's name, then it's safe to assume that he's in league with the monarchy of the Leviathan."

This was all news to Kelloway. King? Monarchy? He didn't personally have any information on the hierarchy of the reds. "I've never heard of a King Coranthis, Elder. Didn't know that the societal structure of the reds was a monarchy, either. That's good intel. Can you tell me anything else about their monarchy or this Coranthis?"

"We don't know where Coranthis is, unfortunately. But I can tell you that he believes himself to be the true ruler of this country, and he has people in positions of power, both human and Ambrogae, spread throughout the American public. And if Olinar knows where you are, then you can be assured that Coranthis knows, as well. The council at our haven no longer believes that we ourselves have had our location compromised, which is a large part of the reason that Jurai and myself were able to arrange for more men and women to be sent to you." The Elder stopped talking, but Kelloway got the impression that he was about to say more, and so the General remained silent in the interim. After another few moments, Kesel spoke again. "Might I make a suggestion, General?"

"At this point, I acknowledge your wisdom, Elder Kesel. Anything you want to suggest, I'm all ears."

"You still have prisoners who are Ambrogae of the Leviathan, yes? I suggest you question them all regarding Coranthis and see if you can learn anything about him. Or about Olinar. His location would be preferable, but any information would be welcome. If we could find out where Coranthis has seated himself, we might be able to consider taking the fight to him. Together."

Now the Elder was talking Kelloway's language. He would love to be able to set up a counterstrike in the future against those Legion fucks. Hit them somewhere it would hurt.

"I am going to put your suggestion into action, Elder Kesel," Kelloway stated. "I will give you full disclosure. Anything I can learn, you'll learn as well."

The Elder's voice seemed pleased as he responded. "Thank you, General. I'll see if I can find anything else on either Coranthis or Olinar once I return to the haven. At least I have a physical description of Olinar, perhaps that will help me find something. Good luck in your own endeavor." Kesel hung up on his end, and the General put down his own receiver.

He pressed his intercom badge and said, "Sergeant O'neil." He waited for the computer to patch him over to the man.

"This is O'neil. What can I do for you, sir?" The sergeant sounded more stable, somehow, since the days leading up to the recent attack. He'd proven to be quite reliable once the heat turned up, at any rate. Kelloway was happy about that.

"Sergeant, I need you to do some things for me. First, I want you to order an interrogation of every imprisoned vampire that we have in the facility. I want you to find out anything you can about both Olinar and someone called King Coranthis. Coranthis is the main threat to this nation. And this Olinar is apparently in league with him. As soon as you do that, I want you to have thirty more quarters prepared for the arrival of another platoon of blues."

"Yes, sir. They're sending more blues our way?" A note of hope entered the Sergeant's voice as he said this.

"That's what I said, O'neil. Snap to it, will you?"

"Yes, sir!" The intercom buzzed and shut off.

Kelloway rubbed his face with one hand. So, the reds had a king, did they? All these years of interrogating prisoners and they had learned next to nothing, but that could very well be because they had never asked the right questions. Now they had two names, and new information. It might lead to something. The General felt at least a little bit hopeful about it. At that moment, he had a thought strike into his mind. He pressed the intercom badge and said, "Seike."

The response came almost immediately. "Yes, General?" Kelloway hoped that his notion bore fruit.

"Any of you four that saw this Olinar able to draw well enough to sketch a detailed picture of his face?"

Again, no hesitation in the reply. "I can draw, General. I was face to face with him, and I am sure that I can give you a perfect portrait of that son of a bitch."

Perfect. Kelloway was feeling even better about the new interrogation tactics already.

"Can you do that for me then, Seike? Gonna ask the locals about him and someone named King Coranthis that your Elder just told me about."

"I'll have the sketch ready for you as soon as possible, General Kelloway. Who do I hand it off to?"

"I'd like you to bring it directly to my office, son. I have a photocopier on hand."

"Alright. I'll get to it, then. Seike out." The intercom went silent.

Feeling a renewed sense of vigor and determination, Kelloway started pouring through his documents, but his mind was now partly on the idea of taking the fight to the Legion. He was still able to focus on the task at hand, regardless.

Rubbing a hand on the scar in the middle of his chest, Olinar reflected on the events of the other night. He had sensed a sudden and immediate danger to himself just as that purple-eyed freak had lifted his hand from his position on the ground. In that moment, he had focused his psionic energy, all of it, into thickening the barrier on the front of himself, and erecting a kinetic shield as well. The bolt that had shot out from Seike's hand had passed through the shield as if it wasn't even there, and Olinar felt sure that if it weren't for his psionic barrier, he would be dead right now.

Almeidra watched him as he rubbed the scar. She looked worried. He wasn't sure if she was worried about him or about her own hide, however. He had hit her a few times after they had reunited at their rendezvous point, furious that she had just turned tail and run away. She had explained to him that she thought he was dead, and that she was next, after he struck her for the third time. He'd relented, and hadn't hit her since, but he was still more than a little pissed. He knew that he had just been directing his anger at being so utterly defeated toward her. It wasn't really her fault. He probably would have run away, too, in her shoes. Still though, she had been acting warily around him since then.

"Does it hurt?" She asked. Maybe she was concerned about him. He resolved to apologize for hitting her, later, once he cooled off some more.

"Not really, no. It stopped hurting a few hours ago. Still itching a little bit, though." He made himself stop rubbing the scar. The damn thing wasn't healing anymore. Just what the hell was Seike, anyway? Olinar had been around long enough to know that no Ambrogae, no matter how old and powerful, could shoot lightning bolts. It just wasn't one of the things on the long list of powers and abilities. But he had the proof on his chest that this Seike could do just that.

Almeidra looked all better, Olinar noted. She had healed up just fine from that blue noble's beating. He'd seen Almeidra fight plenty of blues, and they had always gotten their asses handed to them on a silver platter. He had found it a bit surprising to watch her actually get beaten up by one. That's why he just shot the bastard in the heart. He didn't have the time to do a similar tango, himself. Even if it was certain that he would have come out as the victor, which it was.

Again, he thought back to the events of the other night. He thought he had that violet-eyed motherfucker. Seike could fight better than anyone that Olinar had ever faced. For a minute, he thought maybe he was going to lose in the duel. But in the end, he was sure he had been the better hand-to-hand fighter.

That didn't mean jack shit to a guy that could shoot fucking lightning, though, did it?

He still hadn't reported back on his failure to capture Seike. King Coranthis would probably be angry with him, but at least he knew where that freak of nature was, now. He'd get both Ignusai and Woitan to bring their forces back to Minnesota and also see if King Coranthis would spare any more followers of the Leviathan for a second assault. They were weakened, now. Half of their turrets and half of their people had been wiped out. Olinar was aware that they would in all likelihood send for reinforcements, and maybe even get more blues to tag along, but if he could strike at them fast enough, he might be able to get them before they could bolster their defenses.

"Can you contact Ignusai and Woitan and bring them up to date? They need to get back here. I'll contact one of Coranthis' messengers and see if we can get more troops." He brought his cellphone out of his pocket to do just that.

"Our liege isn't going to like the fact that we failed our first assault. I'll let those other two peckerheads know that you're telling the king, yourself." Almeidra was a thinker. Ignusai and Woitan would likely enjoy reporting his failure to King Coranthis themselves, in the hopes that it would raise their own esteem. "I've got a few more bottles of blood from that nightclub. You want any?"

"Sure, another drink might help... Listen, about hitting you..."

"Don't worry about it. I should have at least checked to see if you were dead, first. It really looked like you were, and that bastard turned and looked at me, and he looked so angry..."

Well, that was good enough for Olinar. He didn't much like apologizing to anyone for anything, but this was close enough to actually count as one. Besides, he didn't want his second to be afraid of him, as he had no intention of killing her. She was still capable of being very useful, and besides, she was the only other one that had seen what Seike could do and was willing to vouch for Olinar. He needed her in his corner if he was to appease the king successfully and get a second assault under way.

She walked over to him and handed him a bottle, popping the cork first. He smelled it. It was no Cherry, but it still smelled pretty good. He'd been too irritated to feed himself very much for the last couple of days. Maybe the scar would heal a little more, once he consumed this bottle of blood. He didn't have much hope of that, but it was a possibility.

Once he finished having this drink, he was going to call the king's messenger. Last time, the king had spoken with him personally after he was contacted, but usually technology was limited within the king's domain, for obvious reasons. Whenever he had to make a call to the king, it was through someone who relayed information. An irritating fact, but there it was. He hoped the messenger would be able to convey the details in a favorable manner.

Almeidra had her own cell phone in hand, but she was waiting for him to make the call first. She knew it was better to get the message to the king themselves than have one of the other two prattle on to a messenger about how they had failed to capture Seike.

He hoped that the king would find the information about the S-47 facility to be a balancing factor, as well as knowing where Seike presently was. Coranthis might be angry, but Olinar felt like he was going to get his army. He would lead a second and successful assault, and after the king found out about Seike's power, perhaps he would reconsider the order to capture him.

After finishing the bottle of blood, Olinar found himself smiling for the first time since the encounter.

CHAPTER ELEVEN

Elder Ludia knew the risk she was taking. She paced around the hallways of the Western Haven as she considered her current circumstances.

She had sent a human into the belly of the beast to spy for her, months ago. So far, Crawley had no idea that one of the human scientists working under him was actually a sympathizer to her cause. The man's name was Harold Lapointe.

The humans that worked for Triaclon Industries were all kept in the dark as to the true nature of the corporation. So, as far as Robert Crawley was concerned, Harold was just another unwitting cog in the machine. Thus far, he had been able to ferret out quite a bit of useful information. Over the last couple of months, Ludia had been able to make several successful moves against Crawley as a result. Furthermore, she had been made aware of his general plans for the future. Robert Crawley was a madman.

Thanks to Harold, she had learned that the Ambrogae within the corporation had been experimenting with ways to enhance their natural powers and abilities.

What scared Ludia was the large measure of success that they apparently had in that regard. As luck would have it, Harold had recently managed to overhear part of a conversation between two of the men on the board of directors. Crawley was trying to find a way to make them all immortal. No more natural death. An elimination to the prospect of the final thirst.

Was such a thing even possible? Ludia suspected that if anyone could manage a feat that seemed to her to be a pipe dream, it would have to be Robert Crawley.

She had to find a way to stop him from achieving his ambitions. She wasn't sure what kind of power the man already possessed due to his willingness to experiment on himself and his own people, but she was beginning to consider the possibility of leading an assault on the corporation's main building, which hosted a series of laboratories that she would dearly love to destroy. Doing so might prevent him from becoming even stronger than he already was.

The problem was that Robert Crawley himself rarely left that same building, and the labs were located on the upper floors, not far below the offices of the board of directors, where Crawley tended to reside. The good news was that the council of the Western Haven would support her, whatever her decision was. The Ambrogises and Ambrogesses of their haven all supported the same cause, united in their determination to put a stop to a man that they had all come to believe was even more dangerous than King Coranthis, himself.

Until now, Ludia had not told the Central Haven or the Eastern Haven councilmen and councilwomen of the threat that was Robert Crawley. She hadn't had enough to go on. That was going to change if she decided to go ahead and assault Triaclon Industries' headquarters. She would most certainly arrange to send a detailed report to both of the other American havens, before she commenced the operation. The Western Haven had nearly four thousand individuals who were members, and the underground complex that was the haven itself housed over two thousand of these as permanent residents. By contrast, they had more members than the Central Haven, but not as many as the Eastern Haven, which had the most by a fair margin, about seven thousand members.

Ludia wished that more blues were willing to join the three American havens, but alas, the majority of Seline's brood formed their own smaller cliques and colonies. These other factions wanted little to do with what they considered the political affairs of their kind. All they wanted was to survive and thrive in their own ways.

Still, though, by her count there were less than a thousand Ambrogae working for Triaclon Industries that were employed in their main headquarters. Around seven hundred, give or take. She also knew that Robert Crawley employed only half bloods and was no fan of the king of those of the Leviathan in America, Coranthis. This was information that led her fellow council members to favor the idea of an all-out assault on the building. The other option was subversion. They could reveal Crawley and his true nature to the world, to the government, and let the humans deal with him. But that might not end well for anyone.

The problem was Crawley himself. Ludia suspected that despite being younger than she was, he could perhaps be the strongest Ambrogae in the entire world. He tried his best to hide his power, but she had discovered some time ago that he was a telekinetic. She did not know how strong his telekinetic powers were, but if he had been administering treatments on himself to expand them, then it was safe to assume that he was on a level that was previously unheard of. Even a moderately powerful telekinetic had the capacity to destroy a small army of humans, no matter how well-equipped they were. And she knew of no living pyrokinetics that she could enlist the aid of. She suspected that there might not even be any left in America. She was still waiting to hear back from Canadian sources that were on the lookout for any of those of Seline in that country that were pyrokinetic. That was the main reason that she had decided to hold off on an attack. Revealing Crawley to the world wasn't a very good option, as much as she would love to subvert him in that regard. Too many lives would inevitably be lost as a result, both humans and probably plenty of her own people, as well.

She rounded a corner in the halls and saw someone that she was hoping to see this day. Councilman Marosavek. He had been integral in their efforts to train their army of volunteers in the fight against Crawley, arming them with knowledge and information about their enemy as well as helping them to realize their own levels of potential with psionics. Marosavek was a master psionicist. He had a rare power, which was to be able to erect an abnormally large shield capable of protecting from gunfire and artillery, as well as the fires of explosions. He could cover an area nearly as large as a baseball field with this special kind of shield. Most kinetic shields failed under the impact of a fiery explosion, but Marosavek had perfected his own over the years to compensate for the large area of incoming force and heat that an explosion brought upon it. Not only could he form a shield of such large size and stability, but it didn't take much effort for him to hold it in place for a lengthy duration. He was considered quite a marvel.

He was also the next in line to take her place should anything ever happen to her, or should she have to leave the haven for any reason. At over thirteen hundred years old, he was almost as old as she was. Her own special gift was that she could manipulate psionic energy to speed up the healing process for any wounds that she herself sustained, as well as other Ambrogae. This gift extended to ordinary humans as well, though to a lesser extent, as its effects merely amplified the individual's natural capacity to heal themselves. Psionic healers were not extremely rare, but they were quite uncommon. And she had never met one with her own level of skill.

"Greetings, Elder Ludia. I was just looking for you." Marosavek smiled warmly at her as she approached. The two of them had grown close over their years presiding over the council of the haven, as well as looking after the haven itself. She considered him a dear friend. "I have news. Care to walk with me?"

Ludia fell in step beside the councilman. "I was hoping to see you today, as well, Marosavek. I wanted to discuss matters pertaining to our mutual problem." That was how she normally referred to Crawley among her fellow council members. Their mutual problem. The sources she had in Canada were actually Marosavek's sources, and she was hoping they might have found a lead of some kind.

The councilman's smile wore off as he prepared himself to speak. "What news I have may be of interest to you in that respect, Ludia. I received a report this morning from the council of the Central Haven. They informed me of a present situation that they are dealing with, and an aspect of it was rather interesting to hear about. Apparently, there's a pyrokinetic somewhere in their vicinity. A powerful one, too." His face grew grim as he said those final words, which concerned Ludia.

She sighed, then said, "Don't tell me. He or she is of the Leviathan, aren't they?" She already knew the answer, though it still dismayed her greatly to hear his response.

"Unfortunately, yes." He drew a sharp intake of breath, his face growing even more troubled. "Even more unfortunate is what I have to tell you about how they discovered this fact. I'm afraid Xiang Lau is dead, Elder." Ludia gasped at hearing this, and tears began to well in her eyes of their own volition.

"That is most unfortunate news," Ludia said. She was trying to maintain an air of stability, though her voice wavered as she said it. "Tell me all that you know of events in the central zone." A few tears slipped from her eyes. Damnit, not Xiang Lau. He had been a dear friend of hers, and his life had been hard earned. She imagined Kesel must be beside himself with grief, though she knew he would have shed no tears. Kesel rarely let his emotions show in any way physically. A fact which had played a role in their separation.

"I know he was very dear to you, Ludia." Marosavek said softly, voice tinged with genuine sympathy. Then he visibly steeled himself and went on. "He was also an extremely strong telekinetic, however. Someone burned him from the inside out, as well as fatally igniting several other followers of Seline. You know only a pyrokinetic could do that. Councilman Jurai strongly suspects that the individual is a pure blood who works under Coranthis. He didn't provide a name, as he isn't certain of the person's identity. But, given the rest of the circumstances regarding their present predicament, it only makes sense that it is someone who serves the king of the followers of the Leviathan."

Marosavek then went on in detail about what had been going on over in the central zone. A deeper level of cooperation had been established between the Central Haven and General Kelloway of S-47, as a result. That part was interesting, due to the reasons for that level of partnership. Seike was at the center of it, which was no surprise to Ludia. The reason why, and the new facts they had discovered about those of the Leviathan, stunned Ludia.

"Emilio is dead?" She murmured as Marosavek finished his account of the report. "Truly? And Seike was the one who killed him, was he?" Ludia felt a mixed series of emotions at this news. Relief. Anxiety, because of the part of the news detailing the pheromones. Vindication. She had never blamed Seike in any way for what had happened to her daughter Selinda. The fault lay at the feet of the Central Council and at the hands of Emilio. Seike had tried to have Emilio unceremoniously terminated, along with her husband and Jurai. If they had succeeded in that endeavor, perhaps Selinda would still be alive today.

Truly, she was glad that Seike had rid the world of that monster, despite the cost. And from what she could tell, his mission of revenge had led to the acquisition of information of vital importance. The pheromones. That explained a lot of seemingly coincidental occurrences of encounters with the enemy over the years. Also, she had always been a progressive thinker. She greatly approved of the Central Haven's deepening alliance with the members of S-47. That part of the news was welcome to hear.

Marosavek said nothing as he allowed Ludia the time to digest all this new information in her own way. After some minutes, as the two of them walked the halls of their haven, she spoke.

"So, this pyrokinetic is likely a pure blood serving under Coranthis… Do you think to use this person in some way, somehow?" The wheels were turning in her own head, she had to admit to herself. She wasn't above trying to render the services of a pure blood in order to get rid of a problem that she considered much larger than Coranthis. She might even appeal to the king himself, if it meant getting a weapon to use against Crawley. Now that she had thought of it, why not tell Coranthis about Robert Crawley? She had never considered that option.

As if he had read her mind, Marosavek said, "Coranthis doesn't know about our mutual problem. Perhaps it's time that he be given some information on the subject." Great minds and all that. The question was, how to go about their approach in leaking the information to the king.

Should they attempt some sort of parlay with Coranthis? Or perhaps a more indirect approach was called for.

"It seems fortune may have favored us in its most strange way, yet, my friend." She said thoughtfully. They met one another's eyes as they continued their slow walk through the maze of halls that was their haven. "Good that we ran into one another. Today is a day for much discussion, it seems."

"I couldn't agree more," Marosavek said, smiling again. "After we're done with our own discussion, we may have to call the council together for yet more debate."

"My thoughts exactly." She would grieve more for Xiang Lau, later. There was too much planning to do at the moment.

CHAPTER TWELVE

King Coranthis contemplated on what to do as he looked down on the two individuals before him. Olinar and Almeidra were on one knee at the foot of his dais, heads bowed. They had been in that posture for several minutes now, while Coranthis had been silent and considering.

He was not pleased at what these two had done. They had gotten nearly one hundred pure bloods killed in their arrogance and had failed to capture Seike, besides. And yet, they had brought to his attention some very valuable information. The present location of the violet-eyed one, as well as the fact that Seike had some sort of completely unique power.

After Olinar had sent a messenger to the monarch stating his failure and requesting more Ambrogae for a second assault, Coranthis' first thought was to have both him and Almeidra killed for incompetency. But he had learned long ago not to knock his own pieces off the board. After years of successful endeavors, one failure, however large, was not enough to warrant killing these two. They could still be useful.

With that thought in mind, he had recalled them both to the palace, to discuss their future under their king.

"In the report you gave my messenger," Coranthis began, directing his words at Olinar. "You stated that the wretch Seike left a scar upon your body from his... attack. Show me." The king leaned forward on his throne as Olinar stood slowly and unbuttoned the top of his shirt, pulling the front of it down. The man kept his head lowered in shame while he did this.

The scar looked almost the shape of a sunburst pattern, though more ragged and uneven in appearance. The wound itself had healed, but Olinar was left with this permanent reminder of his failure. Perhaps that was punishment enough, Coranthis mused. He'd never heard of any Ambrogae, pure blood or not, that had any kind of scar on their person. His kind healed too efficiently from any sort of wound to scar, even from burns. But this energy blast that Seike had struck Olinar with had indeed left a permanent imprint upon the man's body. It had been days, so Coranthis was not inclined to believe that the ugly thing was going to go away.

"That's enough, you may cover it again." As soon as Olinar had finished doing so, he immediately went back down on one knee. The monarch found looking upon that scar to be disconcerting, he had to admit. The implications behind its existence were unsettling. As were the implications behind Seike's existence. What if that creature ever managed to reproduce? Would he spawn even more violet-eyed offspring? Coranthis couldn't take the risk of such a thing ever happening. Seike would have to be eliminated as soon as possible. The king had already sent out orders for Woitan and Ignusai to return to the palace, and it was they whom Coranthis had decided to send back to this S-47 facility. The two before him now had wanted to take an opportunity to glorify themselves, so their punishment would be to sit on the sidelines while their cohorts succeeded where they had failed. It would add to their humiliation.

The prisoner that was brought to the king's palace when Olinar had led the initial scouting mission to the location of Emilio's demise had yielded some truly valuable information. A passcode for the elevator that led into the human facility, as well as a detailed description of its interior. Coranthis was extremely adept at compelling humans using mind control, a power he had honed well over his long years of life. He could force a human to tell him anything they knew. If Olinar and Almeidra had reported in when they had found out that Seike was again at the human fortification, the king would have shared the vital information he had learned with them, as well as sent Ignusai and Woitan to double the size of the attacking force. Success would have been ensured.

It was unfortunate that events had proceeded as they had, but Coranthis saw the silver lining. There was a great deal more information to work with now, plus he considered Olinar and Almeidra to be overall more valuable than either Ignusai or Woitan. Once those two returned with their company of pure bloods, he would put them under the command of a much larger force of half bloods that were loyal to the king. Their orders would be to destroy the entire S-47 compound and kill Seike. Coranthis was no longer desiring of killing the nuisance with his own hands. He saw now that the violet-eyed one needed to die by any means possible.

And if this second assault somehow failed, it wouldn't matter as much to Coranthis to lose only two pure bloods and however many half bloods. Half bloods were fodder to the king, though he was careful to avoid letting any of them know that those were his feelings about them. Some more intelligent half bloods might surmise as much, but those who were loyal to him were not the thinking types. He gave them material wealth to incent them into believing that he valued them to an extent. In truth, he had copious amounts of money and other material things that he placed next to no value upon, aside from using to achieve an end such as gaining more followers.

He decided to let the two before him know of his intentions.

"I'm going to send Ignusai and Woitan to the hole in the ground that the humans have dug themselves into." Coranthis smiled as he saw Olinar flinch slightly. Good. "You two are confined to the palace, for the time being. I'll be giving your two companions the larger force that you requested, comprised of half bloods. They will not fail, as you have. Rise, and depart." There was no protest from either of them, though Coranthis saw that they were clearly unhappy to hear this news. Their heads had both lowered more as he told them of his intentions, and as they rose and left, disappointment clearly showed in their body language. That would be something for them to think about the next time they were too arrogant with their planning.

Marikya was deep in thought as she sipped from a glass of blood that she had warmed in the microwave that was in her quarters. She had always disdained feeding from humans directly. She also didn't like the feeling of her incisors as they came out more sharply before biting down on some part of a person's body.

She didn't hate what she was, by any means. It was simply that she was too considerate of how humans felt as they were being fed upon. Most of them tended to think at least for a moment that she might kill them in the process, if they were awake and aware while she consumed their blood. Luckily though, the Central Haven had no shortage of human sympathizers that were willing to donate blood to their stores. Of course, none of those humans were aware of where the haven was. Blood banks had been set up throughout the central United States just for the purpose of collecting for the haven itself. Since it was public knowledge that those of Seline fought against the followers of the Leviathan, each of these special blood banks had been set up completely legally.

She was once again brooding over the pheromones and the issues they presented. Her and Doctor Peterson's people had discovered pretty much everything that there was to discover about them in a very short time. Now, the problem of Legion Ambrogae feeling their dying brethren was being tackled. They were researching a way to stop the release of the pheromones short of lighting an enemy on fire, for future encounters. Doctor Peterson had come up with the notion of using some kind of injecting dart on their foes at the beginning of any encounter, but that could prove problematic. If they had to use a non-lethal and otherwise unharmful attack on each of those of the Leviathan for every encounter, it could mean the difference between winning and losing a fight. She herself was thinking that perhaps they could come up with an airborne agent of some kind, something that could be spread across a vast distance and had lasting effects. Maybe even a permanent effect.

The real problem was time. Research and development took a lot more time to do than identifying and cataloging something new. Time was something that the people of S-47 and her own people did not have enough of at the moment. It would likely take at least a few months to create something to counteract the pheromones, whatever form of dispersion they ended up settling upon. They were expecting another attack any day now, though it wasn't really possible to tell when it would come. Or if it would come.

Marikya knew enough about Coranthis to know that he was not one to make the kind of move you would expect in most given circumstances. She wondered again why the king wanted to capture Seike. He'd never actively sought out he of the violet eyes in the past. Was she missing something? At any rate, with more soldiers arriving at the base every day, and with over seventy of her own kind that were used to combat in the facility, she didn't feel like they were very highly at risk. But she wasn't a soldier and couldn't really think like one. It might have been her own mind trying to alleviate any fears that she might have about their situation.

On further consideration, she did sort of feel like they were all just sitting ducks. She was aware that Kelloway and some of her own people were trying to get information from prisoners as to where Coranthis might be, but so far, she didn't know how much success they'd been having. She knew they wanted to formulate an attack plan of their own, but to do that they needed to know where the enemy was. And they didn't know. Not yet anyway.

Suddenly overcome with a sense of claustrophobia, which she knew was because of the idea of being stuck waiting for doom to arrive, she got up from her desk and went to the door of her room. She thought maybe going for a walk and perhaps finding someone to talk to could help ease the feeling.

As she got to the door, she felt the presence of another blue on the other side of it. She had been too distracted to notice before, or perhaps whoever it was had just arrived. Seemingly in response to her own thoughts, a knock sounded at the door. She opened it.

It was Samaiel. He looked unusually happy, considering the gravity of the situation that they were all in.

"Hey Marikya. We got it. We know where Coranthis is." He sounded pretty eager about revealing this to her, which after hearing it made her eager to hear more. "We were lucky enough to have a half blood prisoner that never really liked Coranthis. One who knew where his palace was located. An underground palace! The prisoner wanted freedom in exchange for the information, and Kelloway told him he'd get it if the information proved accurate. I have no idea if Kelloway plans on following through on that promise, but it was enough for the guy to start talking. It's in Wyoming. The guy was detailed in telling us how to find it, and Kelloway already sent a small platoon out to look for it. A few of our own people are in that group, including Isaius. They left about twenty minutes ago."

"Then we should catch up with them, don't you think?" Marikya wanted to see this palace for herself, or at least wherever it was precisely located. She rushed back into her room and began to put things in a backpack for the journey.

Samaiel put up his hands. "Whoa, settle down a bit, would you? They left by helicopter, Marikya." He grimaced as she suddenly threw down her pack angrily. Where the hell did they get a helicopter? She asked Samaiel that very question.

"They have a few of them hidden in special landing pads just under the ground of the surface, apparently." He responded. "They had to leave by the elevator to get to them. And before you ask, yes, they took every chopper they had. What's wrong with you, anyway? I thought you were researching some way to stop the pheromones."

She sat down on her bed. "I was. I am. We don't really know where to begin with the research." She looked at Samaiel, noticing the expression of concern on his face. "Don't you think we're just sitting ducks here, waiting for death?"

"That's uh, pretty dark." He said to her. She was feeling scared at the moment, she couldn't help it. Samaiel invited himself into the room and sat down on the bed beside her. "I know being in constant danger isn't something you're used to. Most of the people here are used to danger, though, and I like to think we have a pretty good handle on the situation. Besides, more people are coming from the haven. Another forty, I hear. They all volunteered to go not long after hearing about Isaius and his group coming here to help."

That was a relief to hear. "Why didn't you tell me that first?" She asked as she punched his arm. Hearing some people had left had only increased her feelings of impending doom. But knowing that more people were coming from their haven did make her feel a lot better.

"Sorry. I didn't know you were going through some stuff. I was excited to tell you about finding Coranthis' lair." He put an arm around her as he said this. In this case, she didn't mind. She leaned into him a bit.

"I'm not a warrior, like you, Samaiel. I'm actually a bit of a coward, you know. I hardly ever leave the haven, unless it's to go to my lab in the city."

"You could have fooled me. The other day, you were right beside me to shield us from enemy fire."

"Actually, I was behind you."

Samaiel looked at her with his eyebrow raised, then he laughed. After a moment, she started laughing too. The man had a way of making her smile.

"So what's our next move?" She asked him. "I mean, once we make sure the palace is there."

"Kelloway has already contacted everyone in S-47. Every other base. They're all making plans to coordinate a strike on the palace once we know the exact location. He was also on the line with Kesel, which is when the Elder informed him of more of our own people being on the way. Kesel now knows as much as we do about the palace, and he's going to inform the other havens. Once we know more, Kesel plans on getting at least some people from both our own haven and the Western Haven to join in on that coordinated strike."

Marikya gazed at Samaiel. He really sounded like he was in his element. She didn't know altogether too much about him, now that she thought of it. How many fights and battles had he been in? Clearly more than her.

"We're going to take the bastard down, then." Marikya said, feeling confident.

"As long as the lead isn't false."

She had a good feeling that the information they'd extracted from the prisoner was the truth.

Olinar had no plans on staying in the palace. He had said as much to Almeidra after they were well out of the king's earshot. She'd agreed. He was loyal to his king, but not to a fault. To be grounded like a child for doing something wrong was something that just didn't sit well with him. And it evidently didn't sit well with Almeidra, either. They were presently in a private chamber, discussing the matter.

"The king is going to be furious if we leave, but I think I am getting sick of his bullshit anyway." Almeidra said. Olinar knew that she hadn't been in the king's service for as long as he had, but he had to agree with her statement. He was sick of that old bastard, too. Not sick enough to plan some kind of coup, of course, but that wasn't what they had in mind. They were thinking of moving to Iowa, maybe to find out a bit more about the blues and where they might be holing up. He had a feeling that they had a main base of operations in that state.

"When we leave, though, I say we should still at least see if we can find out something that will curry favor with the king in the future. So he doesn't send out one of his death squads to look for us." Olinar wasn't ready to simply abandon Coranthis, he had a motivation behind his desire to leave.

Almeidra nodded in agreement. "Yeah, I just need a break, you know? Travel around a while, eat whoever we want, whenever we want. Maybe kill some of those blue-eyed pricks if the opportunity comes up." She sighed and sat more deeply into the chair that she was sitting in.

Olinar was glad of Almeidra's company in this endeavor. If the two of them left, and perhaps left some kind of note stating their intentions, it was more likely that the king wouldn't send people to kill them. If he'd been alone, he might have just stormed out of the palace after that little meeting with his liege. He was fortunate to have someone to talk things out with, instead. It had been her idea to leave a note in the first place.

They'd been in this chamber, discussing leaving, for the last half hour, but Olinar knew that they were stalling in order to grow the balls to do just that. They'd basically just been convincing each other the entire time, as they had their general plan fleshed out in the first five minutes.

"Well, I guess we had better get to work on that note." Olinar said, getting up from his own chair. He went to the chamber's desk to fetch a pen and paper. "It's got to be polite, with an air of still being in his service. We really don't want to have to deal with a bunch of assassins."

Almeidra chuckled, then grimaced despite herself. "Yeah, I don't want to have to kill our own kind if I can help it, either." Olinar smiled as he rifled through the desk drawers looking for a pen. The first drawer contained some blank paper, but no pen. Fucking hell, where was a pen when you needed one?

He was aware that Almeidra had also gotten up and was walking over to where he was standing. She laid a hand on his hip, which he found unusual. He met her eyes.

"You seem stressed. Maybe we should have some fun before we go on our little vacation." A sultry note was in her voice as she said the words. Olinar had always found her attractive, any Ambrogis would, but he'd always considered their partnership to be strictly professional. In the several years that they had completed various missions and assignments together, she had never given him any indication that she was interested in him in that way. He hadn't even been sure that she was interested in men. Her hand wandered from his hip towards his groin. He found that he was beginning to harden down there.

After a moment of consideration, he decided to go along with it. It had been a long time since he had a good consensual fuck. "Alright. Yeah. Maybe we both need to have a little fun." He turned toward her, picking her up roughly and throwing her across the room and onto the chamber's bed. She laughed as she bounced on the mattress, which came out almost as a snarl, then crooked a finger at him, beckoning.

He began to walk toward the bed. He had always lived dangerously, but he knew that despite writing a polite-sounding note, Coranthis might decide to order their execution, anyway. So, he was going to bang Almeidra like it was his last night on earth.

CHAPTER THIRTEEN

The old priest prayed at the Altar of Christ for God to rid the world of the red-eyed menace that was Legion, looking up at the giant crucifix as he did so. He knew that they were demons from hell, no matter what the rest of the world thought.

Simon Martin had been a devout man all his life and had entered the priesthood at a fairly early age. He worked for the Catholic Church, not one of those heathen offshoots like the Anglicans or the Protestants. The Church maintained that the blue-eyed ones were sent from God to rid the world of the evil that was Legion, but Simon didn't believe that. They still drank blood to maintain their immortality, so they must be demons from hell sent to deceive the people into feeling a false sense of safety. The sheep would believe in any shepherd, these days. Of course they would, because humanity was in the end times.

Simon had never been perverted. He didn't touch little girls and boys and didn't personally know of any priest who did. Sometimes he was inclined to believe that those stories were all a ruse made up to slander the

Church. He spent his days in prayer, mostly, ever since it became public knowledge that demons walked the earth, back in the eighties. He had put on the cloth shortly after the demons had revealed themselves. Typically, on Sundays, he would ask his flock to pray with him at the end of mass for God to purge the world of the monsters that walked in it. Today was Wednesday, however, and so he prayed alone.

He prayed to Mother Mary, blessed virgin of the immaculate conception, as well as to the Son and the Father. He was feverish in his devotion to these prayers. Someday, God would hear them and answer. All in due time, as God willed it.

Simon liked to fantasize about being an exorcist. Not just any exorcist, but one who was able to purge the people who had been turned into these creatures and restore them to their human selves. He didn't know any exorcists personally, nor the work that they did, but he wondered if there were any that had managed to do just that. It didn't seem beyond the realm of possibility to him.

He also prayed for himself, sometimes, as well. For forgiveness.

He hadn't wanted to take his granddaughter Marissa's life, but she had been bitten. He had seen the bite marks, and when he confronted her about them, she had refused to talk about it. She was only twenty-one years old. She had had her whole life ahead of her, but she was going to turn into one of those things.

She visited him that day at his own humble home. She had never minded the fact that he had turned to the priesthood shortly after he had his son, her father, even though she wasn't overly devout herself. He knew she had been too scared about the prospect to say anything to him, but something had told her to visit him that day. God, of course. And God had spoken to him on that day, as well, and told him to save her. So, he had saved her, the only way that was possible for her to be saved. He had used a knife from his kitchen.

That was four years ago, now. He had known back then that his son would never understand what he had to do, so he had covered his tracks. He'd brought her body to the local dump, along with some ordinary things, so as not to arouse suspicion there either.

Simon had known that he couldn't stop saving those who had been damned. He began going out into public more, into large towns and the city, looking for bite marks on people. He had discovered that a lot of folks who left those dens of the devil called bars and nightclubs tended to leave with bite marks on them. They could be on the neck, but also sometimes the arms and legs. The demons were using those places of sin to propagate themselves.

He would wait until he found someone who walked out with these marks, and if they were alone, and didn't get into a cab, he would follow them as they walked. Simon was seventy-three years old, but he was very healthy and fit for his age. God must have wanted him to be, for his personal mission.

Once they were alone, and when he was sure there were no prying eyes, he would use the same knife that he used on his granddaughter. A knife he had since blessed many times. So far, no one had caught on to him, and he knew it was because God wanted him to continue his good works. Simon was a devout man, and so far, he had managed to save sixteen people, including his Marissa.

The sound of a helicopter began in the distance while he was in the midst of his prayers. At first, Simon continued praying. The helicopter drew nearer, and within a few moments Simon could tell it was more than one. The sound became loud enough to break his concentration. He stopped midway through his usual routine, becoming curious enough to go outside and have a look.

The church was in a very rural area of the Wyoming countryside. There were few houses in the area, and no businesses of any kind for miles. As Simon opened the doors and stepped outside, he could see that the helicopters were almost overhead, and they were flying quite low. He counted five of them, and noted that they were most likely military, as they were a dark green in color.

He watched as they passed over him and began to fly over the wooded area behind the church. After they had gone a certain distance over the trees, he saw them slow down, then stop in midair. Then he watched them begin to descend. He knew that there was a large field in that area of the forest and was fairly certain that that was where they were landing. Had he been caught?

He gave a rueful shake of his head as he smiled at himself. Why would they send five military helicopters after him if he had been caught? Of course, whatever this was, it had nothing to do with him. It was a curiosity, but he wasn't curious enough to go trekking through the woods for a mile or more just to see what they were up to. Chuckling to himself, he entered the church once more to resume his daily prayers.

Isaius looked down on the church as they flew overhead. He saw the old priest come out to see what the racket was, and smiled as he thought that seeing the choppers might be the most exciting thing that had happened to the old guy in a long time. Then he chuckled, thinking of the irony involved in there being a church so close to the primary lair of the most evil sons of bitches in the whole damn country.

They touched down on a field roughly four miles out from the lake that they had been told to go to. It was an unnamed lake near the Flaming Gorge Reservoir. They had been given some pretty exact details, so he was sure that they were close to the place. Apparently, there was a cave that led deep underground in the woods right by this lake, to the southwest of it. The field they had landed in was directly south of the lake.

Their mission was to provide reconnaissance, and nothing more. They were to go to the cave, and hope that he or one of the others could feel any presence of reds. Their kind could usually feel reds before the reds could feel them. Usually. They didn't feel anything yet, so he was sure they had picked a good landing spot, at least. Close enough to get back to the choppers quickly, but far enough that the copters wouldn't be heard by any within the palace. If they were as deep underground as the prisoner had claimed, they probably could have landed right on top of the cave and been alright, but there was no telling when any reds might be coming and going. It wasn't a risk to take.

Everyone was geared in forest colors, as the situation called for. There were twenty-five of them including the helicopter pilots, who were to stay in the choppers, and be ready to fly out at a moment's notice. Twenty of them would go in quiet and fast. They would find the cave, ascertain it as being the authentic location, and get the hell out of there. There were four other Ambrogae with Isaius. One per chopper.

He looked down at himself, dressed as a soldier again. Damn it felt good. He liked blue well enough, but he felt more like the part of a soldier now that he was dressed like the rest of them. He might ask if he could keep the uniform on when he got back.

They fanned out into the forest in groups of five, all heading toward the lake. All with one Ambrogae per group aside from Isaius' group, which had himself and one other man. They were armed and ready for anything, he knew. He reminded himself that this was just a quick scouting trip, though. It was imperative that they confirmed that this cave was there and reported it back to Field Base S-47.

Once they had found the cave, they would radio the choppers, who would get on the line with the base, just in case. If they couldn't confirm an Ambrogae presence upon reaching the cave, they would go in far enough to get confirmation, then radio the choppers again. Just in case. The army always thought things through. It was part of the reason Isaius liked them so much throughout his life, and had made himself a part of that experience.

In no time at all, they could see the lake ahead of the trees. His own team was to the southwest, but so far, he hadn't found a cave that matched the description.

He radioed the others, who all confirmed a negative on finding the cave. He told them to head to his group's general location. They were all equipped with a special GPS that helped them find each other with pinpoint accuracy.

After some more searching, he saw a group of boulders that perfectly matched the description that prisoner had given. He couldn't feel any red Ambrogae's presence, but the man had said it was at least two miles if not deeper under the ground. He approached the boulders with the hope of finding a cave entrance.

Bingo. There it was. It wasn't much more than a crack in the wall, but it was big enough for even a large man to fit into. He radioed the other groups an affirmative on finding the cave entrance, and they finished closing in on his location. Then he radioed the choppers.

Once all twenty of them were together, they quickly formed a plan. Isaius would take five of the human soldiers in, and they would only go far enough to either feel a presence or confirm in some other way that this was the place. No one argued. They had thus far kept words to a minimum, which was how Isaius liked it. Everyone's focus was on the same thing, their mission. God it was good to be back in the action. He had missed those days.

He went in first, and waited for the five men that were accompanying him. It was a definite descent. From the first step into the cave, it went down.

As they progressed, the cave twisted and turned, but it never stopped going down. After about two hundred meters, the walls broadened, and there became much more space to move. Still, it went down. Isaius and his men noticed that the ground was well trodden, but that wasn't enough evidence. They needed something more.

After another four hundred meters, they approached a part of the cave that was clearly man-made. It was an arch and had been carved into a gothic-looking style. Beyond the arch, the floor of the cave dropped even more. It became a large incline going down, quite steep. For a moment, Isaius imagined he could feel a presence, but it was just his nerves at the prospect of being so close to the king of all the reds. He didn't feel anything, but he didn't have to. His gut told him this was the place.

He radioed the choppers again. The signal was a little bit staticky, but he got through with no issues. Now they knew. This was definitely the place; the prisoner hadn't lied.

He got those men out of the cave on the double. Without incident, they returned to the choppers and began the trip back to the base. The entire time he and the others hadn't felt a presence, but he saw that arch, and the ground had been walked upon a *lot* over the years. That was enough. It definitely wasn't a coincidence.

As they flew back, Isaius' mind wandered to thoughts of the prisoner that had revealed this to them, and General Kelloway's promise to release the man. Isaius hated those red eyed murdering bastards, and resolved to kill the man himself, to spare the General from having to fulfill that promise, or to spare him from going back on his word, either one.

"I'm telling you, I thought I felt one of those Seline cocksuckers," Olinar stated again. "Maybe we should inform the king."

Almeidra scoffed at him. "And what? What's going to be your reason for being in the tunnel, where you *could* feel the blue? I didn't feel anything. I think you're a little on edge about us disobeying our liege."

She had already stated as much. When Olinar had thought he felt a blue's presence, he had grabbed Almeidra by the shoulder, turned her around, and forced her to retreat about a hundred feet back toward the gates that led into the palace. They had been arguing in the tunnel for the last ten minutes. As soon as they had gone ten feet back, he stopped feeling the presence, but he was almost positive he *had* felt it. A blue, or maybe…

"What if it was Seike?" He wished he hadn't blurted it out as soon as the words left his mouth. Almeidra just laughed.

"Ok, you being defeated once by him must have really gotten to you. I'm telling you, Olinar, I didn't feel a damn thing. And I still don't." She crossed her arms and stared at him with one eyebrow raised, a half-smile on her face. "Don't you think if one of the blues had been on the way in, we'd have felt them still coming by now?"

"Maybe whoever it was felt us too. They might have left after that." Olinar was feeling less sure of himself by the moment, though. It had been a bare feeling, almost a ghost of a presence. Almeidra could be right, he might just be on edge after the crazy week they'd had.

"Tell you what," Almeidra said. "We keep going and if we don't feel anything by the time we get to the archway, we leave. I'm betting we won't feel anything, even after we get to where the car is parked." They had a car parked at a house that Coranthis had the deed to. He had deeds to a lot of houses in the area, though most of the time, they were abandoned. Vehicles for his people were in all the driveways, so passersby would assume that someone lived in those houses, but most of the sometimes occupants spent most of their time in the palace, or elsewhere in the country. There were also standing orders that no one in the area was to be fed upon or otherwise killed. The king didn't want this countryside to have any kind of reputation for being an Ambrogae feeding ground. He was wise in that, not drawing any unwanted attention.

"Yeah, okay. You might be right anyway. I might have been imagining it."

Almeidra laughed again. "You were. But let's just prove it to ourselves, just in case."

They started back up the winding tunnel that led to the surface. It had been tricky to get out of the palace without being seen, anyway. They had waited until the guards by the gateway left for a shift change, getting out in the two- or three-minute window that they had before the next pair of guards arrived. Olinar wasn't certain that the guards had been notified of their temporary incarceration within the palace walls, and neither was Almeidra. Probably not, as king Coranthis would just expect to be obeyed without question. Best not to take any unnecessary risks, though.

Sure enough, they reached the archway in the next twenty or so minutes without incident, taking their time as they walked up through the tunnel. Nothing. Not even a ghost of a presence. Almeidra was right, after all, it seemed. He was glad that she was with him. Not just because of the fantastic sex they had recently finished having, but also because of that.

After another short stroll upwards, they reached the mouth of the cave entrance. As they exited through the crack, Olinar could faintly hear the sound of a helicopter in the distance, fading. Nothing new there, he'd heard helicopters in this area more than once over the years. Still, he felt no presence of any blues.

They made it through the forest and to the house that had their car in its driveway without any problem. He really did need to get a handle on his nerves. For a minute there he had been imagining that Seike had somehow found him. He felt like an idiot.

As he got into the driver's seat and settled down, Almeidra got into the passenger seat and turned her face toward him.

"See? No problems." She assured him.

"You were right." He admitted. Turning the ignition, he pulled out onto the road and started driving. He felt better already.

CHAPTER FOURTEEN

Ludia listened impatiently as Kesel berated her on the other end of the cell phone. The man just couldn't see reason, and because of that he might put her plan in jeopardy. She was in a house on a property she owned in the Californian countryside, somewhat near Los Angeles. This was the place she usually came to from the haven, which it was also near enough to, whenever the situation dictated a need for direct communication with either one of her human allies or someone from one of the other havens.

"Ludia, we can't just sit around and wait." Kesel said. "We have people at Kelloway's base of operations that are in danger of being attacked at any moment. Not to mention the General's own people. We can't rely on the foolish notion that Robert Crawley may make a move against Coranthis before it's too late."

Kesel had already known about Crawley, which surprised her at first. It had been almost a decade since the two of them had spoken with one another, even over the phone. Of course, she had failed to consider that some of the other council members from the Western Haven might tell him about their own dilemma. He'd been informed of Crawley years ago but had apparently kept the information to himself upon request. He wouldn't say which of the council members had informed him, but she knew it hadn't been Marosavek. It wasn't overly bothersome, as she trusted Kesel with such information. That's why she had told him about Crawley herself, during this conversation. Kesel wasn't up to date, however, and as such he was not aware of the extent of the danger that was Robert Crawley.

"I know what I'm doing, Kesel, and you could save yourselves a lot of trouble if you could just convince Kelloway and your own people to wait for a day, two at most. I feel certain that our plan is going to work."

She and Marosavek had hatched a plan to incite a war between Crawley and Coranthis. Just a few hours ago, Harold, her man on the inside, had employed some hacking skills that she found out he had in a recent conversation with him. After speaking in the halls of the haven the other day, The Elder and the councilman had decided to wait until Harold reported in to see if he had any particular skills with computers, as their best of several discussed plans hinged on whether or not the human could hack into the company's emails. It had turned out that Harold did indeed have skills as a hacker. It was apparently a pastime of his, despite the fact that he was primarily a chemist.

He had reported his success not three hours ago, and now all they had to do was wait and see if Crawley would react as she predicted he would. She was relying on the monster to send his forces against Coranthis openly. If he did that, and the two factions went to war with one another, it would serve her own cause against Crawley, and create a safer situation for Kesel's people and General Kelloway. Crawley had always been decisive in his ability to carry out his own designs. If he fell for the trick, he would act fast. Ludia was absolutely positive about this.

She heard Kesel sigh on the other end of the phone. "I haven't heard back yet as to whether or not Kelloway has confirmed the location of Coranthis' palace. He'll likely want to act immediately upon knowing where it is, but perhaps I can convince him to wait. He's going to inform me the moment he finds out, which should be any time now. I'm staying here in the city until he calls."

It had been fortuitous that she had been able to get hold of Kesel in the first place. She had decided to call the Central Haven's council cell phone to see who, if anyone, was in possession of it at the time, hoping to inform them of her plan. She had made the call while waiting for Harold to potentially call back with further news. She was setting aside six hours or so in total in the hopes that the scientist would call her back and inform her of some kind of information that confirmed for them that the emails had worked. Getting hold of Kesel had been paramount, though she hadn't known it until she got on the line with him. She had no idea that they had been planning to strike at Coranthis as soon as possible, themselves.

"Okay," she said. "I'm going to be here for another few hours at least. If I hear anything, I'll call you back. If you get a report, you call me back." She had to admit that the timing of things so far today had seemed rather serendipitous. Perhaps that luck would continue.

"That sounds agreeable." Kesel replied. "I hope that things turn out favorably for us both, Ludia."

Ludia hoped that things worked out, too. After they had hung up, she began pacing around the house, once again waiting. She was hoping for a miracle of some kind.

"You're sure, Gregory?" Robert Crawley was drumming his fingers on his desk, feeling irritated.

"Yes, Mr. Crawley. I went over the emails myself. They had been deleted a few days ago." Gregory's brow was furrowed in consternation. He didn't like that a few of their half blood brethren had betrayed them, either.

Some of those who *were* loyal to him discovered the emails less than an hour ago. Even deleted emails were monitored within his company, and a good thing too. Otherwise, these rats may have escaped notice. The messages had described a 'most recent' report to King Coranthis, though they had been in a kind of cipher, and the king's name wasn't directly mentioned. The employees who sent the emails evidently had some skill with computers, because they had managed to cover their tracks until now. Deleted emails were monitored weekly and flushed from the system automatically every two weeks. The technician that had discovered them only found them because one individual who sent the emails to a few other individuals had made a coding error while trying to hide them from the system.

Evidently, the Leviathan was presenting Crawley with an opportunity. Who knew how long these disloyal half bloods had been leaking information to the king? If Coranthis was aware of even half of Crawley's plans and intentions, then the monarch was going to be a problem.

The so-called king of America seemed to think he was being devious, keeping tabs on Crawley with a small network of spies. But what to do, exactly? How to resolve this little issue?

"You've always had a sharp mind, Gregory. What do you think we should do, here?" Crawley began to drum his fingers a little more rapidly as he finished asking this, then abruptly stopped. Gregory spoke into the silence.

"Perhaps it is time you pay the king a visit, Mr. Crawley. You could ask him about this yourself." The man's expression didn't change a whit as he said this. Gregory was a man who simply calculated the different factors of a situation. He was a cold, hard thinker. And he had just voiced a very good idea.

"So you're saying we don't do anything with these employees." Crawley stated. "Not yet. Go to Coranthis first and see what the king has to say about this new discovery of ours." Gregory only nodded.

It was so simple, it was genius. Until now, Crawley had been playing games with the king. He'd feared the potential repercussions for his company if he openly spoke out against Coranthis. Gregory was saying that not only should he speak out against the monarch, but he should confront him. It only made sense, now that they had found these emails, proving that Coranthis had been keeping tabs on him all along. The king could have possibly even been making moves against him that he hadn't discovered, as of yet.

Robert Crawley decided then and there that he was going to get to the bottom of this situation as quickly and efficiently as possible.

"Gregory," he said. "Please have my private helicopter prepared for a little trip to Wyoming."

Gregory smiled his small smile as he bowed his head in response. "Right away, Mr. Crawley."

As soon as Gregory had left the office, Crawley began going over in his head just what he would say to Coranthis, the questions he would ask. The king would no doubt be irritated at the CEO and owner of Triaclon Industries for showing up unannounced, but he would allow it. Crawley would stride into that palace himself and figure out what was going on between them. He would broker some kind of resolution that worked out in his favor.

And if the king proved to be uncooperative, then there was always plan B.

This could be a disaster, Ludia thought.

She had received a call minutes ago from sources that were always watching Crawley's corporate headquarters from the outside. They had seen his private chopper leave the roof of the building, heading northeast. Towards Wyoming. She wouldn't have known he was going to Coranthis' palace if it weren't for her previous phone call with Kesel. Until then, she hadn't known where the monarch operated from. Serendipity. And yet, even with that happy little coincidence of being armed with the appropriate knowledge, she felt helpless.

Crawley was going to talk to the king about those emails, she felt it in her gut. If he discovered that Coranthis had nothing to do with them, things could sour for her and for Kesel, very quickly. She was still debating on just what she would say to her estranged husband once she called him back.

Just then, her phone rang. She checked the display out of habit, but of course the number was private. Everyone she spoke with had a private number. She picked it up.

"Kesel?" She knew her voice sounded strained as she said his name.

"Yes. Ludia, what's wrong?"

She swallowed as she prepared to reveal the potentially bad news to the other Elder. "Crawley just left his headquarters by helicopter. He was heading northeast." She waited as Kesel digested this information. When he spoke, he sounded rather strained himself.

"I also have something to report. Kelloway flat out refused to wait. His team still hasn't returned, but they contacted him from the site of Coranthis' palace, confirming that the location is indeed where the king resides. He's mobilizing as we speak."

"You need to tell him not to go there now! Crawley will be there in a matter of hours, and if he's still there when Kelloway's forces arrive, they're done for. Crawley is perhaps the strongest telekinetic that has ever walked the earth, Kesel! Every S-47 soldier in America coming at him at once might not stand a chance."

"I tried my best to convince Kelloway, already, Ludia. He wasn't having any of it. He wants to attack the king as soon as possible, and so he and every other S-47 base commander out there are coordinating their assault right now."

"This could be very bad, husband." She hadn't called him that since she had left the Central Haven, she realized. He didn't seem fazed as he replied.

"There is potential here, Ludia. Crawley will be there before Kelloway. Their forces are going by land, not air. It's going to take them considerably longer to arrive there at roughly the same time together than it would take Crawley to fly there, meet with the king, and be on his way back."

"Tell Kelloway to wait just a few hours. Please, Kesel."

"I will call him again, but I make no promises. The man is a force all on his own, and he likely will dismiss my warnings, as he has already done. He doesn't feel threatened by one man, telekinetic or not. He's never dealt with a telekinetic before and doesn't know what they are capable of."

"Please try."

"I will. And if my words do not work, have faith that this could still all work out with the end of Coranthis' reign."

"I tried to tell you before, Crawley is the real danger. Coranthis is just a distraction in comparison."

Kesel was silent on the other end, taking in the words she had just spoken.

"I just have trouble believing he is as strong as you claim, Ludia. I told Kelloway he was a powerful telekinetic, but to exaggerate that description of him probably won't help."

"The truth is, I don't know how strong Robert Crawley is, exactly. As far as I know, no one does. But your description of him being a powerful telekinetic is at least accurate, even if it is possibly underexaggerated. Make clear to Kelloway just how strong an Ambrogae telekinetic typically is and see if he can't make his move just a little more slowly."

"I will, Ludia. Goodbye for now."

"Goodbye for now, Kesel."

Hanging up, Ludia sat down roughly in a chair in the house's living room. She prayed to any God that would answer for Crawley to be gone by the time the soldiers and those from the Central Haven reached Coranthis' palace.

CHAPTER FIFTEEN

The atmosphere in S-47 Command and Communications was tense, and that was putting it lightly. Samaiel could feel how on edge these humans now were after it had been revealed to them that there might be an additional element of danger involved in an already extremely precarious mission, though Samaiel wasn't yet aware of what specifically that danger was.

Kelloway had called him, Seike and Isaius into the main operations room to give them a briefing on the new circumstances they now faced.

Isaius was dressed in the same soldier's uniform that the rest of the S-47 men and women wore. He had put it on for the scouting mission, and had only been back a short time, so he hadn't gotten around to taking it off yet. At least, that's what Samaiel assumed. He thought that Isaius looked more comfortable dressed like a soldier. The man definitely looked the part.

Seike had been the last to arrive, and he came only moments ago, a couple of minutes after Samaiel. Isaius was already there when Samaiel showed up.

"Well," Kelloway said, as he stood on the upraised section of the command room. "I just got off the line for the second time today with Elder Kesel, gentlemen. It seems we might have another guest showing up to the party." Samaiel and the other two Ambrogae were standing below the upraised section, looking up at the General. Before he said the next part, though, Samaiel caught the word 'telekinetic' among the man's thoughts and let out an involuntary groan.

Kelloway just gave him a strange look and pressed on with discussing the matter. "Do any of you know about telekinetics among your kind? And if you do, please share as much as you know with me. I'm afraid I have zero experience with any such kind of Ambrogae."

"Fuck," Isaius cursed. "Does Coranthis have a telekinetic at his palace, sir? If he does, I advise we rethink the attack plan. Maybe even reconsider it altogether."

Kelloway raised an eyebrow at Isaius, then moved his gaze onto both Samaiel and Seike. "Do you two agree with the Sergeant here?"

Samaiel spoke first. "Yes, General. I do, anyway. A thousand soldiers might not be enough to take out a telekinetic. Even with Ambrogae among them. I don't say this lightly, General. Those people are rare and almost unstoppable."

Seike just nodded as Samaiel was speaking. Now he asked, "Is this telekinetic working for the king?"

The General looked from one to the other of them before he replied. "No. This guy is someone named Robert Crawley, from California. He left there not long ago by helicopter to meet with this King Coranthis. Apparently, he's a telekinetic. That's what the Elder said, anyway." Kelloway inhaled deeply, then said. "According to the Elder, there's a good chance that this Crawley will be gone by the time our forces arrive, anyway. So, I'm going ahead with the operation. We're gonna approach the target site a little more slowly, just in case."

Samaiel had never heard of anyone by that name. He looked over at Seike, who just shrugged. Isaius shook his head and gave a little shrug as well. So, none of them knew who this guy was, including General Kelloway.

"What does the Elder think we should do?" Samaiel asked.

Kelloway looked at him with those piercing blue eyes. Human eyes, but still pretty sharp when he turned them on someone. "He thinks we should proceed but approach our destination a little more slowly. Which is what we're doing."

A strange thought suddenly crossed Kelloway's mind, and Isaius must have noticed it as well, because he spoke up with the question before Samaiel could. "Sir, if you don't mind my asking, what happened with the prisoner who gave us the intel?"

Kelloway grimaced. "Burned him." That was all he said. Before anyone could respond, he added, "Any more questions, or are we ready to get this show on the road, gentlemen?" So, that was why the General's mood seemed a little off. It wasn't because of an element that might end up compromising the mission. It was because he had killed someone that had provided good information.

Samaiel knew that Kelloway was a hard man, but he found himself reflecting on the difficult kinds of decisions the man must have to make almost on a daily basis. He could sense that Kelloway wasn't happy about breaking a promise, even if it was to a monster, but he caught Isaius smiling in response to the General's answer. He seemed to stand up a little straighter as he smiled, if that was even possible. Isaius was clearly happy to hear that answer.

"Nothing else from me, sir." Isaius stated in a voice tinged with enthusiasm. "I'm ready on your command."

Samaiel glanced again at Seike, then Seike said, "We're good to go, General." Samaiel nodded in agreement.

"Good, then." Kelloway said. "I already informed Marikya that I want her to stay here on the base. She was reluctant to agree but relented. I suggested to Kaisimir that he might want to stay on hand as well, but he wouldn't have it. Wants to prove himself after what happened in the last battle. Fine by me." The General put his hands on the railing, then suddenly seemed to deflate. His eyes took on a faraway look.

"I know there are risks," he said, looking at nothing in particular. "Especially with how small the entrance to the palace is, but we need this victory. My whole damn career has been riddled with my people dying, with our side hardly getting in any good shots. We need this. After we take out Coranthis, we can all rest easier."

Not the best of pep talks, Samaiel thought. How much had the General slept in the last week? Not very much, that was for sure. He worried that the man desperately needed some sleep. He wasn't about to suggest that, though.

Kelloway seemed to reinvigorate himself to a degree. "Alright, I'll have you three make your way north, about fifteen miles." A note of authority had crept back into his voice. "Our transportation depot is there, near a highway. My troops are already there, mobilizing as we speak. Half of your own people are to go with them, the other half are to stay here. I'll leave it to you three to figure out who stays and who goes. Sergeant O'neil is already topside, he and a small platoon will lead you all to the depot. Those are my orders, gentlemen, now hop to it!"

Isaius offered his usual crisp salute. "Yes, sir!" he said, practically yelling.

Samaiel and Seike both said "Yes, General." He didn't offer a salute, and neither did Seike. They hadn't done so thus far, and neither of them were about to start now. The three of them left the operations room.

Once they began walking through the corridors, Samaiel addressed Seike.

"Do you think this Crawley is going to be there when we arrive?" He asked his friend. "I mean, I really don't want to run into a telekinetic, do you?"

Seike frowned as they walked, still looking straight ahead. "Kelloway is right. We need this victory." He said. "I don't think we can back out now, just because of one man. Even if he is telekinetic."

Samaiel thought about that, and he had to agree. "Right," he said. "And besides, if we run into this guy, you can just blast him with lightning. Problem solved." He knew Seike didn't have control over his power, but his friend seemed to appreciate the joke. Samaiel had elicited a smile to take over that frown. Good enough for him.

"Do you think we're gonna make it through this, Seike?" Samaiel asked.

"Hard to say, no one knows the future." Seike replied. "I intend on trying my best to make it through today, though."

"Yeah, me too." Samaiel wasn't about to give up now, and he was glad that his friend felt the same way. They continued walking for a few moments in silence.

"We all have to die sometime." Isaius suddenly said. Samaiel grimaced, but he had to admit that was true, too. He wasn't ready to die before he had at least kissed Marikya once, but if today was the day, then so be it.

The three of them walked on toward the elevator in silence after what Isaius had said, but with a grim determination in their stride.

God had spoken to Simon again, telling him to go to the city shortly after he had finished his prayers. He had to find another soul to save.

The aged priest was still in the church. He had a change of clothes on hand for the occasion and had donned them a few minutes ago. He always kept casual attire in his church, in case he needed to get dressed for walking around in the public eye.

Cheyenne wasn't a big city, but it had enough people to attract the demons. They could disguise themselves to look just like ordinary people, and preyed upon anyone who dropped their guard. At this stage, there could be tens of millions of them throughout America already. God needed soldiers like Simon Martin to help stop the spread of the evil ones. It was his duty.

He finished up his preparations and was on his way to his car when he heard a familiar sound. Another helicopter was approaching in the distance. This one was flying pretty low too, but he observed it to be of a civilian design. He watched as it flew overhead. Strangely enough, it was flying in the same direction that the Military helicopters had gone. They had left an hour or so later, going back in the direction they had come from, albeit at a higher altitude. This one kept going past the field. It wasn't completely unusual to see helicopters in the area, but this many in one day?

The end times were strange times indeed.

He shrugged it all off as unimportant and got into his brown station wagon. It was time to search for a soul to save from eternal damnation, and he couldn't delay just to wonder about strange sights in the sky above his church. It wasn't like Mother Mary Herself had appeared in the clouds.

He pulled out of the church parking lot and began the drive towards the city. Already, his mind was focused on the great work that God had bestowed upon him. He had all but forgotten about the helicopters.

The helicopter hovered above the group of rocks that served as the entrance to Coranthis' little palace of pure bloods. It was about twenty-five feet from the ground, an easy jump for Crawley. He leapt down after instructing the pilot to land in a small field on the northern side of the lake, with further instructions to return and hover above the rocks one hour from now.

He was still wearing his business suit. He almost always had a suit on, preferring that style of dress to any other since the turn of the twentieth century.

He made his way through the crack that served as the entryway to Coranthis' lair, getting a little dirt on his suit as he passed through. He took a moment to brush it off. How distasteful. It had been quite a long time since Crawley had last been here, almost a century. The last time, it was to curry favor with the monarch for some finances to invest in a project that would eventually become Triaclon Industries. At the time, he probably had enough of his own wealth to succeed, but his primary motivation had been to convince the king that Robert Crawley was in his debt. All a part of his long and elaborate scheme to someday undermine Coranthis.

As he made his way into the tunnels, he tried to imagine how this was going to go. If the king knew enough about his plans, he thought it might lead to violence. That was alright by him.

It took a while for him to finally reach the large ornate doors that served as an entryway to Coranthis' palace. There were two guards standing there, just as there had been nearly a century ago. Crawley smiled at them as he approached.

"State your business." The guard on the left said bluntly. It seemed that some things would never change. Crawley was highly amused at the medieval attire these guards still wore, even after centuries of progress in the real world. They were even holding large halberds and had crossed them together over the doorway as the guard had recited the same phrase that he had probably been saying for his entire career. And what kind of job was it, anyway? Door guard. Really? So very droll.

"I'm here to see the king, on matters of utmost urgency. Tell him it's Robert Crawley." Crawley decided to play along as if it were still the Middle Ages. He truly found that Coranthis had an inability to adapt to change.

The guards looked at each other in surprise, then back at him. They recognized his name, at least. The one on the right spoke next.

"Wait here." He said, opening the door on his side of the large double doors, and slipping inside the palace's interior.

The other guard wouldn't meet Crawley's eyes, as he knew the man wasn't supposed to. Though, it could also be because Crawley was a half blood. The guard stared straight ahead, halberd pointing up now, rigidly at attention. Crawley stood with his hands in his suit pants pockets. They stood like this for nearly ten minutes until the other guard finally returned.

"The king will see you." He said, opening the doors further to admit Crawley into the cathedral-like interior of the palace.

Of course he will, Crawley thought. He wouldn't put it past Coranthis to try to kill him here and now. Crawley was ready for that, however. The guard looked him over suspiciously as he passed.

There was another guard inside, ready to escort him to the king's throne room. "Follow me," was all the man said as he turned around and began walking, expecting Crawley to do just that. Crawley began to follow the fellow. A slight annoyance had tinged his initial amusement by this point. The guards were being rather curt with him, which was no surprise since he had shown up without an invitation. He suspected that it also had to do with the fact that they were pure bloods, and he wasn't.

They made their way through passageway after passageway. Crawley noted the many curious faces that watched him pass. The nobility of Coranthis' court, as well as the servants. The servants were mostly half bloods, or very young pure bloods who were learning their place in Coranthis' hierarchy.

After quite some time of this, they finally approached the large gothic doors that would lead into his royal majesty's throne room.

There were four guards by these doors. Two of them pushed the doors open to allow Crawley into the throne room, regarding him with a disdain that they didn't bother trying to hide. As he entered, he saw that there were four guards just inside the doors as well. Exactly the same as the last time that he had been here.

Crawley saw the old silvery-haired king sitting atop his throne, full of pompous authority. He walked along the red carpet that led to the dais that the throne sat upon. As he approached the dais, the king spoke.

"This is most unexpected. On your knee, Crawley."

There was no way that Crawley was going to bow or kneel in any way for this fool, not this time. Already he could tell that courteous words were not going to be exchanged. He abandoned the thought of wordplay altogether, deciding instead to take as direct an approach as was possible.

Still standing, Crawley spoke, looking directly at Coranthis. The king was becoming visibly angry, now.

"I know that you've sent your people to pose as my employees. How long has this been going on?"

For a moment, the monarch's anger faded and Coranthis looked confused. Crawley was suddenly unsure of the authenticity of the emails. Then the king spoke back.

"All of your employees are my people. As are you. I'll say it again, Crawley. Kneel before your king."

Suddenly it dawned on him. Ludia. She was behind the emails, somehow. This old fool had no idea what Crawley was talking about, a fact which was evident after only a few words exchanged. He had been played. There was still no way he was going to kneel, however.

Crawley was aware of footsteps approaching behind him. He glanced back to see all eight of the guards that were at the door were now approaching him, menace in their expressions.

"Guards. This half blood shows me no respect. Perhaps some time in the dungeon to ruminate over his lack of respect for his king is called for. Take him away." The king gave a dismissive wave of his hand after speaking.

The guards were almost on him, now. Calling upon the enhanced primordial forces within himself, he turned around and flung his hand toward the group of them. They came apart. Heads, arms and legs were all torn away from the bodies of the insufferable fools. Crawley turned back toward the king, who had stood up from his throne and was trying to convey rage in his facial expression when he was obviously terrified. The king hadn't known about his power. He had been oblivious to all of Crawley's activities this entire time, it seemed. He silently cursed Ludia.

Things had gotten out of hand, quickly. Crawley adjusted his tie as he faced the stunned king. It became apparent that the Leviathan had something else in mind for him, something other than what he had initially thought. A different sort of opportunity.

Clearly, it was time for plan B.

CHAPTER SIXTEEN

Ignusai couldn't believe what he was seeing. The palace was in ruins. Debris and bodies, or pieces of bodies, were everywhere. He and Woitan had come to the palace alone, leaving their men elsewhere in the state of Wyoming, with orders to be ready to move out on a moment's notice.

He knew something horrible had happened at the palace. They had felt the deaths of many of their brethren shortly after they had arrived in Wyoming, coming from that direction. A thousand death screams within minutes. In the forest, they had felt no presence of their fellow Ambrogae. By the time they had reached the crack in the rock, the stench of death was overwhelming. Ignusai knew what they would find, but still, he had to see it firsthand. They made their way into the cave and through it and their fears were confirmed as soon as they had arrived at the main gate, which had been blown off its hinges, with pieces of guardsmen strewn about the entrance.

As they had made their way inside, they witnessed a scene that Ignusai had never imagined would ever come to pass. Neither of them had spoken as they combed through each passageway and chamber. It seemed that everyone was dead, and their deaths had not been pleasant. The smell had become almost unbearable. The underground structure itself was heavily damaged, with parts of columns crumbled, and rock from the walls and furniture scattered all around.

The two of them were rushing now, making their way to the throne room. Ignusai still couldn't feel the presence of any Ambrogae other than Woitan. Whoever had done this had left no survivors. Still, he clung to the hope that he would feel something before he reached the throne room, though a rational part of him knew if there was anyone alive to feel, he would have felt them back in the forest. But perhaps some had managed to escape. Maybe the king had survived and was now somewhere else.

That hope was dashed to pieces, just as so many of the pure blooded Ambrogae had been, as he and Woitan entered sight of the throne room doors. They had been blown off their hinges, as well. He could already see inside, though he made himself continue walking. A part of him refused to believe that the worst had come to pass, at least until he got close enough to see it in detail.

As he and Woitan crossed the threshold and into the throne room, Ignusai's heart began to beat even more quickly than it already was. Atop the throne was Coranthis himself. The king's body sat as if granting them an audience, but his head had been placed neatly in the body's lap, face forward. The crown still sat atop that head. A look of horror was on Coranthis' face. Whatever had killed their king had struck fear into his heart before ripping his head off.

"I can't believe this." Woitan said as they slowly walked into the throne room, echoing Ignusai's own thoughts. "Who or what could do such a thing, Ignusai? What could accomplish such devastation?"

"I don't know." Ignusai replied. Fear and awe were in his voice, he knew. "I can't help but think it was the violet-eyed one, maybe. He managed to defeat Olinar, a feat that I have never heard of happening in all my years." Ignusai was over eight hundred years old, and Woitan was nearly his age. He had known of Olinar prior to his entering the service of their king, and the man had never been defeated in all his life, as far as Ignusai knew. Ignusai himself had been born in this palace and had always served Coranthis. So had Woitan.

Woitan began to inspect the parts of the bodies of the guards that littered the throne room floor. "It seems our king tried to have whoever it was restrained before they began their massacre. Here, in the throne room itself."

"Either that, or a fight broke out elsewhere and eventually led into the throne room."

Woitan shook his head. "No, see how these bodies are the only ones in the throne room? I count eight. There are no corpses near the doors themselves, or within the antechamber beyond. These men were the ones posted at the doors. Whoever did this had been allowed in to see the king. I'm sure of it."

Ignusai wasn't about the deny his partner's appraisal. Woitan had always had a keen mind for detail. On his own closer inspection, it did seem that his partner was right.

"Well, it couldn't have been Olinar." Ignusai stated. He turned back toward the body of his late monarch. "Coranthis was stronger than Olinar, I'd wager… I… I find it hard to believe our king is actually dead, even now looking upon his body." Ignusai had almost forgotten something. He had found a curious letter in a chamber that Olinar sometimes frequented. It was addressed to the king, and so he hadn't opened it. He did so, now, however, after taking it out of the pocket he had slipped it into.

Woitan grunted as he nodded. He was looking at Coranthis now, still disbelieving. Ignusai's focus had turned to the words on the page he held in his hand.

"What do we do, now?" Woitan asked after a moment.

"We return to our forces and inform them of the news. Some may want to see it for themselves, but we can't allow that. I don't truly believe that whoever it was is coming back, but we shouldn't take any chances. After we get back, we should try calling Olinar. Look at this." Ignusai handed the note to Woitan, who began to read it, his expression growing odd as he did so.

"It seems Olinar and Almeidra were lucky to leave when they did." Woitan said, handing the note back to Ignusai. "And perhaps we were lucky to be slightly delayed in coming here."

Ignusai agreed with that statement. They had taken some extra time to arrive, due to the process of organizing their men to meet up with them in the respective states they had been investigating in their search for Seike, and then meeting up with each other, afterward. Olinar and Almeidra had had no men left, and so were able to arrive before them. As chance would have it, they had decided to disobey an order from their king to remain in the palace, and so it seemed that they had survived this massacre. Ignusai considered the notion of having no one to serve, now, and found that he didn't know what to do with himself.

Olinar had always been a good leader, he knew. He wouldn't swear fealty to the man or any such nonsense, but he thought that Olinar may have a better idea of what to do next. Ignusai had no idea what to do, so any suggestion would be welcome.

They had felt their people die, so very many in such a short span of time. When it had happened, they were both in denial that such a disaster had actually occurred. Ignusai still couldn't fathom what force could have taken out not only their people, but their king. The thought of it left him terrified.

"We should get out of here." He said to Woitan. His partner merely nodded, and the both of them turned to leave the throne room, heading out of the palace. He didn't know when or if he would return, but he wanted to be out of there for now. The smell and sight of it all was going to haunt him.

Seike regarded the grim faces of the people who were sitting in the back of the heavy utility truck with him, as they finally crossed the border of South Dakota and Wyoming. He and Samaiel were both in the back of the vehicle, along with several of Kelloway's people. Samaiel had been teaching him a few words and phrases in the ancient tongue during the many hours they'd been on the road. They'd left Wednesday night, and it was now just past dawn on Thursday morning. He found it hard to believe that it had only been a little over a week since this whole mess had begun with him killing Emilio.

He hadn't known that Samaiel was adept at speaking Ambrogaeic. Apparently, Marikya had convinced him to take over Seike's lessons in her stead while they were on this mission. She'd managed to get Seike alone to teach him for about an hour of every day that they had been on the base, except for the day of the attack. Things had been too hectic at that time for either of them, but for her, especially, with her work in the lab.

Their transport was only one in a much larger convoy. They had stopped to fuel up a couple of times throughout their trip, doing so at publicly known military bases stationed near the highways they were driving upon. When it came to the military, there was a need-to-know basis for a lot of activities within the nation itself, and the people at these bases did not need to know. They knew only that Kelloway's people were on their way from point A to point B, and they required refueling. That was enough, along with proper credentials.

Isaius was in a different vehicle than they were, and Samaiel had mentioned being happy about that. The man's words minutes before they had entered the elevator leading to the surface bunker of Field Base A-92 had caused Samaiel to think rather darkly about the possible outcome of the situation they were heading into. Seike and Samaiel both knew that they were true words. Of course everyone had to die eventually, even the Ambrogae. Samaiel just hadn't been able to let the words go, however.

He had let them sink in. Seike wasn't bothered at all by them. A part of him kind of wanted to die, anyway. Life without Selinda had been full of pain, every day. Pain that he had to do his best to hide from everyone else.

"Are we there, yet?" Samaiel blurted out in a child's tone of voice, after a lengthy silence where no one had spoken. His words drew smiles and chuckles from most of the men present. He might be thinking of things in a more somber way than usual, but Samaiel always had a great sense of humor, and Seike found it nice to see that it had survived Isaius' grim words.

"We'll be stopping for a bathroom break and some ice cream soon, so hush up." This from one of the soldiers, a woman, who was grinning after Samaiel's little outburst. More people laughed at her own quip. Seike couldn't help but smile, himself. It was good to ease the tension, even if just a little.

Suddenly, the speaker at the top front of the back of the transport activated, and Sergeant O'neil's voice came through from where he was positioned, at the front of the convoy.

"Alright, people. We will be arriving at our destination in about an hour. We'll be rendezvousing with every other S-47 company from around the nation at that time. Most of them are there already, and those that aren't will be arriving at about the same time that we will. We'll move in on the target location upon arrival at the rendezvous point. We're not going to waste any more time."

The speaker went silent. It had taken them over half a day to get to where they were presently at, and Kelloway was of the opinion that that was plenty of time for this

Crawley character to have come and gone. The total number of soldiers that were assigned this mission was over fifteen hundred, including the soldiers from all the other S-47 bases. The total number of Ambrogae sat at just fifty-five. According to the now deceased prisoner that Kelloway had received the intel leading to the palace's location from, there were under one thousand Ambrogae in the palace at most given times, though there was an inflow and outflow, so that number could sometimes go beyond one thousand.

The plan was simple enough. They were to enter the cave with flame throwers and napalm at the front, getting as many people into the tunnel as they could manage. And when they arrived at the entrance to this palace, they were to light it up. They were relying on heavy firepower in close quarters to give them the advantage, as well as the element of surprise. No Ambrogae were to enter the cave, unless needed as their incursion progressed. Kelloway didn't want to let the enemy know that they were coming.

After O'neil had made that statement to all the people of the convoy, no one in Seike's own transport said another word for the rest of the drive. A sense of readiness permeated the cramped atmosphere of the back of the vehicle. It was almost do or die time.

Justin O'neil was no coward. He had always been a man of courage, but he was a realist, as well. He didn't mind the fact that he was afraid as he and his men made their way through the crack that served as the entrance to the cave that would lead them to their battleground.

Fear sharpened his senses, made him more aware of his surroundings.

It took them longer than he anticipated, once they were in the tunnel. It wound down further and further, growing steeper as they progressed beyond the arch that Isaius had reported finding. After a while, though, they came to their destination, armed and ready.

What Justin wasn't ready for, however, was the sight that greeted him as he and his squad finally came within visual range of the main gates to the palace. The doors were on the ground, and there were pieces of the men that had been guarding them all over the place. Bits of armor and heads and limbs were haphazardly lying about the ground all around the exterior and interior of the entrance to the palace.

He could see inside the doorway and saw that the interior beyond was a field of destruction.

He put his hand up in a motion for the men behind and beside him to stop their advance. "I've got to radio the men topside. We need to inform General Kelloway of the situation, pronto." As soon as he finished saying the words, he got on the horn with the rest of their small army that were still outside, letting them know that someone beat them to the punch.

"Pass the word along to the General." He finished after describing what he was seeing.

A part of him began to feel a sort of glee all of a sudden. It seemed like he was not only going to survive this, but that no one else was going to die, either. Still, they had to be thorough. He knew that they had to finish entering and sweeping the entire palace and communicating back what they saw. He already felt pretty sure that they weren't going to encounter any of the enemy, however.

He and his squad and a few other squads that were in the tunnels streamed through the broken palace doors, organizing themselves to search for anyone who might still be alive.

They found no living individuals after an hour of searching the entire palace's interior. The place was huge! He could easily imagine over a thousand Ambrogae living in this maze-like complex. It was made easier to imagine due to the fact that there were probably close to a thousand dead Ambrogae that they found while sweeping the area. Most of these creatures were torn apart. O'neil couldn't imagine how one man could have done this, but he knew it had to have been that telekinetic everyone was talking about. The man named Robert Crawley. Based on the intelligence they had up until this point, it truly seemed to Justin that there could be no other culprit.

He and the other squads made regular reports to the surface as they swept the area, searching for anything that could give them a more solid idea of what went down here. It almost looked to him like hundreds of grenades had been thrown all around the inside of this palace. And they all went off at once, killing everyone.

He knew that couldn't be true, of course. Too many inconsistencies to be the result of explosions. No residue, and the body parts had no signs of being singed or charred. It looked more like a wild animal had ripped them apart. Chunks were missing from the walls and among many of the pillars and columns that were located throughout the many rooms, and many of those chunks had evidently ended the lives of a lot of the red eyes. They were found lying on top of bodies and embedded into other parts of the interior. Telekinesis could do all this? Seriously? Justin had trouble believing that, just as he had trouble believing that one man, potentially otherwise unarmed, had been the one responsible for it all.

After some time, others entered the palace to see the destruction for themselves. Among those were the blue-eyed Ambrogae and Seike. The one named Samaiel and Sergeant Isaius confirmed O'neil's suspicions. It had been the work of telekinesis. And that meant Robert Crawley.

He found himself feeling lightheaded after over an hour down here in this mess. They eventually catalogued the entire place, most notably the throne room, where they found the body of this King Coranthis still sitting on his throne, though he was headless. His head was there, it just wasn't attached to his shoulders anymore.

After they had all returned to the surface, there was a sort of celebration. People were clapping each other on the shoulder and commending one another as if they had something to do with it. Sergeant O'neil understood the comradery. They were all alive, no one was going to die today. He let them have their jests and their smiles and said nothing.

Once they were on the road back to the base, he radioed Kelloway, telling him that he and the Ambrogae that were here all believed it was Robert Crawley's doing. The General agreed but said there was no need to discuss it further until everyone was back at the base, safe and sound.

As the convoy made their way home, Justin O'neil felt a strange mix of positive and negative emotions. At first, he was happy, like the rest of the soldiers. Not a single man's or woman's life had been lost in this endeavor. After a while though, a sort of terror began to set it.

A terror at the notion of one man who could personally destroy anything in his way.

CHAPTER SEVENTEEN

After Olinar and Almeidra had felt it, they pulled over to the side of the road. They had barely made it out of Wyoming when it happened. Olinar still couldn't believe that it was true, but there was no denying the indescribable feeling of so many of their own dying within minutes of one another. The one death that Olinar found himself really trying to wrap his head around was Coranthis'.

Coranthis had been a lot older than Olinar, and extremely powerful besides. That he should be killed seemed highly improbable, but there it was.

After a heated discussion about the mass death that he and his second had felt, they had resumed driving away from the direction of the palace and were now well on their way through Nebraska. They'd been driving in complete silence for over five hours, and Olinar imagined that Almeidra must have felt as scared as he did. They were nearly at Lincoln, now. They'd put gas in the car over three hours ago and didn't even have the nerve to kill the attendant at the gas station, though the man had been alone and would have made for an easy meal. Instead,

Olinar had wordlessly put the money for the gas on the counter and left.

The only thing he could think of was that it had been a telekinetic, likely a blue telekinetic. He thought back to the blue presence he had briefly felt in the tunnel, the one he had allowed himself to be convinced was just his imagination. He no longer thought it was. After more than five hours of not saying a word, he decided to broach the subject with Almeidra, now.

"Remember when I thought I felt a blue in the tunnel?" He began to say, but Almeidra cut him off.

"I'm not sorry I convinced you to leave, that it was your imagination. We're alive."

Olinar sighed. He had initially wanted to go back to the palace and investigate after they felt the death screams of their brethren. Almeidra had convinced him it was a stupid idea, and they had argued about it by the side of the road for several minutes. She had won the argument by convincing him that whoever had killed them all might still be around, and it would be a better idea to get as far away as possible. Olinar had a sense of honor when it came to serving his king, but he had relented, because Coranthis was dead, now, anyway.

"I wasn't going to blame you or anything." Olinar said, looking at the woman with a frown. She pouted at him and turned her face forward to look at the road ahead of them. "Can I say what was on my mind, or are you gonna cut into me again?"

"By all means. I'm curious, now."

"I think it was a telekinetic. The blue, I mean. A powerful one, probably."

She regarded him, considering this possibility, which had evidently not occurred to her. "Shit." Was all she said.

Yeah. Shit. If Olinar had stayed, everyone in the palace might still be alive right now. Or some of them at least. Maybe Coranthis would have survived.

"Still not putting any kind of blame on you, though, Almeidra. Things have a funny way of happening. Maybe this is for the best, to be honest." He sighed again, keeping his eyes on the road. "We're free of obligations, now."

Just then, his cell phone rang. He and Almeidra looked at each other, puzzled at first. He checked the display and saw that it was Ignusai.

"Seems we're not the only survivors." He said to his second. He swiped right on the phone and put it up to his ear. "Hey, Ignusai. We felt it, before you ask."

"What could have done this, Olinar? It was horrible. Woitan and I left our men elsewhere in the state while we investigated the palace, ourselves. No one survived." Yeah. Obviously. Hearing that those two idiots had decided to investigate made him feel dumb for thinking of doing the same thing, himself. Thank fuck for Almeidra.

"I believe it was a telekinetic. Probably a blue telekinetic. That's my theory, anyway. I have experience with their kind, and they're definitely capable of it." He listened as Ignusai relayed the information to Woitan, basically just repeating what he had said almost word for word.

"That makes sense. We don't know what to do, Olinar." A note of pleading entered Ignusai's voice as he said this. "Without a king to serve, I feel lost. So does Woitan." Olinar hoped that they didn't expect him to be the new king, because there wasn't a chance in hell of that happening. A thought occurred to him. Maybe someone should contact Coranthis' parents, over in Europe. It wouldn't be him, of course. He was done with the monarchy for now, but these two would be perfect candidates to do so. They had been born and raised in that palace.

"Call the king's parents. Or if you don't have a way to do that, find some way to contact them. They'll send one of their other children over to take Coranthis' place, eventually. Then you'll have a new king to serve. Or maybe a queen." The Monarchs of the Leviathan in Europe had one daughter who wasn't presently ruling over anything. At least, Olinar was fairly certain she wasn't ruling over anything.

"Of course. We should have thought of that. That's a good idea. And it just so happens that we have contacts in Europe that can reach them." Ignusai paused as if expecting Olinar to say something, so he did.

"Good. Keep me posted." That ought to keep these two out of his hair for a while.

"Yes, sir. What are you going to do in the meantime?"

Olinar suppressed a sigh. "We're going to Iowa. We were going to do some digging as to where the blues might be hiding. We suspect that they have a main fortification of some kind in that state, as there's been a lot of activity there in the past. We were going to do this for the king, but now..." He let himself trail off, to allow Ignusai time to agree.

"You're going to do it anyway. It sounds like you have your work cut out for you. You and Almeidra better be careful out there. It might take a while before we hear back from Europe, but we'll keep you posted, like you said." By the sounds of it, Ignusai and Woitan had found purpose again after losing their way. That was nice for them. Olinar just wanted to be rid of them for a while. Maybe not forever, but for a while, at least. He looked over at Almeidra, who could easily hear Ignusai's voice on the phone. She rolled her eyes dramatically at him.

"We will. You be careful too. Talk to you later." He hung up without waiting for the man to prattle on any further.

"I don't really want to serve another king or queen. Not for a while." Almeidra made a good point in saying so. Olinar felt the very same way. He wanted to be free of bullshit for a while. After that phone call, he didn't feel very scared anymore. He still had some Ambrogae in his corner, and he had secured his reputation without having to devote much of his time. It had worked out nicely. He knew that Ignusai and Woitan might tell the monarchy in Europe that they had disobeyed their king to pursue a lead, but that wouldn't sound so bad coming from them. They would talk he and Almeidra up, put in a good word. He was certain that it wasn't in any way going to come back to bite him in the ass, or her, and he said as much to her.

"Yeah, I feel that." She said, her hair blowing slightly in the wind of her rolled down window. "I know it's really quite a shitty thing, what happened. But we should still try to enjoy our vacation. That's what I think."

He agreed. He could tell that she didn't feel that frightened anymore, either. Others had survived. Notably, the two men they had both worked with for quite a few years. Olinar thought back to when it had just been the four of them doing things for their king. That had been an easier life. A more enjoyable one, compared to having command of a bunch of pure bloods. Olinar had never cared about having too much responsibility. He preferred simplicity. When it had just been him, Almeidra, Ignusai and Woitan, things had been simple. It had been a good life.

Then Seike went and killed Emilio, who had been older than even Coranthis, and every bit as renowned. Shit became complicated, after that. He hated that freak for that reason as well as for beating him in a fight. Not that it had been a very fair victory, as far as Olinar was concerned.

"We should find some food once we get to Lincoln," Almeidra said. He glanced her way and saw that coy smile. "What do you think?"

"Yeah, I'm down." He replied. Maybe they could find someone as tasty as Cherry had been. Or even tastier. It was good to leave an old life behind, and to have someone familiar with him as he did so. "Maybe we could just paint the town red." He smiled as Almeidra laughed at his joke, even though he was only half-joking. Of course, they should keep a low profile, but that didn't mean staying out of trouble altogether.

The news that Elder Kesel had received was better than he could have hoped for. An ancient enemy was dead, and the threat to the people of S-47 was over. It was true that there was still a threat out there, but that threat was unaware of them, and if he had it his way, he would convince Ludia to let things be, for now. He didn't want her to draw the ire of Robert Crawley, now that they knew how formidable he was.

Of course, the situation here at the Central Haven wasn't entirely favorable, as right now he and Jurai were arguing with the rest of the council about what should be done with their people who were currently at the base. The old buggers wanted to have everyone back, and Kesel couldn't disagree more.

"For the last time, no." Elder Kesel directed the statement at Kaolirus, but allowed his eyes to fall across each of the council members in turn. "Seike will return, but if the others want to stay, or to go back and forth from here to there, that is up to them. I've said it before, and I'll say it again. We don't rule the people of our haven, we only try to guide them as best as we can. It's as simple as that."

The other council members murmured in dissent to what he was saying, but at least Gerlanyeil was holding her tongue. She had been rather vocal at the beginning of this meeting. Her and Kaolirus had the support of the rest of the council regarding the notion of bringing their brethren home from Field Base A-92.

Jurai saw the sense in it. His son had already contacted him and was adamant in his desire to remain in Kelloway's employ for at least a little while. Kelloway had a use for Kaisimir's psychometric talents, and the boy appreciated having his skills recognized. Elder Kesel could easily understand the young noble's desire to be of use, especially after all they had been through in the last week. The lad had been cooped up in the haven far too much over the years, anyway. Even Jurai acknowledged and agreed with his son's ambition to be out in the world, putting his talents to use.

"This discussion is pointless," Jurai said after allowing the muttering to go on for a minute or so. "We don't own the people here, we never have. They can come and go as they please. Besides which, the larger portion by far still remains housed within our haven. It's not like many hundreds have found a calling elsewhere, only a hundred or so. A bare handful of people when compared with how many actually live here."

"And as I stated earlier," Kesel interjected before Kaolirus or Gerlanyeil could voice another argument. "We are now going to be cooperating on a deeper level with the humans of S-47 than we ever have. It wouldn't be prudent to issue a statement of our desire for all of the people we have at their base to return post haste to the Central Haven. It just wouldn't look good when considering the partnership we are trying to develop with these humans."

"You mean the partnership that *you* are trying to develop," Gerlanyeil had finally come out of her period of quietness. "We never wanted this in the first place."

"Oh, quit it, you bitter old woman." Jurai spat. "As I said, this isn't a discussion that we have any right to be having. The men and women we have at the base will choose their future for themselves. Period."

Gerlanyeil had obviously been offended by the remark. She crossed her arms and stared venom in Jurai's direction. She did stay quiet, however, choosing not to say anything further. The rest of the council appeared to have run out of steam, as well. Good. Elder Kesel was quite frankly sick of speaking with them on the matter, and it was obvious that Jurai was also done talking.

"If there's nothing else…?" Kesel waited only a moment before giving the closing statement. "This meeting of the council of the Central Haven is now concluded."

As he left the room, Jurai followed quietly behind him. Once they were in the halls, he spoke.

"I'm proud of Kaisimir, you know."

"Good, Jurai. I'm glad that you can be happy for your son."

"I know that he will be doing good work over there, besides just being happy for him." Jurai hesitated a moment, then said what was really on his mind. "I understand that this new threat out west bears speaking about. It's too bad no one wanted to bring that up in the meeting."

"Oh, we'll be talking about Robert Crawley before long. He's the main topic at the Western Haven and has been for years." The two men were ambling along the halls now, side by side. They were in no hurry to be anywhere except out of earshot of others. "Have you any information on this Olinar that Seike fought in Minnesota?

"He could be our pyrokinetic," Jurai said in answer to the question. "The sketch that Seike drew was sent over to us by Kelloway. I had Brad print it out at Just for Kicks. So far, I haven't found anyone that has seen him before, or any records regarding him. In short, there's no evidence to suggest he *is* our pyrokinetic. It's just a feeling I have."

"You and I both, old friend." They continued walking for quite some time in silence, both of them considering the implications of Ludia's notion of using a red pyrokinetic to further their own agenda. If the man had true loyalty to the late king, perhaps he would want to seek vengeance. It would be an interesting conversation to have, at any rate, if only they could find this Olinar.

Kesel had a feeling that Olinar was still out there, somewhere. He would ask Seike more about the man once he returned to the haven. After he got the young Ambrogis to recite whatever he had managed to learn of the ancient tongue, of course.

Kesel smiled at the thought of having Seike around again. The boy had only been gone a week, but the Elder missed him.

CHAPTER EIGHTEEN

The headquarters of Triaclon Industries was a massive building, capable of housing its more than one thousand employees. It towered above the surrounding buildings, with a large TI attached near the top of the north side. The logo was an emboldened red. Robert Crawley had the place locked down. He was technically breaking the law, but he was so rich that he somewhat stood above the law.

The moment he had returned to the helicopter after his visit to Coranthis' palace, he had called Gregory. He'd ordered that no employees who were on shift at the time of the email's discovery were allowed to leave the building, and any who were not on shift at the time were asked to come in for questioning at the beginning of their next shift.

The orders stood for all Ambrogae employees as well, but the true targets were the human employees. Crawley strongly suspected that whoever had falsified those emails was a human under Ludia's employ. He knew that none of his half blood brethren would ever consider such a thing. They'd sooner kill themselves than be an informant for a blue. They were there to keep an eye on the humans as they were lined up for questioning. About seventy percent of all their employees were Ambrogae, so the process of questioning wasn't going to take very much longer.

Presently, Crawley was in the primary laboratory. It was a secret facility, not on the building's maps. It was simple enough to create a top floor that was hidden from the humans and would have fooled a lot of Ambrogae employees had they not been made aware of it. It was a smaller structure in the middle of the roof of the building. Smaller by comparison to the dimensions of the rest of the building, as it was still a sizable place. It was written off to officials as a large emergency generator room, but in reality, it was the location of all of Crawley's most notable achievements.

He was watching a half blood inject himself with a new serum. This was Crawley's twenty fourth attempt at creating a cellular stabilizing nano device. A handful of units, perhaps three thousand, were required according to all the charts. So far, the devices had been too foreign within their bodies to do more than begin the process of nullifying the cell's requirement to age. This would eliminate the need for consistent cellular regeneration and theoretically halt the cell's aging process indefinitely, by causing all cells to adopt certain characteristics that were programmed into them by the nano devices via a special mode of rapid cellular alteration, essentially rebuilding the cells, then programming them to rebuild each other in the same fashion. The result was supposed to be that harmful oxidants would not damage any molecules within the cells, making far less work for them and not requiring them to nearly constantly have to regenerate themselves. The result was a cell that would, in an Ambrogae, never die.

The foreign material that was in the devices thus far hadn't been found. It was a poison to the bodies of the Ambrogae, but Crawley had been unable to identify the culprit material or materials within the nano devices. They were complex little things. Bio-machines, essentially.

He'd been making educated guesses and swapping out the various components within the nano devices, which unfortunately had resulted in the deaths of twenty-three volunteers so far. He was hoping this wouldn't add one to that count. His assumptions on the switching out of certain materials had all been quite reasonable so far, but each time the result had been the same.

Instead of stabilizing, the body would attack the devices. A severe immune response would be triggered. They weren't nanobots exactly, more like nano bio-computers. More advanced than typical human nanobot technology. He just referred to them as devices. They did their work in the body fine. He had what he was looking for in terms of the performance of the little machines and had successfully halted the need for consistent cellular regeneration in all of his subjects. The problem was merely the fact that the composition of their components needed some small adjustment that he hadn't yet pinpointed.

The devices would be unharmed by this attack of the immune system, but each white blood cell that came into contact with them would die from whatever this material was. The process took several days, but with each passing day, the subject would become gradually weaker, then begin to take on a rather ghastly appearance. The result was the complete collapse of the immune system and an increased rate of decomposition after death. The opposite of what the intended result should be. After four or five days, each Ambrogae test subject expired from convulsions. Crawley wasn't put off though. Any number of half bloods in his employ would gladly make the attempt to become the world's first true immortal.

Robert Crawley wouldn't be sure about this subject until tomorrow, after reviewing a series of tests that would be performed shortly after the injection. And probably also by simply looking at the man the next day.

He wasn't undertaking any of his company's questioning of the humans personally. That responsibility fell to his aide, Gregory. The man was gifted with a potent level of psychometry, which had only been further enhanced by a special serum that he had years ago injected himself with. It had proven to work flawlessly, and the degree to which it enhanced Gregory's psychometry was a fair amount, indeed. The man could shake a hand and know all physical actions that that person had performed with their body for the last week in vivid detail, by seeing through the body's eyes. It only took him a minute to digest this information in a very accurate manner. Robert knew from personal experience that the individual's subconscious mind merely sifted through it all, coming up with only the important and relevant imagery of the person's activities for conscious review.

It wouldn't take Gregory long to do a brief period of inane questions that acted as a cover story for the lockdown, all the while judging for certain the person's innocence or guilt. He had to do this for over three hundred human employees, however, so it didn't surprise Crawley that it was taking some time. Gregory would find the little rat, and then Crawley would find Ludia.

"Thank you for volunteering for this trial injection," Crawley said to the man moments after he had been injected. "Perhaps you will be the first."

The man looked sure of himself, as all the Ambrogae who had volunteered up until this point had. A typical Ambrogae had a tendency to begin feeling invincible, to a detrimental degree, shortly after their first century of life. Robert Crawley had always been too practical to inherit such a nonsense psychological trait.

"I will be the first, rest assured." The man said confidently. They'd all said something to that extent after the injection. Crawley kept his reservations to himself, projecting an air of confidence right back at the volunteer.

"The doctors will perform a series of harmless tests on you now, to see the results, so that they may be recorded." Crawley shook the man's hand before he went off with today's laboratory assistants. He was hoping this most recent exchange of components within the devices would prove to have removed the element that was causing the immune system's reaction. Not for the man's sake, of course, but for his own.

He left the lab and headed to his office, nodding to the familiar faces along the way. Once there, he settled in to wait for his Five PM dinner to arrive.

Ludia was listening to Harold on her phone over what she was sure was a secure line. The man had hacked into the company's system and deleted his record of employment within, as well as all files pertaining in any way to himself. The fact remained that he was in danger.

Ludia was again at the house that she kept not far from Los Angeles. Harold had called one of her Ambrogae associates begging to talk to Ludia as soon as was possible. Through an arrangement, he had called her at the house about five minutes ago, in quite a panic. He wasn't allowed to leave the building. He'd been working when they began to enforce the lockdown.

"I don't know what to do," Harold said after a long-winded explanation of what was going on in the building, and what he was up to as a result. "They'll find out about me eventually." The man sounded scared, which told Ludia that he was no idiot. She didn't know what to do either.

"Just stay calm, Harold," she said soothingly. "I will have a council meeting to see if my people can send a team to rescue you before they find you and question you." She knew they would use mind control to find out everything that Harold knew, which was enough to worry her. The cold part of her that was considering herself and her people above the value of Harold's life was only concerned about him revealing sensitive information, but the part of her that was humane and caring was genuinely scared for the man. Still, though, she didn't know if sending a team would be something that the council would go for.

There was only one way to find out, of course, and that was to call the council together as soon as she arrived back at the haven. She didn't know how long it would take them to come to a decision, but she knew that every moment was precious time wasted.

She would hurry back toward the haven as fast as her car would take her. It was hidden among the concrete jungle that was Los Angeles, so she wouldn't take long to get there. She hadn't predicted that Crawley would simply eliminate Coranthis and his entire palace. She hadn't been sure that he was that strong of a telekinetic. She strongly suspected he was, but she had reserved some hope that he wouldn't turn out to be so powerful.

She couldn't deny that having Coranthis out of the picture was a good thing for all of those of Seline in America, but there would be repercussions, plus the encounter that Crawley had with Coranthis had evidently pointed the finger at her in some way. She had a lot on her plate, at the moment.

The only thing she could hope for now was to be able to get Harold Lapointe out of that building in time. She had finished hearing what he had to say and had assured him as best as she could. After saying to one another that they would speak later, she hung up the phone and immediately set out for the haven.

It happened again last night. Simon had rescued his seventeenth soul from the clutches of evil. He had had to stay up for quite some time, watching the people flow in and out of several bars and clubs that he watched carefully from the outside. It wasn't until after midnight when he had finally found a young man who walked off alone with a brand-new blood red set of holes on the back of his neck.

Salvation had arrived for the young man, however. Simon had followed him until finding a dark corner of the street where he could run up and slit the boy's throat, deeply and quickly. He knew that the wound was going to kill the lad, but he never stuck around to watch them finish dying. He simply walked away as soon as the deed was done. He wasn't a morbid man; he was just doing the work of the Lord. He had to remember to stay humble in his crusade.

Simon always felt invigorated after saving a soul like that. Today was no different. He felt like a million dollars. He was presently at home and had finished his litany of morning prayers hours ago. He was in the dining room, enjoying an early afternoon coffee while he read the day's paper.

He'd heard through the grapevine of his neighbor's gossip that a huge military convoy had passed by their way, starting just before dawn that day. He'd still been coming back from Cheyenne at the time, but he told the man that he hadn't noticed it, that he must have been asleep. It was interesting to hear about, though, considering what he had witnessed just outside his church yesterday. He wondered if there was any connection there but came to the conclusion that it was beyond him to figure it out and had nothing to do with him anyway. That was better than being bothered by it.

The neighbor had told him late this morning of all the military trucks and vehicles passing by, and not all at once either. It had happened several times over the course of an hour or so.

Very interesting, to be sure. Simon still dismissed it, preferring to be on with his day. He was going to visit Marissa's grave today, before Friday's mass tomorrow. He usually visited her on Thursday afternoons.

God bless and receive his wayward child. May she be saved forever and ever, amen. That was one of his many prayers.

CHAPTER NINETEEN

After returning to Field base A-92, Seike had been told by General Kelloway that Elder Kesel had sent word that Seike must return to the haven and intensify his studies in learning the ancient tongue. He was in his quarters, in the midst of gathering his belongings together, and was mentally preparing to say his farewells to Samaiel and the others. They had all decided to stay for a while, especially Isaius, who had switched out his blue shirt and jeans for the same military fatigues that the rest of the soldiers at the base wore. A number of others of the Ambrogae of Seline had also switched their clothing to that of Kelloway's people.

Seike wasn't looking forward to spending the next undetermined length of time holed up in the Central Haven with his nose buried in books, but he had fully come to terms with the punishment that had been set out for him. A part of him was glad that he could at least relax for a while, not having to worry about anyone's safety, or his own.

After a few more minutes of packing, he was ready to leave. He left his room to meet with his friends in the mess hall. They were all there already, awaiting his arrival, an arrangement made via their intercoms about a half hour ago. The way there from his quarters wasn't an overly long trip. When he got there, he saw Marikya, Samaiel and Kaisimir sitting at a little round table, where they had reserved a seat for him.

"I wish I could stay here a little while longer." Seike said as he walked up to the table and took the empty seat. "I'd like to be able to help out with whatever you guys are going to be doing over the next few months."

"We'll keep you updated," Samaiel said with a grin. "We'll make sure that Elder Kesel lets you know about our activities in our regular reports. I'll bet that you won't miss much, anyway."

Marikya added her own thoughts. "With Coranthis out of the picture, Kelloway's focus is going to turn to forming ties with the Western Haven, now, and helping however he can with gathering intelligence on Crawley. I imagine it's going to be mostly boring work, honestly, Seike. We won't be personally involved with a lot of it, anyway. You just need to hurry up and become comfortable enough with speaking Ambrogaeic, so you can come back." She patted Seike's hand reassuringly as she finished speaking. He let out a resigned sigh.

Kaisimir looked at Seike without any sort of prejudice whatsoever. "I hope you come back soon." He said plainly. "I personally think you should be awarded at this point, not punished. But I'm not on the council, so my opinion on that doesn't count for anything."

Seike studied Kaisimir for a moment as the young Ambrogis finished his words. It seemed that there was no animosity or hate left in the noble as he gazed back at the violet-eyed vampire. Seike had apparently found a new friend in Kaisimir over the course of the short time they had spent together. It was nice to have more than just Samaiel as a friend. He now considered Marikya to be a friend as well. The four of them had certainly bonded over recent events.

"I have every intention of coming back to help General Kelloway with future threats." Seike stated.

"That's good to hear, Seike." The General said as walked into the cafeteria and toward the table they had seated themselves at. They were all mildly surprised at his sudden appearance. He stopped only a few feet from them and gave them all a smile that Seike was sure he once only reserved for his own people. "I'll be glad to have you back as soon as possible."

The General pulled a vacant seat out from one of the other tables and sat himself down in it. He looked Seike in the eye, his expression suddenly serious. "I know we got off to a rough start, you and me. I hope we can both let bygones be bygones. I wanted to personally tell you that I've come to consider you to be an individual of value to the people of this base. Hell, I actually like you, Seike. I'm happy to know that you want to come back when you finish your studies. You might not be one of my soldiers, but you're a damn fine warrior."

Seike was taken aback with sudden emotion. "Thank you, General." He replied. He wasn't used to being in any way praised or endeared towards by the people around him. He was more used to suspicion and ridicule, unless he was mingling with humans in Iowa City and disguising his eyes as he did so. He wondered what his drinking buddies were up to at that moment. He hadn't thought much about either Jack or Ferg since he began this little adventure. It hadn't been much more than a week since he last spoke with Jack, but he knew it would be a lot longer than that before he spoke with either of them again. He intended on eventually reconnecting with them, but he didn't feel as lonely as he was used to feeling, sitting here among friends.

He wasn't sure if he would feel lonely in the future either, now that he had these companions of his. It was a good notion to consider. He found that he was feeling a little less resignation about having to leave, knowing that he would be welcome back so openly. After a moment, Kelloway spoke up again.

"I also came here to tell you that your transportation back to Iowa is ready when you are. They'll drop you off at a location of your choice, and you can make the rest of the way to your haven on foot." The General swept his gaze across all four of them. "I want to thank you all for everything you've done for us. A lot of people have been feeling more at ease today, including myself. I even got a few good winks in."

Seike chuckled. "That's good to hear, General. I'm sure everyone here is glad to know that you finally got some sleep." The rest of them nodded and murmured their agreement. The five of them sat and talked for a few minutes about mundane things like Isaius' haircut, and Marikya's tendency to get ink from pens on her fingers. They smiled and laughed as they talked, even General

Kelloway, who seemed much more relaxed since they had returned to the base from Wyoming.

Afterward, they each said their goodbyes to the violet-eyed vampire. Seike felt much better about leaving as he got to the surface of the base and began to make his way to the transport depot, where he would meet with a group of soldiers that would drive him the rest of the way to Iowa. He figured he would get them to stop at Brad Hennick's bar, Just for Kicks. He wouldn't mind seeing Brad again. The man had never really judged him for his eyes, instead treating him like just any other person, which was well enough.

Brad had a rough sort of personality, and a dry but good sense of humor. He got on well with Samaiel. The two of them just clicked.

After reaching the depot, he saw that Sergeant O'neil was among the men who were responsible for taking him to his designated location. The sergeant nodded and smiled at him in greeting.

"Had to take you home, myself, I figured." O'neil said as Seike walked into the garage where his ride awaited.

"Thanks, sergeant. It'll be good to have another familiar face around just before I have to do my time."

Justin O'neil scoffed good naturedly at him. "Oh, it's not so bad as all that. You're going to be in a familiar environment, learning more about the language of your kind. Doesn't sound so bad to me."

Seike had to laugh. The man had no idea how uninterested he was in learning Ambrogaeic. "Books have never really been my thing. And I'm going to be around them the entire time."

O'neil chuckled at that. "Old dusty books?"

"The oldest and dustiest. The people I'm going to be around are pretty old and dusty, too."

That comment elicited a genuine laugh out of the sergeant. He clapped Seike on the shoulder as the violet-eyed one entered the rear seat of the jeep that they would be taking. In short order, they were on the road. The other two soldiers with O'neil seemed amiable as well during the whole ride. It wasn't an unpleasant trip.

As they drove, Seike couldn't help but think of Selinda during the moments of silence between himself and his present company. He thought of how proud she would be of what he had been a part of recently. How happy she would be that he was making new friends.

As he thought of these things, he couldn't help but notice that having her on his mind didn't hurt quite as much as it once did. He didn't know what to think of that, really, but he welcomed the reprieve.

He eventually considered that he hadn't slept at all since being back at the haven, and settled down for a nap as the vehicle drove along the Minnesotan roads.

Ignusai was on the hunt for new recruits, which meant turning humans into new half blood Ambrogae. He and Woitan had scouted the area of the state relatively close to where the palace was located, as most of that region was very rural and secluded. They had been looking for a place where humans habitually gathered and had decided that their target would be a church just south of the lake where the cave entrance was.

The church was in the middle of a Friday mass and was filled to the brim with people from all around the area. Ignusai had the place surrounded by twenty of his men, including Woitan, of course. The slightly younger Ambrogis deferred to him due to his being older, as was their way.

By Ignusai's count, there were over a hundred people in there right now. The plan was for him and his men to go inside and use nonlethal force on everyone there, subduing them by incapacitation. They would render everyone unconscious, feeding only a little on each person, then share their blood with all those inside.

Sharing blood was the only way to guarantee that a human would turn into an Ambrogis or Ambrogess. Merely biting a person would rarely cause them to turn. It was a very small chance, overall, and so the strategy they would employ today would involve them cutting themselves after everyone was knocked out, then cutting the people as they lay unaware and mixing their own blood with the humans'. They would then tie and bound each individual until the three days had passed and the transformations were complete. Anyone whose eyes turned blue would be killed instantly.

Ignusai had mixed feelings about creating an army of half bloods, but it was needed. Their numbers were too few, now that everyone in the palace had been killed. He wanted to have more of the Ambrogae on hand for whenever word got back from Europe about a potential new king or queen. He had sent word to a contact in England, where he knew that King Vaysalvar and Queen Ermaillein resided, and was waiting on that contact to get word to their royal majesties. It could take a while, as getting an audience with the European monarchs wasn't as simple of a matter as Coranthis had made seeing him on a moment's notice. His king had been the kind of man to make time for any who entered his realm, seeing to them personally. A fact which could have played a part in the monarch's downfall, as far as Ignusai was now concerned.

Coranthis' parents were another matter altogether. They tended to be hard to find, moving around from one fortification to another at a whim. They also rarely granted an audience to any who managed to seek them out, preferring instead a written account of the inquiry from the individual.

"Are you ready, Ignusai?" Woitan's words brought Ignusai out of his thoughts. He refocused himself. The church had a back door, side door, and front doors. A group of them were all around the structure now, awaiting their leader's word.

"Yes. Everyone knows the plan, so let's do this with utmost efficiency." Ignusai gave the signal, and every one of the Ambrogae around the church burst inside at the same time.

Upon their entering, the priest, an old man, was giving his sermon to the people sitting at the pews. He stopped, confused and shocked, once he saw all the unfamiliar faces that were now barring all the potential exits. The people sitting down for the service turned their heads, a mixture of curiosity and confusion among their expressions.

Ignusai and his troops had entered in disguise. Their eyes were all varying shades of brown and blue now, and they all looked very human to these people. That was about to change.

Ignusai revealed his true nature to the onlookers, his irises morphing into a shade of scarlet red. Gasps and shouts began to rise from the people sitting at the pews, and some of them began to stand up as if to flee, though there was nowhere to go.

"Demon!" The priest yelled. Woitan and the rest of Ignusai's men allowed their eyes to turn to their natural state, and the priest yelled again. "Demons! You are not welcome in the house of God!"

Ignusai had to smile at the stupid old fool's apparent bravery. The man had no idea what was about to befall him and his flock.

Within moments, chaos ensued. People began screaming and scattering in all directions, but the old priest just stood where he was at the pulpit, staring with anger directly at Ignusai. The majority of the Ambrogae left their positions by the doors and began the process of incapacitating all of the panicked humans.

It was simple enough, they used psionics to jolt each person, knocking them out cold. Ignusai watched as his men efficiently dashed from person to person, barely hitting each one. There were a few children and babies among the crowd. These were destined to become meals for the others of Ignusai's forces that awaited in the forest beyond the church. The hidden Ambrogae would also partake of feeding in smaller amounts from those who would become Ambrogae themselves, enough to sustain themselves until they found yet more prey, later. Ignusai watched as some of the children were killed to be later fed upon. So did the old priest.

The man was displaying only rage visibly. Ignusai could see no fear in the man. He felt a measure of respect for the priest in that moment, and advanced toward him. The man saw this and met his eyes as Ignusai walked closer to the pulpit amidst the carnage. Once the Ambrogis was within ten feet of the priest, he was surprised by what happened next.

The man suddenly lunged at him, brandishing a good-sized knife. "Demon from hell, go back to whence you came!" He screamed as he stabbed at Ignusai with the blade, aiming for his throat. Ignusai effortlessly grabbed the aged man by the wrist, forcing him to drop the knife. In that moment of contact, he experienced what the man had recently done. He had used that very same knife on a young man in a city. He had killed that person in cold blood, seemingly without reason.

"Murderer," Ignusai whispered fiercely at the old priest, swatting the man's attempts to strike at him with his free hand. "Killer of innocents. You'll make a fine addition to our ranks. I have a good feeling that your eyes will be red, soon enough."

Now Ignusai saw the fear that he had expected to see from the priest earlier. The man began to struggle to get his good hand free of Ignusai's grasp, though his efforts were futile. The Ambrogis ignored the man's attempt to free himself as he slowly bent down and picked up the knife that had fallen. He was curious, and the knife would reveal more deeply into the past than a body could.

As he picked up the blade, he felt flashes of the numerous lives it had taken. He couldn't identify the victims, other than to say that they were all young and hadn't seen their deaths coming. He smiled at the man, showing teeth that were now as sharp as the knife he held.

"You've been busy, it seems." Ignusai said softly. The priest suddenly froze. "How many have you managed to kill? Why? I'm curious."

"My reasons would be beyond you, demon!" The priest said, his voice finally taking on a tone of fearfulness. "I was saving them all from becoming what you are! Legion! Soldier of hell!"

Ignusai laughed. The man was clearly mad. He thought Ignusai was a follower of the being that religious folk call by the name of Satan. Furthermore, he had been killing humans that were not in the process of turning, thinking that somehow they would, unless he stopped them. Still, he imagined what he must look like to this priest, with his men leaping about the room striking down the people of his church. Red eyes, sharp teeth. He knew he certainly fit the description of what humans thought of as demons. But this priest was vile in his own way, tainted with madness as he was. He would most definitely become an Ambrogis of the Leviathan.

"Soon, you and all the people here will be one of us. Then you will see that your God is just a fairy tale, when you feel the presence of the true God. The Leviathan. You will be young again, and you will kill for your God, just as you have been doing as a human being."

The priest looked absolutely horrified now. Ignusai was truly enjoying this. He decided to keep the man conscious for the entire duration of the turning.

Still holding onto the priest's wrist, Ignusai used the knife to make a small incision into his own wrist, enough for a decent amount of blood. He then plunged his knife into the arm of the man, enjoying the resulting scream. Finally, he put his wrist over the man's wound, blending his own blood with the priest's. The man screamed in denial of what was happening. He began to recite prayers in his desperation, all the while still trying to break free.

In a few days from now, Ignusai was betting that the man would insist upon a new name.

CHAPTER TWENTY

Long ago, when the Ambrogae were still living deep under the earth, his people fed upon one another. Olinar knew the history of his race as well as any other Ambrogae. All were taught it while they were young, with their people's history being passed down by word of mouth from sire to fledgling, or from parent to offspring.

His people once reproduced more quickly than any human and were capable of having dozens of offspring between one mating pair within only a year's time. This compensated for the fact that they had consumed one another for sustenance. At some point, his kind had found a way to the surface. They found humans there and began to feed from them.

His people discovered that consuming humans caused certain mutations within them, leading to their future evolution into what they now knew themselves as. The Ambrogae.

They had always been a long-lived and powerful race. However, consuming human blood led to a far lengthier life and far more strength, besides. They eventually developed a resonance with psi, the ethereal substance that acted as a medium for allowing them to perform feats that seemingly defied the conventional rules of reality. Their people could feel the presence of their Creator some time after developing this resonance. The Leviathan whispered to them the secrets to uncovering the mysteries of the universe, expanding their consciousness and understanding. It told them of their place at the top of the food chain, their destiny to rule the world.

Sometime after they had stopped consuming each other and had used humans for a food source consistently for many generations, the Ambrogae began to have trouble conceiving. It seemed that an extraordinarily long life and great power along with it had its price. Bolstering their numbers became something that was much more difficult than it once used to be. This caused a sense of togetherness within the social structure of the Ambrogae that had survived the test of time, existing even until this day. They placed a high value on one another's lives.

Then came the blues, a relatively new mutation of their people. Historically recent, comparatively speaking. Those Seline worshipping fuckheads had really fucked everything up.

Before the rise of the blue-eyed Ambrogae, his kind had numbered in the tens of millions, if not more. All it took was the last several thousand years of war with each other and both those of the Leviathan and the blue eyes combined now numbered not much more than four million on the entire planet.

Ignusai had called and told Olinar of his plan to turn a large number of humans into an army of Ambrogae under their new monarch, whenever they got one. He didn't think it was a very bad idea. This world could use more Ambrogae, even half bloods. Olinar considered himself a member of an endangered species, even if they were at the top of the food chain.

He continued along the highway in Iowa, with no real destination in mind. He and Almeidra had filled their bellies in Lincoln and were still more than sated. They didn't technically need to feed again for a while, even weeks, but he felt sure that they would find someone to kill and eat before then. They had originally intended on coming to Iowa to seek out a blue hideaway, potentially a big one, but now that Olinar was here, he didn't particularly care anymore. It's not like he had a king to report to, now, nor an army behind his back.

They hadn't found any blues so far, and Olinar knew that Almeidra didn't really care whether they did or didn't, either. They'd been in the state for hours, now. If they did come across any, they would kill them, maybe even question them, but he no longer considered it any kind of priority.

On a whim, he turned off the main highway and onto a road that seemed to lead to nowhere. There was nothing but nature itself on either side of the road for miles as he drove.

After driving for a while, he eventually felt the familiar presence of a blue nearby. It was coming from somewhere ahead of them.

He turned and looked at Almeidra, who looked at him in a way that told him she had begun to feel the blue as well.

"What do we do?" She asked. "Kill or keep driving?"

"We could always use more sway when a new monarch finally arrives from Europe." He replied. "I say we grill them for information, just in case, before we kill them."

Almeidra seemed to think about this, though she didn't seem reluctant. "Yeah. I guess you're right, more sway can always be good. Are you ready, then?"

"Always."

Shortly after this exchange, Olinar saw the first building he'd seen on this road since turning onto it. It was still far in the distance on a straight stretch of the road, but Olinar could make out the words 'Just for Kicks' on the big sign close to the road on its parking lot. He could also make out the shape of a figure in that parking lot, apparently looking in their direction.

Moments later, he saw that the figure had black hair and pale skin. It seemed that their mystery blue had felt them as well. The way that the man in the parking lot felt at this point was a little different, somehow, now that Olinar had gotten closer. He did feel like a blue, and yet something was off.

He kept driving and as he approached the building, which he saw now was clearly some kind of bar, he recognized the face of the Ambrogis in the parking lot. He was so shocked that he had to laugh. It was Seike. Of all the people it could have been.

"Oh shit," Almeidra said breathily beside him. "Oh shit, turn around." She made a motion as if to grab the wheel herself, then withdrew her hand.

"We're gonna see this through, Almeidra. I'm not turning around."

She looked at him with surprise, then said, "Like hell you aren't! He'll blast us! He might not even wait til we get out of the car!"

"I survived it once. I'll take my chances again. Stay in the car, if you want, but I'm taking the keys with me."

A calm had settled over him. Within the next few moments, he was pulling into the parking lot. Seike had recognized him and was merely watching as he parked the car near the roadside sign. He turned off his cherished green Mustang and looked at Almeidra once more.

"Staying in the car?"

She was obviously scared. "Why do you have to do this? You really feel like you have to prove something to this guy?"

"If we're being honest, I want to talk with this guy. I don't really want to fight him, especially if he can just fry my ass. He doesn't have blue eyes, so I don't feel like I am betraying my own kind in just wanting a few words with him."

"What? I thought you hated him and wanted to get him back for what he did to you."

Olinar let out a sigh and waited a moment before he replied. "You know, ever since we felt the whole palace get snuffed out, I've been thinking about how few Ambrogae there are in the world, these days. When Ignusai called a little while ago and laid out his plan, I thought damn, that's a pretty good idea. Just turn as many humans as we can to bolster our numbers. We've grown too used to being obsessed with keeping the blood pure, we didn't see the solution right there before us. Humans can become Ambrogae."

He turned his head to regard Seike, who was still standing there, looking back. "I look at this guy and right now I don't see a blue. I see a question. And the only way to answer a question is to ask more questions, which is what I feel like doing now. What are the chances that we happen upon the very same man that killed Emilio and unleashed this chain of events? I'm not going to waste this opportunity. I want to know what makes the man tick, why he's sided with the blues. For all we know, he could be convinced to change his mind about things with the right words.

He met Almeidra's gaze. "Imagine if the violet-eyed one fought for the survival of those of the Leviathan, instead of those of Seline. I know it probably won't happen, I have no illusions, but he hasn't blasted us with a lightning bolt yet. I think it may be fate that this man and I exchange more words. Who knows what we could learn in the process? So, are you coming or staying in the car?"

"Staying. You might think I'm a coward, but I just think there's less chance he'll attack if I just stay in the car."

Olinar didn't argue. It sounded like it made sense, actually. In a way, she was just looking out for them both, not being a coward.

"Alright, here goes something." He said as he opened the door. He got out of the vehicle and looked again at the violet-eyed Ambrogis. Seike merely waited, standing there in the middle of a parking lot that was mostly empty. His was the only presence that Olinar could feel. It was just the two of them, other than perhaps some nearby humans, and Almeidra.

He decided to change his eyes into the shade of blue that he once used to present himself to the Viking people, ages ago. He didn't know why he did it, exactly. He supposed that he just wanted to appear less likely to attack.

Walking up to Seike slowly, he kept his two hands raised, palms out. "Really wasn't expecting to run into you. I thought to myself, why miss a golden opportunity? A chance to talk on even terms. You willing to talk, or are you going to do your thing and try killing me again?"

Seike just stared at him for a moment, then said, "Still deciding. You killed Tannik."

He must be talking about the blue that had won in his fight against Almeidra. The one he shot. Olinar ventured to exchange tit for tat. "You and your friends killed all of my pure blood brethren."

"Your kind kill humans and those of Seline. And you were attacking us in the first place."

"That's fair. I had orders, though. I was just acting under them. And my kind kill humans because we need to eat. We're just trying to survive. The humans you've been working with are trying to make us extinct. You think they're gonna stop once they get rid of all the followers of the Leviathan? Think they'll draw the line there?"

Seike seemed to be getting visibly angry. "My allies and I don't kill people. The humans have no reason to fear us."

"There aren't many Ambrogae in this world," Olinar retorted. "And there are plenty of humans. The herd could stand to be thinned out a little bit."

Seike seemed to master his anger, though he still looked at Olinar as if he wanted to kill him. The violet-eyed vampire said nothing for a few moments, then asked Olinar something he wasn't expecting.

"Are you aware that your king is dead?"

How could he know that? Olinar thought for a brief moment that maybe it was Seike that he had felt in the tunnel that led to the palace, after all. Not a blue telekinetic. He couldn't believe that, though. He didn't think this man could kill a thousand pure bloods in minutes, even if he was able to shoot lightning. It could have been one of his allies, though…

"Do you know who killed King Coranthis?" Olinar felt a sudden tension form in his body as he asked Seike the question. "If it was one of your friends, then maybe I have a bone to pick with you, after all."

"It was a red that killed your king. One of your own."

Olinar couldn't believe what he was hearing. None of his kind would ever cross Coranthis. None would even desire to kill their king, it went against who they were as a people.

He spat on the ground. "That's fucking impossible." The tension in his body increased. If he and Seike were going to fight it out, then he felt ready.

"Are you a pyrokinetic?" Seike asked. The question stunned Olinar to the point where a lot of the tension left his body. "Some of those from my haven seem to think you might be."

Word must have gotten around about what he had done at that nightclub in Iowa City. That was the only thing that Olinar could think of. But what did he say now? Should he be honest with the violet-eyed Ambrogis? After a moment, he decided honesty couldn't hurt.

"Yeah. Heard about what I did here in Iowa, did you? I had to defend myself. Just trying to survive, you know?"

"So, it was you." Seike stated matter-of-factly. "I know a lot of people who would be interested to know that. That you're a pyrokinetic, I mean. Have you ever heard the name Robert Crawley? He's the one that took out your king, and all the rest, besides."

Olinar was stunned into silence at mention of the name. The half blood business tycoon from L.A. Olinar knew of the man, had even met him a few times over the centuries. He was loyal to Coranthis and had helped the monarchy establish itself throughout America. His ties with the human world had provided Coranthis with plenty of helpful information over the years. What Seike said next stunned Olinar even more.

"Crawley is a telekinetic." The violet-eyed one said nonchalantly.

It fit. Olinar knew that only a telekinetic could have been the one to take his liege out of the picture, and cause that much death in that short of a time. He didn't want to believe that Crawley would do something as terrible as killing so many of his own kind, but he knew that there could sometimes be tension between the more powerful half bloods and those of pure blood. Could it have evolved into this kind of scenario?

"Can you prove these things you're saying?" Olinar asked, not sure how he would react to an answer in the affirmative. "You gotta understand, I'm finding this to be a hard pill to swallow, my man."

"I've got no reason to lie to you. We have a common enemy in that man. He has his own agenda, beyond the normal scope of our kind. If you still want proof though, there's a printer and fax machine in that bar over there." Seike pointed his thumb over his shoulder, indicating the one building around for miles. "I can arrange to show you enough documented information that will likely convince you that Crawley is a threat to us both. I can also get you a conversation with Ludia, a follower of Seline from the West Coast. She's been trying to find a way to stop Crawley for years."

Olinar knew the name Ludia. He had heard about her war against Crawley but had always figured that it was just a typical feud that played out between the blues and the followers of the Leviathan. Maybe there was more to it, though. At any rate, he had wanted to talk with this Seike, and now they were talking. May as well continue the conversation.

He began to follow Seike towards the bar. Then he heard Almeidra yell behind him.

"Hey! What's happening right now?" Her head was sticking out of the car's window.

He smirked at her. "We're gonna go discuss something interesting that just came up. Just wait in the car."

She looked confused, but she stuck her head back inside the vehicle. Olinar thought that Almeidra might not understand his desire to avenge his king, if he could. Even if it was a half blood who was the culprit. Hell, maybe especially then. The audacity of someone of his own kind killing their king sort of made his blood boil.

If Seike convinced him of the truth of the matter, there would be incentive for further discussion. He really did still feel a degree of loyalty toward the Ambrogae monarchy, for they had helped him survive the many centuries of his life. And if Robert Crawley really was a telekinetic, and had done the unthinkable and killed Coranthis, there was further incentive to do something about it.

After all, life was about survival, and maybe Crawley didn't care so much about the survival of the rest of the Ambrogae. Maybe even to the point that he would murder over one thousand pure bloods to further his own ambitions.

Olinar never really liked business types, anyway. This was turning out to be an interesting day.

CHAPTER TWENTY-ONE

The clever little rat had thought to hide, but Crawley had found him, anyway.

The man's name was Harold Lapointe. A human, as Crawley had surmised. He had cleverly deleted himself from the company's databases, leaving no trace. What he hadn't counted on, however, was the human social element. One of his human coworkers had reported him for suspicious activity, saying that he was acting oddly ever since the building had been locked down. They gave his name, and when it had been looked up by one of Crawley's subordinates, they found that there was no such person in the system. It became rather obvious at that point that they had found their spy.

Harold had been quickly apprehended by some of Crawley's half bloods, and he and Gregory had been peeling away at his mind ever since, compelling him to reveal everything he knew about Ludia and the Western Haven. They'd both used psychometry on him to start with, but that had only revealed a phone number that he had dialed several times in the last week. The man hadn't met anywhere with Ludia in person in the timeframe they could see back to, using that talent. Crawley didn't plan on calling Ludia himself. He had other ideas.

They were in Crawley's office, where he was presently trying to get information out of Harold that the human couldn't recall with accuracy.

"Think." Crawley said, growing impatient. "You were in the car, going to the safehouse. You know it's outside of Los Angeles. Try to remember where the driver took you, in detail."

"I can't remember." Harold said again. Tears were streaming down his face, and he was drooling slightly. Psychic coercion took its toll on a human. "It was a white house, in a nice neighborhood. It had rust colored shingles on its roof. It was somewhere in Riverside. That's all I can remember. Please… it hurts."

It was unfortunate that mind control couldn't improve a person's natural ability to remember things. Crawley felt sure that the right information was in the man's head. He had one method left to employ, but Gregory was unaware of his special gift. He resolved to ask his aide to leave, to allow him some one-on-one time with the human.

"Gregory, could you please leave the room? I have some more in depth questioning to perform, and I need our friend here to gather all his focus together in order to answer these questions. Less people around to distract him will be better."

His aide didn't even so much as bat an eye at being asked to leave. Gregory bowed his head. "Yes, Mr. Crawley." He then left Crawley's office, closing the door behind him.

Good employees were hard to find, but Crawley had always been able to rely on Gregory. His aide never asked too many questions, nor did any deep thinking on Crawley's motivations. It was too bad that he didn't have more than one Gregory.

He turned back to regard Harold after seeing that the door had closed tightly. It was designed to open only from inside the office without the key, so there was no need to see if it had been locked. The human had snot dripping from his nose now, in addition to the tears and the drool. What a pathetic little creature, this clever rat. Crawley didn't at all regret that he had killed Coranthis. He considered it a good move, overall. He had left no survivors, so the blame wouldn't fall on him, in any case. What annoyed him was that he had been fooled by the emails. By Ludia.

"I have only one more question." He stated, looking at the sniveling human before him.

"What's that?" Harold asked. A spark of hope had entered his bloodshot eyes. Crawley found that humorous.

"What is the totality of your knowledge, even that which you cannot remember?"

Harold looked so confused that Crawley barked a laugh right before he leapt upon the man and bit into his jugular, knocking him out of his chair and onto the floor. He drained the sweet essence of life from the human, gorging himself rapidly. Harold was so stunned, he didn't even cry out. Within several seconds the human passed out from lack of blood flow to the brain. Crawley kept drinking, until the man's heart stopped. Still, he drank, until it became too hard to get blood from the wound, and the body looked grey and emaciated. Only then did Crawley cease the exsanguination of Harold Lapointe.

Feeling pleasantly sated, Crawley got up from the floor where Harold's body lay, walking around his desk and seating himself in his comfortable desk chair. The process would take several minutes, possibly a bit longer, but soon he would know exactly where Ludia would eventually be. He had thought to get the human to call her in order to lure her out of her cursed haven, wherever that was. Harold hadn't known, but Crawley was intent on getting the information from Ludia herself, somehow. Psychometry might work. But if he saw unfamiliar imagery, even if it did lead to the haven, he wouldn't know how to get there. She might need to be tortured for information.

He had asked enough questions of Harold to ascertain that Ludia frequented this house often. Almost any time she needed to make a phone call, or receive one, the house in Riverside was where she ended up going. He was willing to divert himself from his normally scheduled activities and go there to wait for however long it took. He knew she probably went there nearly every day, so he didn't think he would be waiting for long.

Several minutes went by, with knowledge and imagery flashing through Crawley's mind.

Suddenly, he smiled to himself. He saw that Harold's eyes had seen the sign with the street name, and he saw that Harold's eyes had seen the numbers on the house as he had walked up to it. 83 Marigold Lane.

And as a bonus, he found that he now knew more about computers than he previously did. His smile deepened. He picked up his phone and dialed Gregory's personal line. The man would be in his own office, now, waiting for word from Crawley. After two rings, Gregory picked up.

"Hello, Mr. Crawley." He said. "I trust everything went well with Mr. Lapointe?"

"Wonderfully. Gregory, you and I are going to go for a little drive to Riverside."

"Very good, Mr. Crawley. I shall ready your favorite car at once."

Crawley hung up. He could always depend on Gregory to know when a situation called for a ride in his favorite car. This was most certainly one of those instances.

After getting off the phone with one of Ludia's associates, Seike had been doing whatever he could to ease the tension in the little bar. Brad didn't like having a red there, at all. He couldn't understand why Seike had brought Olinar into the place to begin with, but he trusted the violet-eyed one enough to allow it, so long as Olinar behaved. Seike was still having trouble believing that Olinar had just come to him out of the blue like that. It seemed like long odds, but it had happened.

They had been waiting for well over an hour since Seike had hung up from contact with the Western Haven member he'd got on the line with. It had been a hard atmosphere to deal with in the place ever since. Olinar's friend or whatever she was, Almeidra, had remained in the car the entire time. She had no interest in going anywhere near Seike, which was fine by him. Seike wasn't sure that

Brad would accept having two reds in his bar, anyway. He was on the verge of conniption ever since he had discovered that Olinar was of the Leviathan, shortly after they had entered the place.

Olinar had had the nerve to ask Brad for a drink of blood, and the angry hysterics had begun.

For a human, Brad Hennick was imposing. He was almost as tall and heavy as Olinar, which was saying a lot. His sandy hair was longer and fell down past his shoulder blades, and he had bright brown eyes which were still fiercely looking Olinar's way every ten seconds.

"There had better be a good reason for this." Brad said, glancing Seike's way before looking back hatefully toward Olinar. Seike sighed. The bartender had said the same thing at least a dozen times over the last hour or so. Olinar was just ignoring him, thankfully, not trying to incite the man's anger any further. The large Ambrogis was pouring over documents that Ludia had forwarded to Kelloway, and that Kelloway had faxed over to Seike upon request. They were all about Robert Crawley.

"The enemy of my enemy, Brad." Seike replied. He really wanted to kill Olinar, truthfully, but the man had a skill that Seike and his allies desperately needed. Seike had only heard of pyrokinetics, he had never actually met one. He knew enough to know that the big bastard was their only chance. Kelloway had known it too and hadn't fretted too much over sending classified documents to a bar in Iowa. Besides, Seike knew that he wasn't able to just shoot lightning out of his hands and wasn't too keen on fighting the big Ambrogis without being able to use his strange power at will. Olinar was by far the strongest red that Seike had ever come across. Still, the violet-eyed one had been playing it like he *could* just blast the large man, if he misbehaved. Seike knew that he had a good enough poker face for the ploy.

"Ludia is taking her sweet ass time." Olinar said, the first words he had spoken in almost a half hour. He didn't look up from the papers in his hand, though.

"She'll call. Her safehouse is close enough to L.A. It won't be much longer." Seike said, sighing again.

"A man can't even get a drink in this place."

Brad had refused to give service to Olinar, not blood nor booze. He wanted the red out of his bar as soon as possible. Seike understood and felt bad about putting Brad in this situation. The bartender surprised him at the moment though, pouring a glass of whiskey and sliding it down the bar toward where Olinar was seated.

"Cheers." Olinar said, still not taking his eyes from the files as he took the glass in his hand and began to sip from it.

Brad was staring hard at Seike, now. "I don't know much about this Robert Crawley, other than what I've heard today, but can he really be that dangerous?"

Seike was about to respond, but Olinar spoke up first.

"Oh, he is, but not to me. I'm the V.I.P in this little show."

Brad turned his hard stare toward the shaggy haired Ambrogis. He crossed his arms before saying, "What makes you so special in all this?" Olinar merely smiled as he continued reading, still not looking their way on the other side of the bar.

"We'll be out of your hair after we touch base with Ludia, Brad. I promise. I won't bring any more reds your way down the road, either." Seike was beginning to feel exasperated. He hoped that Brad could hold in his rage.

"See that you don't." Was all the bartender said, before turning his attention to arranging the various bottles on his shelves. They were already in a neat order, Seike knew, but he understood that the man had to busy himself somehow.

Seike was hoping that Ludia would hurry up and call, and that she would have a plan already in store for them to move in on Crawley. He thought about how he might not have to go back to the haven, now. He knew it was a selfish thing to be thinking about, but he couldn't help it. He had always preferred a life of action and adventure, and the chance to take out a foe like Crawley was something he didn't want to miss out on.

Once Crawley was out of the picture, he would be able to rest a lot easier. He knew that Kelloway and the people of the Western Haven would, too.

Ludia was almost at the house. She had been in a foul mood until one of her people had reported that Seike had found the pyrokinetic who had killed Xiang Lau. She was tempted to call Seike back and tell him to just kill the man, but she knew better. They needed this follower of the Leviathan, and according to what her associate had said, the man was willing to help in order to avenge King Coranthis. She would have to be careful. This Olinar couldn't know that Coranthis had died in large part because of her own handiwork.

The council had refused to vote in favor of a rescue squad for Harold. That had been the reason for her dour state of mind. She hoped the human was still safe, keeping himself hidden. She didn't know if she would be compromised in any way if he was caught, but she hoped that in the worst case of him being questioned by Crawley, that the half blood would find nothing out. Nothing of note, anyway.

Harold had once been to her safehouse, but he had been driven there, and it was a fairly long time ago. She was betting he wouldn't know how to get there if asked, even if he was being truthful. A part of her hated herself for thinking in such a cold and calculating way about the man's predicament, but the safety of her people was paramount.

At last, she reached the house and pulled into the driveway. She got out of the car and headed inside, immediately going to where the cell phone was on a coffee table in the living room. She picked it up and dialed the number to Brad Hennick's bar. It rang several times, but the bartender finally picked up on the other end.

"This is Brad." He said, sounding upset. "Tell me that's you, Ludia."

"It is. Something wrong, Brad?" She hoped not. The man was an important contact and supporter of the followers of Seline.

"Just some unwelcome company in my bar, is all. Things are fine, other than that."

Ludia breathed a sigh of relief. Good. Seike had the red in Brad's bar. And behaving, apparently. She considered this a good sign. "Is Seike there? Can you put him on?" She waited for a response.

"Yeah, he's here. Hang on." She heard a small series of thuds as the phone was passed over to Seike. Brad had a landline, and a corded phone besides. In this day and age, that was quite rare.

"Ludia. I found Olinar, and he is what you and the others suspected he is. I hope you have a plan." Seike was trying not to sound dubious. His patience must be worn, having to deal with Olinar for over an hour without a fight breaking out.

"I do, but it's going to require him to come to California."

"I figured as much. I plan on tagging along."

She was about to respond, but a voice spoke up from the living room entryway behind her.

"Ludia! How wonderful to see you. I thought I'd have to wait here a while, but you got here before me!" A terror had gripped her. She knew that voice. She wanted to turn around, but suddenly found that she couldn't move a muscle. It was like the air itself had clamped down over her entire body.

She heard footsteps as the owner of the voice made his way into her field of vision. It was, of course, Robert Crawley. His black hair was slicked back and well cut, and his red eyes were glaring victoriously. She couldn't believe that he had found her. Harold must have been caught, and somehow was able to point Crawley to this safehouse.

"Who are you talking to, Ludia?" Crawley purred menacingly. The phone was still up to her ear, and she couldn't move it, nor any of her fingers. It was like she had been frozen solid. "Let's find out."

He reached for the phone, taking it out of her hand gingerly. He put it up to his own ear. "Hello, who am I speaking with?" He sounded very polite.

Crawley waited for a response, but Seike wasn't saying anything on the other end. Ludia felt sure that he was stunned into silence rather than simply not answering. After a few moments, Crawley spoke in a not so polite manner.

"Tell me who you are, or I'll kill this bitch here and now."

"Seike." Ludia was able to clearly hear the violet-eyed Ambrogis on the other end. He had never been a very good liar, unfortunately.

Recognition dawned in Crawley's eyes at mention of the name. Ludia groaned. Why did it seem like everyone knew who Seike was? She hollered out. "Forget about me, Seike. Hang up!" Crawley casually backhanded her, hard. She hadn't seen it coming and so had been unable to put up a barrier to protect herself from the blow. It sent her crumpling to the ground. She was still conscious, though her ears were now ringing.

"I wouldn't hang up, if I were you, Seike. Are you really *the* Seike?" Crawley's eyes had taken on a fervor that Ludia found horrifying. She knew what Crawley was thinking. What he said next told her as much. "What I wouldn't give for a vial of the violet-eyed Ambrogis' blood. How about you and I make a trade?"

From her position on the ground, Ludia could still hear Seike as he replied. “Whatever you want. Just don’t hurt her.” Damnit Seike, she thought. Damnit. Why did he always have to try to be the damn hero?

Crawley smiled and met Ludia’s eyes. She felt more scared at that moment than she had ever felt for herself. The only time she had ever experienced fear like it was on the day that Selinda had died.

“Alright, Seike.” Crawley said, still looking down at Ludia. “I won’t hurt her. So, have you ever been to California?”

CHAPTER TWENTY-TWO

He'd been told to come alone, and within two days. That didn't leave Seike much time to prepare. He'd just finished hanging up the phone after his brief conversation with Crawley. His mind was racing. It would take thirty or more hours of steady driving just to reach Crawley's headquarters, which was where he had been told to go, and he had to be there in under forty-eight, or Ludia would be killed. He didn't picture Crawley as the type to make idle threats.

Olinar was staring at him curiously, and Brad was looking dumbfounded. The red Ambrogis would have been able to hear the words spoken on the other end of the phone clearly, but not the bartender.

"What just happened?" Brad asked. "It didn't seem like you were talking to Ludia after a minute there."

"Robert Crawley just happened." Olinar said when Seike didn't immediately respond. He leaned forward, facing the violet-eyed Ambrogis from his seat at the other end of the bar. "I hope you're not actually thinking that you're going to go alone. We're going. We'll plan something on the way."

Brad's expression had become shocked at Olinar's words. He looked back and forth between the two Ambrogae. "So this Crawley's got Ludia." He said. "We should tell the Elder. He might be able to help. And besides, I think he has a right to know."

Brad's words sparked some thoughts into Seike's head. Crawley didn't know about his connection to Kelloway and S-47. The General would be able to communicate any essential information that Seike gave him over to both the Central Haven and the Western Haven more quickly than Seike would be able to on his own. He could leave any plans up to them. He didn't know if he was up to giving the bad news to Kesel personally just then, anyway. Right now, his only plan was to get to California as fast as possible.

There must have been something in his facial expression, because Olinar said, "Ludia is particularly important to you."

He met the red's eyes, which were still a watery blue in color. Part of him just wanted to attack Olinar right then and there, but he decided that he was going to need the red Ambrogis. It might be going against his better judgement, but Seike chose to go the route of sharing a little about himself with the hulking red.

"She is the mother of my sire." He said. "I'll say no more of it."

"No problem here. So, you need to leave, and I have a car. I just need to convince Almeidra to let you into it. She might want to be let off somewhere. No guarantee she's gonna come along. She'll see it as a suicide mission. I personally think we can work something out, some kind of an apt plan, especially if you do pass word along of Ludia's kidnapping."

Seike wasn't sure of Olinar yet, but he reminded himself of the need of him, once again. "You really want to get revenge badly enough to go?" He felt the need to ask. He wanted to hear the red's answer.

Olinar smiled coldly. "You should understand the logic of taking the opportunity to avenge the death of this continent's king when you were loyal to that king, and in his service. Whatever else you may believe about my kind, we value one another just as your kind does the same. I wouldn't be too surprised if Almeidra decides to go, but she's reacting a little differently to the death of Coranthis than I am."

That was good enough for Seike. The man seemed sincere somehow in his shared desire to stop Crawley, even though he didn't prioritize saving Ludia, obviously. Even so, he thought they could work something out where they could just both walk the other way after they rescued Ludia. Even if it did involve killing Crawley.

He thought that if they were to succeed, a little more planning than he and Olinar simply talking it out in the car would be needed. He met Brad's eyes.

"Can you connect me to Kelloway, Brad?"

The bartender immediately took his phone out from under the bar, as if he had been ready to do just that. He picked up the handset, passed it to Seike, and began to dial out. The violet-eyed Ambrogis waited as the connection was made. The voice that answered was familiar to him, now.

"This is Corporal Lisgard." S-47 didn't announce themselves when taking a call. Not even from the red line.

"Corporal, this is Seike. Is General Kelloway available at the moment?"

"He's in his office, I'll patch you through."

"Thank you, corporal."

Seike heard a click from the receiver as he was put on hold. He imagined that Kelloway was not going to like what he had to say, but he hoped that the General would be able to quickly get in touch with the havens. He knew that Ludia's survival, and his own, probably hinged on whatever kind of plan that they would be able to come up with.

Kaisimir was with Isaius and Samaiel in Kelloway's office when the General took Seike's call. Kelloway had called them in to discuss what they were going to do now that it seemed that they had enlisted the aid of a red pyrokinetic. They had been in the midst of talking about Olinar and what kind of move they could make against Crawley when the General's phone rang.

Kelloway kept the call with Seike short and had already issued an order to Command and Communications to contact both the Western Haven and the Central Haven and inform them of the news. They would hopefully have a plan fleshed out within the next couple of hours. Kaisimir wasn't too keen on the idea of Seike being alone with Olinar and Almeidra. He had absolutely zero trust in the two reds. He could understand why Seike had decided to go with them, though. Time was of the essence, and the violet-eyed Ambrogis had been more or less forced to suddenly rely on the man who had been a hated enemy before today. As far as Kaisimir was concerned, Olinar was still an enemy. He hoped Seike wouldn't let his guard down while they traveled together.

The young noble had a sudden notion and shared it with the others in the office.

"If we left now, we could make it to Los Angeles in time, ourselves." Kaisimir hoped that they would agree. He still felt that he had to prove himself in some way after his act of cowardice on the field of battle.

General Kelloway furrowed his brow just as Samaiel began to shake his head.

"It's too risky." Samaiel said. "Seike's not going to be in contact with us again, and we might end up throwing a wrench into whatever plan he and Olinar come up with. We should leave things to the Western Haven, I think. They know Crawley better than we do. It's likely that they'll know when Seike arrives, since they have eyes on Crawley's building. They'll be able to determine when to make any kind of move."

Kelloway and Isaius were both nodding at Samaiel's words. Kaisimir felt a sense of disappointment, but he couldn't fault the logic that Samaiel had just presented. Still, he wished there was something that he could do. It pained him to think that they were all just going to end up sitting this one out.

"I hope that red doesn't double-cross us." Isaius stated. "I have to say, I am not liking this situation, not one bit."

"None of us like it, sergeant." Kelloway retorted. "Especially since if Olinar ever finds out that Ludia is basically the reason that his king is dead, the whole thing will probably go sideways."

"Well, he's not gonna hear it from us." Samaiel put in. "And we can only hope that he doesn't hear it from anyone else."

Everyone in the office fell silent, lost in their own thoughts. Kaisimir briefly considered trying to convince them all to reconsider going to California, but he relented. He knew that there was no sense in trying to help when they would be going in blind. Rushing headlong into danger was Seike's thing, anyway. He would be alright.

"So, what do we do, now, then?" Kaisimir asked the others, breaking the momentary silence.

"We wait until we get calls from the havens." Kelloway replied. "Once the message about Ludia's kidnapping and Seike's current circumstance spreads, someone is bound to think of a plan. We wait until then, and hopefully we'll be able to help in some way with whatever they come up with."

Kaisimir didn't like it, but he knew that was all they could really do. He took comfort in knowing that everyone in the room felt the same way. Hopefully, they would hear back from the havens soon.

It was the worst news that had come to Elder Kesel's attention in a long time. If anything went wrong, Ludia would be dead. And it was likely that Seike would be killed, too.

Hearing that Olinar was the pyrokinetic that had killed Xiang Lau and was now with Seike on the way to California had frayed the Elder's nerves. He felt more helpless than he had in quite some time. The rational part of him knew that Olinar was the only real chance that Seike and Ludia both had for survival. Another large part of him hated that fact. Too many things could go wrong. Olinar had no loyalty to Seike, and their partnership was based on the most tenuous of strings. If the Ambrogis of the Leviathan discovered the real reason that Coranthis was killed, he would most definitely betray Seike.

After receiving the news back at the haven, the Elder had immediately set out to go to Brad Hennick's bar, Just for Kicks, in order to make some calls of his own. He had already spoken with a contact from the Western Haven, as well as called Kelloway. The basic plan had been formed, and now there wasn't much else that the Elder could do. The Western Haven would wait for Seike to arrive, give the young Ambrogis some time once inside, and then storm the building. They would contact local authorities before doing so, however, to let them know that Triaclon Industries was a den of half bloods and that they were going to take care of the situation before Crawley could do more harm to the local human population.

That was as much information as the Elder had been able to glean from the Western Haven contact. He had relayed it all to Kelloway, but the General had already heard as much from a different contact. Elder Kesel would stay at the bar for the time being, until he heard back from either Kelloway or one of the Western Haven council members. He needed to know more about what would be done, though he didn't hold out hope that much more information would be forthcoming.

He was presently sitting at the bar, his mind a jumble of unpleasant thoughts. Brad could evidently sense his unease, for the bartender poured a glass of blood and offered it to him wordlessly. Kesel accepted it with as much grace as he could muster.

"Thank you, Brad." The Elder thought his own voice sounded worn and frail, in that moment.

"I don't know about that red," Brad said. "But I would bet on Seike coming out of this on top, somehow. And with Ludia alive and well."

The Elder took a swallow from the glass. He knew that Brad was just trying to comfort him. Still, he appreciated it.

"If anyone can succeed, it will be Seike." The Elder couldn't stop thinking about Ludia, and how she was now at the mercy of a monster capable of ripping her to shreds with his thoughts alone. The years they had been apart hadn't diminished his feelings for her. She was his wife. They had been together for almost a thousand years before separating because of the death of their daughter.

Brad must have been able to sense that further words wouldn't be much help right now. He gave the Elder some space to think and said nothing more.

He began to think of the day that Selinda had died. Emilio had been a force too powerful for him to stop, and he had been the only one who witnessed the death of his daughter. Ludia and Seike had both been elsewhere in the haven when Emilio had broken free of the cell that had been holding him, killing anyone that got in his way in his effort to escape.

Kesel and Selinda had both fought the ancient one, but she had died in the ensuing battle. Emilio had been old. Older than Coranthis had been. With his age came strength unlike any that Kesel had ever dealt with. The old creature had been a master at strength-enhancing psionics. Selinda had been strong too, but she was only a little over five hundred years old, and no match for the ferocity of such an ancient being.

Emilio had held Selinda by the throat, promising Kesel that he would allow her to live in exchange for directions out of the haven. In his desperation, he hadn't even hesitated. He had told Emilio how to escape, then watched helplessly as the ancient one laughed before snapping Selinda's neck. Emilio had then stated that he would allow Kesel to live, knowing the pain of what he had done would be worse for the Elder than any method of death could ever be.

That horrible laugh still haunted Kesel to this day. The sound of it, and the sound of his daughter's neck snapping that followed it. He tried to think of something else, but he found that his mind was in no shape for any sort of positive thinking. He feared for Ludia's safety. If he lost her too, he didn't know how he would find the strength to carry on.

All he could do now was wait, and hope that Seike and this Olinar were able to pull off a successful rescue.

CHAPTER TWENTY-THREE

It had been a long and arduous drive so far, and they were still only in Colorado. Seike didn't know if he possessed enough patience to deal with Almeidra's remarks and comments throughout the entire ride. She had vehemently disagreed with the entire notion of going to California on a mission of vengeance with the violet-eyed vampire in tow, making it perfectly clear to Seike that she didn't care about rescuing Ludia. As Olinar had suspected, she thought the entire idea was a suicide mission. Seike still wasn't sure why she had decided to go.

Seike was in the back of the car, behind Olinar, who was driving. Almeidra didn't want him to be sitting directly behind her in the front passenger seat. There had in fact been an argument about the seating arrangements. Almeidra had wanted to be in the back so she could keep her eyes on Seike, with him sitting in the front passenger seat. Seike didn't trust her at all and had stated as much. They had argued about the lack of trust and who was going to sit where for several minutes before Olinar had told Almeidra that Seike was going to sit in the back, or she could start walking. She hadn't taken that well and had lashed out at Olinar verbally about his ridiculous sense of honor toward a dead king. She had admitted that getting revenge on the man who destroyed the palace and killed everyone inside would be good, but she didn't believe that they stood much chance of succeeding. After all, over a thousand pure bloods had died at Crawley's hands, so what chance did they have?

In the end, Olinar had placated her by saying that she didn't have to go inside Crawley's headquarters if she didn't want to. She could go hang out in Hollywood or something until the whole thing was over. In response, she completely changed her mind about the situation, saying that Olinar would have a better chance of coming out of that building alive if she went in with him, and so she was going to do just that.

While they drove, they worked out a basic plan that would get all three of them into Triaclon Industries headquarters. Seike was invited, so for his part, he would just walk in and announce that he was there to see Crawley. Olinar and Almeidra would wait just a little while, then they would go in and pass themselves off as half bloods. Olinar knew a guy in Nevada who did excellent fake IDs. He had already called the man and arranged to pick up an ID for both him and Almeidra. The IDs were just to lend credence to the human names they would be giving to whoever received them at Triaclon Industries. Olinar wasn't sure that they would be needed but was getting them just as a precaution.

Seike found it interesting to learn that the Ambrogae of the Leviathan couldn't readily discern any difference between someone who was a pure blood and someone who was a half blood, despite the glaring prejudice between the two. The difference was purely knowledge and reputation based. If a pure blood like Olinar wasn't known to any of the half bloods that he encountered while in the building, he and Almeidra should have no issues getting in and somehow finding out where Crawley would be.

For his own part, Seike only planned on getting Ludia safely out of there, whatever steps were required. He didn't imagine that Crawley was going to immediately show him where she was, but the man had promised that he could periodically call and hear her voice, to be rest assured that she was still alive. He'd taken one of the cell phones from Brad's bar to do so and was just finishing up one of those calls. Ludia had said he should forget about her again before Crawley had cut her off. Seike had decided not to stay on the line with Crawley, so when the half blood asked if he was satisfied, Seike had simply said that he was and hung up.

Olinar spoke shortly after that phone call.

"Dangerous game that you're playing, calling Crawley like that. That's the second time you've called just to make sure Ludia is alive. He could be tracking that phone by now."

Seike didn't care. "Let him track it, then. He'll see that I'm on my way, and as far as he knows, I'm driving there myself."

Almeidra turned and sneered at him from her seat. "You wouldn't care if you exposed us, anyway. You just want to save your precious Ludia."

That wasn't altogether untrue. Seike didn't really care about Almeidra. He needed Olinar. Otherwise, he would be completely at Crawley's mercy once he came face to face with the half blood. There was a very real chance that Crawley would just do whatever he wanted with Seike and then kill Ludia anyway. Olinar was the only person that could perhaps turn the tables and allow for a real negotiation to take place, though Seike still couldn't picture how they would get to that point.

"Can it, Almeidra. He's not going to stab us in the back. The situation's too dire for that." Olinar flashed a look in the mirror at Seike, as if daring him.

Olinar was right, Seike knew. Almeidra should be able to catch on to that, but it wasn't the first time they'd had a conversation like this. Almeidra would insult or otherwise attack him verbally somehow, Olinar would say something to quiet her for a while, maybe hours, but envitably she would snap at him again.

Seike's solution for it was to just stop talking, usually, but he felt he should say something more this time.

"Without Olinar, I likely won't stand a chance against Crawley. He'll probably kill Ludia and capture me." He didn't mention that he thought Almeidra could very well screw up the entire scheme, instead keeping that part to himself.

"That's right." Olinar said immediately, before Almeidra could come up with any kind of snide response. "And I know you're no stranger to a little espionage, Almeidra. This should be a walk in the park for you."

"Yeah, if you want to call it that." Almeidra said. "We're going to walk into a building full of half bloods and try to find out where their boss is so we can kill him. Shouldn't be hard at all." She said the last part with more than a little sarcasm. It wasn't lost on Seike or Olinar, but for a while no one said anything more. They just drove on in silence.

Seike might not trust Olinar, but he had to admire the man's sureness of himself. It seemed that the large Ambrogis was the least nervous one in the car. Seike's nerves weren't for himself, of course. He was worried about Ludia. But he felt like Olinar had already decided that they were going to win in this little game they were playing at. They would take out their mutual enemy and rescue his hostage, and then walk their separate ways. That was what was agreed upon, anyway. Once Crawley was out of the picture, Seike didn't really know what was going to happen between them. He was willing to let Olinar walk away, but would the red Ambrogis be willing to do the same? With a little luck, they would get to a point where they could find out. One thing at a time.

It was going to be very interesting to be able to have the violet-eyed Ambrogis to study. Crawley had no intention of letting Seike go once he had him, nor did he have any intention of keeping Ludia alive and well. He was feeling mildly irritated at not being able to find out the whereabouts of her base of operations through the psychometric process of coming into physical contact with her. The images he had received were blurred and jumbled. It was to be expected with an old Ambrogess like her.

The downside to psychometry was that it did not work well on someone who had the same innate ability. It was clear to Crawley now that Ludia had at least a fair degree of skill with it. It wasn't an intentional shield preventing him from finding out anything, but rather it was simply that she was also psychometric. He wouldn't have been able to glean anything from contact with Gregory, either, even if they both would have allowed it.

He had just finished a meeting with his board of directors that had mostly been regarding the business climate of his company's endeavors. But he had also let the board know that the most recent candidate for true immortality was dying, as the others had. An annoyance, but progress would be made. He had of course brought it up that he was going to be visited by the violet-eyed one, and the other executives seemed to enjoy the news, commenting on how they might be able to create superior products with the knowledge they could gain from examining Seike. They were all on the same page as Crawley in that once they had the violet-eyed Ambrogis, it would be preferrable not to let him go.

Crawley was on his way from that meeting to pay Ludia a little visit. She had specially arranged accommodation on the same floor as the board's and his own offices. Floor twenty-seven, near the top of the main building of Triaclon Industries. He had been visiting her frequently, trying to wear her down emotionally and physically in order to get her to surrender the information he really wanted from her, which was the location she operated out of. He might keep her alive for a while yet, even after he acquired Seike. He particularly enjoyed torturing her, even if she hadn't given him anything he could use, yet. There was always the chance that she might, and his visits to her made for an amusing pastime.

It didn't take him long to get from the boardroom to the door that served as an entryway into Ludia's new prison. The door looked like wood on the outside but was actually an especially hard alloy that Crawley's company had developed years ago, which dissipated psionic energy to a good enough degree that he hadn't been able to find anyone that could break down the doors that were made from this material thus far. Even so, two of the stronger Ambrogae on his company security team were stationed just outside the door. The walls inside were thickly lined with the same metal, so he didn't anticipate that Ludia would be able to make any kind of an escape.

"Mr. Crawley, sir." The security guard on the left side of the door said as Crawley walked up to them. "Here for another visit with the prisoner? She's been quiet." Initially, Ludia had been very vocal, but after a few sessions with him, she had dialed it down considerably.

"Good. Open the door please." Crawley stood ready to grab the woman with his telekinetic grasp if she had somehow escaped her chains and made any kind of move once the door was open.

The guard nodded and turned to use his sliding passkey on the high-tech locking mechanism under the doorknob. The machine beeped after he slid the card through it. A green light flashed on it, and he turned the handle to open the door, moving back to his position on the left side of it outside in the hall. Crawley moved past him and the other guard, pushing open the door and walking into the room. It was empty except for Ludia, who was chained in a splayed-out fashion to the wall on the room's far side, opposite the door.

She looked positively haggard, Crawley was delighted to see. She hadn't been with him long, but he had been spending plenty of quality time with this woman who had been a thorn in his side for quite a number of years. He'd visited her four times in just the last day, and by the look of fear in her eyes, Crawley could tell that his visits were beginning to have their desired effect.

"Ludia, darling." he said soothingly. "I was thinking that perhaps we could swap some stories. I could tell you some of my past, and you can tell me some of yours. What do you think?" He slowly walked up to her with a small smile on his face. The fear stayed in her eyes, but she still wasn't flinching at having him this close to her. And she didn't respond to his question immediately. That was alright. He cuffed her hard across the temple, knowing that the blow would leave her head feeling sore enough to make sure she didn't forget her position here.

"What's your connection to Seike?" he asked in a mild voice, after striking her. He hadn't questioned her about that, yet, and it seemed to take her off guard. Her eyes widened slightly, taking on a defensive look.

"You'll get nothing out of me, Crawley." she bravely said. "I don't place a high value on my own life, you should know that by now. You might as well kill me and get it over with."

Blood was trickling down the side of her temple. He had struck her hard enough to break the skin there, causing the bleeding. No matter, it would heal quickly enough. With each wound Crawley caused her, forcing her body to heal, her condition would deteriorate. She would eventually begin starving, and hungry Ambrogae were far more likely to talk, in Crawley's experience.

"He's on his way, you know." He said. "I was on the phone with him not long ago, and he was already in Colorado at the time. He will be here sometime tomorrow." Crawley searched Ludia's face for any kind of emotional reaction to this information, but her expression remained passive.

Crawley knew that Seike might try to arrange for some help with getting Ludia back, but the ambitious businessman was prepared for such an eventuality. He wasn't exactly expecting the violet-eyed one to lead a charge into his headquarters, but if his people saw Seike approach and enter the building with anyone other than just himself, they had orders to detain him immediately and bring him and whoever was with him to Crawley. He thought that it was more likely that an individual such as Seike would come alone, however. From what Crawley had heard, the violet-eyed Ambrogis styled himself as something of a hero. And heroes were foolish enough to walk headlong into certain danger without any kind of backup plan. Crawley had killed plenty of heroic people throughout his long history of being alive.

"It's alright, Ludia. You don't have to share with me if you feel it is inappropriate." He began to caress the side of her head that was bleeding.

She tried to move out of the way, but her restraining chains, which were made of the same alloy as the rest of the room, prevented her from doing so. She yanked on them uselessly as he stroked her head, eventually moving his hand down to her left shoulder and along her arm until he got to her elbow. He rested his hand on her elbow for a moment, then viciously gripped and yanked on it with all his might, snapping the limb at the joint. Ludia screamed in pain, a sound which Crawley thought he might never tire of hearing.

"I'll give you some more time to think it over." He stated. "All you need to do is tell me a little bit about how you know Seike, and I'll tell you something about myself. It's a fair trade, really." He patted her cheek gently, before turning around to leave the room.

Marosavek had made all of the arrangements. The attack on Crawley's headquarters would begin one hour after Seike entered the building. His haven had more than enough eyes on the place to give a timely report when that moment came to pass. He had people positioned around Los Angeles, outside of the haven and relatively close to the main building of Triaclon Industries, though not close enough to be detected. He himself was outside of the haven and had just finished making all the necessary calls to human law enforcement and the local politicians, informing them of Crawley and his true identity as a many centuries old half blood bent on taking over the country. He told them of the madman who experimented on both human and Ambrogae subjects in his quest for greater personal gain and power. Marosavek had a good reputation throughout the human world within California, and they took him at his word on the matter, though he had arranged to give supporting documentation as well.

They would keep quiet and make no moves to stop Marosavek's people once they began to storm the building. He was presently with one other council member, a man named Huilanios, in a small apartment rented by the haven for the purpose of communication and reconnaissance. Huilanios was a capable combat veteran and would be leading the forces of the Western Haven alongside Marosavek.

"It's almost a guarantee that Ludia will be kept near the top floor, possibly somewhere close to Crawley's main office." Marosavek said to his companion. "We're going to let Seike and the red pyrokinetic deal with Crawley. Rescuing Ludia is our priority."

Huilanios nodded his assent. "Of course. And we'll succeed. I just hope that Seike and Olinar are able to take out Crawley. It wouldn't be very good to put a man like that on a forced offensive. And that's what will happen if we take out the headquarters and he survives."

"I'll count the mission a success if we can get Ludia out of there, and Seike as well. Even if Crawley manages to survive, somehow." Marosavek didn't want that to happen, of course. They all wanted Crawley to meet his end in this assault, whether at Seike's hands or Olinar's. Whoever managed to kill Robert Crawley wasn't as important as the need for the man to die.

"I'd relish the opportunity to rip the bastard's head off, myself." Huilanios said. He was a man of medium height and a thick, stout build. He was very strong, physically. Much stronger than Marosavek. Still, Huilanios tended to think with his muscles, more than his head. He was no fool, of course, just a bit too aggressive in certain instances.

"I know you would, my old friend." Marosavek responded. "But that's not very likely. Remember, we must rescue the Elder. Once we're in that building, I want you to only concern yourself with that. We're not going to be there for Crawley. We can only hope that those that will be, will get the job done." He was thinking of Olinar, the red pyrokinetic. Obviously, it must be difficult for Seike to ally himself with an enemy, especially one that might not be very trustworthy. Even if the alliance was to be temporary. He hoped that Olinar's desire for vengeance was sincere and strong. Marosavek knew from experience that revenge could be quite a motivating factor. He also knew of the strange sense of loyalty that those of the Leviathan felt towards their monarchy, especially their kings and queens, so he didn't have much reason to doubt the red's desire and intention to get his revenge on Crawley.

Olinar was a means to an end, though. Nothing more. He hoped the red would not find out the truth about the destruction of the palace and all those inside. He knew he wasn't the only one with such a hope. Marosavek wasn't above letting the man walk away from them once Crawley was dead, but if he found out the truth, he could become dangerous in the future.

"It is a delicate plan that we are executing." Huilanios said, inferring Marosavek's current thoughts. "But we won't get a better opportunity. I don't believe so, anyway."

"Nor do I, Huilanios. Nor do I."

This could be the moment they had all been waiting for. The chance to take out a powerful madman. Even if it cost them, it would be worth the sacrifice. And Marosavek had no illusions about that. Lives would be lost, even if they were victorious.

CHAPTER TWENTY-FOUR

Once they had arrived in Los Angeles and were within a few miles of Triaclon Industries, Seike was left to drive the rest of the way in Olinar's green Mustang. Olinar and Almeidra got out of the car to walk the remainder of the distance to the headquarters, to give Seike time to get in and meet with Crawley.

As soon as they got out of the car, Olinar bent down toward the window before Seike began driving away.

"Just try to keep Crawley talking until we get in and make our way to whatever floor you two will be on." The big Ambrogis said reassuringly. "Hopefully some cavalry from your side get there in time, too."

Seike had no idea what kind of plan, if any, had been devised by Kelloway and the havens. He hoped there was something in the works but had no way of knowing for sure. He couldn't risk calling anyone after he had been on the phone with Crawley a few times. For all he knew, the evil bastard could have traced and digitally tapped his phone and was now able to listen to any calls he might make.

"Let's hope it all works out for us both." Seike said. For a wonder, he meant the words. Olinar would deserve to go his own way as far as Seike was concerned, if the man was truly able to help him defeat Crawley.

"Just remember," Olinar said warningly. "Our best chance of walking out of there with Ludia is to kill Crawley. Hell, that's our only chance of walking out of there. I got a read on you now, Seike. You don't feel like a typical blue and I'll be able to sense you wherever you're at in that building once I get in. It'll be easy for me to sift out one unusual Ambrogis among a bunch of my own kind. We'll find you once we get in, one way or another."

"Okay, good." Seike tried his best to feel like the plan was going to work out. Olinar seemed confident, and the violet-eyed vampire could stand to let a little bit of that confidence rub off on him. "I'll do my best to keep Crawley distracted until you get to wherever I end up."

Olinar nodded at his words, then said, "We just gotta stay focused, and we'll get through this. There are a lot of my kind in this city, I can feel them. It makes it easy for us to blend in."

Seike nodded as well, then saw an opportunity to pull from the spot he had parked on the side of the busy street. He pulled out and merged into traffic, leaving Olinar and Almeidra to walk in the same general direction.

L.A. was a busy city, and even though Seike could see the building he was heading toward in the near enough distance, with its big red TI logo on top, it took what seemed to him a grueling amount of time to make his way there through the traffic. Finally, though, he found a parking spot within sight of the building's front doors.

He felt that he was being watched. It was vague, but he could feel the presence of those of Seline around the area, though that feeling was dwarfed by the mass of reds he could feel inside the Triaclon Industries building. Feeling allies at all gave him hope that there was some kind of plan in motion, other than what he and Olinar had come up with. If more help arrived and the timing of it was good, that would increase the chances of survival for both him and Ludia. Seike's people would know what Olinar looked like thanks to the picture that he drew for circulation, so the big red should be good too.

He took his time getting out of the car, deliberating over whether to take the cell phone with him just in case. He decided to take it after a minute of consideration. It wouldn't hurt to have it on him.

After leaving the vehicle parked where it was, and stuffing the key and phone into his pants pockets, he made his way in what he hoped would seem like a leisurely fashion toward the steps that led up to the large front entrance of the corporate headquarters. The feeling of being watched only got stronger as he walked. He hoped it wasn't just the reds that were watching.

He approached the doors but was unable to get a look inside. They were somewhat tinted and highly reflective. All he could make out was his own reflection and the street and other buildings behind him. Taking a deep breath, he opened one of the four doors and went inside.

The interior was very modern looking, with mostly white walls and white marble floors striated with grey, and an eggshell white ceiling. The furniture he could see was all seemingly expensive, from the polished wooden receptionist's desk to the posh chairs that were meant for waiting guests. He saw a woman sitting behind that desk, and she was looking his way. He could immediately sense that she was an Ambrogess. While he had travelled into the city, he had shifted his eyes from their natural violet color to the brown that they were in his human life. As he approached her, he allowed his eyes to shift back to violet. She smiled at him, and it didn't seem like a menacing smile, though he assumed she was quite practiced at it.

"Seike, I presume?" She said from her seated position behind the desk. He nodded.

She pressed a button on the phone next to her. A voice came through on the speaker. It was Crawley.

"Yes?" Was all he said.

"Mr. Crawley," she said in a perky voice. "Seike has just arrived to see you." She flashed him that smile again, but this time he could see a predatory look in her almond-colored eyes.

"Gregory will meet him in the lobby shortly, please tell him to take a seat in the meantime."

"Yes, Mr. Crawley." She said, pressing a button on the phone to end the call. She gazed up at Seike with that smile of hers. "If you'll just take a seat, Mr. Crawley's aide will be here shortly to escort you the rest of the way."

He was already done with this game and didn't offer the woman a reply. He also chose not to sit down. Instead, he went over and stood by one of the chairs, with his arms crossed. He waited there like that, not even sparing another glance at the receptionist, for about five minutes.

The elevator doors off to the side of the front desk suddenly opened, and out strode a somewhat tall, thinly built man. He was dressed in a suit and had a look of self-importance about him. He looked over to where Seike was standing, and a plastic smile crept onto his face. The violet-eyed Ambrogis was getting angry just looking at the way this man approached him.

The man got within three feet of Seike and offered his hand. "Greetings. My name is Gregory."

Seike just looked at Gregory's outstretched hand, then up at his face. He was aware that the man could have some talent with psychometry and had no plans on letting the man touch him in any way. That would screw everything up for sure.

"I'm not shaking your hand. I'm not playing this game where we all pretend to be friendly with each other. Just bring me to Crawley."

The man at first looked shocked at the vehemence in Seike's voice, then annoyed that his attempt at a handshake had failed. He withdrew his hand after a moment, a sour expression on his face.

"Very well." Gregory said. "We'll be taking the elevator, if you'll follow me."

Seike followed the man but kept his distance while they stood inside the elevator. Gregory took a keycard out from the breast pocket of his suit and passed it along a scanner just above the elevator button panel. A light flashed green, and Gregory hit the button for the twenty-seventh floor. At that moment, Seike wished he could text Olinar what he had just seen, but it was too risky. He might yet get a chance to do so, but not while he was inside the elevator.

As the elevator ascended the floors, Seike felt progressively more and more tense. He began to feel like he might be in over his head this time. He didn't look Gregory's way but kept a watch on the man in his peripheral vision. The thin man made no move toward him, and for that he was glad. He didn't want to have to explain to Crawley that he had been forced to kill Gregory. He didn't think he could make up a very good reason for such an act. That, and there was a camera in the elevator, looking down on the both of them. He imagined that Crawley might be watching him at that very moment.

At last, the elevator reached floor twenty-seven and stopped. The door slid open, and Gregory motioned for Seike to continue following him. Neither of them said another word as Seike was led down a hallway containing many doors on one side, and windows on the other. Most of the doors seemed to be made of a strange reddish colored wood.

Eventually, they reached a door that was a bit more elaborate looking than the others Seike had seen. It was still made of the strange looking wood but had a more elegant design. Gregory knocked twice on the door.

After a moment, the door opened, and there stood a man who was slightly taller than either Gregory or Seike, with a thin but strong looking body. His black hair was slicked back, and Seike found himself thinking that this man looked like a modern businessman version of the fictional vampire, Dracula.

"Thank you, Gregory." The man at the door said. "You may go, now."

"Yes, Mr. Crawley." Gregory said, bowing his head in acquiescence. He turned and left without another word or even a look in Seike's direction.

"At long last we meet, Seike." Crawley said. "Please, come in and have a seat."

So, this was the man that single handedly killed more than a thousand pure bloods and levelled their entire palace? Seike knew he should be afraid, but he felt calm as he accepted the man's offer, walking past him into the large space that could only be Crawley's personal office, and taking a seat at a slightly out-turned chair near the exquisitely expensive-looking desk. Seike had to keep the man talking, he reminded himself. So, he would play the game as well as he could, now.

Crawley walked over to seat himself in a chair that looked something like a throne, behind the desk. He smiled at Seike as he folded his hands and placed them on the desk's surface.

"I know I said I wanted a vial of your blood, Seike, and I still do. But I was thinking, I could use a man of your talent here at my company. I hear you're very adept at killing."

Seike made himself smile back. He had to play along. "It comes naturally to me. I've been told that I'm stronger than most Ambrogae who are over a thousand years old. It sure seems that way to me when I fight."

"Interesting. And how old are you, exactly?" A glint in Crawley's eyes told Seike that he was genuinely interested to hear the answer.

Play along, Seike thought. "I'm almost one hundred and thirty years old."

Crawley raised an eyebrow at him. "You're that young, truly?"

"Yes. I was born in eighteen ninety-six. A human by birth."

Crawley seemed content to ask more questions, and Seike was going to answer them as honestly as he could manage.

"Ah, so you weren't born an Ambrogis. That's very interesting. Neither was I." Crawley seemed relaxed, and Seike could understand why. The man was presently very much in control, and he knew it. "How much do you know about me, Seike?"

"I know from Ludia that you're a telekinetic. I'm not here to fight you, I know that would be a mistake. I'm here to negotiate a trade, as you said you were interested in doing on the phone. Ludia's freedom in exchange for my own, if necessary. You want me to kill for you? I'll do it, if she gets to live."

Crawley chuckled lightly at hearing those words from Seike. The violet-eyed Ambrogis didn't want to sound too desperate, but he also wanted to seem compliant towards Crawley.

"Well, that's an offer that I most certainly must consider." The half blood said. "Perhaps you would like to know more about what we do here at Triaclon Industries?"

"I am kind of interested in knowing. Honestly, Ludia never told me much about you or your corporation. I think she wanted me to steer clear of you."

"And we can't blame her for that." Crawley's eyes seemed to hold their own smile. "After all, I'm a dangerous man. But so are you, Seike. And dangerous sorts ought to stick together, I've always thought.

"So, with that in mind, allow me to tell you a little bit about my company and the kinds of activities that we engage in."

Seike leaned back in his chair, attempting to look like he was in no rush to see Ludia. It was a difficult thing to do.

Olinar hadn't wanted to let Seike know how much he now knew about Crawley and his little headquarters. The documentation that he had spent time going over told him a lot. He felt certain even before he and Almeidra arrived at the building that Crawley would meet with Seike on the twenty-seventh floor. That was where most of the executives on the board of directors were housed, including Crawley's own main office. It had been almost an hour, but they were now on the doorsteps of the building.

"You ready?" He asked Almeidra. She gave him a sardonic look that said it all. She didn't like the situation, but she was ready.

"Alright," he said. "Let's go."

They made their way up the steps and into the building. A receptionist at the front desk was there to greet them. She was attractive, with glasses that were obviously on her face just for show, as Olinar could tell right away that she was an Ambrogess. Their kind didn't need their vision corrected.

"Can I help you?" she asked as Olinar and Almeidra walked up to the desk.

"My woman and I are new in town." Olinar began. "We felt that this place might welcome people like us. Thought we'd apply for a job."

The Ambrogess looked Olinar up and down, seeming to size him up, then she did the same with Almeidra.

"Triaclon Industries could always use more people like yourselves. I'll contact Gregory. He specializes in interviewing potential employees that have particular... merit." The woman pressed a button on the phone at her desk.

"This is Gregory." A voice said out of the phone's speaker.

"Gregory, there are two people here looking for a job. I told them I would call you. Are you available?"

After a brief hesitation, Gregory responded. "I am available, Natasha. Please ask them to take a seat, I'll be right down."

The receptionist motioned towards the chairs near the front desk. Olinar thought they looked pretty comfortable and confirmed it by sitting down. They were good chairs. He patted the cushion on the one next to him, looking Almeidra's way. She sat down, looking perfectly in her element as a prospective employee.

Gregory? If Olinar remembered correctly, that was the name of Crawley's right-hand man. That would mean that he would have a keycard that could take them to the twenty-seventh floor. He could feel Seike clearly up above him and felt certain that was where the violet-eyed

Ambrogis currently was. It seemed that they might be in for a lucky break.

After a few minutes, a thin man in a suit exited the elevator door, setting his eyes on where Olinar and Almeidra were seated. They stood up from their seats, and Olinar went over to where the man was still standing near the elevator. Almeidra was only a pace behind him.

The thin man extended his hand to Olinar. "Greetings. My name is Gregory."

Olinar was aware that the man might be able to tell some things from a handshake, but he also knew that it took at least a minute for psychometric review in the mind's eye. So, he took the man's hand in his own and shook it. "Randall Davidson. This is my woman, Sarah Jones."

"A pleasure. If you'll follow me, we can go to my office and discuss matters. Have you heard of Triaclon Industries?" Gregory had already turned around and gone into the elevator. Olinar followed him inside, as did Almeidra.

"We were on the east coast for a long time." Almeidra put in. "The name rings a bell, but we don't know much about the company. We didn't know it catered to our kind of people until we felt it nearby, here in L.A. We decided to investigate, as we plan on staying in California for the foreseeable future."

"Excellent. Well, we can certainly discuss-"

The door to the elevator had closed and Gregory had already pushed the button for the eleventh floor. He stopped talking in mid-sentence, though, so Olinar knew the game was up. Olinar nodded to Almeidra, who quickly worked her talent for technology manipulation on the camera in the elevator. It would freeze the image, but seeing as how they were all standing there when the image became frozen, it wouldn't fool whoever was in the security offices for long.

Gregory turned toward Olinar, his face no longer friendly-looking. His eyes had gone red, and he sneered with a mouth full of sharp teeth. Olinar was unimpressed and punched the man in the chest with full force, breaking through his rib cage and obliterating the heart behind it. Gregory had a moment of life left for his face to take on a shocked expression, then he dropped to the elevator floor, dead.

Olinar didn't waste any time. This fucker had a keycard on his person, and the big red Ambrogis needed to find it as fast as possible. He bent over the body and began to pat it down. It only took seconds for him to feel the hard square in the man's breast pocket. Olinar's punch had missed that pocket by an inch, which was intentional.

The elevator was almost to the eleventh floor when Olinar passed the keycard over the reader that sat above the elevator button panel. He saw a light flash green and pressed the button for the twenty-seventh floor. Seike was still up above. He could feel the violet-eyed one clearly. Olinar couldn't yet tell if it was the twenty-seventh floor that Seike was on, but he was betting his life that it was.

"Twenty-seventh? You're sure?" Almeidra posed the question.

"I read a lot of reports and files on this place. I'm feeling pretty damn positive that's where Seike and Crawley are."

Almeidra looked doubtful but said nothing more. As the elevator approached the twenty-seventh floor, Olinar could feel Seike's presence more clearly. Upon reaching the floor, he and Almeidra exchanged looks. They could tell that it was indeed where Seike was. She looked relieved as the door opened, but that relief was short-lived.

They were greeted by a dozen armed security personnel as the door finished sliding open. Shit.

Oh well, Olinar thought. He hadn't really expected that this was going to be easy. The security guards said nothing and immediately opened fire. But they didn't know who they were dealing with. He and Almeidra were a pair of Coranthis' most elite warriors. Bullets ricocheted off the kinetic shields that the two pure bloods had erected before the elevator door finished opening.

Some of the bullets bounced back and hit the security team. Within seconds, three of them had dropped to the floor, not dead but injured. The guards stopped firing.

"Time to die, you fucking filth." Olinar said just as he and Almeidra simultaneously leapt out of the elevator and began their attack. The guards were too slow to react, at first. It took only moments for the two pure bloods to kill half of them before the remainder began trying to fight back.

Almeidra kicked two of them in the head so hard that their necks completely snapped, while Olinar did to three others what he had done to Gregory, smashing into their chests with such force that their hearts were destroyed.

The guards tried to retaliate, but to no avail. The ones who were left standing threw a few punches that Olinar easily parried and countered. One of them decided to try shooting Almeidra, but she moved behind him faster than he could pull the trigger, and twisted his head so violently that his faced turned a full one hundred and eighty degrees to look in surprise at Almeidra's own face before the life went out of his eyes, and his body dropped.

The entire fight lasted less than a minute. Olinar felt sure that they had to keep moving or more would come. He could feel Seike not too far down the hallways of this floor.

"This way." He said to Almeidra. She only nodded as they set forth, running as fast as they could towards where they could feel the violet-eyed one.

The large pyrokinetic had been spotted going into Crawley's headquarters less than fifteen minutes ago. Marosavek had been getting ready to move his forces in when Olinar had been seen. He had relayed orders to his two full companies of soldiers, five hundred men and women in total, to hang back just a little while longer.

Now, he pressed a button on his military-grade walkie talkie, opening a channel to the leaders of every squad that was presently near Crawley's building and waiting.

"Alright, everyone. This is it. We can only hope those inside already are getting their part done. If you see Olinar and the woman he's with, do not engage. Everyone's seen the composite sketch of his face, so no mistakes on that front. We move in now. Go!"

It would only take his forces a matter of minutes to get inside the building from their various positions. At this stage, though, it was likely that those inside would feel the followers of Seline coming.

It was almost certain that Ludia would be held on the twenty-seventh floor. Marosavek hoped dearly that Seike and Olinar would be able to kill Crawley. Otherwise, Crawley might kill them all.

CHAPTER TWENTY-FIVE

Seike began to feel the presence of a lot of those of Seline closing in on the building. He knew it wouldn't be very long before Crawley would feel it too and he had to wonder if any of the other Legion Ambrogae within the headquarters had already felt it, especially those on the lower floors.

The leader of these half bloods clearly loved to hear himself talk. Crawley had told Seike about the many expenditures of his company and the results of those expenditures. How they had led to not only more money, but also more power for the individuals who were Ambrogae within the company. Literal power in the sense of heightening whatever their natural powers and abilities were, as well as power in terms of influence, both political and economic.

Crawley's office was big, with plenty of floor space among the sparse furnishings. There were bookshelves filled with books on either side of the room, but other than those shelves, the desk and the two chairs were the only furniture. A large, patterned carpet took up most of the floor, and the desk and chairs were both on the carpet.

There were no windows, as the office was located within the interior of the building.

He of the violet eyes was already feeling on edge, but that sensation increased when Crawley's desk phone suddenly rang. Seike figured that the situation was about to intensify.

"One moment, Seike." Crawley said.

He had been blathering on about trading stocks just before the phone cut him short, a topic which Seike knew next to nothing about. The violet-eyed one understood very little of what the businessman had been talking about.

Crawley picked up the phone.

"Yes, Natasha?"

Curiously, Seike couldn't hear the voice on the other end. Crawley's eyes were staring off at nothing at first, but suddenly they focused on Seike, narrowing.

"That's unfortunate." Crawley said to Natasha on the other end. "You know the procedure." He hung up the phone.

"Something wrong?" Seike ventured.

Crawley didn't answer him. The man just stared coldly towards him, folding his hands on the desk once again. Seike could guess what that phone call was about. He hoped Olinar would arrive soon. He couldn't tell amidst so many Ambrogae of the Leviathan in such close proximity to him whether any of them were the large red.

Just as Seike was about to say something more, he felt a force grip his entire body. He found that he couldn't move at all. Crawley's telekinesis was at work. Seike had no experience with telekinetics, but he knew that the power he felt immobilizing him couldn't be anything else.

"I'm disappointed in you, Seike." Crawley said moments after Seike found he could no longer move. "I know that your primary motivation in coming here was for Ludia, but I was hoping that we could work something out. Some kind of partnership. I was originally going to kill Ludia and imprison you, but during our conversation, I was thinking of keeping Ludia alive for as long as you would work for me. I wouldn't have let her go, of course. But I wouldn't have killed her. It seems as though I'm going to have to stick to my original plan, however."

Seike knew he should feel afraid in his present circumstances, but he didn't. Instead, he felt a heated rage begin to boil beneath the surface of his mind. It was like the inky void of the Serpent, that cold and calm part of his mind, had been set aflame. The bastard had never planned on giving him Ludia. He noticed that he could feel the energy that was gripping him as something tangible. It felt like he could feed from it, somehow. Almost like it could sustain him, if only he could… yes, there. It was like a mouth had opened up somewhere inside of his body. The thick energy gripping him flowed into that mouth and was consumed.

An expression of surprise dawned on Crawley's face. Seike could feel the telekinetic energy inside of his own body now. It flowed and roiled within him, and he knew it was at his disposal. He could use it. A burning force just waiting for him to throw it back at its source. He felt himself grasp this power with his mind. It was like taking a stone in his hand. And then he threw that stone.

Crawley made a sudden swiping motion with his hands, and the energy that Seike had just directed toward the telekinetic's body was thrust outward, somehow. Seike could feel that he had thrown it into Crawley, and he could feel that Crawley had redirected it just a foot or so outside of his body. The air exploded beside the businessman. Fire seemed to come from nowhere and the flames were hungrily lapping at the air beside Crawley. After a moment, the fire died out. The right shoulder of the telekinetic's suit was singed from the flames.

Crawley's expression of surprise remained on his face as he said, "You're a pyrokinetic! Now I really can't let you live. Once I've dealt with you, I'll deal with Ludia. You won't be the first pyrokinetic I've killed over the centuries."

Seike felt surprised, as well. Having absolutely no encounters with any telekinetics throughout his life, he had been completely unaware of the power that he possessed to fight them. Crawley had also surprised him by actually pushing the fire away when it had been aimed to burn the man from the inside out. As it stood now, most of the energy that Seike had felt inside of himself had been used up. He doubted he could use what little was left to any effect.

Suddenly the desk between him and Crawley flew up from its position on the floor, right towards the violet-eyed Ambrogis. It struck Seike with a great deal of force, carrying him with it to be slammed up against the wall, pinning him there. Seike could feel the energy from Crawley's telekinesis permeating the area surrounding the desk, and he began trying to absorb it.

At that moment, a loud crash from the door to the office brought Seike's attention snapping toward it. Someone had just hit the door hard from outside of the office.

"What the fuck is this door made of?" Olinar muttered after slamming into the door with full force. It had shuttered but had not given way to his strength. A door like this should have ripped off its hinges with the amount of physical and psionic strength Olinar had put into shouldering it.

Olinar could feel the telekinetic energy on the other side of the door. He knew Seike was probably in trouble, but he could still feel the violet-eyed Ambrogis. Seike was still alive. Almeidra was standing a few feet behind Olinar. She seemed surprised that the door remained in one piece, as well.

"Don't just stand there." She said. "Hit it again."

Bracing himself and preparing to hit the door even harder than before, Olinar backed up a few paces to charge it with a running start. Like a raging bull, he slammed headlong into the door, shoulder first. This time the door flew open. It remained on its hinges, but at least Olinar had managed to break through it. The scene on the other side was not what Olinar expected.

Seike had been pinned against the wall by a large desk, apparently made of the same wood-like material as the door. But that wasn't what was surprising to Olinar. The violet-eyed one had an arm free and was leveling his hand at Robert Crawley, who was standing at the back of the room. Crawley was moving his hands as if blocking physical blows, and each time he thrust his hands and arms off to one side or another, bursts of fire exploded into the air on either side of him. Olinar's surprise left him frozen there to witness the display.

Seike was a pyrokinetic! Not only that, but somehow Crawley was fighting Seike's pyrokinesis, while maintaining his own telekinetic abilities. After several of these fiery explosions had enveloped the air to Crawley's left and right sides, the desk dropped. Olinar could no longer sense telekinetic energy permeating the room. Seike had absorbed and used all of it.

The violet-eyed Ambrogis was clearly tired, but Crawley didn't seem so fatigued. Both of their heads turned to where Olinar and Almeidra stood in the doorway.

"Who are you?" Crawley demanded to know. "I don't recognize you, but if you're some of my employees, I suggest you detain this man at once. Or kill him, if you can."

The only way Olinar would be able to fry this prick is if the owner of Triaclon Industries started using his power again. Crawley didn't know it yet, but right now the situation was a standoff. He decided to move toward Seike and the desk as if obeying Crawley's orders.

"Stay back." He said, looking at Almeidra before heading into the office. She raised her hands in a gesture that said she had no intention of setting foot in that room. Olinar went in and went over to where Seike was laying with the desk partially on top of him. He made eye contact with the violet-eyed one as he approached. Seike looked angry. Not with Olinar, but with Crawley. As Olinar got to the desk, he bent down as if to grab at Seike, but then gripped the desk with both of his hands, heaving it with all his might toward where Crawley was standing at the back of the office. It felt heavier than it should, but it still flew through the air towards Crawley. It stopped only feet away from the half blood, halting in midair. Olinar could feel the telekinetic energy holding the desk in place. He began to absorb it.

"Another one!" Crawley exclaimed. He said nothing more as Olinar focused his fire into Crawley's body. The large Ambrogis was amazed as he felt the fire pull out of the half blood's body and push off to the side, with Crawley making the motion of blocking with his hands. The air beside the half blood exploded briefly into flame. The desk dropped at the same time.

"I've killed more than a few pyrokinetics in the course of my life. It seems this day I'll be adding two more to that tally."

The words were confident, but Crawley did not make another attempt with his telekinesis. The desk lay on its side on the floor in front of him now. Olinar couldn't get to it. There was no more remaining energy in the room for either he or Seike to try to use against the half blood.

"You're going to die, Crawley. Coranthis will be avenged. As will all those you killed." Olinar stated. Crawley looked momentarily confused, but then a smile crept onto his face.

"A pure blood! A pure blood pyrokinetic that Seike here recruited to help him take me out. Of course." Crawley began to laugh mirthlessly. "You should know something, pure blood. I killed Coranthis, yes, but I was incited to do so by the woman you two have come here to save. By Ludia herself. Of course, I would have gotten around to killing that so-called king eventually, regardless. But it happened when it did because of her meddling."

Olinar took a moment to digest this information. He felt mildly surprised and somewhat like he had been used as a chess piece in someone else's game. But he registered all of Crawley's words, not just the fact that Ludia was responsible somehow for Coranthis' death. It wasn't she who did the killing. And as this insane half blood just stated, he had wanted to kill Coranthis anyway. Whatever Ludia had done had just given him the excuse to do so.

"Seike? Can you shed a little light on what he's talking about?" Olinar still planned on killing Crawley but was interested to hear what Seike might have to say.

"I'm not sure of the details, Olinar. All I know is that Ludia wasn't expecting Crawley to murder your king. Crawley made that move all on his own." Seike picked himself up off the floor as he said this. For a moment, Olinar stared at the violet-eyed Ambrogis. At least Seike had the decency to look apologetic. The large Ambrogis decided that now wasn't the time to settle this matter. He had come here to kill Crawley, and that's what he intended to do.

"We can figure this out later." He stated as he turned back toward the half blood. Seike faced Crawley from his side of the office, as well.

"Very well." Crawley said. "I have no compunction with killing another couple of pure bloods along with the lot that I've already dealt with. The three of you will die.

Ludia will die. And I will go on fulfilling my dreams of becoming the true ruler of this world, unimpeded.

"Even as I say this, my people are taking care of this little incursion you've set up, Seike. Everything important to this company isn't just located in this building. I have locations all over this country where I can continue my business and research from if this place were to fall to those wretched Seline worshippers. But after I take care of two more pyrokinetics, I'll be free to set about destroying all those who are now invading my property."

Olinar could suddenly hear footsteps coming down the hallway, and he could feel that they were followers of the Leviathan, and not the cavalry. He glanced at Almeidra.

"I got this." She said, disappearing from the doorway to head down the hall toward the direction of the incoming security forces.

Crawley still made no move to use his telekinesis again. The three of them stood in the office, Olinar and Seike facing Crawley. The half blood was sweating, now. Olinar knew it wasn't from exertion, but rather from the situation that Crawley had found himself in.

"So you've killed some pyrokinetics, have you?" Olinar said. "I'm betting you haven't dealt with two at a time, before."

"I've barely begun to show you what I can do." Crawley said, suddenly smiling.

At these words, every book on the bookshelves flew out and shot toward Olinar and Seike with tremendous force and speed. The large Amrogis wanted to retaliate, and was absorbing some of the telekinetic energy, but the assault was too much. It was all he could do to shield himself as book after book flew at his body and head. Seike seemed to be in a similar predicament, and one of the books caught him on the side of the head, drawing blood.

The desk was suddenly airborne again, flying towards Olinar. He leapt out of the way just in time as it crashed into the wall behind him. Still, he gathered as much residual telekinetic energy as he could manage with his distracted concentration. He hoped Seike was doing the same.

The chairs were flying at them now, and the desk, which was still in one piece, flew from its position on the wall toward the violet-eyed one. Seike didn't see it coming and it crashed into him, taking him to the ground and pinning him there.

Olinar managed to hit both of the chairs out of the air as he kept his gaze focused on Crawley. He was almost brimming with Crawley's telekinetic energy now, and decided to play things out a bit differently. He focused a small amount of the energy onto the carpet under Crawley's feet and set it aflame.

Crawley hadn't been expecting this, and he jumped back as the books and chairs stopped flying around the room and dropped to the ground. Olinar then focused on Crawley himself. He had enough energy inside of him for a few good attempts. Inside of aiming for inside Crawley's body, he aimed for the businessman's suit. Crawley anticipated it, however, and made a pushing motion with his hands. The air in front of him exploded into fire briefly.

From his position under the desk, Seike suddenly kicked the large piece of furniture out from under him. The desk went sailing towards Crawley and connected with him, sending him to the ground. The half blood recovered quickly though. The desk flew off him and back at the violet-eyed Ambrogis, who was ready for it this time. Seike dodged nimbly as the desk crashed into the corner of the room on his side.

This was Olinar's chance. He aimed inside of Crawley and began to use his fire to try to burn the man from the inside out. Again, it didn't work. The fire was pushed out of Crawley by the man's telekinetic force and exploded into the air around the center of the office.

Seike thrust out his hands and did the same, but also to no avail. Crawley telekinetically parried yet another attempt at torching him, the fire exploding harmlessly a few feet away from the half blood.

"I could do this all day." Crawley said as they stood and faced each other again in a room devoid of telekinetic energy. "Can you two say the same?" Crawley was smiling, his light perspiration indicative of perhaps a little strain, but more likely just because of nervousness at being confronted by two pyrokinetics.

Olinar was sweating, himself. And for his part, it was because of strain. He was tired, almost spent. He noticed that Seike was practically dripping with sweat, as well. If the violet-eyed one hadn't known he was a pyrokinetic, and this was his first go at it, it was likely he was just about used up.

"Seike, what about that other thing?" Olinar said to the violet-eyed Ambrogis. "You know what I'm talking about."

Seike furrowed his brow together and gave a small shrug. That wasn't the reaction Olinar had been expecting. Was Seike too tired to call upon the lightning that Olinar knew he was capable of using? The big Ambrogis hoped not.

Suddenly, Olinar had a notion. The moment Seike had used his power was right after Olinar had said that he was going to kill all of Seike's friends. Olinar had noted the rage in Seike's eyes at that time. It was what allowed the big red the opportunity to bolster his psionic barrier in preparation for the incoming attack as Seike had raised his hand towards him from lying on the grass of the open field. He thought now that maybe Seike needed some kind of motivation like that.

"This guy is going to kill Ludia." Olinar said to Seike. "And he won't stop there. He'll kill every blue that's now in this building fighting to help us win this. I can feel them inside at this point. There are hundreds of them. He'll kill everyone you know and love, Seike. If he wins here, he wins, period. He won't stop after everyone on this side of the country that opposes him is dead. He'll make his way over to your neck of the woods. To your friends."

Seike looked at Olinar then. There was rage burning in those violet eyes of his. Olinar recognized it as the same look that Seike had given him on the night that Olinar had attacked that S-47 base.

Olinar was right. If Seike died here, Robert Crawley would become unstoppable. Seike's people didn't know any other pyrokinetics. He could feel a white-hot righteous rage burning inside of him at the thought of all of his friends dying at Crawley's hands. A rage that told him that he could do anything. He felt it, then. The energy inside of him that was his own, that was unique to whatever he was. It was like a thousand burning suns.

Crawley looked confused as Seike raised his hand toward him. The half blood didn't have a chance to react to the thick bolt of electrical energy that suddenly shot out from Seike's palm. It struck Crawley in the head, which exploded into chunks of skull and blood and pieces of brain, splattering mostly on the wall behind him.

For a moment, the half blood's body was still standing. The bolt had struck with such a particular force so as to not create any inertia within the rest of Crawley's body. The businessman's corpse then dropped to its knees before falling forward onto the tattered and burned carpet of the office.

Seike stood where he was, disbelieving. He had actually done it. Hundreds of books, the chairs and the desk were lying haphazardly all over the room. And Crawley's headless corpse.

"You did it." Olinar said into a silence that had stretched on for close to a minute, with the two of them just standing there, breathing heavily and looking at the corpse that was once Robert Crawley. Olinar slowly walked towards Seike. "Whatever Ludia did, I heard what Crawley said. He wasn't planning on letting my king live, even if Ludia hadn't given him whatever nudge in that direction. That insane fucker was a danger to us all. My kind, and yours."

Seike met the red Ambrogis' eyes. "Thank you for your help in this." He said. "I know we're not friends. We probably can't ever be that. But I'm going to hold up my end. I'll see that you and Almeidra walk out of here, even if the place is crawling with those of Seline right now."

Olinar nodded at this. At that moment, Almeidra reappeared in the doorway. She wasn't alone. A group of those of Seline were with her, holding her at gunpoint. Olinar looked from them towards Seike.

The seven men and women of Seline looked over to where Crawley's body lay. One of them, a stout man, stepped forward, looking at Crawley's body and then at Seike.

"The name's Huilanios. We found this one standing amidst a bunch of half blood corpses, so we figured she was the one who came into the building with Olinar. Still, she's a red, so I admit we pointed our guns at her. She volunteered to lead us to you."

Almeidra didn't look happy. She looked hatefully towards Seike. "Coranthis might still be alive if not for your damn Ludia."

Olinar interjected. "You heard what that lunatic was saying Almeidra. He was planning on killing our king eventually, despite Ludia's intervention on the matter. We're not in a position to argue, at any rate."

Almeidra scoffed at Olinar, but then her expression softened. "You're right, Olinar." She stated. "Plus, I really would like to not die, right now." She looked around the forces of Seline that were still pointing guns at her, though some had turned their guns toward Olinar.

Seike met Huilanios' eyes. "I couldn't have done this without these two. I would be dead, right now, and likely so would you and your people. What's the situation out there, anyway?"

"Most of the half bloods turned tail and ran." Huilanios replied. "They seemed organized in doing so. Plenty stayed to fight, though. We lost close to a hundred men and women, all within minutes of entering the building. There was a body and keycard in the elevator. Without that keycard, my squad and others wouldn't have made it up to this floor."

"You're welcome." Almeidra put in. "Can you please stop pointing guns at us now?"

"That was your doing, was it?" Huilanios asked.

"The body in the elevator was Gregory. Crawley's right-hand man." Olinar said. "We needed his keycard. I must have dropped it when we were met with some resistance once we got to this floor."

Huilanios chuckled at the comment. He raised one hand. "Stand down, people. We're letting these two go."

The rest of Huilanios' group lowered their weapons.

"Thank you, Huilanios." Seike said. "I gave them my word they could walk away after this, and I'll be glad to keep that promise."

Olinar and Almeidra were standing together now, still encircled by the soldiers of Seline. "You got my car keys?" Olinar said to Seike.

Seike had forgotten about the car and the keys. He still had them in his pocket, though, and fished them out now. He tossed the keyring to Olinar, who caught it effortlessly. The large Ambrogis looked around the room, meeting each of the eyes of the followers of Seline encircling him and Almeidra.

"Don't worry." He said to them. "I got no plans on trying to take over the world, myself. I just wanna survive, is all."

In response to his words, the soldiers made way, allowing a clear path to the doorway of Crawley's office. He and Almeidra left, but not before he gave one last look towards Seike. That look spoke volumes. They could never be friends, but it was almost as if Olinar wished they could be. Maybe they weren't friends, but they were now brothers in arms. After they had gone, Huilanios approached Seike and clapped him on the shoulder.

"We found Ludia shortly before we found Almeidra. She's a little worse for wear, but she's alive and well. She wants to see you."

"Take me to her."

Huilanios led Seike and the other Ambrogae of Seline out of the office and further down the hall. Seike didn't see Olinar and Almeidra, and assumed they were already halfway out of the building by now. Eventually, they came upon another group of blues, Ludia standing amongst them.

"Crawley?" She said to the violet-eyed one.

"Dead."

Ludia was visibly relieved at hearing the news from Seike. She sighed audibly, seeming to relax.

"And what of Olinar and his cohort?"

"We let them go, Ludia." Huilanios said to her. "This wouldn't have happened without them. Didn't seem right to put bullets in their heads after they risked their lives for us."

Ludia nodded approvingly. "We kept our end of the bargain then. Crawley is dead, and Olinar and his woman are gone their own way. I met her briefly. Fiery woman, that Almeidra."

Seike looked questioningly at Ludia. "You met her?"

"Yes, just a few minutes ago. She had just finished killing a half dozen of Crawley's security guards when we came upon her."

"Oh. Yeah, Huilanios said so already. I didn't know you were there too."

Ludia chuckled. "Well, I was."

"So what now?" Seike asked. "Is the fighting over already?"

"Just about." A man standing next to Ludia spoke up. "You've done your part, Seike. We'll finish up here."

Seike didn't know who the man was, but he radiated authority. Ludia introduced him.

"Seike, this is Marosavek. He'll be the Elder of the Western Haven, now. I'm coming back to the Central Haven with you."

This information seemed to surprise everyone there, including Seike. The violet-eyed Ambrogis certainly hadn't expected such a proclamation. It seemed that it was the first time these others present had heard as much, as well. Marosavek turned wide eyes towards Ludia and began to protest. But Ludia forestalled him.

"I need to go home, Marosavek. I've been away too long, and now that Robert Crawley is dead, there's no pressing need for me here."

Marosavek still seemed like he wanted to argue, but he relented. "I understand, Elder. I imagine Kesel will be glad to have you back."

"I'm sure he will be glad." Ludia smiled.

Seike knew that Kesel would be happy to have Ludia back at the Central Haven. The Elder would be happy just to know that they were all still alive, and that Crawley was dead.

Huilanios seemed like he wanted to say something. He wore a perplexed expression, as if something didn't add up in his mind. Seike was pretty sure he knew what the man was thinking. Other than a small scorch mark on the shoulder of his suit, Crawley's headless body had been untouched by any fire. The violet-eyed Ambrogis had his suspicion confirmed when Huilanios finally spoke.

"Crawley wasn't burned to death." The well-built Ambrogis turned towards Seike, his gaze questioning. "What exactly happened in that room? How was it that you two managed to take down Robert Crawley?"

Seike wasn't sure that he was ready to talk about his unique power. He still didn't understand it, or how to use it at will, even after successfully using it for a second time. If he was being honest with himself, it still kind of scared him. That much power made him feel completely invincible. When he could feel it inside of him, he felt not only like he could create lightning, but like he could do anything. It was as if he could run full speed without losing breath. Like he could fight forever. Like he could tear the entire world down, if he wasn't careful.

"Crawley was able to deflect our pyrokinetic attacks."

"Our?" This from Ludia. She had stepped forward and was looking at Seike as if seeing him for the first time. "Do you mean to tell me, Seike, that you are also a pyrokinetic?"

"Yes. I just found out today. In that office."

"Fire's Light..." Ludia whispered. "The name Selinda gave you, and the reason. It seems connected, don't you think?"

Now that Ludia mentioned it, Seike thought for the first time since the fight about what his name meant. Fire's Light. It did seem to be quite a coincidence that he should be named so when he ended up having the gift that he had just found out, minutes ago, he possessed. He was a pyrokinetic. More than that, but also that.

Selinda had named him that because the first time she had seen him, his eyes had been shining with tears and they had reflected the light from the fire of his burning house perfectly.

"But how is it that his head was missing?" Huilanios said in reference to Crawley. He was pressing the matter, but Seike couldn't blame the man for being curious.

"I... have another power. Kesel and the others know about it now, as does Kelloway and the rest of my team at Field Base A-92. And now I'm telling you guys, I guess..." Seike was feeling self-conscious as everyone's eyes focused more heavily on him upon saying those words. He couldn't leave it at that. He had to tell them, now.

"It seems to have to do with when people I care about are threatened. I feel some kind of energy inside of my body, and I can channel it through my hands. It looks like lightning, but I don't think that's what it is."

There was no need for him to tell them about how the power made him feel. That was for him to work through on his own.

"An unheard of power for the man with unheard of eyes." Ludia said. Oddly enough, there was pride in her voice. Seike didn't mind that she said it like that. It was better than being reacted to fearfully.

"Well, that's something for the books, then, isn't it?" Huilanios laughed and grasped Seike by both his arms before enveloping him in a big bear hug. He of the violet eyes was both surprised and warmed by the gesture. He still wasn't used to being regarded amiably and with respect.

Marosavek looked thoughtful, but he too wore a smile. "You'll have to come to our haven, Seike. I think that food and celebration are in order after an ordeal like this one. You and Ludia can depart for Iowa together, tomorrow. For tonight, we must give our thanks to you and your role in taking down Crawley, who we surely thought of as the direst threat this world had ever faced."

"There was something else." Seike said. "Crawley was on the phone with someone and told that person about knowing the procedure before he hung up. I can't help but think this may not be completely over."

Marosavek's smile faded and his expression grew serious. "As to that, many of the half bloods escaped, taking valuable data and research with them. They destroyed the hard drives of any computer that might have contained something of value to us regarding Triaclon Industries. The executives on the board of directors were nowhere to be found, either. I imagine they put into operation a contingency plan just in case of an invading force like the one they met with today. Despite Crawley being killed, that plan was executed.

"But it's of little consequence, right now. We have won a great victory this day, and we will celebrate it this night."

The other Ambrogae were nodding at this, and before long the smiles and laughter and shoulder clapping had returned. They had accomplished what they had set out to do. Ludia was back with them, safe and sound. Crawley was dead, and they had taken the headquarters of Triaclon Industries.

They set about with new orders to have the building manned at all times, and for it to be completely combed through for anything that could give them information regarding the activities Crawley had been up to. They would look for any clues pertaining to his research and discoveries.

After some searching, they found the laboratory at the top of the building, but everything inside of it had been destroyed. There was nothing they could gain insight from left in the lab. Seike left them to do their assigned jobs, going with Ludia back to the Western Haven to rest and recuperate.

He found himself wondering about Olinar and Almeidra. It was an odd thing, to find himself concerned about how two reds were faring out there. During the couple of days they had spent in each other's company,

Seike had to admit he could see things from the large Ambrogis' perspective. Olinar considered himself part of an endangered species and wanted to survive. It was a mindset that the violet-eyed one could understand. He expected the man to be evil, like he had always thought all of those of Legion were. But he had found both Olinar and Almeidra to be very... human. They would hate the comparison, Seike knew, but they had expressed themselves and talked about things much like any of those of Seline or any ordinary human would have. Yes, they murdered humans and drained them of blood, but they themselves didn't consider such acts evil. They considered it simply a part of their nature, of what they were. And a matter of survival.

Seike thought that maybe Olinar and Almeidra could be persuaded to live life differently. Be a little less murderous, maybe. But he knew it was just fanciful thinking, and that those two would likely never change.

If he ever came across them again, they might meet as enemies. Seike found himself hoping a day like that would never come.

EPILOGUE

He had been Simon Martin, priest of the Catholic Church. Now, he wasn't sure what he was, besides starving.

It had been days since he and his congregation had been imprisoned here in his church. He had been offered no food or water. He was a man used to fasting, but right now he felt an aching hunger inside of him unlike anything he had ever been capable of imagining. It grew worse with each passing hour. He felt that he would die if he didn't eat something soon.

During the course of the days that they had been imprisoned, many of his flock had succumbed to the darkness of the beast. Their eyes had turned red, and once that happened, they were allowed to feed from some of the people that hadn't been turned and were kept just for that express purpose. Most of those people were dead now, drained of life by those that had once been their friends and neighbors. Some of the church goers that had been turned didn't turn into those with red eyes. Instead, their eyes had turned blue. Not many, maybe eight or nine in total. Those people had met a gruesome end at the hands of Ignusai and his group of demons. They were tied and bound in the first place, and as soon as each of them had gone blue in the eyes, their hearts were ripped from their chests.

Simon had found himself fantasizing about Jesus coming down from the heavens on a white horse to save him and the others many times during the first couple of days, but today was the third day, and no such help had come. He now found himself hating God for abandoning him and his flock in their time of need. He couldn't understand why Mother Mary and the Lord hadn't come for them. They were devout people, all.

They *had* been devout people. Now, as Simon looked about the large interior of the church, he saw only monsters. Ignusai saw him looking around and then began to approach him. Simon had been tied and bound like the rest, but unlike the rest, he had been kept awake for the entire time. The demon approached him with a bundle in his arms.

"You look positively famished, Simon." Ignusai said as he stepped up to where Simon was, sitting at the front of the pews. "You should have something to eat."

Ignusai presented the bundle. It was a baby. Simon knew the child's name was Jonathan. He had baptized the boy not two months past. For some reason, looking upon the babe intensified Simon's hunger. He could smell a scent wafting off the child that was unlike anything he had ever smelled before. A sweetness, alluring and intoxicating. After a moment, Simon realized that he was smelling the boy's blood underneath the flesh. He wanted to scream his denial at what he was experiencing. Instead, he found himself leaning towards the boy. It was as if something else had control of his body.

Before he knew what he was doing, his mouth had closed around the boy's neck, and his teeth had bitten into the child's flesh. He began to drain the baby of all of its blood, feeling it seep into him, sustaining him. A feeling of warmth and invigoration overcame his entire body. He felt strong. Stronger than he had ever felt before in his life. Stronger than he had been in his prime.

He couldn't stop. The baby was crying as he fed, but the mewls grew quiet after a few more moments, and suddenly Simon felt his body break free of the cords that had bound his wrists. A small part of him thought that he would attack Ignusai now that he was free, but his hands only grasped the child in the demon's arms, yanking it free from Ignusai's grasp. He greedily drank until the child stopped making any sounds. He drank until there was nothing left to drink. Then he reached down toward his ankles and snapped the cords that bound them.

Life! He could feel a force in his mind, whispering to him that he had joined it entirely. It spoke to him of the grand design that had been planned out for him now that he had given in. In his surrender, he would find that he was truly free.

"More." He said to Ignusai. One of the prisoners, a woman in her mid-forties who he knew as Wanda, was brought forward by two of Ignusai's men. She screamed and struggled and looked at Simon as if he was some kind of terror to behold. But he was no terror. He knew that now. He was connected to the true God of this world, for the first time in his long and boring life. He compared the presence in his mind with the fanciful imaginings of the God he had thought he knew. There was no comparison. Legion was the true God. This being inside of him now granted him true freedom, and true power to make a difference in the world.

As she was brought closer, Simon stood up from the pews. He approached Wanda and whispered, "Your sacrifice will help save the world, my child. I must be strong in order to save it."

He sank his teeth into her neck, and listened to her heart beating faster as he drank from her lifeblood. He grew even stronger than he had already grown from feeding on young Jonathan. As her screams died out, and he continued drinking, he felt a power inside of him that was exponentially larger than what he had felt after feeding on the child. He felt limitless. The whispering inside of his mind grew louder. It spoke to him of the secrets of the world. He understood that this was truly what communing with God was. The whispers told him that his purpose was to bring about a new era, a new time for the people. Not the humans, no, but what he was now. A perfect being. He could see, now, that they had never been demons, these vampires. They were something else entirely. A different race of beings altogether. God's true chosen.

"I can see that we're going to have to take you out for a night on the town." Ignusai chuckled.

Simon had been the last human left in the church that had been put through the process of turning. He had clung feebly onto his humanity, like it mattered, for longer than the rest. Now, everyone inside was an Ambrogis or

Ambrogess. He knew that was the name, now, for Ignusai had told him the stories while he had still been human.

He had thought them lies, but he saw now that it was the truth. The Ambrogae had lived within the earth for hundreds of thousands of years, walking among the humans as they pleased once they had discovered the surface world. The perfect predators, undetectable until it was too late.

Woitan came up to him, with the knife he had used on Marissa, his granddaughter, and the other humans he had killed in his ignorance. "You can have this back, now, if you want. Welcome, brother." The Ambrogis said to him, presenting the blade.

Simon took the knife, holding it balanced in the palm of his hand, looking at it. He did not close his hand on the handle of the blade. Instead, the whisperings of the God inside his mind told him of a particular secret, and he decided to try it out on the knife.

He felt an abyss of power inside of him, flowing from his body and into his hand where the blade lay. It floated up off of his palm, and just hung there, in the air. Ignusai and Woitan and the other Ambrogae nearby gasped in shock and surprise.

"You're telekinetic!" Ignusai exclaimed. "I've heard stories of your kind that state it takes at least a hundred years, sometimes longer, for such power to express itself through an Ambrogis! And yet you display that power moments after turning to the Leviathan. Such a thing is unheard of."

Simon felt himself smiling at what Ignusai had just stated. He had been chosen by the true God, and the man's words only confirmed this thought in his mind. A hundred or more years for this power to manifest? And it was only a fraction of what he knew he was capable of.

He focused on the knife and watched it crumple into a ball before him in the air. The whispering in his mind continued as the onlookers exclaimed over what he was doing. Those of his flock who were now Ambrogis were watching him with an awe especially strong, as they had known Father Simon Martin in their human lives, and were now witnessing his beginning, along with theirs, in the new life that they would all lead.

Finally, the whispering stopped, and Simon fully understood. He looked at the crumpled metal ball hovering in the air above his hand and felt the force that was holding it there increase in temperature dramatically. As he concentrated, the metal ball turned bright red within seconds, then burst into flame and was consumed in moments.

"That's impossible." Ignusai stated, his mouth hanging open.

"Obviously not." Simon said.

Ignusai and Woitan exchanged glances, both wide eyed and slack jawed. Then they turned back toward Simon and simultaneously dropped to their knees before him. The Ambrogae that were with them when they had attacked the church were only a moment behind in doing the same. The people of his flock joined them. All of them were on their knees before him.

"With you, Simon, we can accomplish more than we ever have before. Say you will lead our people into glory."

Ignusai said, awe tinging his voice. "Say that you will take our dwindling numbers and make them greater."

"Dwindling numbers? How many of us are there?" Simon was genuinely curious.

"Not more than a few million left both within the earth and on its surface. We've been at war with the blue-eyed ones for thousands of years, and our numbers have dropped significantly in that time."

"We shall have to change that, then." Simon stated. Ignusai was looking at him with a hope in his eyes that Simon had never seen anyone look at him with before in his mortal life. Such hope could not come from a demon's eyes. Simon understood that now.

"My flock." Simon said, addressing the hundred or so people there that he had known for years in their human lives. "Tell me, what do you see before you?"

"A savior!" A voice rose from the crowd. "A miracle!"

"You look young and vibrant, Father!" Another person chimed in.

Simon looked at his hands and arms. They were the hands and arms he had once had, when he was in his mid-thirties. He realized he was no longer an old man, a short way from death's door. He was again youthful. Just another gift from the true God.

"Do you see a shepherd before you?" Simon asked.

"Yes!" voices rose in unison as they agreed with his words. Shouts and cheers came from his flock.

"Then I will lead you, my people." He said. He looked upon Ignusai and Woitan kneeling before him. "And if you who have turned me to the truth will have me, I shall help to lead you, as well."

Ignusai looked up at him in surprise. "Of course, Simon. Do you want to be called Simon, still? Usually, a sire gives a new name to their fledgling, but this is a unique case. I do not feel right in trying to come up with a name for you."

Simon smiled. He looked upon his flock, both the new people in it and the old and usual ones.

"I shall remain Simon, but no longer can I think of myself as Simon Martin the human. Instead, call me Simon Magus. It is a biblical reference, for those of you who do not know. But I deem it fitting, as I shall not be attempting to fly any time soon." This brought chuckles from many of the former church goers.

"Simon Magus." Ignusai seemed to be tasting the name. "May we simply call you Magus, then?"

"Call me Father Magus, if you like. Or just Simon."

"Father Magus." Woitan whispered reverently.

The whsipers that had been in his head seemed to be coming from the people in the room, now. Voices passed on the word to one another. He heard the name Father Magus whispered, until it became almost a chant.

"There's a place nearby…" Ignusai suddenly said. "The palace of our fallen king. His name was Coranthis. He was a just ruler but fell before his time. At least, that's what I thought. Now, I'm thinking that you should be the one to preside over that palace, and Coranthis fell precisely because it was his time to fall. To make room for you, Father Magus."

"Please, Ignusai, you are my sire. You, at least, can call me Simon." A palace? Simon was intrigued.

"Very well. Simon, if it would please you, the palace has been partially wrecked by an enemy, and we would have to clear out the bodies of the former occupants, but it is miles underground, and an excellent defensive bastion. It is only several miles from here, through the forest. I can take you, if you like. To show you, at least, so that you may make a decision on the matter."

"Very well. I must say I am quite curious to see this palace. It has always been there, so close to this church… and yet, am I right in assuming it is much older than this church?"

"It is thousands of years old, Simon." Ignusai responded.

"Come then, let us all go and see this remarkable piece of history with our own eyes." Simon was addressing his entire flock now. Everyone made ready to leave.

Within minutes, Ignusai was leading them all through the forest behind the church. Simon knew that he was going to see his new home in this world. He would save these people from extinction, and in doing so, he would be saving himself. It was all in service to the true God, the Leviathan.

He would save them all.

Manufactured by Amazon.ca
Acheson, AB

11707605R00210